1794

THE CITY BETWEEN THE BRIDGES

Also by Niklas Natt och Dag
1793: The Wolf and the Watchman

1794

THE CITY BETWEEN THE BRIDGES

A NOVEL

Niklas Natt och Dag

Translated by Ebba Segerberg

ATRIA BOOKS

New York London Toronto Sydney New Delhi

ATRIA
BOOKS

An Imprint of Simon & Schuster, Inc.
1230 Avenue of the Americas
New York, NY 10020

Copyright © 2019 by Niklas Natt och Dag
English language translation copyright © 2022 by Ebba Segerberg
Originally published in Sweden in 2019 by Forum as 1794
Published by arrangement with Salomonsson Agency

All rights reserved, including the right to reproduce this book or portions thereof in any form whatsoever. For information, address Atria Books Subsidiary Rights Department, 1230 Avenue of the Americas, New York, NY 10020.

First Atria Books hardcover edition February 2023

ATRIA BOOKS and colophon are trademarks of Simon & Schuster, Inc.

For information about special discounts for bulk purchases, please contact Simon & Schuster Special Sales at 1-866-506-1949 or business@simonandschuster.com.

The Simon & Schuster Speakers Bureau can bring authors to your live event. For more information or to book an event, contact the Simon & Schuster Speakers Bureau at 1-866-248-3049 or visit our website at www.simonspeakers.com.

Interior design by Silverglass

Manufactured in China

1 3 5 7 9 10 8 6 4 2

Library of Congress Cataloging-in-Publication Data has been applied for.

ISBN 978-1-9821-4591-0
ISBN 978-1-9821-4593-4 (ebook)

Please sit down—but always fend!
Look around as tankards smack,
For the one you thought your friend
Plans a dagger in your back.
—Carl Michael Bellman, 1794

Cast of Characters

Jean Michael Cardell: known as "Mickel," formerly a sergeant in the Artillery; after losing his left arm at Svensksund, employed by the Stockholm Watch, whose duties he conscientiously ignores; would rather earn his keep as a hired heavy.

Cecil Winge: formerly a lawyer, last year temporarily appointed to the police; afflicted with consumption.

Anna Stina Knapp: formerly a flower girl in the parishes of Maria and Katarina, later sent to the workhouse; as of the winter of 1793–1794 managing the Scapegrace pub under the name "Lovisa Ulrika Blix," the forenames belonging to the publican's runaway daughter.

Isak Reinhold Blom: secretary to the Chamber of Police; a poet and disciple of Carl Gustav af Leopold, upon whose example his own poetry leans heavily.

Johan Kristofer Blix: a surgeon's apprentice from Karlskrona; husband to Anna Stina Knapp in an unconsummated marriage; perished on the ice of Knights' Bay; dead and buried.

Petter Pettersson: a custodian at the workhouse on the Scar.

Jonatan Löf: a watchman at the workhouse.

Dülitz: once a Polish refugee; now a merchant who trades in people's lives.

Gustav III: by the grace of God, the King of Sweden; shot at the opera and dying of his wounds in March 1792.

Gustav Adolf: the only son of Gustav III; king in name only, he turns sixteen this November; still a minor while the kingdom is ruled by others in his name.

Duke Karl: the younger brother of the late King Gustav; guardian of the young crown prince; a lightweight who would rather enjoy the fruits of power than endure the work entailed.

Gustav Adolf Reuterholm: a baron and a prominent nobleman of the land, and in his role as trusted confidant of Duke Karl, the true ruler of the kingdom; dubbed the "Grand Vizier" behind his back; vain and superstitious; a sworn enemy of the late king, constantly occupied with reversing his legacy.

Gustaf Mauritz Armfelt: a favorite of the late king, and the last hope of the Gustavians; fled into exile after his conspiracies against the regency came to light.

Magdalena Rudenschöld: a lady of the court; once much admired by Duke Karl; lover of Gustaf Mauritz Armfelt and his coconspirator; arrested for her involvement in the plot; known as "Malla."

Karl Tulip: known as the "Flowerman"; the owner of the Scapegrace; a willing accomplice in the deception by which Anna Stina Knapp impersonates his estranged daughter.

Magnus Ullholm: Stockholm's chief of police since December 1793, when he succeeded Norlin, who was transferred to the north; notorious for having embezzled the ministers' widows' fund; a willing lapdog of the regency.

Carl Wilhelm Modée: Governor of Stockholm, one of the most powerful men in the land, loyal; to Baron Reuterholm.

"Master Erik": the watchmen's nickname for the cat-o'-nine-tails used at the workhouse on the island of Scar.

PART ONE

From the Tomb of the Living
WINTER 1794

What borders restrain him who might with crime will pair,
Who cries he's above the law, and doesn't have a care—
Who'll stop his arm in time from the violence he'll do,
Who else but God above, to punish and give due?

—Isak Reinhold Blom, 1794

1

It is January now, the year just turned 1794.

Earlier, I was disturbed in my chamber, chased out of my bed, and asked to dress, for the year was new, vermin and filth had been allowed free rein for long enough, and now the stale air would be smoked with fir and the floors splashed with vinegar. I clumsily knotted my trousers, tied my shoelaces, and swung a coat over my shoulders, now grown so lean the cloth hung loosely. I headed down the stairs and out for the first time in what must have been weeks, out into the day that my narrow window had reduced to a shard.

....

The linden trees in the garden had for months stood robbed of their leaves, but what debt autumn had left, winter now repaid with snow. The branches stood swathed in shrouds trailing the earth as far as the eye could see. The sun was shining and its beams shimmered all in white with a force that would admit no other colors. I blinked and was blinded, forced to cover my face with my hands. Other invalids crowded the stairwell or staggered across the snow, swearing at the sensation of their shoes first getting cold, and then wet. Rather than suffer their company, I took the road down to the water, where the ice spread a quarter mile before giving way to open sea. The unsullied white promised sanctuary. The air was biting cold but the sun offered warmth and, despite my dark mood, I set out across ice that was surely thick enough to reach all the way to the bottom.

Far away on my left, the Stockholm Quayside glittered like a row of yellowed teeth, the church spires forming sharp fangs, and beyond them, the squat mass of the castle. I averted my gaze, as if to avoid drawing this slumbering predator's attention, and instead gazed back along my own tracks, where the valley lay exposed in its entirety in a way that otherwise only seafarers know.

The city had turned its back on Dane's Bay and it is as if time itself has done the same. The days are different here. The hours of light cut short, the darkness long. Two hilltops shear the heavens from either side and curtail the course of the sun. Few who can avoid it visit the hospital, even though many of those who share quarters with me suffer from nothing worse than old age. A place has been prepared for them here by sons and daughters who have wanted to provide for them in their final years but who never seem to find the time to visit, these old people soon reduced to dotage by neglect.

In the distance, along the water towards Finnboda, lies the asylum. From where I was standing, I could count seven storeys stretched across the slope where the foundation had been laid at an angle, like a staircase for a giant emerging from the deep. The asylum is a constant source of gossip in the hospital corridors. They say the building holds twice the population it should. Many windows are boarded up, others covered with bars. When I had reached as close as I could, I thought I could hear a grinding noise from within, a droning crackle, and was reminded of how my childhood curiosity tempted me to sneak up to beehives in the field and how in time I had learned to associate the languid buzzing with the threat of sharp stings. It must be the patients themselves who make the sound in there, in the listless throes of their madness, packed on top of each other in overcrowded rooms. From time to time, ladies and gentlemen from the city travel out in a barouche in order to be astounded by the folly of the afflicted, in exchange for a couple of coins passed to the guards. Those of my carers who have the energy to partake in such things pay close attention to how the guests act as they depart and grin broadly should their faces show pale.

For reasons of which I cannot fully give account, I now steered my course there. As yellow as an unlanced boil, the asylum straddles its crag, the old salt mill, once set apart from populated areas because of its harsh vapors, now because of its residents. At the entrance, I was confronted by a plaque with wording in a kind of verse: A PATHETIC GREED, AN UN-HAPPY LOVE, HATH BESET THE INHABITANTS OF THIS HOUSE—READER,

KNOW THYSELF! How well could these angular stone letters have been hewn to describe myself?

No one barred my way and I found the large gate unlocked. As soon as I opened it a crack, noise flooded out, the same noise I had earlier only been able to hear as a muffled sigh. Now I could make out many voices: chattering, complaining, wailing, and giggling. The light of the hallway was dim, and it took a while until I could see a small man, standing very still as if he had been awaiting my arrival. I gave him a nod and he sped across the floor to my side. His eyes were intense and betrayed a kind of mocking curiosity, his voice smooth and refined.

"Welcome! And exactly on the hour agreed upon. You are to be congratulated on such punctuality."

I did not know what he was talking about. My face must have revealed my confusion, but his radiant mood was not affected and he bowed, waving at the stairs.

"If you will be so good as to follow, I will show you around."

Since I could hardly deny that it was my curiosity that had drawn me here, I did as he said, even though I had been mistaken for another.

I followed him out into a courtyard, surrounded on all sides by walls that stretched four storeys up. Below the wall, there lay a great deal of rubbish, evidently thrown down from the windows above, the panes of many of which were cracked or patched with boards. A group of lunatics were standing in a corner in their dirty shirts, rocking back and forth, trailing drool from their chins. My guide followed my gaze and gave them a dismissive wave.

"Take no notice! They are cattle in human form and not unruly as long as one doesn't scare them to stampede. I have far more interesting patients to display."

A couple of steps led us out of the courtyard on the other side and, after we had climbed even further up, my host positioned himself next to a door leading to a corridor, cleared his throat, and began a short speech.

"From the beginning, we had twenty-seven cells here, each one intended to house a patient in relative comfort. I do not know how you view the world, sir, but if you ask me, it is not very surprising that the need quickly turned out to be far greater. The city robs people of their wits, and we receive an endless stream of lunatics. Today, each room must house a quartet at least. And many are violent so we have to put them in irons to keep them apart, and in many cells we have had to raise partitions for this same reason."

He stepped aside, pulled back the bolt on the door to the corridor, and showed me through. I was met with the sight of a set of double rows of heavy doors, as well as a deafening roar. Wails and whimpers were intermingled with the sounds of fists and objects striking the doors and scraping walls.

"It is close to feeding time. They may have lost their minds but there is nothing wrong with their bellies, and it is by hunger that they measure time." He continued down the corridor, stopping from time to time in order to point out an interesting detail. "Many of the patients are so far gone they can hardly be let out at all, so you will observe that we have special openings in the doors by which the chamber pots can be emptied. Sadly, not all are able to use the facilities as intended, hence the stench. Even the stoves are fed logs from the corridor, although we can only afford to light them at night when it is coldest. The crowded conditions yield some advantages when it comes to keeping the rooms tolerably warm. Will you see?"

He placed a finger over his lips and gingerly opened a hatch which, set at eye height, forced him on his toes. The sight brought a smile to his face and he waved me closer. It took a while for my eyes to pierce the shadows. Inside, a half-naked man was performing a lumbering dance to the rhythmic clanking of the links on the chain that kept his one foot secured to the wall. Along the wall, three others sat on top of bales of straw, and when I saw that they were all kneading their stiffened members with knuckles that shone white through the dirt, I turned away in disgust.

We walked on. My guide showed me the cells at the very end. "Here are the dark rooms, where the French disease has advanced beyond the aid of mercury. It is not possible to peek inside but they are not much longer for this world. Saddle noses and ulcerated sores, and their helpless rages are a sight to behold when the mood takes them. Otherwise they express themselves little, the tips of their tongues having been eaten away by the pox."

I became aware of a rising nausea and an overwhelming desire to leave this godforsaken place for the bleak shoreline that now seemed as enviable as the Elysian fields. My guide, however, made no move but stood quite still as if awaiting a question. "What kinds of cures do these miserable creatures receive?"

He nodded eagerly as if he had anticipated my query.

"As science tells us, madness is a result of a sound mind being wrenched from its seat by outer or inner circumstances, and we know that reason can be tempted to return if the patient is administered a shock as substantial as the one that caused the imbalance in the first place. We have a leather hose to provide sudden cold water baths. We once introduced scabies to the inmates in the hope that the itching would triumph over the insanity, but now it infests the walls so the newly admitted are infected willy-nilly. And there are other methods that we can pass over for the moment." He may have chosen to add these last words because a sudden vertigo had driven me to seek the support of the wall.

Finally he turned and showed me out, but as we passed the cell with the four men, I suddenly felt his hand on my shoulder.

"I see that I left the hatch open and that is just as well, since there is one last thing I wish to show you." He propelled me to the door where the same scene was still in progress. "Do you see the corner in there, at the very back? Where some of the gentlemen have done their business?" His mouth approached my ear and his voice dropped to a whisper. "That is the place we have saved for you. Soon you will return and we will be ready." I drew back and saw his mouth forming a distorted grin, revealing two rows of sharp teeth with plenty of gaps. "You are so young and handsome. So slender, with alabaster skin. You will give your cellmates plenty of joy, I assure you."

"Who are you?"

He peered at me with disapproval. "Oh, it varies from day to day. Yesterday I was King Charlie the Dozenth himself, lost in happy memories of how I led my boys in blue through the snowclad woods of Masuria, where we slew infants with our boot heels in front of their parents on our way to the killing grounds of Poltava. If you had come yesterday, you would have been able to hear the lead ball that took my life rattling when I shook my head. Today? Today my names are far more numerous than anyone can count. I've been called the Old One, the Adversary, the Archfiend, Prince of Darkness, Son of the Morning. You may call me Satan. We are waiting for you. You know better than anyone how much you belong here."

I don't know how I would have responded to this if we had not been interrupted by a strange voice that rose above the din of the corridor.

"Tomas, you know that you have no business here. We have told you many times not to take liberties simply because we choose to give you the benefit of the doubt. Straight back to your bed, now."

A compact man in a stained jacket had appeared at the door at the other end of the corridor and was now approaching with quick steps.

My guide took a step closer to me and fixed me with a stare. "I will leave you with a riddle. They say that I am constrained to my infernal kingdom, locked in hell. How then can I be here among the people? I've left clues for you everywhere. Remember what you have seen, and mind your step as you make your way through the world."

The other man, who must have belonged to the asylum staff, seized the patient he called Tomas by the arm and began to pull him down the corridor, sweat running down his broad face. As Tomas struggled, he was grabbed by the collar and received a series of forceful slaps to his head until his tears and the blood gushing from his nose ran together down his chin. His assailant cast me an awkward glance.

"We sometimes leave his cell unlocked, and he sometimes happens to go wandering around the asylum, all the way down to the hospital. There are only two of us to look after the loons during the day, and I would be most grateful if you would keep this incident to yourself. I hope that Tomas has not upset you. He says the strangest things."

....

Relieved at the misunderstanding, but shaken by Tomas's words, I staggered outside, standing still for a while in order to reflect on this tomb of the living. Suddenly it was as if the world itself had tuned its strings from the pitch of my mood. I felt the light shift, although there was not a cloud in the sky. I squinted upwards. What I saw filled me with terror, for it was as if some strange creature had taken a bite out of the disc of the sun itself, like a segment of freshly sliced bread bitten off by my own teeth. I could not help letting out a scream, and my knees buckled. I lay curled up on the snow, trembling, for a long time, racked with the deepest fear, before I dared to open my eyes again and found that the light had returned. An eclipse, nothing more. It can't have lasted more than a few minutes.

I hurried back along the way I had come until I could shut the door of my room behind me, crawl into my bed, and pull a blanket over my head. It was a mistake to have left my room, one I will not make again. I have been asked to wait patiently for the right cure. Until then I have to bide my time and avoid the company of others. Tomas may have been a lunatic, but he also reminded me of the shame that is mine; I can't look another in the eye without being reminded of my misdeed, and the pain this causes in me is unbearable.

From time to time, it is possible to obtain thebaica, a tincture that dulls the mind and body, assuaging pangs and cramps, allowing me to spend the day in such a daze that I hardly notice even the most persistent visitor. But I have to share these precious drops—dissolved in water and mixed with sugar or honey—with many others. The supply often dwindles, even though we are fortunate, for I have heard that the hospital also controls the portion allotted to the asylum. Those days, when no drops are to be had, I vow to act the part. I will rock back and forth, or face the wall with my eyes half-open, humming tunelessly, and fix my gaze in vacancy until my visitors' patience wears thin and they leave me in peace to ruminate on my guilt. I shall remain in this state until the hour of twilight and, in its wake comes the night, when I am able to set out my writing implements without being observed.

....

My benefactor has asked me to write in order to better document the memories of the unfortunate events that have reduced me to such wretchedness, and perhaps so I may accept the events that have brought me here to the bleak shores of the Salt Sea, to Dane's Bay Hospital. I have been told that I am not in full possession of my faculties and that that which is not right may be cured, that the source of my guilt is not my own but a whim of nature. I nurture little hope that this is true.

A storm rages in my head and my heart holds only emptiness. I raise my hands before me. Red. They cannot be washed clean. The tools of a murderer.

I lacked love for most of my life, but what I would never have been able to imagine is what it would look like when it finally arrived—beautiful but terrible, a fever in the blood, a tyrant dressed for a feast—nor how it would lead me so far down this dark path from which there can be no return. If I were granted one wish it would be this: never to have loved. Without love, we would have been spared all this. I wouldn't be here on this godforsaken rock, and she . . . No, no more. Let the quill rest now. I am not yet ready to write of the end, and so the beginning must suffice this night.

2

Mine could have been a childhood without sorrow, one where I lacked for nothing, but fate had a different plan. I was born under a velvet canopy on my father's estate, passed down over generations, which like my family itself bore the name Three Roses. The grounds were far from the city, overseen by a long line of fathers and sons with little interest in politics and who were therefore viewed as harmless by the outside world. The soil yielded good harvests and my father took good care of his tenants, wise enough to realize how much the appreciation of his subordinates benefited his affairs.

I came into this life seven years after my brother, Jonas, my only sibling. My mother, accustomed to the bustle and flair of the city and bored by her staid country life, had again begun to long for a baby. She was advanced in age and the risks were considerable, but my mother was a brave woman who knew her own mind. My birth was preceded by more than one miscarriage, which my mother took very hard. In order to taunt me, my brother related a private conversation on which he had eavesdropped, in which an elderly physician she consulted tried to dissuade my mother from bearing another child at her age, which he had previously assumed had already robbed her womb of fruitfulness. He offered her a variety of methods to end her pregnancy. She gave a derisive laugh and told him to go to hell. And when I arrived, some three weeks later than expected, it was at the cost of her life. Only once did I feel the warmth of a mother's embrace, and of that moment I have no memory. Her arms grew cold around me.

....

The unfortunate circumstances of my birth indelibly marked the relationship between me and my father. He was at peace with the heir he already had, felt too old to raise an infant, and I assume that the sight of me was a constant reminder to him of how he had been robbed of the wife with whom he had planned to gild his ailing years. Perhaps he felt particularly shortchanged since I soon proved to be poorly suited for any of the skills he most valued. I never comfortably sat on horseback, I missed the easiest shots when hunting, the foil slipped from my hand as soon as it crossed my opponent's steel, and my constitution often brought me down with a fever or cough that prevented my participation even when the will was there.

I was increasingly left in the care of my tutors, and when the day became a long line of duties and frustrations, I made the night my own. While the house slept, I left my bed. My mother's portrait hung above the stairs, and it was said that we looked alike. Many times, I carefully pulled a stool across the floor in order to lift down the heavy mirror and place it under her portrait in order to more clearly see her face in mine, moving the low flame of the candle back and forth to allow the light to caress every likeness between us: the line of a chin, the roundness of a cheek, the curve of an eyebrow.

I had not yet turned eleven when my brother left us to begin his military career. My father took the loss of his companionship hard. They were close, and the time that my father had left after taking care of his business affairs, they had spent together either hunting or riding, or in marksmanship—all activities from which I was excluded on account of my age and incompetence. I don't think I ever saw him smile again, except during one of my brother's visits. On those occasions when we could not avoid each other's company, I sensed in him a simmering rage at the hand he had been dealt. I went to great lengths to avoid meeting him in the hallways of Three Roses, and increasingly regarded him with fear. He began to seek his comfort in the wine cellar. From time to time he performed his fatherly duty by disciplining me when I had broken one of the rules of the house, and for a few days after the beating he could be milder than usual. For my part, I shed bitter tears, more from indignation than pain, and withdrew still further.

....

At Easter that year, my father invited friends, acquaintances, and the more well-to-do of the tenants on our estate to a feast, the first large celebration in years. During the preparations, I noticed for the first time in a long while a degree of enthusiasm in my father, but soon we received the message that Jonas's regiment could not spare him, and the spark that had been lit in my father's eyes was immediately extinguished. He likely wanted to cancel the whole thing, but the invitations had already gone out. During the festivities, he had soon drunk too much and the melancholy that grew with each glass of wine spread inexorably to the rest of the party.

Towards evening, dinner was served, the place beside my father left empty in memory of my mother. When I glanced towards him from a few seats down the table, I saw how a flush had begun to spread across his face and heard his speech becoming slurred. He rose unsteadily to give a toast to my mother, tears running down his beard. In the solemn silence that followed, I reached for my glass from the monogrammed service my mother had brought as part of her dowry and that was so rarely used, but misjudged the distance and knocked it over so the stem snapped. I grew quickly at that age and had had trouble judging the length of my arms and legs. My clumsiness was a source of irritation for my father, and I saw how his grief now transmuted into rage. Before I knew it, he was lifting me by the collar and delivering a barrage of blows. As soon as some guests who had jumped up were able to free me from his grasp, I ran sobbing from the room, curling up behind a bank of snow piled up on the colonnade, and made myself small and invisible when the servants came to look for me.

I lay there for a long time, crying, until I felt the presence of another. When I lifted my head, it was a girl, as pale as the snow and with hair as red as embers shining on a copper kettle. She stood calmly in the snow, which was starting to fall more heavily now, as if unaffected by the cold, although she had not bothered to wrap anything around her simple cotton dress. Without saying anything, she lifted her hand and I saw that she was carrying a glass exactly like the one I had broken. She held my gaze as she dropped it straight down on the flagstones, where the shards were lost among the fallen icicles. Such was our first meeting.

That celebration was the last event when my father managed to show even a glimmer of happiness. He allowed himself to sink ever deeper into melancholy.

3

I searched for her as if I knew where to look, as if I had been gifted with the ability to pick up the scent of her trail and I only needed to follow my instincts. And find her I did, in the forest where spring had thawed the ground and meltwater babbled around tree roots. A glimpse of a white dress between dark tree trunks, a face as pale, her hair a mocking flame. Limbs as slender as a twig.

Although my search for her was successful, I was awkward at first because she seemed to me a creature born of the landscape itself, some fairy or sprite. She immediately perceived my eyes upon her and stopped in the middle of the fallen tree on which she was balancing. She did not run away but made a pirouette on the slippery bark and turned around, casting a glance over her shoulder, her green eyes full of question and challenge, and forces unseen lent me the courage to follow.

Her name was Linnea Charlotta, her father, Eskil Colling, one of the many who rented the land that had belonged to my family since time immemorial. Colling was an energetic and industrious man who, after much hard work, had been able to better his lot considerably. He knew how to work the land in the best way. Since arriving at Three Roses a few years earlier, he had been able to increase the scale of his tenancy and, thanks to efficient management, the family rose in position and reputation. But he was shrewd enough to know that more than sheer labor was required for anyone who wanted to raise himself above his station; he carried himself more as a gentleman than a farmer, although subtly, so as not to give offense. He dressed his wife and daughters in clothes attractive enough to flatter their beauty, and he himself wore a golden chain with his watch, silver buckles on his shoes. His strategy paid dividends. Among our tenants, it was Colling that my father held in the highest regard and, whenever we received cancellations or had empty chairs at our table, it was Colling and his family who were next in line to invite, as had been the case that Easter when I first laid eyes on Linnea Charlotta.

In the forest, we played tag. We were children, and the friendship between us was evident but fragile. Linnea was steered by her impulses. Her patience would give way without warning, and her eyes would shoot thunderbolts; I learned to run rather than fight fire with fire. But she was always there the next day, waiting for me, often to my surprise, and I learned the word *sorry* in a language that was hers alone: a crooked smile under a bashful gaze, an apparently accidental touch, a jingling laugh at something that I said that was hardly worthy of such appreciation. And then we were friends again, and she would lead me to places that I otherwise would never have found, for the forest seemed as unable to keep secrets from her as I was. An old elk bull's drinking spot by the edge of the tarn, the concealed nest of a woodpecker and a tawny owl's hole in a rotten tree, an eagle's palace of branches at the top of a pine . . . I didn't have much to offer in return, but what little I had was hers. According to her whims, I wrestled young branches in arches to the ground, swallowing my tears if they happened to spring back and whip me across the cheek, covering them with spruce and creating a shelter for us both.

How much better would it not have been for us both if we had been allowed to linger in these innocent games of childhood? But the years went by, and they did not leave us untouched. Linnea's thin body, once hardly indistinguishable from my own, altered according to nature's will. At Three Roses, everything stayed the same, and despite all the days we spent together far from the gaze of others, time seemed to me so brief, so very brief. Memories of the changing seasons flow together, many summers become one, one wintertime game of hide-and-seek among the snowdrifts is impossible to distinguish from another. Suddenly we were fourteen years old and children no longer. Maturity crept up on us stealthily. Neither of us wanted it. I remember how we were once surprised by summer rain in a meadow, where the shower made Nea's dress a mere veil, and she wrapped her arms to cover herself while I bashfully lowered my eyes to the ground. After that, she began to dress differently, but our games were sometimes rough and we could hardly avoid touching each other, whereupon we would jump apart and the silence would grow long, without either of us knowing how best to break it. A couple of days each month, she stayed at home rather than appear at our meeting place, and afterwards she made all kinds of excuses. I had also grown, was stronger now than Linnea, and when we fought I had to pretend in order to preserve the impression that we were still evenly matched. Neither of us had wanted to taste the apple of knowledge, but our paradise had nevertheless changed.

Her moods became more volatile. A single poorly chosen word or action could spark the fire of rage, enough for her to either storm away or banish me from her forest with a gesture worthy of a queen. It was summer when I at last challenged her, in a willful mood myself after having lain in bed with a fever for a few days. Her shoves were like nothing to the muscles of my budding manhood and, when she jumped on me intent on scratching, I only laughed because one of Linnea's bad habits was to bite her nails down so far that they were useless. Before I knew it, she had grabbed my hand and sunk her teeth into it, not in jest, but so hard that she drew blood.

I screamed as much in surprise as in pain. She let go, our eyes met, and I saw the tears of despair streaming down her cheeks. With trembling breath, she turned and ran away among the spruces. Although I wanted to follow her, I remained where I was, red drops watering the moss.

To this day I bear the marks of her teeth, on the very hand writing these words.

The next day, it took me a while to find her, my hand bandaged and supported in a sling around my neck to ease the pain. She had chosen a clearing far away as her hiding place, a site she had shown me once, long before. She gave herself away with her sobs. She sat with her arms wrapped around her knees, shaking like aspen leaves in the wind. A twig snapping underfoot betrayed me, and I sank down into a crouch as close to her as I dared.

"What is it, Nea? Don't mind the hand, it's hardly a scratch, let's forget all about it."

It took a while before she answered, and when she did, her face was buried against her knees.

"You should hear how they speak about you, Erik."

At first I did not understand what she meant.

"Who?"

"My father is so proud to work your father's land. He speaks about Old Three Roses as if he were the sun itself, as if the crops couldn't possibly grow without his leave. My sisters gossip about your brother and his officer friends as if they are prizes in a competition, the rules of which they all know. They spend every free moment preening their feathers. They are learning to sit nicely in beautiful dresses, to embroider flowers with needle and thread, to manage a household and hold a tune, and make their eyes lecherous while the words stay chaste, all accomplishments which will be useful to them to catch a man richer than the one who fathered them."

She lifted her face and dried her eyes and nose. Not even swollen eyes and a blush of sorrow could rob her of her beauty.

"And I have to sit there quietly and listen. My father wants me out of the forest and on a loom, or with my nose in the catechism. My sisters tease me about you, they've seen us together, they're encouraging me because they judge others by their own standards. The injustice of it all passes over their heads. One is born a Colling, the other a Three Roses, one with nothing, the other with all. Father has to grovel and scrape for crumbs from your table, and is so used to it that he swoons with delight each time his flattery hits the mark. My sisters want nothing more than to one day look down on others as others now look down upon them."

I had never heard her speak so before.

"But Nea—"

She did not let me finish.

"I don't want what they want. I want to be myself alone. I have never wanted a man."

My bewilderment must have been apparent on my face. When she continued, her voice was barely audible.

"But you I want, Erik Three Roses. You and no one else. You have slain my old dreams, and which ones I should now dare to dream, I no longer know."

A wild happiness grew inside me. The words came of their own accord.

"I want you too. No one else. I know how your dream should look because it is the one I've dreamed myself many times. You and I before the pastor, Linnea, husband and wife."

She shook her head sadly. "I don't want to be a noblewoman cooped up in a manor house, sitting in judgment over others, waited on by those whose friendship is only a disguise for envy."

I laughed.

"My brother will inherit Three Roses. My lot hardly amounts to anything. If you crave freedom for the price of poverty, I could not make you a better offer."

I was shaken by sudden doubt, and the manly voice that had just sprung out of me was once again the stammer of a young boy.

"If you want to, that is."

She was still crying but her tears were different.

"Yes! A thousand times yes."

And she wrapped her arms around me with a force I had never felt before. We sat like that for a long time and as she was unwilling to part ways, she followed me all the way back to the meadow outside Three Roses.

She held her lips up to mine in farewell. I had never before shared a kiss, but the art is as old as mankind and so I closed my eyes and answered while the darkness behind my eyelids swirled with shapes and colors. All of the love that life had denied me now streamed into me through the single point where she and I were one. I was granted what I had been lacking, whole for the first time. My entire body trembled at this enormity, my knees buckled and our tears mingled with the same salt tang as where our lips met.

4

My brother, Jonas, who had been granted leave in order to assist with the harvest, was the first to make me aware that my love for Linnea was no secret at Three Roses. The day after he arrived, he took me along to the stables with the excuse of showing me his horse, and gave me a sly pat on the shoulder, and a smirk.

"So, little brother, the stable hands tell me that you spend your summers rolling in the hay with the daughter of one of our tenant farmers." I stood silently, staring at the floor while he continued with a laugh. "She is said to be a beautiful girl, but a peasant's daughter, Erik—surely you can aim higher? Even if I have never had much good to say about your other qualities, you have always been pleasing to the eye." I blushed, which amused him even more. "People also say that she is a bit strange, that she keeps to herself and puts on airs, even that she is quite thick in the head, which I'm tempted to believe since she puts up with your company." He jabbed me in the side with his elbow to mark the jest, and insisted on hearing the lascivious details that existed only in his imagination.

When I remained silent, he wagged a finger and warned me to be wary of any unwanted consequences of the affair. His warning would prove well founded as soon as the harvest celebrations were over, days during which my duties prevented me from meeting Linnea Charlotta— not in the way he had meant, but by way of a summons to my father's chamber. I wondered who had given us away.

....

I had not seen my father alone for several weeks and only now noticed how much his last episode of melancholy had sapped his strength. He appeared to have aged a great deal this short summer: his face was more lined, the hairs on his head ever more scarce. He must have lost at least twenty pounds, which had caused his once full cheeks to sink in and had changed his appearance in a way that frightened me. His private chamber was somber despite its magnificence, with the curtains drawn to banish the afternoon sun. He gestured me to sit in one of the two chairs that he had evidently arranged across from each other for the sake of the meeting. He sighed deeply before speaking.

"I hear from your tutor that your studies go neglected."

I hung my head and kept my replies brief rather than resorting to lies, and soon my father decided to take the bull by the horns.

"I take it that you are sleeping with her?"

I blushed, and I could feel my heartbeat in my ears.

I shook my head, and it took him a while to ask the next question.

"Why not?" In the silence that followed, he rose and walked over to the window, where he remained standing in front of the gap between the curtains, his hands clasped behind his back. "Erik, you are a second son. That is no fortunate circumstance. It is your brother who will inherit and become the master of Three Roses, and effort will be required if you seek to advance our family. You will have to make a good match. If you are interested in women, I know of several daughters whose fathers are prepared to pay a substantial dowry in order to have earls for grandchildren."

Tears of indignation sprang to my eyes. This did not escape my father, who shook his head in displeasure before returning to his chair. "Do not misunderstand me. I don't say that you have to break off contact with this girl. Not at all. Enjoy yourself with her, Erik, and sow as many wild oats as your heart desires. If her belly swells, we can afford the bastard even if we will have to find some man to marry her. If you want to keep her as a mistress afterwards, I have no objection. But she can never be your wife, Erik. No Three Roses marries a peasant's daughter."

I dried my eyes as I prepared my answer, and heard how childish my voice sounded, muffled as it was between bookshelves and floral tapestries. "Her family is rich enough for me."

Now it was my father's turn to redden, but from anger. "So the rough-hewn floors of some cottage are to be preferred above the estate of your forebears? A lousy hay mattress better than silk sheets, as long as she lies in your arms? Do you think we have gained all this without sacrifice, and that you are free to cast off the labors of your forefathers for some youthful infatuation?"

I had rarely gone against my father, and never without regretting it. I found the courage I needed in my love for Linnea. "I love her above all else. We are already engaged, and even though it has not been declared at the altar, I am certain that God heard every word."

My father's riposte spouted from his mouth like water out of a boiling kettle.

"Your mother gave her life for yours. You hid in her belly for too long, and when you finally came out you tore her in two. How many happy years would have been ours, me and my beloved wife's, if it hadn't been for you? You stole her from me. And what are you doing to repay that debt, Erik? You want to throw your life away on a pauper."

My father was silent for a long time. I sensed that he was searching for a way to regain his calm. After a while, his breathing slowed, his hands stopped trembling, and when he began to speak again, his voice was controlled once more. "You will be fifteen in December. Three years remain until you are of an age to make decisions for yourself."

"I will wait as long as is required."

He raised his hand to stop further interruptions. "I shall send you south, Erik. I have associates in business on Saint Barthélemy, our Swedish crown colony, and I will ask them to find a position for you. When you turn eighteen, I cannot prevent you from returning home and cannot do anything other than appeal to your reason. But I hope you may change your mind after seeing more of what the world has to offer."

I rose so abruptly the chair was pushed back.

"Never. I will not leave her." I began to walk to the door on trembling legs. His voice followed me out.

"You will depart, and if you refuse to go, I will have no other choice but to cancel her father's lease. The choice is yours."

I rushed to my room, aware that my father had dug a hole for me from which there was no escape. I felt rage well up inside, to a degree I had never felt before. A red veil clouded my gaze, expanding until the world was consumed by a roaring haze. When I regained my senses, I found myself standing among the wreckage of the furniture in my room. I blinked in shock at the devastation, uncomprehending, as if I had witnessed a theatrical performance where the curtain had just been drawn and opened, but where by some mishap an entire scene had been left out and all context had become lost. Pain caused me to look down. My knuckles were bleeding and my fists were swollen and bruised. If it had not been for the evidence of my own hands, I would have been convinced that some unknown perpetrator had seized the chance to wreak this havoc while I was unconscious.

This was how the kiss that Nea and I had shared revealed a previously unseen side to my nature. A repressed rage lay ready to explode each time my love for Linnea Charlotta met with obstruction. In her, I had won something I could not afford to lose, and forces I had never before had to call upon stood at the ready to spring to its defense. This outburst was the first. To my grief, it was not to be the last.

5

As soon as I could, I went looking for Linnea Charlotta, but she was not to be found in any of our usual meeting places, and when I saddled a horse and rode over to Eskil Colling's farm, I was told that she had gone to stay with relatives. When I met her father's gaze, I sensed fear. In my person, a boy of only fourteen, he saw an ogre that threatened to lay his future to waste. I started to lead my horse home, bitter tears on my cheeks, only to find Linnea Charlotta's mother waiting for me by the side of the road where the fields ended and the forest began. She was sitting on a rock and she offered me a place next to her.

"I have seen you, of course, you and my Nea. Even back then I thought that this would never end well, but there was nothing I could do. She is a strong-willed girl and I could only hope that passion's wick would burn down of its own accord." She met my gaze. "For a long time, I was afraid that she was only a plaything for you. A farmer's daughter for a young nobleman to dance with while summer lasts."

"I have never touched her. I want her for my wife. I seek your blessing."

It took a while for her to reply, but first she sighed deeply. "She cried, Erik, so that my heart came near to breaking. She hung on to the doorway harder than any grown man would. I know your father is sending you away, but though we gave him a promise to keep Linnea Charlotta from you until you left, I will give you a promise also, and hope that will be a comfort to you: she will wait. Nea will remain unmarried until the day you come of age. She does not want anyone else, and we have never been able to make that girl do what she didn't want. If you return then, and you both still want the same thing, you will have our blessing."

I fell into her arms and, after we had said our farewells, I was struck by a sudden thought and turned around. "If I write to her and send the letters here, will you make sure they get to the right place?"

She hesitated for a moment, then nodded, and I returned home to write the first of many.

....

My date of departure was set for late in October, which gave me plenty of time to prepare. I went to the library in the hope of finding something about Saint Barthélemy. My father was no scholar, however, and the volumes he added to the collection of the house were few. After a few hours of fruitless pursuit, I gave up and instead placed my hopes in my tutor. As usual, Lundström was sitting in his room, curled over a stub of a candle and a book. He gave me the kind of admonishing look that he so often had since my meetings with Linnea had started to impinge on my studies. I made an effort to look contrite, and we briefly spoke about my situation. He softened a little. Rumors of my upcoming departure had naturally spread like wildfire, and he did his best to cheer me up, and was much aided in this once I related the meeting with Linnea's mother.

"But in that case, Erik, what could be better? She is waiting for you without any expectations of duty from your side, and in the meantime it is high time for you to have an adventure or two. You can't go from school-boy to husband without first having experienced something of life. The fact is that I wish I were in your shoes. Both Euphrasén and Carlander have already visited Saint Barthélemy to gather specimens, and Fahlberg, who remains there, frequently sends his findings back, to the delight of the Academy, but I am sure there is still much to discover."

When I began to question him in more detail, his expression changed from boyish enthusiasm to the wrinkled brow of the pedagogue, and I realized he was concentrating in order to recall the various aspects of his knowledge. He told me that the colony was turning ten this year and that the late King Gustav in his great wisdom had acquired it from the French in exchange for toll-free rights in Gothenburg harbor, as good a deal as anyone had heard of. The island was one of many on the other side of the great Atlantic Ocean and was said to be a tropical paradise as if sprung from the pen of Defoe, well suited to those crops that would otherwise cost vast sums of money for the nation to buy: cotton for clothing, sugar to season food, molasses for drinks and for sweetening. The capital, Gustavia, was named after the king himself.

"Who lives there?" Lundström tapped his front teeth with his thumbnail. "Many Swedes, would be my guess, but you will also get good use of your French."

When his knowledge of the subject appeared tapped, I bashfully begged his forgiveness that my antics had cost him his position, but he simply shrugged. If I promised to collect him some natural specimens, we would be even. I gave him my word.

....

The weeks dragged tediously by. As the date of departure approached, Johan Axel, my cousin, arrived with his bags packed. He was going to accompany me to Saint Barthélemy, and it was impossible to mistake how much he was looking forward to the adventure. This was only natural: like me, Johan Axel had arrived too late in this world to be able to count on an inheritance. He had several older brothers and was planning to study, but welcomed the possibility of first acquiring experience elsewhere. Also, our relationship, which had at times been close during our childhood, had grown less so during the months when I spent all my time at Linnea Charlotta's side. He appeared happy to renew our friendship, and his enthusiasm was a comfort to me.

My own packing was easily completed. Not many of my possessions were suited to the tropics. My shirts and trousers were altered by the maids for a warmer climate than we were accustomed to in the far north. A shoemaker came to measure both me and Johan Axel, and returned a few days later with two pairs of leather shoes that, with a little luck, would accommodate our growing feet for a year or more to come. The farewell between me and my father was dispatched in as few words as one could have imagined, a brief meeting during which his desk prevented us from getting closer than five paces. He drew my attention to an object on its surface: his parting gift, a wooden box of fine marquetry. The lid was fastened with a clasp, and when I opened it and lifted the lid, I found a pistol inside, the barrel of which was of tempered steel and the handle inlaid with an intricate design in brass. There were also a few bullets, a powder flask, and a bullet mold. Our coat of arms appeared above the barrel of the gun, along with my monogram.

6

The trip to Stockholm, from which we would embark on the ship that would carry us south, took only a couple of days, and on Friday, the thirty-first of October, at eight o'clock in the morning, we carried our trunks up to the ship's purser, Schinkel. The travel documents were completed and we were helped with our luggage the short distance down to the ship's berth on the Quayside. The ship was moored with heavy ropes, which was still not enough to keep the gangplank from scraping back and forth across the gravel of the quay. It consisted of little more than a few planks strapped together, yet it marked a border of a fateful kind. It was with an ominous feeling that I took the four steps that led me up on deck to find my entire world changed: here everything was in constant motion, to the accompaniment of groaning and creaking from boards and rigging. The smell of sea and tar was strong.

Everything happened quickly. Experienced sailors cast off, hoisted the sails, and a gentle wind pushed us out towards the Baltic. The colorful rows of houses along the Quayside grew increasingly distant, eventually to be lost from view altogether behind King's Pasture. We did not get far that first day, but in less than a week we left the archipelago behind and had to get used to being surrounded by water in all directions as far as the eye could see. I soon learned how the mood of the sea could shift from one moment to the next. When a storm whipped up, terror reigned on board, and the hand that rested on the rudder could mark the difference between life and death. On other days it was calm, and the sea would lie still as a ballroom floor, with a surface so shiny and transparent, it allowed us to see the remarkable fish that swam close to the ship. At sea, the sight of land is not necessarily comforting. In fact, a leeward shoreline is a source of fear for every seasoned sailor who knows that a capricious breeze can be enough to drive a ship onto the rocks.

Her name was *Unity*, a name that was often the subject of ridicule by the passengers and crew, in light of all the quarrels that inevitably arise in such limited space. She was to be our home for three and a half months. Of life on board, much can be said without truly doing it justice. Everywhere was cramped, solitude nowhere to be found. Our bunks, to which we were often consigned when the waves made us nauseous or because the weather was too violent for us to be allowed above deck, consisted of rolls of cloth hung with ropes from rings in the beams, easily stowed when not in use. To sleep well in them was an art in and of itself, but with much practice we were soon adept. Johan Axel and I were both plagued with seasickness at first, but within a few days we had found our sea legs.

....

We sailed past the island of Gotland after two weeks, went through Kattegat in the middle of December, and celebrated a feeble Christmas in a storm by the shoals of Dogger Bank, where the ship leaned enough to put the port-side railing under water before attempts to lower the mainsail ended with it tearing to shreds. After the white cliffs of Dover were lost behind the crests of the waves, we did not see land again for a long time. Johan Axel and I worked together to create a checkered board and fashion simple chess pieces, and even though I had to rely on luck to even win a game, we did not have anything better to do to make the time go by.

The change of climate crept upon us so slowly during the Atlantic passage that we hardly noticed it from one day to the next, until, after several weeks had passed, both Johan Axel and I could sit next to each other by the railing with our fishing lines, wearing nothing but our breeches. The sun was beaming down, at first making our shoulders red and tender but after a while tanning them brown. Of the passage itself, there is otherwise not much to say.

....

One incident that occurred I would later recollect with regret. It was a gray day, when no one could say for sure if the clouds had sunk low or the fog grown tall. I had climbed into the mizzenmast, where I had found a good seat on a crossbeam. By that time I had learned that the further you get from the ship's center, the more violent the motion, but the sea was so placid and calm that I hardly felt any motion at all, even here. To climb the masts was the only way to be alone, and here I was surrounded by a vast expanse of water and sky in which it was soon impossible to discern where the one ended and the other began. For once, sorrow and longing were not the strongest feelings in my thoughts of Linnea Charlotta. Instead I remembered the joy we had shared, and the tenderness, and I stayed until the damp air plastered my linen shirt to my chest, my hair hung in greasy ringlets, and my body was shivering. I found my way back down with numb fingers and went below deck in search of dry clothes.

Back at my bunk, I found Johan Axel far too engrossed in his activities to hear me until it was too late. He had opened my bag and was in the process of reading my long letter to Linnea Charlotta, the one I had started after leaving Copenhagen and that I would not be able to send until after we reached our destination. When he became aware of my presence, he turned, blushing with shame, trying to stammer out an explanation.

It was as if I had intercepted an eavesdropper while I was baring the deepest secrets of my soul, intended only for her. For the second time, my feelings for Linnea Charlotta transformed my otherwise calm demeanor. I ripped the letter from Johan Axel's hands, trembling with fury. With shaking hands, I smoothed the tainted pages and turned towards him. Once again, it was as if a swathe of time had been removed from my mind. When I regained my senses, I was not sure where I had been: I was standing on the deck of the *Unity*, and at first I did not understand when I found Johan Axel lying on the deck before me, bleeding from his nose, his shirt ripped. Shaking to my marrow, I let my fists fall to my sides and I tried in vain to control the panting that had left a stitch in my side and a taste of iron in my mouth. Johan Axel also lowered the hands he had raised in defense, and the concern in his gaze changed to wonder as he slowly realized what had happened. I had hardly begun to say some confused words before Captain Damp came towards me, freshly roused from his nap by one of the crew. He grabbed me by the collar and roared that I was a hairsbreadth away from spending the rest of the journey in the hold, but he let go of me when I offered no resistance.

Johan Axel, who was now back on his feet, dried his face on his sleeve. He gently took me by the shoulder and led me aside, and the shame I heard in his voice was no less than what I felt.

"Forgive me, Erik. Your father paid my fare on the condition that I make sure you don't do anything ill-advised. He suspected that you had found a way to communicate with your beloved and he insisted on being told what you were writing. I accepted his terms, not for my own sake or his, but for yours. I deceived myself into thinking that my snooping was in your best interests. I won't do it again. You have my word on that, and henceforth we can write the reports back to your father together. Let us be friends again, and I will be a better squire to you than any knight could ever boast of."

He smiled at this allusion to our childhood games, and held out his hand. I seized it, with gratitude and regret in equal measure.

In the middle of February, we sighted Antigua and, after battling a headwind for a few days with the harbor in sight, we were guided in towards Saint Barthélemy.

7

Let me describe Saint Barthélemy the way she appeared when I first laid eyes on her.

We had ample time to observe the island from a distance while we lay at anchor. I had imagined a flowering Eden in the midst of all the blue, where a tight jungle of exotic trees framed cultivated fields laden with sugar and tobacco. Instead, I found her to be more of a dry, bare knuckle of rock, in shades of brown and ocher, thrust above the surface of the water. The only visible vegetation was a bed of thorny brush hugging the hills. Sandy earth, pierced with stone shards, formed an unclear boundary against the waves in the form of shallow swamps. Saint Barthélemy did not look like much, and I couldn't help but make Harcourt's words from de Belloy's tragedy my own: *The more I saw of foreign lands, the greater my longing for home.* I comforted myself with the fact that we were only seeing her from the windward side and that she might do herself better justice from a different vantage point. Many other ships were in the same predicament as us, impatiently waiting for a change in the wind. Whatever her appearance, she did not lack for suitors.

....

The pilot ship, an old cutter by the name of *Triton*, set out for us after we had been waiting our turn a long time, guiding us in between the rocks. The harbor was a natural basin. From between two jutting cliffs stretched a lagoon, with water so clear, the sandy bottom looked near enough to touch. Even so, the depth was enough to allow passage to all but the longest keel. We slowly passed a number of ships, flying every imaginable flag.

At the very end of the bay was the town of Gustavia, named in honor of the founder of the colony, the late King Gustav. Gustav III was also the name of the fort presiding on the hill above the town and whose guns stood mounted to protect the inlet, and every morning hailed daybreak with a boom. As we approached, a flag was raised in greeting on the dock and our captain responded in kind. We were directed to our berth, and after another hour, Johan Axel and I were able to climb down into the rowboat that bore us onto the first dry land we had felt under our feet in many weeks.

The town itself was not yet ten years old, and even though she may lie on the far side of the world, she is nonetheless Swedish and was already counted among one of the nation's most populous. We stood at the edge of the quay for a long time, taking in all the novelty. Life and motion were everywhere. Barrels were hauled ashore while smaller vessels arrived laden with fruit and fish we had never seen before. The more elegant houses had stone foundations on which their wooden walls and roofs rested, and some were surrounded by an attempt at a garden that fought a vain struggle against the sun beating down on us now, and causing us to sweat profusely under the fine clothes we had donned to make the best impression. The men of dark skin were everywhere. I had hitherto only seen their like depicted in illustrations, which hardly did them justice. They worked half-naked and so too did the women. The whites, whom we also saw in great number, wore long, light-colored trousers, with shirts and hats to shade their faces. We quickly became aware of how clearly our dress marked us as foreigners, so it was with some hesitation we made our way along the dusty streets. The men we spoke to for directions to the governor's house all turned out to be French, and even though we were both accustomed to the language, their pronunciation was often strange and presented difficulties. We strolled past houses that appeared increasingly humble the further away from the Carenage— this was the name of the harbor—we strayed. Soon there were only huts with earthen floors, patched together with boards, which did nothing to prevent their inhabitants from conducting commerce of all kinds. We found ourselves in a labyrinth of streets completely without marks of any kind. In this tangled place, the mood was different, full of animosity. Drunkards stumbled about, forcing us to make way for them while they swore at us in French and English. Old women sitting under awnings of palm leaves yelled out the price for which their services could be secured and, when we turned our backs on them, they called our manhood into question. The men were not much better: with insolent expressions, they offered us rum, their dismissive comments burning in our ears as we hurried on. Naked children followed us at a distance to stare at our breeches, silk stockings, and ornate jackets.

....

With some effort, we found the governor's dwelling, announced ourselves at the front door, and were shown into a sitting room, the furnishings of which were a strange mixture of roughly hewn pieces and beautiful objects that must have been shipped from Sweden. We were given lukewarm beer and eventually waved further into the house by a uniformed valet.

Governor Bagge himself, a portly man of between forty and fifty, sat at his desk in his shirtsleeves, sweat stains large as barrel lids under each armpit. When we bowed, he wiped his rosy face with a handkerchief and acknowledged us with a nod while he riffled through a pile of papers to take out a letter in my father's hand.

"Young Masters Three Roses and Schildt, we were expecting you a few weeks ago, but the passage is, of course, always uncertain, and I must confess I thought you long since lost. You see that I am receiving you with a notable degree of informality, and in future I will not ask that you dress more than is necessary on my behalf. A meridian such as this invites us to be a tad more practical than at home, and you will do best by swiftly adapting to our customs." He poured himself a glass of a dark, richly scented liquid from a carafe, which he drank greedily. "We are too few for the assignments to which we have been entrusted, and I always have vacancies in my ranks. We shall soon see which positions best suit you. But that can wait. Allow me to tell you a little of your immediate future, and if you find me too frank, I can only advise you to get used to it. All newcomers to Saint Barthélemy soon fall ill with fever. It tends to last a fortnight, give or take. We have all tried to escape it. None has succeeded. The sickness lingers in the air we breathe, or in the water we drink, or in the food we eat. Most recover, though, and are thereafter no longer bothered by it. But not everyone; the weak submit, here as everywhere. You will surely see the sense in me not wasting more time than necessary until I know how you will fare, and therefore my first order to you is the following: return to the Carenage, ask around for the establishment of Alex Davis, and rent yourselves a room. Spend the short time you have before the fever comes in acquainting yourselves as much as you can in Gustavia. If you can, find Fahlberg, who serves as our provincial physician. He has been with the colony ever since the beginning, just as I have, and what he doesn't know about Saint Barthélemy is hardly worth knowing. Tell Davis that I would like to see you cared for during your convalescence, and unless fate has something different in store, I will see you here again once you have regained your health. In the meantime, it can be useful for you to know that even though we formally follow Swedish Law here, there is considerable difficulty in its application, since the garrison is small and the sins many. Be on your guard. Might makes right, and he who does not possess the strength would do well to proceed with caution. I wish you the best, gentlemen."

He dismissed us with a wave of his hand, already refocused on his papers. We bowed and retraced our way back to the harbor. The ground rocked under our feet, not only because our bodies seemed unable to forget the constant rolling of the ship's deck, but also from our concern over the governor's ominous words.

On our way down to the water, we were met by a remarkable sight, which caused us to come to a complete halt. A black man was coming towards us, making his way with a crutch under one arm. At first we thought he was one-legged, but as we looked closer we saw that this was not the case. Around his neck he bore a collar of iron to which a chain had been fastened. The links ran tightly down his back and held his right leg pulled back so hard his foot rested on the small of his back. On both his neck and ankle, the metal had cut deep enough to draw blood, and with each new step he gave a whimper. When he slowly passed us by, we stared after him and saw that his back was a crisscross of wounds. We did not know what was the matter with him. I turned to Johan Axel.

"Is the man a penitent?"

Johan Axel, who ever since our arrival had been churlish in sharing his thoughts, shook his head thoughtfully, but kept his silence.

8

Alexander Davis, who went by Alex, was a sinewy Englishman who supported himself as best he could, partly from his income from one of the island's modest cotton fields but more so as an innkeeper. His establishment bore the marks of popularity in more ways than one. Everything was worn. Worn-out oak barrels had been set in long rows to serve as tables for the guests as Davis himself walked up and down, chatting with all and sundry, making sure that no one went thirsty, all the while meticulously marking his board to keep tabs.

He took a nonchalant measure of us when we arrived. In the dialect of the island, where Swedish and English words laced a base of simple French, he roared that his rooms were full but allowed himself to be convinced to provide something temporary for us, so long as we were prepared to pay extra for the trouble. He did not give us much to choose from, and quickly recited the services we could expect when the fever struck. Water, a thin soup, rum, help from a maid with the necessities. He poured us some rum to seal the deal, and I could hardly decline. At first I found it revolting, but after the numbing power of the first few sips, I tasted molasses and anise, and I did not find it unpleasant, especially when diluted with a little water. It also took the edge off the anxiety I had been experiencing ever since our arrival on Saint Barthélemy, with everything around me seeming strange and threatening. Dusk and dawn hardly exist at these latitudes. Night rushes in with surprising speed and grows darker than one would imagine, given how piercingly bright the sun is by day. This first evening on Saint Barthélemy we thought we would have plenty of time to unpack our belongings and see more of Gustavia, accustomed as we were to the light hours of the

Swedish summer. We were mistaken and, outside our door, encountered a darkness so thick we could not see our hands in front of our faces.

We were therefore stranded at Davis's establishment and made our way to the public bar in search of an evening meal, where we found some unusual goings-on. A circle had been cleared in the middle of the room, strewn with sand, and people were streaming in from the street. Some of them were carrying cages. As the crowd increased, we were served bread and meat, and in each corner of the room, money started changing hands and small tickets were distributed. Soon, two cocks were set loose in the ring and pushed closer together than either would have preferred, until they each started to attack, eagerly cheered on by the audience. Tiny blades had been tied to their feet. Within a few moments, one had sliced the other's belly badly enough for the innards to well out, and while the conquered animal lay on its back, its legs quivering, those who had bet wisely cashed in their money. This went on, and the heap of slaughtered cockerels slowly grew by the wall.

The room was now so full we could hardly move, and we found it wiser to remain standing than try to push our way through. So we became witnesses to an escalating altercation: a man who had clearly had far too much to drink was demanding the return of his coins from the one who had given him the odds. Soon a thug stepped between them, apparently in the latter's employ. No less drunk was he, but so superior in size and skill that this hardly mattered. The complainant received a few blows before pulling a long dagger out from his boot and cutting the larger man in the side, which caused the thug to lose his temper altogether. A kick disarmed the drunkard, and he was knocked to the ground with a strike to the temple, whereupon the larger man started stamping his foot on his throat and face until blood was spattered everywhere.

It was only when his employer patted him on the shoulder as a sign that enough was enough that he desisted and walked off to get his wound bandaged. His broad back had obscured our view of the man lying on the ground, but now we saw that his face had been disfigured beyond recognition, the eye sockets red pools, his jaw hanging to the side, and only a crater strewn with fragments of bone where his nose had once been. Davis elbowed his way over to listen to the bubbling breaths, then shrugged, shooting a few meaningful glances at those nearest him, all of whom turned around while the innkeeper placed a hand over the man's mouth and nose. The fallen one, barely conscious, made a few attempts at resistance, but Davis shushed him until his heels stopped hammering the floor and his breathing had stopped.

"Welcome to Saint Barthélemy, boys," Davis snarled as the corpse was carried to the side and laid next to the dead cocks. "If you liked tonight's show, we have dog fights here every other week, and every third, negroes." Before we had the chance to escape, we saw a youth use his knife to pry a gold tooth loose from the dead man's jaw, to the objection of none.

I lay awake for a long time that night, and not only because of the heat and the presence of so many unseen insects, some with wings and some with many legs, that haunted our chamber and seemed to like nothing better than to crawl over my skin. In this strange town, which was now to be my home, I felt the longing for Linnea Charlotta more keenly than ever.

....

The next day, we went looking for Samuel Fahlberg. We found him in his home, a man who radiated a healthy vigor, somewhere between thirty and forty but still of a youthful frame of mind. He had just finished his morning meal and we were invited to join him for coffee. He was about to make a visit to one of the patients in his care, but we soon found that surgery was only one of his gifts. Fahlberg had a great knowledge of the island and the town, and confessed to having divided up the land and planned the design of the streets when he had first arrived on the *Sprengtporten*, the first Swedish ship to take the island into possession. "Not that it would be anything to brag about—you can see the results for yourselves. There are forces at work here that will heed neither plumb line nor ruler."

I told him about the scene we had witnessed at Davis's last night; Fahlberg showed little surprise.

"When we first arrived, Saint Barthélemy was sparsely populated, and she needed people if we were to be able to count on any income from taxes. Word was sent out that the island was now under Swedish rule and that only Swedish Law had jurisdiction. Every crook in the Caribbean saw his chance of starting a new career, and they emigrated en masse. Thieves, pirates, and murderers: these are the feet of clay on which this giant stands. Small wonder there's much employment here for one who knows how best to dress a wound."

I mentioned to Fahlberg that I had heard his name before, through my tutor Lundström at Three Roses. The doctor took this as an invitation to talk at length about the various matters of scientific interest on the island, from its geology to its flora. Just then we walked past a woman with a basket of fruit on her head, her skin tone quite light, and Fahlberg was quick to catch our unspoken question as we followed her with our gazes.

"Most men around here take dark-skinned mistresses. Saint Barthélemy may not have been Swedish for longer than a decade, but the English and Dutch have been here for centuries and have reproduced to their heart's content." He went on to list all of the variations in nomenclature he knew.

Johan Axel's expression was grim as he forcefully posed his question. "There doesn't appear to be much fertile land here, and the salt basins by the water can hardly yield a fortune. So how can this island support itself?"

Fahlberg gave him a long look. "If the governor hasn't let you in on that, I think it's best to await his explanation. Have patience until then." Then he bade us good day and promised to visit us at Davis's as soon as our fever started.

....

The chills came on that same evening, first to Johan Axel, who began shaking with cold despite the heat, and, only a few hours later, to me as well.

9

My memories of the days that followed are patchy. Johan Axel and I lay in bed, sometimes overcome with heat and other times quivering with cold. One of Davis's maids occasionally brought us broth, into which she dipped pieces of bread which she held up to our lips. The little I managed to swallow I could rarely keep down, and I had often to fumble for the chamber pot to vomit. Often the spasms came on too quickly and my sick instead hit the floor, where beetles and other insects gathered around to feast. Faces flickered by: the maid, Fahlberg, Davis, Johan Axel—pale and frightened in the few moments his legs managed to carry his weight. No longer could I distinguish night from day.

When the fever was at its worst, I made my peace with the thought that my life would soon trickle out of me entirely. Johan Axel raved in the bed next to me without the ability to put any strength into his words. I started to hallucinate, reality no longer discernible from dreams. Scenes of my life were played for me in random order, eventually only to fixate on one single image, and stay there: her kiss, the one Linnea Charlotta and I had shared, the pivot of my short life. Everything else that I had experienced paled beside this memory. With all the life force that remained within me, I swore to do everything I could to experience that moment again.

....

My next memory is one of blinding light and sudden breeze, and when I opened my eyes, Samuel Fahlberg was standing by my side with a look of satisfaction, the window behind him wide open to air the room.

"So, Erik, the fever has broken. Welcome back to the land of the living."

I turned my head, and found the bed next to mine empty. "Johan Axel? Is he . . . ?"

Fahlberg shook his head. "Between the two of you, it is young Mr. Schildt who has been blessed with the stronger constitution. He has been back on his feet these past four days and is now strong enough to run errands for the governor. So will you, within a day or two. Make sure to eat enough. You have lost much weight, and you were already skin and bones to begin with."

By the afternoon, I was able to stand up, albeit with some difficulty, for the first time in what I learned was two long weeks. I stumbled down to the beach, where I sat on the warm sand with a blanket over my shoulders.

As my fingers dug absently in the sand beside me, they encountered a strange object which, when I lifted it up, I found to be a stone, of a kind I had never before seen. It most closely resembled a branch, pocked with tiny holes, bleached white. I could not discern its nature, but it felt good in my hand, and I recalled the promise I had made to Lundström to save some specimens. When Johan Axel came to find me, a little while later, I slipped the stone into my pocket.

....

Two days later I was ready to work, and presented myself to Bagge, my feverish sweat long since washed away and in newly laundered clothes.

He congratulated me on my recovery. "If you turn out to be as quick-witted as your cousin, you will be an asset to the island."

Johan Axel had already been appointed Notary, but because of my youth, the governor was unwilling to make an immediate decision, preferring to first test my abilities at various tasks. I was close to objecting, somewhat petulantly, that Johan Axel was only a year older than I was, and that I should not be penalized for being of slighter build and looking younger than I was, but I held my tongue.

"To begin with, you may accompany Schildt and inspect the cargoes on the newly arrived ships. He knows the ropes already."

The sudden change in status that separated us caused some embarrassment to both me and Johan Axel as we walked down to the Carenage. He appeared more uncomfortable than I, and just before we climbed into the longboat that would row us out to the anchored ship, he drew me aside.

"Erik, I have learned much about the colony these past few days. I visited a similar ship earlier in the week while you were still in your bed. It is better for you to see it for yourself, since I don't think I can find the words, but I advise you to control yourself. Will you promise me that?"

Without understanding why, I nodded sullenly at these words that had, for a second time that day, made me feel like a chastised child.

....

We sat quietly at the back of the boat as the oarsmen set out, dipping their blades and finding their rhythm. The breakers near shore were violent and repeatedly pushed our shoulders together, as if to force us back to unity, but the further away from land we went, the calmer the water. Once we had rounded the promontory, I saw the ship. As we approached, I sensed a rank odor wafting over the waves. Johan Axel was already pressing a handkerchief against his nose, and I had to breathe through my mouth. The rowers did not flinch. When our boat finally pulled up alongside the rope ladder that had been lowered down, there was no longer any doubt: these noxious smells came from the ship itself, and I wondered what cargo it could possibly contain.

The captain greeted us on deck and introduced himself as Jones, I forget his first name. The conversation took place in English, and Johan Axel made notes in his docket. In response to the question as to whether we wanted to inspect the cargo more closely, my cousin answered in the affirmative, waving me to precede him as we went below deck. As I passed him, he leaned close and whispered in my ear. "Stay calm, for both our sakes."

The stench was now so strong it seemed to me to take physical form, and I waved my arms around me as if to ward off smoke or fog. It was dark inside the ship. A sailor with a lantern lighted our way and led us deeper below. Finally he stopped on the steep stairs and lifted his flame to illuminate the darkness in the low space that opened before us. At first, I saw nothing. Then hundreds of glittering eyes appeared, all turned towards us. I don't know what expectations Johan Axel's warnings had raised in me, but I could never have imagined that hell itself had been borne across the sea.

They were all lying down, naked in long rows, each chained to the other. Between the rows there were even more of them, placed at an angle in order to make use of every inch of the floor. Men, women, and children, stuffed into an area that was only one meter in height. They lay in their own waste, in excrement and bloody vomit and pools of urine that sloshed to and fro with the waves. Among them lay a couple of dead bodies, turned over with their faces in the filth. The buzzing of flies was so loud that their groaning voices could scarcely be heard. I will never forget their eyes: not those that were full of murderous rage at having borne witness to every blow and humiliation they had been subjected to, nor those—far worse—that were as blank and devoid of expression as cattle, as if long since dead inside.

Under that first deck there was yet another, identical. Then another, and another. We did not go further. From the deepest hold, where all the waste and bodily fluids must have accumulated, there rose a choir of lamenting voices speaking foreign tongues.

"Each grown negro," the sailor explained, as I kept my knees from buckling by holding on to a rope, "takes up six times one and a half foot, the women somewhat less, and the children five times one. In this way we can fit almost five hundred slaves. Their own kin sell them to us for glass marbles."

I turned in panic and raced up to the deck, where Jones guffawed at my pale visage. Johan Axel followed me up, and the captain turned to him anew.

"Well, where's the current market stand, and how about the price?"

Johan Axel gave him some numbers and Jones's lips moved silently as he did the mental calculation, eventually breaking out in a satisfied grin. My thoughts spun in my head until I could no longer control myself and ran to the railing, where the results of my retching barely missed our transport back. Johan Axel made my excuses. "My cousin was taken ill with the fever and has still not regained his strength."

On the way back, he put his arm around me where I sat shaking in the scorching sun. "You did better than I, Erik. The first time I saw this, I fainted, and Bagge was quick to blame it on sunstroke." He drew a deep breath from the fresh breeze. "This is Saint Barthélemy's secret, Erik, something I have been aware of for a few days now. The largest slave market of the Antilles is on Swedish ground. We have a free port here, free of charge to the vendor and with only a small export charge for the purchaser. Times have never been better than they are now. The English, allied to the Dutch, have declared war on the French. We are the only neutral port in the West Indies, and the westbound slavers have nowhere else to go."

10

Such was my first insight into Saint Barthélemy's rotten heart. Perhaps I should have picked up on the truth of things earlier, but it would not be the first time I needed longer than others to comprehend the truth. Johan Axel certainly developed suspicions much earlier than I did, and was therefore perhaps better suited to adjust to the order that reigned on the island. For me, it was an unbearable trial, and the hardest thing was meeting the gaze of the many black residents of Gustavia, a handful of whom had bought their freedom and enjoyed a liberty of sorts, but the majority of whom were slaves belonging to some white man. I read in their eyes the emotions they must harbor against everyone of my complexion, from whom they had no reason to distinguish me: fear and hatred, cloaked by a veneer of subordination.

In the governor's mansion, I was soon found ill-suited for most tasks. It came as no surprise that I lacked a good head for numbers, but it was as if the island had robbed me of my other gifts. I had never been much of an actor, and it did not take long for Bagge and his cronies to ascertain my sympathies. Soon I was regarded as sensitive and, as such, untrustworthy. They began to make a point of excluding me from their company. Doors were closed in my face, conversations ended as I reached within earshot. With the excuse that it would toughen me up, they soon found me a suitable task. I was to assist in record keeping for the island's judiciary. Bagge laughed harshly when he gave me my instructions. "Even if Three Roses is not known for his skills in arithmetic, not even you should fail at making lines on a piece of paper."

Without knowing the full scope of what awaited me, I took my satchel of writing tools, put sheets of paper under my arm, and set off for the hillside fort, north of the bay. I arrived late, and they were waiting impatiently for me on the ledge where the guns were arranged to protect the harbor's inlet. The view was astounding and, from this distance, Gustavia appeared a beautiful town. A small group was gathered up there, including a handful of soldiers from the fort in sun-bleached uniforms. The commanding officer made a laborious point of consulting his pocket watch as a reproach for my late arrival, but he soon turned his back on me to get the whole occasion moving. Two soldiers were holding a black woman between them. Dressed only in rags, she was so emaciated that I could count each rib. To my horror, I perceived that she was with child and, to judge by the size of her belly, she was already far gone. On the ground in front of us, a set of leather straps was attached to the wheels of the gun carriage, beyond which, slightly further back, two poles had been set in the ground.

When the soldiers led the woman up to this improvised scaffold, a white man stepped forward and there ensued an agitated exchange in a French so guttural that much of the contents escaped me. I understood enough to realize that the man was the slave woman's owner, and I assumed he was asking for clemency in light of her condition. Instead the discussion ended with the officer making a sign to the two soldiers, who stepped forward and started to dig a hole in the sand halfway between the poles and the gun carriage. I understood nothing. The owner read the confusion in my face, stepped forward, and introduced himself.

"My name is Durat. My apologies for the delay." In my halting French, I asked him what was transpiring, and he laughed heartily and gave me a hard slap on the shoulder as if to confirm my youth and naivety. "You are new. This is how it is: rates on slaves vary a great deal. The ones from the coast of Guinea are worth the least. They don't speak the language and have to be taught all things. If things go badly, they are tempted into disobedience by memories of the life they once led. Far more valuable are our Creole slaves, the ones who are born here and have sipped their servitude with their mother's milk. Obedient, strong, savvy."

I shook my head to indicate that I still didn't completely follow.

"Don't you understand? In her belly there is twenty *moit* of pure profit for me, double the price of a new slave. I will not see it hurt. The hole in the sand is for her belly."

In full view of me, they led her over, removed the few rags she wore, forced her down on her knees, and fitted her stomach into the hole. When they were satisfied, they bound both hands to the wheels of the gun carriage and spread her legs to tie them to each pole. She was crying quietly. The officer recited her sentence.

"The slave woman Antoinette has three times been found to sell goods outside after the hour of darkness in the full knowledge that this is not permitted. Thirty blows before the guard."

The flog-master wrenched his shirt off so it hung from his waist. The whip was twelve feet long, a dark coil of braided leather. We backed away and he began. He was skilled enough to strike the body with the tip of the whip each time. It cracked like a gunshot, echoing off the walls of the fort. Flesh and skin were torn off, accompanied by terrifying screams from the victim. She lost control of her bladder, and her water trickled with a gentle gurgle into the hole where her belly rested. Never had I imagined that thirty lashes could be so many, nor the time to deliver them so long. At nineteen lashes, I held up my hand and called out "Thirty!" with a voice that sounded weak in comparison to the cracks of the whip. None questioned my counting. One of the soldiers loosened the ties, and two slaves lifted up their sister, apparently unconscious, but whose body still rippled with strong tremors, onto a stretcher and carried her off. Durat followed them, and gave me a far darker look than during our first conversation.

Stupefied by what I had seen, I soon made my way back to Gustavia. The trade in humans was everywhere to be seen. Down at the Carenage was the slave market, where auctions were held every other day, with the best goods saved for Fridays when large numbers of buyers flocked in from neighboring islands. Ships arrived every day with fresh cargo. Down by the docks, and at Davis's, they traded tales of terror: when I ate my dinner, I sat so close to the group next to me that I overheard a captain in a state of bitter intoxication complain about his misfortune. He had made the trip across the Atlantic back to Holland with a cargo of sugar, buying large amounts of the kind of trinkets that Africans value, sailed the whole way south to Guinea, and there bought himself enough slaves to cause the hull of his ship to groan. On the way back to the West Indies, the ship had been becalmed, trapped in the doldrums. Weeks had gone by on a placid sea, until finally provisions and water were getting low. He then did the only thing he could under the circumstances: the slaves were led up on deck, all linked together on the same heavy chain, and the first ones pushed overboard. They had to keep going for a long time until the weight of the chain and the bodies gained the momentum, and the ones who remained on board were irresistibly dragged in. With a humorless laugh, he described it as a long, black centipede that left bloody marks as the weight grew strong enough to break legs against stairs and edges. The railing followed in a shower of chips until the very last ones, pummeled into an unrecognizable state after having been dragged along the deck across the length of the ship, were whipped into the sea with a flick, to the delight of the sharks that rose from the deep to feast on their prize. He spat on the ground: his entire fortune extinguished in a few moments! More than a year's worth of work, only to have to start all over again! The stains couldn't be washed out of the ship's timber, he said, greeting him each day as a reminder of his hapless lot.

....

I was sent for later that afternoon to appear before the governor. The color in his face betrayed his rage. "François Durat called earlier today in order to make a complaint. He counted the lashes himself. Thirty was the sentence, and by your count, you spared the slave at least ten. My question to you, Erik Three Roses—and I advise you to weigh your answer with care—is this. Are you an idiot, or did you do this deliberately?"

I bowed my head so I wouldn't have to see his reaction. "I may be bad at counting, but not that bad."

He struck his fist onto the desk so violently as to make the inkwell dance. "Listen to me, Erik. It is of the utmost importance that we ensure any disciplinary action on the slaves is carried out to the letter. There's been a revolution in Hispaniola. Freedmen have grown sufficient in number to incite those still enslaved to revolt. Such large areas of the island are beyond control that it appears lost altogether. Here too the slaves outnumber us, Erik. We can never give them a reason to doubt our strength. Do you think the favor you did her will alter her view of you in the least? Alone with her in a room, under the protection of any walls and doors, and if she had a knife, you'd be breathing your last in the blink of an eye. Only the threat of the whip guarantees obedience from her kind. They speak no language but violence. Tomorrow she'll be given the lashes we owe, and if there is any doubt about the count then, the flog-master will err on the side of caution." He rose to his feet. "But you will not be keeping count, Erik. You have lost my trust. I must admit it is a challenge for me to find you any suitable position here on this island. For now, you are simply to accompany your cousin and assist him in his activities. Tomorrow there's an assignment in the interior of the island where even you can't cause any trouble. If I'm forced to call you back here for any similar reason, the consequences will be dire indeed."

I felt a shift in his mood as he pushed a letter across the desk. "What you have done is a criminal offense, Erik, and one that I should punish severely. I have a hankering to shackle you or to let you yourself take the lashes that you owe. The reason for my leniency is a letter that arrived earlier today from Gothenburg. It's from your father. He also wrote to me, and therefore I can be relatively sure of the contents and want to be the first to offer my condolences. Your brother met with an accident. He fell off his horse. He has not survived."

....

The nights on Saint Barthélemy were full of strange noises. In town, torches blazed, and screeching and bellowing could be heard from every pub, and every building seemed to host at least one. Unseen insects would sound in a unified rhythm and give pulse to the darkness. Slaves were not allowed to leave their beds after dark, but many disobeyed this order, and as visibility was so poor, they often did this without any risk, as long as they stayed away from the streets where the night watchman did his rounds. Even those who remained indoors often stayed up and sang, and the same tunes spread from house to house—mournful songs in a language that not even Fahlberg was able to decipher, recollections perhaps of lands lost but not forgotten. They awakened a yearning in me also. Memories of my brother, so much older than me and never particularly close, were soon replaced with the image of Linnea Charlotta, and the shame I felt about this was no match for the pain of my desire.

11

Gustavia was awakened with a boom from the fort, marking the time as five in the morning. Johan Axel was quickly on his feet, shaking me awake, and once we had finished our morning ablutions, we went outside to saddle the bony horses that he had secured from a stable the day before. The slaves had all been hard at work since first light, and many were eating their breakfast on the go. I felt guilty about the meal we had just enjoyed when I saw what they had to eat. While we broke freshly baked bread and were served fresh fruit with our coffee, as well as any fish that had blessed the nets laid out at night, they had the same meal to look forward to every day: salt herring from Sweden, transported across half the world but still the cheapest food there was to eat. They ate with their fingers out of calabash gourds. For dinner, I had seen them served a scoop of flour to mix with water into a thin gruel. Their work slowly leeched the life out of them, as the efforts of their labor were hardly matched by their diet.

Down at the dock, unloading was already in full swing. Bunches of bananas, tobacco, vats of rum, and barrels of fresh water, all of which we would have lacked on Saint Barthélemy had it not fallen like manna from heaven.

We followed the road up the hill through Gustavia and soon found ourselves beyond the outermost houses in a landscape that I was now seeing up close for the first time. Endless bushes, far too thick and thorny for anyone to pass through. Higher up, the ground lay bare, strewn with gravel and stone. Truly an inhospitable place.

Johan Axel could hardly be unaware of the dressing-down the governor had given me, as he did not question my presence on his assignment.

Yet he seemed determined to let me be the one to bring it up, and I indeed felt the need to clear the air. "I take it you heard?" He nodded. "Do you think I am in the wrong?"

He looked at me with something indecipherable in his eyes. "No. And yes."

"Talk plainly."

"Erik, what we see on this island revolts me as much as it must revolt you. I bitterly regret that we ever set foot on Saint Barthélemy and I am counting every moment until we can leave this awful place behind. You lessened an unjust sentence and I can't blame you for it, but I wish you would think more about where your actions lead you. What you did was obvious to everyone. The slave you spared will now be punished even more severely, and the clear stand you took will not be forgotten. Never again will you be put in a position to do good."

I felt ashamed at the truth of his words. "Yes, you're right. Of course you are. And yet I could do no different."

Johan Axel smiled and shook his head, close enough now to reach a comforting hand to my shoulder. "If you were any different, I wouldn't be as fond of you as I am."

"Is there nothing we can do, then?"

My cousin put his thumb in the corner of his mouth and started chewing thoughtfully on a nail as he often did when he was mulling over something that presented a challenge. "I can't say, Erik. Let's bide our time. Perhaps the time will come. Alone, unaided, there's not much we can do."

We sat quietly for a while until I asked him about our task.

"We're on our way to an estate as far into the interior of the island as it's possible to go, a cotton plantation. It belongs to a Tycho Ceton, a Swede who has owned land here for a year or two and who appears to be something of an eccentric."

"And what business do we have there?"

"All slaves who work on the island are at times marshaled into the service of the Crown according to a set schedule, to undertake such tasks as benefit the island as a whole. Maintaining roads, constructing buildings for public use, and so on. Our papers show that Ceton has bought quite a few slaves, but none of them have taken part in labor on the governor's behalf. We have been sent to ascertain the reason and to remind Mr. Ceton of the duties that fall to all landowners."

....

The island of Saint Barthélemy is not large, only six miles or so at its longest, and three and a half at its widest. Nonetheless, our journey to the interior was long, due to the condition of the roads and the natural rockiness of the land. We snaked our way through the brush to higher ground, where the sulphurous soil lay black and red, like slag spread around a blast furnace. The heat grew while tiny flies took the opportunity to feast on every bit of exposed flesh. The horses could not be compelled to go faster than they themselves wished, and it was many hours before we rounded a curve and Johan Axel pointed to a group of buildings in the distance. "There. Fahlberg showed me on the map. The French name for this valley is Quartier de Grand Cul-de-Sac." My lips moved as I translated in my head. "The dead end?" Johan Axel nodded. We rode on.

The main house was worn but otherwise in good condition. A bit further away, there was a long house with newly built windowless stalls, and other small buildings arranged around a yard. A foul smell had descended into the bottom of the valley. At first it made me queasy, but I soon enough found myself able to ignore it.

A man was sitting in the shade under an overhanging roof, watching our progress. Our approach had been fully visible from the house for the last half hour. When we stepped onto the swept yard, he stood up and I laid my eyes on Tycho Ceton for the first time. A little shorter than average, probably not yet thirty, still youthful in appearance, in tidy clothing and a wide-rimmed tricorn. His hair was gathered and tied at his neck, of that blond kind that really can't be said to have any color at all. His face was well proportioned, with high cheekbones and alert eyes that were almost violet in color. Ceton could have been called handsome were it not for the fact that his features were disfigured by an unusual scar, a poorly healed furrow that cut through the left corner of his mouth and continued in a jagged arc up his cheek. The muscles that had been cut in two had not managed to knit back together, but had grown skewed, and it was clear that the wound still bothered him. Where it met the mouth, it wept pus still, forcing him to dab it dry with a handkerchief from time to time. In addition to the cut ruining the symmetry of his face, I soon became aware of its other effect, creating an illusion in the eye of the beholder. The injury had affected his expressivity and gave the impression of a constant smile, if a terrible one. It was not easy to tell when Ceton was being serious and when he was joking.

Ceton lifted his hat in greeting and spoke politely to us in French but lifted a surprised eyebrow when Johan Axel answered him in our shared mother tongue. "Swedes? Well, what do you know. Welcome to Cul-de-Sac. It isn't often that we are given the privilege of entertaining guests." A large, weathered man with ugly teeth came up and took our horses by the reins, as wide as a bull and with muscles like ship's cables. "This is Louis Jarrick, my foreman. He asks little and rarely speaks, perfectly fitted to all manner of confidences. N'est-ce pas, Louis?" Jarrick shot him a sour look back.

Ceton waved us over to a table on the wooden floor under the awning, already set for three with glasses and bread. He offered us rum to quench our thirst, but chose for himself fruit-infused water. We drank gratefully. He soon proved to be an amiable host, polite and cultivated, and very curious for news from Sweden. He also asked us a great deal about ourselves, and refilled our glasses whenever we emptied them. I found myself happy to speak in such a relaxed way with someone other than Johan Axel, and I told him about Three Roses, about my family, and about our laborious voyage across the sea. He listened attentively and made encouraging comments to spur me on. My head began to spin from all the spirits. At one point I lost my thread and fell silent. Ceton gave me a warm smile. "Our custom is to rest during the hottest hours of the day, and I'm sure you also want to have a wash after your ride. Louis will show you in. Once you are refreshed, I would like to show you the grounds." He exchanged a serious look with Johan Axel, who nodded.

....

Once I awoke it was with a pounding ache at my temples, and at first I was unsure of either time or place. My tongue felt swollen in my mouth and I was alone in the room we had been shown to, with a divan for each of us and a bowl of scented water. Once I staggered out, I found Johan Axel and Ceton conversing in the yard, the latter turning to me with a cheerful exclamation.

"Ah! And here I was, worried that our young friend required additional time to recuperate. You are to be congratulated for such a splendid constitution. We were just going to start." He clasped his hands behind his back and led the way, all the while describing what we were looking at and pointing out details when additional explanation was needed. We walked around the main house, passed rows of pens, and looked out across the cotton fields. There wasn't a single bush that wasn't dried up and withered. The crop was neglected, the earth as dry as ashes. Ceton noticed our surprise and held his arms out. "As far as the agriculture is concerned, my luck has abandoned me."

Johan Axel self-consciously cleared his throat. "Mr. Ceton, where are all your slaves? According to our records, there should be at least twenty-three, twelve men, eight women, and three children."

"They have retired for the day."

"So early?"

"You can see the condition of the fields for yourself. I don't have the heart to make them toil for too long for such meager gains."

Johan Axel turned towards the windowless pens. "I would like to see them so that I can count each and every one for the governor's records."

Ceton shook his head. "I would rather not like to disturb them during the short period of time they have to rest."

"I'm afraid I must insist."

"Can you imagine what it would be like to labor in the sun every day? It is more taxing than counting heads, I assure you. I try to make their lives here as tolerable as I can. You have already heard my answer and now you also have the explanation. I trust that is enough to satisfy you."

They stood still, staring at each other for a while, before Johan Axel yielded and turned his head away. "As you wish."

Ceton smiled, and the hard edge he had revealed for a moment vanished immediately. He led us on until we rounded a corner and suddenly found ourselves in front of a large mound on which hundreds of flowers grew. Ceton gestured over the area. "Here my efforts as a gardener have been rewarded with greater success. Frangipani. *Plumeria obtusa.* The pride of the house." Hardly had this remarkable sight in the barren landscape had time to sink in before a breeze came from the same direction and wafted the foul odor towards us more strongly than ever. Ceton brought a handkerchief to his face and gestured an apology. "There are drifts of seaweed rotting down by the water's edge, an annoyance for all of us who have land too close to the beach. The wind and currents bring all kinds of debris here to Saint Barthélemy's east coast."

Then he turned towards his bed of frangipani. "In the evening, the flowers open their petals completely and their scent fills the valley. In this way we at least escape the stench at night, which you will notice if you stay awake long enough. It is too late for you to return tonight, as you surely understand. You are welcome to dine with me, as there is nothing I wish for more than a little company from home."

12

The evening meal consisted of a soup followed by roast pigeon, accompanied by sweet root vegetables that had been cooked in coals, which counted as one of the better meals we had been served on the island, if not much to speak of compared to the food we were used to at home. The wine was another story. Ceton kept an excellent cellar and knew how to elevate a simple meal with his selection. The dining room was modest, like the rest of the house, but richly decorated with beautiful objects. A chandelier hung from the ceiling, the prisms of which scattered the light of the candles around us, and small sconces were attached to the walls, which were hung with wallpaper. A Turkish rug lay under our feet. After a couple of glasses, it was only the heat and the many mosquitoes lured to the flames that reminded us how far we were from home.

Ceton and I provided the majority of the conversation; Johan Axel was more reserved. Our discussion was restricted to trivial matters. The year's salt yield from the island's many basins, the necessity of building more cisterns to gather rainwater, the effect of the French war on trade. Ceton appeared knowledgeable on most matters, and I did my best to keep up with his observations but feared I cut a rather poor figure. The wine and fatigue from the long day soon took its toll and Johan Axel helped me to the bed that had been prepared for me. This early evening did me good, to the point that I woke refreshed only to find that it was still nighttime. I tossed and turned for a while to find a position in which sleep would more easily return, but finally decided to abandon these futile attempts and instead wandered outside to find out if Ceton's flowers really did smell better at night.

A breathtaking array of stars twinkled overhead on their black velvet backdrop, in foreign patterns to which I had not yet had time to accustom myself. Although the moon had already dipped below the horizon, it was light enough for me to see where to put my feet and I set off in the direction I thought was the correct one. I soon became aware of my mistake when I instead found myself in front of the low building where Ceton housed his slaves. The heavy door was secured with a forged iron latch with a padlock. This discovery allowed me to reorient myself and with my newfound bearings I had no trouble making my way to the flower bed, where I could see that my host had not been exaggerating. His frangipani filled the air with a sweet, intoxicating perfume. Each flower had opened and was gaping towards the sky. Under the stars, the petals were robbed of their color. They did not seem to be of this world, more a ghostly vision, an otherworldly view onto Elysian fields. Large numbers of moths fluttered over the bushes and filled the darkness with their muted choir.

On my way back, out of the corner of my eye, I saw a flash of light, and when I drew closer I gleaned that it was Ceton himself, who had come outside with his pipe. Each puff illuminated his face with a gentle glow. He smiled at me. The shadows danced over his scar and I shivered. "Well?"

"It was as you said, Mr. Ceton. They are glorious."

"Please call me Tycho. May I tempt you with some tobacco?" I shook my head. "Would you like to sit with me for a little while anyway? I find the midnight hour to be the most enjoyable that our tropical day has to offer." I sat down in the chair across from him and we found ourselves speaking easily. He had many questions about Three Roses and my family, and for some reason it felt easier to talk about my brother's death with this stranger than with my cousin. Ceton expressed his condolences. "Your only sibling?"

"Yes."

"I have also experienced the pain of a family member's death, although I am an only child. My father has passed, my mother is in a convent, and both left my upbringing and education to my father's brother."

We spoke for a while about the fleetingness of life and it did not take long before I confided in him about Nea and the reason for my exile. He asked me many questions about her. Of all those whom I had met during the months that passed since last summer, this strange man was the first to take my feelings seriously, the only one who listened to my story as if it were something other than a young man's folly. He nodded when I finished. "You may think your fate cruel now, but think about how many go through life without ever experiencing such feelings for another. We are alike, you and I, and you would be astonished if I revealed how similar the reasons for my migration are to your own. I have also nurtured desires that my environment has not been in a position to understand."

He sank into silence and set his pipe on his armrest.

"They call it the Age of Reason, all those who do not understand that man is driven by forces that reach deeper than logic. That which exceeds man's comprehension is often met with resistance. Rather than try to understand, people choose to push it away. But to be fair, we are the ones who owe them our compassion, these poor shadow creatures who have never been touched by passion. Yet they rule the world, unworthy as they are. We see the consequences all around us. Man was meant to be free, but everywhere he is in chains."

Never had I heard more remarkable words issue from the mouth of a slave owner, and my silence gave me away. Although no one was listening, he looked around cautiously, leaned in closer, and lowered his voice to a whisper. "I am not who I seem, Erik. Remember that. I hope a time will come when I can explain everything to you, but until then, I must ask you to trust my word."

For a while he sat there staring out into the darkness, before he shook himself and turned to me. "How old are you, Erik?"

"I will be sixteen in December."

"The years go quickly, you'll see. Soon you can do as you like. How are you liking it here so far?"

Ignorant as I was then of the truth of the matter, I was at pains not to hurt his feelings and made an attempt to veil my own behind misleading words. "Sometimes Saint Barthélemy seems like a place on which God has turned His back."

Thoughtfully he exhaled a smoke ring that floated away in the night. "A believer, are you?"

I nodded, although hesitantly, thrown by a question I had never been asked, one that pointed to a freedom to choose, the existence of which I had never perceived. He continued after a couple of puffs. "I myself find it hard to believe in a God who in every imaginable situation appears to favor the perpetrator and hamper the path of the righteous and the meek."

I remembered an answer from a book I had read, one that had belonged to my mother, written by a Frenchman the sound of whose name caused my father to snort as if it were the devil himself. "God is surely not responsible for all that is evil in the world. It is we humans who have forgotten our original state and instead built a society where his decrees are ignored."

"To each his own belief, but that society is rotten must be apparent to all who have eyes." He leaned over, his face not far from my own. "Perhaps no regulations should bind man other than those that originate from the conditions of nature. How much could we not achieve without such limits, men like you and me? Wouldn't that be true freedom, Erik?" He sat up again and drew deeply on his pipe as he stared up at the stars. "Do what thou wilt should perhaps be the whole of the law."

As I squinted through the dark to read his facial expression, I only saw his injured side and could not know for sure if he was smiling or not. He noticed my bewildered expression and laughed. "Forgive me. My sense of humor is not to everyone's taste, and if I showed it to you too early it is only because I have rarely felt such rapport with someone so quickly."

He knocked the ashes out of his pipe against his shoe and we stood up to bid each other good night. "I know there are many an evil tongue in Gustavia who want nothing more than to speak ill of me to anyone who asks. It makes me happy that you and I seem to understand each other. I hope that you are able to think well of me in spite of these schemers and their fanciful tales." I gave him a mute nod without knowing how I should answer, but it was enough to brighten his face and he made as if to put a hand on my shoulder. "I don't know any more of your father beyond what you have told me, but a man who rejects a son like you can't be other than a fool. You should know that you are always welcome here at Cul-de-Sac if ever the need arises or an opportunity comes along. I will ask Jarrick to keep your room in order from now on, and if you were to feel at home here, I would be honored. Now I must say good night."

13

In the morning, when Johan Axel shook me back into an awareness of the world, it was with the feeling that we had slept longer than we ought. Nonetheless Ceton awaited us at a fully set breakfast table and invited us to join him. There was steaming coffee in a silver pot, bread, and herring. After we had finished eating, Ceton started to count out coins on the table. "I have tried to estimate the sum that the Crown has had to cover for all the labor my slaves have failed to perform. Mr. Schildt, would you be so good as to correct my homework? I have an abacus here, in case that is helpful." He put a page full of numbers in front of Johan Axel, who declined the abacus with a shake of his head and eventually answered, after having traced the numbers with his index finger. "The calculation appears to be correct, though the overall sum is higher than it should be."

"I thought that Governor Bagge can either see the excess as a personal compensation for the trouble I have caused or, if the governor prefers, as a prepayment for future failures of the same kind."

Johan Axel frowned. "I am not sure that this is how the Governor's Office usually conducts its affairs."

Ceton gave my cousin an amused look, and the smile that I for once thought I saw clearly on his lips was that of age humoring the good faith of youth. "If your life has hitherto been peopled by those who turn down the money they are unconditionally offered, you've either been raised among saints or you haven't been paying close enough attention. But let us leave all such considerations to the governor himself, shall we? Put my response in the hands of His Grace, Carl Fredrik Bagge. I have the letter here. Will you write out a receipt for the sum you have received?" With an elegant gesture, he held out a quill from the plumage of some exotic bird, then fetched some ink and a piece of paper that Johan Axel readily signed.

Out in the yard, we found Jarrick with our horses, freshly watered and ready to be saddled. Ceton waved us off from the shade of his veranda, and we set off in the baking sun. It took a while before either of us spoke. My cousin's tension was easy to read in the set of his shoulders. I was therefore the one who broke the silence, when I was no longer able to maintain my patience. "What is weighing on you, Johan Axel?"

My cousin held back his horse so that we rode alongside each other. "There are no slaves on that estate, though there should be more than twenty. The fields are withered and there are no traces that any work has ever been done. When you had gone to bed, I stayed up and talked with Tycho Ceton for a long while. After he had asked me many questions about my view of the Swedish Crown's affairs on Saint Barthélemy, he finally gave me an explanation."

"Well, what was it?"

Johan Axel chewed thoughtfully on a nail, spat a piece onto the side of the road, and started filing the jagged edge against a tooth, a bad habit I had witnessed many times before. "One I would very much like to believe. He told me he had the same distaste for the business of Saint Barthélemy as you and I."

I nodded eagerly. "I also spoke to him alone, and he told me the same thing."

At these words, a shadow of anxiety passed over Johan Axel and he stopped the horse completely. "When was this?"

"I went out to smell his flowers, and he was still awake."

"Erik, I don't want you meeting with him alone, not until I have been able to find out the truth behind his words. Will you promise me that?"

Within me, irritation was growing into indignation. "And will you always treat me like a child?"

He gave me a look so full of consideration it pained me, as if I were not yet mature enough to make decisions in my best interest. "You aren't grown yet, Erik, and you are too quick to think well of others, even when they have done very little to deserve your confidence. That is nothing to be ashamed of, quite the opposite. But the feelings you have are visible to all, which makes you vulnerable. I will not hide anything from you, but first I want to ascertain the lay of the land. Until I know for sure, will you promise me to stay away from Cul-de-Sac?"

Perhaps it was my thirst and the heat that made me more irritable than usual, but his tender tone provoked me to anger. Ceton had spoken to me as an equal, the first on Saint Barthélemy to do so, but I had hardly gone further than a mile or so before being patronized all over again. "Because little Erik Three Roses can't take care of himself, can he? He is only Schildt's strange little cousin, no use to anyone and a danger to himself. God forbid that anyone would ever see anything in him except an opportunity for self-gain! But know this, Johan: we know each other as we know ourselves."

And his gaze also went dark. "What do you mean, Erik?"

"You said it yourself. My father paid for your trip so that you could play nursemaid and keep an eye on my affairs. From now on, I will choose my own friends." I said the words simply to hurt him and would soon regret them, but, in the moment, my blood rose as if of its own accord and without waiting for a reply, I dug my heels into the sides of my horse. The animal snorted in surprise and set off down the trail as fast as it could. My horse was the faster of the two and Johan would have no possibility of catching up.

I must have taken a wrong turn at one of the crossroads and it took me many hours to find the right path to Gustavia. Luckily there were not many roads, and the island barely large enough to become truly lost on. Once I had left the horse at the stables and made my way back to Davis's guesthouse, it was already evening, but Johan Axel was neither to be found in our room nor in the public areas. To my delight, I instead found Samuel Fahlberg, who took pity on me and asked me to share his table. "I didn't see a glimpse of you or young Schildt yesterday." I gave him a brief account of our assignment. "Tycho Ceton? I have never made his acquaintance, but remember his short stint in this town before he purchased land on the other side of the island. One of my colleagues was apparently called to one of the whorehouses in Gustavia to see to the injuries he had left behind. It did not take long before he had made himself persona non grata everywhere. How did you find him?"

I recalled Ceton's warning about the rumors that had been spread about him. "A perfect host. We had a long conversation that I appreciated very much. It can hardly have gone without notice that I have had trouble finding my place here on Saint Barthélemy, and he seemed sympathetic."

Fahlberg studied me for a while, lost in thought. Then he changed the topic. "Erik, let me tell you about a remarkable creature I have found here on the island in connection with my scientific investigations. It is an unusual beast that at first glance looks like an overgrown spider, displaying many of that animal's distinguishing characteristics. Upon closer inspection, however, I found it was no spider at all, but instead belongs to the scorpion family. I was surprised, but in time I had the opportunity to observe the reason for the charade. This scorpion, which lacks both a visible tail and stinger, makes prey of other spiders that mistake the nature of their enemy and allow him so close that he can attack without fear of failure." Fahlberg finished and put his elbows on the table before him, leaning over and looking me in the eyes over the rims of his cracked glasses. "Do you understand what I am trying to tell you, Erik?" The reason behind his description escaped me but I nodded anyway, hesitantly. Shortly thereafter we bade each other good night.

Up in the room, I had counted on seeing Johan Axel, and, if not actually retracting what I had said, then at least explaining my feelings more clearly. But the room was empty and when I looked around, I saw that many of my cousin's belongings were gone, even though he appeared to have packed carefully so as not to make it obvious that he was planning to spend the night elsewhere. When I had a sudden impulse to look through my own belongings, I found that the pistol I had been given by my father no longer lay in its case.

14

I made my way to the governor's mansion early the next morning to ask about Johan Axel. At first I was snubbed by the secretary, but Bagge himself caught sight of me as he was leaving his office, where I had lingered, not sure what else I should do. "Three Roses. He's temperamental, your cousin. I'd never think he had it in him. And do you know where the hell he's gone off to? There are accounts here that need settling." I answered that I didn't know and that I had actually come to ask the very same question. Annoyed, Bagge scratched the rolls of fat on his neck where many a mosquito had drunk its fill. "We had a bit of a row yesterday. Schildt insisted on returning to Cul-de-Sac even though I considered our business there concluded. There are more important things to do here that won't wait on his flights of fancy. Even though I can hardly be held accountable for etiquette regarding clerks, I admit that I went a bit far." Bagge gestured with his arms. "But it was all in his best interest. If I chose to dress him down it is only because I see potential in the boy and consider him worth the trouble, as opposed to . . . well, you, Three Roses, to be frank."

The governor appeared somewhat abashed at the haste with which he had pursued his argument and I realized that he was more than a little drunk. He changed the subject. "What is your impression of Tycho Ceton? Schildt appeared to have reservations, even though the man in question has just paid what he owes and taken the trouble to write me a reasonable explanation." He waved for me to hold my tongue when I started to stammer out an answer. "Never mind. When next you see him, tell Schildt that we shall wipe the slate clean and, if his pride has been hurt, that I did not mean to castigate him for worrying about his cousin, regardless how unworthy said party. It was mainly the dessert wine talking, and in future he should take care not to spar with me so late in the day. Come now, Three Roses, away with you." He left me there, no more the wiser.

....

Up at the stables where we had rented our horses, the hands knew more. Johan Axel had taken the same horse as last time and set off inland at first light. The hefty foreman picked his nose and examined his results with interest as he grunted, "He also wanted a spade."

I did not know what grievance Johan Axel had against Ceton or what his purpose was in returning to Cul-de-Sac without the governor's blessing. I sensed trouble, but Johan Axel had always been clearheaded and capable of taking care of himself, and I perceived these same qualities in Ceton, whereupon I decided that the most natural result of the whole affair would be that the two of them cleared up any misunderstanding and made peace. I decided to wait.

....

Without Johan Axel, I found myself completely without anything to do. No one needed me, and my time was my own. I made my way to the water in order to walk along the beach, back and forth until my path was blocked by thorns reaching all the way to the water's edge. From time to time, I walked further away to the basins that caught the seawater during high tide and then let it evaporate into salt that the slaves gathered with rakes into pearly heaps. Something made me recall the unusual rock I had found earlier in the sand, and the hunt for more of the same kind helped me pass many hours. My harvest was a handful of similar objects, the true nature of which still eluded me. They had a porous quality but were still heavy, each marked in the same peculiar way. Some looked like shards, others were curved and slender.

During my second day of waiting, I grew tired of my pastime and instead walked up and down the streets of Gustavia. The commerce that was the lifeblood of the colony was evident everywhere. Skiffs and longboats were lined up to unload their goods along the quay. Each time a slaver arrived in the harbor, the crew came with new stock bound by rusty chains, long rows that made others hold their noses and turn away until they were led down to the shore to wash off the encrusted filth, and from there led to the marketplace to be auctioned. Many carried the marks of insanity after their long journey: wildly staring eyes; frothing, chewing jaws.

In the hopes of not losing profit unnecessarily, many of the skippers called on Fahlberg, whom I sighted in the crowds. I followed him for a while as he walked from one to another and made brief pronouncements. "Scurvy. Scurvy. Fever. Scurvy." He did not appear to eschew my company; perhaps it even provided some slight relief from his grim task. "Most of those we see carry symptoms of the kind we would expect from anyone who has made a similar voyage, but here on the island there are also cases that present more of a challenge." He paused and showed with a grimace that he wished to see the teeth of the man before him. "We call it the pining sickness, and it is an affliction that strikes many of the newly arrived slaves. I believe it is an obsession with the memory of the homeland of which they have been deprived, so strong that it takes physical expression. Breathing becomes shallow and rapid, the heart slows. They will not take food nor water. The ones who are far enough along do not recover, but succumb."

"Is there no cure?"

Fahlberg turned to the next man in line but shot me a look with a raised eyebrow. "One seems obvious."

I passed the slave market on my way back to the boardinghouse, and although I walked with my face downturned for having seen enough unpleasantness for the day, my attention was drawn to one of the fettered slaves awaiting transport to some far-flung sugar field. He could only grunt as he wore a kind of bridle that fixed his mouth in a half-open position. He was waving his arms around wildly.

I had grown accustomed to the fact that the color of the slaves' skin could be a variety of shades, but I had never seen anyone like this. As naked as the day he was born, he displayed a body as marbled and blotchy as if marked by illness, from the darkest black to lighter areas. He had no hair left and his scalp still showed the traces of the blade that had cut it.

His face, so dark that only the whites of his eyes were visible, had been badly beaten. Tears streamed down his face as he wailed at me, reaching as far as the chain around his neck allowed, and I had time to think that he was likely one of the ones in the final throes of this pining sickness, before a roughly hewn Englishman stepped between us and, with his walking stick, gave the slave a well-practiced blow across the groin.

The young man fell, his entire mottled body curled around the pain. The Englishman snarled at me: "This one claws and fights if given the chance. Even though he cost next to nothing, I feel swindled. Keep your distance." From the slave there were only sobs, which I heard for a long time as I continued on my way.

15

It is a laborious undertaking to write at night, and it is only today that I am reminded of how the seasons shift. The winter has long since been forgotten, spring has passed, and summer will soon be over. Tonight I was struck by the fact that the window in my room had been left open; I noticed at once that I was cold, and I picked up the smell of wet leaves.

It makes no difference to me. I spend my days in the stupor that the thebaica offers me. The daylight hours are simply a dream that refuses to imprint on my mind. They make sure I drink, they let my blood, they turn me in my bed. Only with twilight does wakefulness set in, during the few hours between midnight and dawn when there is no one to dose me. I pass these terrible moments with a goose quill, and long for the sunrise.

....

Earlier today I came to for a while and soon found the reason: two visitors had occupied my room. Judging by their behavior, they had for a long time been trying to get answers from me. I don't remember if I gave them or not. One was large with a frightening visage, a brawler if ever I saw one. The other was his opposite, thin and pale and quiet in his speech. I did what I could to escape from these curious visitors into my opiate trance, but my retreat did not come quickly enough and soon their questions let me divine their purpose. Here was justice, which must have been looking for me for a long time in order to mete out my rightful punishment. A part of me wished that I could throw myself at their feet and confess my crime, but fear and the sedatives paralyzed me, and, although I could hear some of their words, I don't think I betrayed my reaction.

With rising frustration, they attempted to compel me to answer before the futility of the exercise became apparent. The large one nearly lost his temper. In an attempt to regain control over himself, he struck his left fist into the door frame, and the sound of the impact drew my attention to the fact that there was something not right about him; that his hand was missing, and that a carved block of wood had been put in its place. The thin one's name I still remember, because the large one called him by it. His name was Winge.

Perhaps their appearance heralds an end of my time here. I must hurry if I am to write down everything I have to tell before fate calls me away.

16

The time I had given myself to wait seemed endless, my isolation never as apparent as amid Gustavia's jumble of sailors, slaves, and all manner of lowlifes. I rose early in the morning on the second day, paid my fee up front to the foreman at the stables who now knew me well enough to call me by my first name, and then I set off. This third time that I followed the road that connects Gustavia and Cul-de-Sac, I made a better job of finding my way, and on the only occasion that I paused at a crossroads in order to choose between right and left, I heard the sound of a horse approaching behind me, and from around the bend there came none other than Jarrick, Ceton's man. He greeted me with a somewhat startled expression.

I had not found myself alone in his company before, and he did not appear to be a particularly sociable man. He pointed me onto the right trail, and he kept me company for about a mile. He was suffering severely from a hangover which he made no attempt to conceal, and at regular intervals he assuaged his thirst with greedy drafts from the flask he carried in his jacket pocket. In his crude French he said that he had been to Gustavia on his master's behalf, to deliver some goods. He interrupted himself with a sudden chuckle that I did not understand, but his speech was not always easy to follow and, as he was likely making an attempt at humor, I laughed along politely, which made him even merrier. As his horse was much faster than mine, he soon excused himself after confirming that I knew my way, and rode off.

When I entered the valley, I saw Tycho Ceton in the distance sitting on his veranda with a glass in his hand, and as soon as I made it to the yard he walked over to meet me. He bade me welcome, as well mannered as ever, but could not hide the fact that the moment was marked with gravity, for reasons I did not understand. "Come with me, Erik. We have much to discuss." To my astonishment, he waved me over to the slave quarters, which were unlocked, the door wide open. He stepped aside and led me in, and I shuddered at the thought of being greeted with a sight like the one beneath Captain Jones's bloodstained deck. As soon as my eyes had grown accustomed to the dark, however, I found that I had worried for no reason, as all the rooms were empty. Surprised, I turned to Ceton, and he answered gravely. "The reason that you and your cousin did not find any slaves here is that they are now all free men. I have no interest in the enslavement of others and this island fills me with disgust. There are a few of us who think alike and I have formed a pact with one of them, an English skipper. I buy slaves at the marketplace and house them here only to await his arrival. He knows every shoal and reef along the eastern shore. At regular intervals, he sets anchor and sends a longboat for the slaves. Afterwards he sets a course to Hispaniola and sends them ashore among their brothers, the rebels, where they can support the fight for an independent nation, free from oppression." Ceton led me out and peered out over the sea with a hand at his brow. Then he turned back and looked me right in the eyes.

"Schildt came to me three days ago. He demanded that I answer all his questions, and although he is Bagge's man, at least in title, I had no choice but to lay my cards on the table. I lack the talent to mislead a man of such keen mind. Instead I put myself completely in his hands, divulged my secret, bared my throat, and hoped for understanding." Ceton leaned closer. "And Schildt gave it to me, with all his heart. He abhors slavery as much as I do, and did not hesitate one moment before deciding to join our cause."

"But where is Johan Axel now?"

"He took the ship to Hispaniola, to make sure that the last cargo safely reaches its destination and to see what contacts he himself can make that will further advance our fight. Those of us who are united in this have long looked for a man like Schildt, who can speak on our behalf on that opposing shore, and the value of his contribution can hardly be overestimated. They set off yesterday, with the turn of the tide."

Ceton let what he had had to say sink in and waved Jarrick over. "Schildt left a letter for you." He handed me a single page, folded and sealed with Johan Axel's signet. I broke the wax and found the message brief. Only a few sentences, written in haste. His handwriting was unmistakable. A heartfelt adieu was inscribed above his name. "There wasn't much time, otherwise he would doubtless have written more. His decision to accompany the freed slaves was made swiftly, from the heart, and haste was of the essence as the tide will wait for no man."

Then he threw up his hands. "And now it all comes down to you, Erik. All power over our fates lies in your hands."

"What do you mean?"

"You have learned all of my secrets, just as your cousin did. If you choose to return to His Grace, Governor Bagge, and tell him everything, I won't be able to stop you. He would surely reward you handsomely for your loyalty, and my life will be forfeit. I stand before you humbly and await your sentence." To my great amazement he fell to his knees before me. Even though I couldn't find the words, Ceton read my silence correctly. Gratitude could be read in that ragged smile. "We will be needing your help, Schildt and I."

....

I remained at Cul-de-Sac until the shadows had grown long, and we spoke at length about the path I now had to tread before I took my leave. Just before nightfall, I glimpsed the firelight in Gustavia and managed to emerge victorious in my race against the dark. In my bed at Davis's, I read Johan Axel's note again and again, touched by the fact that the farewell must have caused him a significant amount of pain, as the page was stained with tears.

17

I made excuses for Johan Axel to Bagge and told him the tale that Ceton had supplied me with after I told him about my last meeting with the governor. I let it be implied that Johan Axel had been so affected by their final exchange that he had felt compelled to board the first outbound vessel, a Frenchman on his way to Le Havre.

Bagge spat at the gravel, flushed, and gave me an open look of disdain. "Goddamn it, Three Roses! They send me two young men, one a dunce and the other clever, and still the useful one turns out to be the worse of the two. To hell with the both of you. Out of my sight!"

....

The weeks passed. I visited Cul-de-Sac regularly, each time with the hope that Johan Axel would be there waiting for me, back from distant Hispaniola with news of his good work, and that our mutual delight at the reunion would disperse the clouds that had lately gathered around our friendship. But I had to satisfy myself with a handful of letters that he addressed to Cul-de-Sac, the brevity of which left out too many details and mostly bore witness to the weight of his labor. He did, however, appear to be in good health, and certain that the choice he had made was the right one. The tidings from Johan Axel were unfortunately not the only news that reached me: one day when I returned to my room, Davis called for me and held out a missive that had just arrived from home. The sender was Johan Axel's father, writing to tell me that my father had taken ill. He had made an effort to be tactful, but was also honest enough to give me a clear picture. Ever since my brother's accident, my father had rarely been seen sober. One day he collapsed, was found to have a fever, and when he was helped into bed, it was revealed that his legs were covered in festering wounds that he had concealed and that were now copiously suppurating. My uncle guessed that my father had suffered these injuries from wandering around the house at night and, in his intoxicated state, walking into the furniture. His condition did not show any signs of improvement, and my uncle promised that he would send further word when there was more to tell. News of his death followed shortly in the next mail package. I had no one left to turn to but Ceton. I had learned that he preferred not to have physical contact with others and so it meant all the more when he embraced me. I moistened his shirt with my tears and when I calmed myself, he gave me his handkerchief to dry my face. "I wonder," he said slowly, "if it would not be best for you to come here to Cul-de-Sac for good." The arrangement struck us as so natural that we were both amazed we had not thought of it before. The practical matters were quickly attended to: with Jarrick's help, I carried my sea chest to his waiting wagon, put the amount I owed Alex Davis into his calloused palm, and turned my back on Gustavia without the least ounce of regret.

Even though Cul-de-Sac did not offer much in the way of entertainment, it was far more dear to me than Gustavia. Calm ruled the night and I soon saw the wisdom in dividing the day like my host. We rested in the afternoons and in return we could spend many a cool, nighttime hour in conversation by Ceton's flowering frangipani. But despite all that Ceton did for my diversion, I missed the companionship of someone my age, and my thoughts dwelt more often on Nea. In my melancholy, I worked at long epistles to her, in which I clumsily tried to dress my feelings in words. It was this lovesickness that led to one of the few episodes at Cul-de-Sac that disturbed the peace we shared. Perhaps as an overture to friendship, Jarrick started to ask me about the beloved he so often saw me sighing over. "*C'est l'amour, hein?*" he grunted, and I answered as well as I could in the language that I could read much better than speak, in spite of all the lessons. He asked me to describe her, and after I had done so to the best of my abilities, I saw to my disgust how he fondled his groin to more comfortably rearrange the bulge. For an apology, he simply grinned, showing his brown teeth, and I felt my blood rise like it had before, at home in my room after my father's decree, as

well as on the ship with Johan Axel. The world glazed red, and when I
came to my senses I was caught in Jarrick's arms, staring straight into
his face that now bore marks where my nails had scratched and where a
dark swelling was beginning to emerge around one eye.

He held me until my breathing had returned to normal. He let me go
with some trepidation and I became aware of Ceton, who was taking in
the scene from the shadow of the veranda, his carved pipe in his mouth.
He waved Jarrick aside and showed me to a chair next to his own. "What
is this, Erik? I wouldn't have thought this of you. Rarely have I seen such
an outburst." I bent my head to hide tears of shame. Ceton gently began to
ask me questions, concern evident on his face. "Has this happened before,
eruptions like this? And afterwards you recall nothing?"

I explained as well as I could, and the more I unburdened myself, the
more easily the words came. It was a relief to lighten my heart as this rage
pointed to a darkness in me that I had not been able to explain.

Ceton listened without interrupting, and when I finally fell silent, he
sat lost in thought for a while. "This seems a simple matter, Erik," he
said finally. "You are not a whole person and cannot be expected to act
like one. You have given your heart to another."

"What should I do?"

He set his pipe aside and knit his fingers together. "If you would like
my help, I will do my best to find a solution, and as you now stand without
a father or brother, I would very much like you to see me as half of each
from now on. All I ask for in return is your patience."

If there was a pause before I managed to stammer out my gratitude,
it was only because I had felt no greater joy since I first set foot on this
godforsaken island.

As the week progressed, I noticed Ceton started to suffer from a growing restlessness. He often stood looking deep into the countryside for the
post, or out to sea for an approaching ship, to no avail in either case. He
appeared unwilling to share his troubles with me but in the end could not
contain himself. "It is Schildt. He has not written as he should, and I beg
your pardon that I have not shown you this before, but here is his latest
letter, addressed to me alone." I took the note with trepidation. The message was even shorter than normal: a warning of danger. "We agreed on

these exact words before he left, and Schildt would not have written them if he had not feared that he would fall into the hands of our adversaries. We can't know for sure if this has actually happened, but it is a risk we can hardly afford. We must flee, Erik. They have methods to make even the most stalwart of men sing. Cul-de-Sac is no longer safe." He quickly gave me instructions, and before the hour was at an end, I found myself on Jarrick's horse bound for Gustavia to deliver a letter for Johan Axel to Davis, where he would surely stop if he returned and found Cul-de-Sac abandoned. The journey before me was too long to be made twice before darkness, and when I returned at dinnertime the following day, I saw a plume of smoke over the estate from a great distance and pressed my heels into the flanks of my horse to hasten its speed. I feared the worst.

It was the slave quarters that had burned. When I rode in across the yard, there was only a smoking crater left, carefully monitored by Jarrick with a bucket and a wet switch to dampen flying sparks. He had pounded the smallest piece of wood to pulp with a sooty mallet. Ceton stood at a distance, arms crossed. "Even if the next owner will surely miss them, they will never again be used to imprison those who should be allowed to go free. Now pack your chest."

"Where are we going?"

With a gesture, he invited me to walk alongside him. "I have been think-ing about what you've told me, Erik, and I have a proposition for you. You may still not be of age, but a guardian would be able to speak with the same authority as your father. Even to the point of blessing your marriage." My heart flew into my throat only to die down just as quickly. I had no family left and could only shake my head. "But who would that be?"

Ceton stopped me and grabbed both of my shoulders. "Would you do me the honor?"

I threw my arms around him.

"Then, to Sweden!" he shouted. "And to Linnea Charlotta!"

In my euphoria over this future which just a moment ago had seemed out of reach, I had suddenly forgotten all I had learned of the world, and a sense of shame at the benevolence I was being shown suddenly overcame me. How could I, ever unworthy, possibly be deserving of Ceton's help? "Why are you doing all this for me, making all of these sacrifices?"

He must have misunderstood my question and behind it heard some suspicion and a half-expressed accusation, for he appeared flustered and, if my eyes did not deceive me, he even blushed. He drew his hat from his head as if he were a miserable wretch ready to confess his sins before the magistrate. "I wish I were a better man, Erik. I wish that the only motivation for my actions were the goodness of my heart. But that is not the whole truth. I have not dared to burden you with this confidence before, Erik, but the assistance I extend to you contains an attempt to help myself. I once belonged to an honorable order, but I did not part from my brothers in friendship. The fact is that our conflict drove me to my exile. But they would place great value on you, Erik, and if I return with you as a future member, I am sure that they would be more likely to look kindly upon me. Would you do this for me?"

Just as I was going to answer, I happened to look over his shoulder and cried out in confusion. All of his beautiful frangipani had been dug up, already brown and withered under the sun's punishment. In the place where they had once grown, there was only a wide ditch, a gaping hole the depth of which bore witness to the effort the digger had made not to leave a single root in the soil.

Ceton followed my gaze and grimly shook his head. "Damned if I was going to leave such beautiful flowers for the slaver who will surely take Cul-de-Sac in possession once we are gone."

18

Saint Barthélemy took no notice of the farewell we were preparing. The colony bustled as ever. It did not take long for Jarrick to procure a buyer for Cul-de-Sac. The thought of Johan Axel in captivity was like a vise on my heart, but Ceton did what he could to comfort me: "Your cousin is a clever man, Erik, wiser than us two combined. Leave yet another letter for him with Davis, and make it a wedding invitation! With luck, he will join us at home in Sweden on the day when Linnea Charlotta becomes your wife. Who would be a better choice to take your father's place by your side at the altar?"

Our trip home was arranged, and on an overcast morning we stood in front of the vessel, the crew busy unfastening her moorings. It seemed to me that there was no one left on Saint Barthélemy to whom I owed a goodbye, but as I stood on the Carenage awaiting my turn to board, I caught sight of Samuel Fahlberg. He saw me at the same time and we walked over to each other and shook hands.

"So young Erik is leaving us so soon."

"You at least I leave with my best wishes, Doctor." We spoke for a while to dissipate the melancholy we shared. Somewhat distraught, I put my hands in my pockets and found one of the strange stones I had collected. I took it out and showed it to Fahlberg. "Would you happen to know what this is?"

I held it out to him, but he did not make the least attempt to take it from me. Still he nodded in the affirmative.

"Yes. But I don't know if you really want to know the answer, Erik. You who are a child of Rousseau and surely a proponent of the concept of the noble savage."

I insisted, and he shrugged.

"I have spent many years here on Saint Barthélemy. I also have gathered my share of strange objects. One often finds these on the beach here by the Carenage. I have shown them to the old ones on neighboring islands, and they gave me an answer." He sighed heavily before continuing. "Many hundreds of years ago this island was home to a people who called themselves the Arawak. One day another tribe came in canoes out of the west. They were famished after their long journey. They brought all of the Arawak men and boys to the beach, where they made a meal of them. Of the women and girls, they made provisions. They roasted the bodies in pits filled with red-hot coals. The stones you have collected are their cracked bones, turned to stone with the passage of time. The marks they bear come from the teeth that once gnawed them free of flesh."

At first I did not know what to say, and simply stood with the little stone in my hand, this innocent object whose nature had so suddenly taken on a different meaning. I was struck by a thought, and for a few short moments found it was a comfort to me. "Are we not then better than that, Doctor? Slavers we may be, but never cannibals."

He smiled sadly and shook his head. "You've never visited the sugar fields, Erik. The Antilles are one big slaughterhouse, one that would not have been possible without our assistance. The profit is so large and the slaves so cheap that many choose to let them starve. When they collapse, they buy new ones, and greet them with the spade they must use to bury those they have just replaced; men, women, and children, joined in a mire of rotting flesh to make a bed for others when next the grave is opened."

He turned away and raised a hand to his face, overcome with emotion. "Maybe the savage was never noble. Maybe mankind was blighted from the very beginning. Maybe the world becomes older but never better. Maybe all these advances we call civilization only allow us to practice our evil on a scale never before seen. Everywhere on these islands, sugar blooms by the ditches of the dead. We use it to sweeten our food. God help us, Erik, would we not have shown the greater mercy if we had simply gone straight to Africa and eaten the negroes?"

19

M y journey to Saint Barthélemy had been made the longer by missing Linnea Charlotta, but my impatience to be reunited with her made the return journey endless. The ship bearing me home was so alike the one that had carried me away that I have trouble distinguishing them in my mind. Ceton taught me a number of card games, and we spent countless hours in conversation. His ceaseless curiosity and evident investment in my happiness flattered me. The ever-present Jarrick was hardly noticeable at all, which was quite a feat considering his size and the modest dimensions of the vessel. We were the only passengers, and the crew preferred to keep to themselves. Ceton gave me unfettered access to his small portable library and, to pass the time, I chose Galland's *Thousand and One Nights*, as well as a French volume whose curious title I laboriously translated as *The Misfortunes of Virtue*, even though my deficiencies in the language probably led me astray, for surely the intentions of the author must have been other.

The passage over the Atlantic took its toll, and in Southampton we were forced to dock and refit; the sails needed patching and the torn rigging replacing. Powerless in my eagerness, I had to remain patient while the crew spent days on end sitting with their legs crossed on deck, splicing rope. I had been hoping to present my news to Linnea Charlotta in person, but instead I wrote a letter and sent it on with a merchant on his way to Gothenburg, with a request to her that she send me an answer that could be waiting for me in the harbor in the event that I encountered additional delays there. I struggled with how to best express myself, and Ceton could not hold his amusement at bay when he saw all the crumpled pages that had gathered under the desk. I finally abandoned all attempts at elegant formulations and wrote freely from the heart, the trembling of my hand visible in each letter: *"Nea, I love you more than ever. If you will be mine, I ask for your father's blessing of our union."* I included a separate note to her father with a more formal version of the same, for Linnea to deliver or throw away as she saw fit. Both of their replies awaited me in the mailbag of the Gothenburg customs office. Linnea Charlotta gave me an elated yes, far more expressive than my clumsy proposal. Her father's response had a more restrained tone, but I imagined that one could read joy between the lines.

For once, there was no way to mistake Ceton's smile, and his emotions were touching to see.

"Well then, Erik. We shall make the arrangements for a wedding."

From Gothenburg, he wrote a number of letters sent over land while we continued to sail through Kattegat and up along the coast towards Stockholm.

And so, after many a lengthy mile at sea and by carriage, I finally laid eyes on my childhood home again. For the first time in generations, our ancestral estate had been left in neglect. Never before had I stood alone in my father's library, strewn with his neglected and forgotten papers. Debts needed to be repaid, others to be collected. Without Ceton, I would surely have been lost, but as my guardian, he showed his new responsibility the gravity it required and took possession of my father's desk in order to review the accounts, whereupon he said he needed to head back to Stockholm, the same way we had just come, to buy all the goods he felt essential for the wedding, and to deliver the document to the court that was required to make the marriage legal, despite my minority. I shifted my weight nervously from side to side, finding myself at the end of the journey deprived of the courage needed for its final step. Ceton sat up in the saddle and pulled on the reins to test the mood of the horse that had once been my brother's. "Leave the practical matters to me. Now go to her! You have tarried long enough." And with that he rode away.

....

I first steered my course to our church in order to pay my respects to my father, long since consigned to eternal rest under his memorial slab. Tracing the letters that spelled out his name with a finger, I said a prayer for the blessed resurrection of his soul, and directed to him an apology, such that he might forgive me all the disappointment I had occasioned him over those years we spent under the same roof, along with a wish for his blessing of the marriage he had gone such a long way to prevent.

It was warm outside but I shivered as I knelt on the floor of the church. The stone was cold. My grief over my father's passing was diluted by bitter memories and followed by the realization that I now stood alone in the world. But of my friends, one yet remained, and Linnea Charlotta would be mine. Who could ask for more? With a pounding heart, I took the path across the fields in among the trees in whose shade I had known such joy during the summers of my childhood.

20

M y feet followed the old paths of their own accord, and they did not carry me to the Collings' farmstead but down the hill to the tarn, that summer meadow where Nea and I had sat so many times: in the mornings watching the osprey dive, in the evenings to catch a glimpse of the elk bull's antlers as he strode from between the trees to nibble at the lily pads, and at night to wonder at starry skies. The grass and flowers grew tall, and I did not see her until I was very close. A dress shone white among all the colors and showed me how destiny itself had sped our reunion. She sat with her back to me, her arms around her knees, but was on her feet as soon as she heard my steps disturb the stalks. And then we stood face-to-face, equally surprised, and became for the first time aware of the fact that a year had gone by since we had parted.

She had changed, grown both taller and slimmer, her cheeks stretched out to reveal the high edges of her cheekbones. I had left a girl, and now I found a woman. And yet her red hair was exactly as I remembered it, braided in the same pattern, her freckles still more numerous than the stars in the night, and none of the changes I saw in her had deprived her of any of her beauty. Quite the opposite: the treasure I had been forced to abandon had grown richer by a year.

I could not prevent my smile, but it froze as a sudden worry wrenched my gut. What about me? How had I been changed by all that I had gone through? What did she see, this girl whose green gaze scoured me as if I were a stranger? The thought of Saint Barthélemy's ugliness haunted me. How could anyone pass through such a place without carrying its taint for the rest of their life? But she came closer, close enough for me to feel her quick breaths against my skin, reached out a hand, and placed it on my cheek. It was trembling, as I was, as if our bodies were a note reverberating at the same pitch. A voice that cracked until only a whisper remained: "Is it you, Erik? Is it really you?"

I was speechless, nodding, dampening the warm hand that caressed me. Now the tears also sprang up in her eyes, and with my voice distorted by my emotion, I asked the question that I could no longer keep silent. "Nea, do you still want me, now that you see me?"

She put her forehead to mine, opening again the eyelids that her tears had closed until my entire world took on the color of her eyes. "Yes. A thousand times yes."

....

We sank to the ground and sat close together, as if the sun could give us no warmth, and we talked of the year that had passed. The shadows grew long and the sky red, and we walked back hand in hand through woods that already cradled the night. I took her home. Her father and mother greeted me, at first with the dignity that befitted the owner of Three Roses, but as the light faded from the highest branches of the trees and I was forced to bid my beloved good night, her mother followed me out, took both my hands in hers, and leaned close. "Without you it was as if life itself had abandoned her. At first she lay in her bed for days on end, facing the wall. The words that came across her lips tonight are more numerous than all I have heard her speak since last summer. Thank you, Erik, thank you for giving us our daughter back." She gave me a kiss on the cheek and hurried back in, clearly moved by the moment.

21

Our marriage banns were read in church to no objection; a date was set. Ceton was indefatigable in his zeal, traveling to and from Stockholm in order to reassure himself about all the arrangements, since only the best was good enough. Ungrateful and oblivious, I hardly noticed him at all as my place was now always at Nea's side. At first I was amazed at how different everything appeared, but soon I realized that the grounds of Three Roses were the same, and that we were the ones who had changed. Between us lay the promise of our future together. It was both enticing and frightening, making me at once ecstatic and agitated. There were also other sentiments of the kind we generally don't like to name, and I noticed them even in Nea. And if I hadn't already known the importance of keeping these desires in check during my final days as a bachelor, Ceton's reminder brought it to the fore. He had drawn me aside earlier. "It's not seemly for an engaged couple to be running about the forest alone, Erik. You hardly want to bring your wife before the minister surrounded by gossip of lechery. It would be best for you to walk where others can see you, so that your wedding night will be all the more memorable."

His words made me blush but the advice was sound, and soon I found that the company of others lessened the tension between us. Although we made sure to be surrounded by their gazes, we could keep them out of earshot, and thus undisturbed we talked about the future. I knew Nea's feelings, and found that the estate I had inherited had become a millstone around our necks.

"Nea, what do you think your father would say about managing the lands in their entirety? That would make us free to do whatever we wanted. We can see Stockholm, or even travel further south."

At first she furrowed her brow and allowed her grip around my hand to harden. "Only if you want to, Erik. I don't want to force you to leave your home for the sake of my whims. If your preference is to stay, I will have to ask my sisters to teach me everything they know of gossip and embroidery and make you a wife as tame as I can muster."

I laughed because I knew the dreams hidden behind her beautiful words. "I would always have you wild. So then let us leave Three Roses in the care of Eskil Colling. The only happy memories I have from here are of you." She brought my hand to her lips and held it there for a long time.

....

I waited impatiently for the day that promised to be the happiest of my life, and although the sun itself seemed to want to extend my bachelor days by slowing its course, the morning came and I was fetched at an early hour. Water had been warmed on the stove, I was scrubbed clean and sprinkled with scent. Then I was dressed for church. My clothes were new, unworn, splendid, and scented with the lavender sprigs that had come packed in the chest. Ceton himself examined me with the knowing eye of a connoisseur. "Many of your wedding guests belong to the order I've mentioned. These are men of the world, Erik, and even though I know that they will appreciate you for yourself, I advise you to comport yourself in the manner befitting a gentleman. Do not ignore them, even though you will have trouble averting your eyes from your bride. I still have much to attend to, and in the church you will be on your own, but tonight I will be at your side."

I thanked him profusely, aware that no words could spring from my mind that would be able to do justice to his benevolence.

A garlanded carriage waited outside, and I saw that it was Jarrick himself sitting on the coach box, dressed in livery in honor of the event and with an unaccustomed expression that seemed to pass for a smile. And in this way I was brought to the minister, and Eskil Colling himself placed his daughter's hand in mine. On the way up the aisle, the train of her dress caressed the stone that bore my father's name, and in that motion I saw reconciliation. I repeated the words after the minister in a daze, but we stood alone before the altar, Linnea Charlotta and I, in our own world, only vaguely conscious of all the bustle around us. The pews were full of elegantly dressed gentlemen; there was cheering. We exchanged rings and were carried out by the people into the warmth of summer, to be brought in triumph to the festivities at Three Roses. They put glasses in our hands and I drank, already woozy with bliss. The first kiss we shared as man and wife was not the one I longed for, only a chaste approximation fashioned for the gazes of onlookers, but in Linnea's eyes I saw my own desire reflected back at me. Soon! Soon.

The celebration began, with Linnea Charlotta by my right side at the table of honor, our arms linked. One course followed another without my tasting a morsel, being already full to the brim with emotion. One speech followed another, and no single word did I hear, the speakers all being acquaintances made just moments before. They were an unusual bunch, more magnificent than any company I had enjoyed before, gilded and splendid in the finest fabrics, elegant in both their speech and manner. I was moved by the joy and kindness that they clearly felt for me, astounded at the friendship they so easily extended. Again and again, they pressed my hand, and my shoulder grew tender under their pats. Never was I allowed to glimpse the bottom of my glass. After each toast, new wine was poured, and soon my head started to buzz with a wondrous intoxication that heightened my euphoria. When it threatened to go to my head, Ceton was there to pep me up with tiny pastilles spiced with anise. The tables were pulled back and the floorboards cleared for the dance, the musicians who had been brought in from the town tuned their fiddles, and then we started. Polonaise, minuet, a whirling storm. Linnea Charlotta's rosy face against an increasingly fuzzy backdrop. Everyone wanted to dance with such a bride. I remember how I laughed out loud several times at nothing at all. My neighbors joined in. Towards evening, all memories ended, despite Ceton's enlivening cure. The exertions of the day took their toll, as did the wine.

22

I woke with a start, and my first thought was what an underwhelming figure I must have cut during the first night we spent together. Soon it was followed by the joyful knowledge that this night would only be the first of many.

....

At first I took them for rose petals, spread about the entire room as a felicitation to us both. A deep red. When I lazily reached for one of them, I grasped at nothing, and when I lifted my hand to my face, I saw that my fingers bore the same red color. My naked body was stained and spotted. When I got to my feet and threw the blankets from the bed, it was her shroud I disturbed. Her skin was as white as the sheets. Her face was no more, lips in shreds over a gaping hole where the jaw hung broken. From this silent shout, the tongue lolled blue and swollen. Eyes unseeing out of the grimace bore witness to the terror of her last moments. Arms and legs wrenched out of place. The body that had just now lived was now simply a broken rag doll. Fragments of her were everywhere: strips of hair glued to the bedposts, blood on the rug and on the wallpaper, stains on the ceiling. And over all of her a cracked, yellowed membrane, fractured and faintly acrid, as if she had been painted with a varnish that was already starting to set. I screamed aloud for an eternity, vainly trying to shake life back into her. Her head rocked heavily on a snapped neck, and with my embrace I tried to give her back the warmth that death had stolen.

....

It was Jarrick who pried away my twitching arms and held my shoulders as if in an iron grip. Right behind him there was Tycho Ceton with an expression of shock and disbelief as he whispered in desperation. "Erik, Erik, what have you done?"

23

I never stopped screaming. It was only my mouth that fell silent. That same cracked voice has echoed in my head ever since that moment, without ever stopping to draw breath.

....

Ceton took care of everything and, docile, I let myself be led. He set me on my feet, he and Jarrick, and they took me from the bedroom I had painted a death chamber, put me in the tub, and brought in soap and water. I found that I had been injured during the tumult of the night, badly enough that I could only with some difficulty straighten my midriff. I felt a sharp pain in my rear, and later found that the bleeding was sufficient to redden the bathwater, although no wound could be seen. In time, the pain subsided to a muted pulsing, but even today, as I write these words, I feel it, and every trip to the privy is agony. I bleed still. In some way she must have put up a struggle, although not enough of one. I can't stand it. I can't stand it.

I sat in the tub all day. My body seemed as if it were dipped in a dried mucus, white but yellowed, flaking from the skin at the touch, and from which others now scrubbed me clean. From time to time, they came with more hot water, rubbing my hair with soap. Jarrick displayed a circumspect agility with such tasks. Without a word, he scrubbed the red accumulations from under my fingernails and combed the clots from my hair. Ceton returned in the evening and they wrapped me in a blanket and led me to the bed that had been my father's. I was not myself. Every thought was as if muffled.

Ceton sat by my side, and it was only after a couple of hours of troubled sleep that I regained enough consciousness to address him. "What has befallen? Tell me it was a nightmare."

He put down the book he was reading. "All has been taken care of. You need not worry. The guests have all been sent home, ignorant in their hangovers. The room has been scrubbed, the bedclothes burned." I did not need to ask my question. "She's lying in the cellar, wrapped in her sheet. She is safe there, Erik, for the short time above ground that still remains to her. Louis has put a chain on the door. No one has seen her; those who left think she is still sleeping, too exhausted from the exertions of the evening to bid adieu."

I could only sob, and repeat my question as if I were a small child: "What has happened?"

"I have made inquiries as discreetly as I could manage, and have found someone who says they heard your quarrel begin. Linnea Charlotta tried to tell you about another towards whom she had nurtured tender feelings in your absence, and you lost your temper. That has happened before, hasn't it? Of course, I knew about your outbursts of rage, but never could I have imagined . . ."

He allowed the words to sink in as he went on.

"Erik, you are not well. Don't blame yourself. The root is some kind of ailment, a disorder of the mind for which you yourself cannot be held responsible. I know people who can be of assistance. The message has already been sent. We leave tomorrow."

"Where are we headed?"

"To Stockholm. To Dane's Bay. If there is anywhere you can be helped, it is there."

"To the asylum?"

He shook his head. "No, to the hospital. They only put those in the asylum for whom no hope remains."

....

I will soon have written all I have to tell. None of the curatives they have given grant me anything but a moment's respite. For a long time, I thought that Ceton's words to me before we left Three Roses had simply been a naive hope, and that help for my condition was beyond the power of any man. The nightmares grow ever worse. Carved bedposts painted with her face. I wet my bed more times than I awaken dry. My bedclothes are changed, but the mattress remains damp in the absence of a replacement and the hay turns rancid.

....

And then today Ceton came to me. Under his arm, he had a wooden case which he placed at his feet as he sat. "I hear that you had guests here, Erik, only a few days ago, and that many questions were asked."

I nodded in agreement, clearheaded since no one had given me thebaica since the beginning of the week, and Ceton's expression grew concerned.

"Time is starting to run out for us. In the worst case, these gentlemen will take you away from here, and I will no longer be able to act in your best interest."

"If they are the servants of justice, do I not then deserve the punishment that they may give me?"

Ceton shook his head with a level of animation that was not typical of him. "No, Erik. Don't ever say that. You are not to blame for what happened. Your illness was Linnea's bane. If you fall into the hands of the police, they will not care, wishing nothing more than to fill their quota. But we can punish your illness, Erik, by curing it."

He cleared his throat and lifted the wooden case onto his lap.

"All of your doctors have washed their hands of you, Erik. Yet I have never given up hope, and therefore I have turned my gaze outside our borders. I have found a gentleman in service to Francis II, a superb *medicus* of unparalleled experience, which also includes a handful of cases such as yours." He hesitated for a moment before going on, caressing the marquetry on the lid with the palm of his hand. "You must understand, Erik, that the treatment that remains is drastic in nature. And yet I believe it is our only hope of giving you any relief."

I shook my head faintly, expecting yet another bitter decoction with no effect. Ceton drew closer, pulled the case's clasp out of position, and opened the lid.

On an interior of deep-blue velvet there sat a number of shiny instruments, each in its own designated place, polished to a mirror sheen and carefully fastened with ties. Ceton pointed to one of them. "With this one, we drill a hole into the skull, a few inches above the hairline." He lifted the piece from its appointed place in the fabric and held it out to me. Astounded, I took the tool and held it up to the light. The steel was spotless and freshly sharpened. "Once the bone has been pierced, the brain, the seat of reason, lies exposed, where the source of your condition is to be found. We keep the blood away with the help of a pump that gathers the flow into a vessel and affords the surgeon line of sight." I was also allowed to feel this remarkable item, equipped with bellows and a short leather hose for the collection and dispersal of the blood. "And thus to the most important part of the procedure. This rod is intended to be held over a flame until it glows red. We then guide it through the hole, thereby to burn away the disease that afflicts you. But I must warn you, Erik. This procedure is not without danger, not even in the hands of as accomplished a surgeon as ours. This is a decision that no one can make but you, and it is yours alone. It may be that you will no longer be the same afterwards. By your leave, I will return with him tomorrow."

Images and recollections flickered inside me. There were the cannibals of Saint Barthélemy. My conversations with Fahlberg. My wedding night. Slaves and their chains. Frangipani, uprooted. And in a flash it came to me: the answer to the riddle that the fool Tomas, the one who in his confusion had claimed to be the devil, had asked me. The reason that Satan can walk by my side is that the world in which we live is itself infernal, a purgatory we built of our own accord, where we fan the flames with our lies. What difference did it make that Tomas was acting a part when Satan himself could hardly have made his case with more eloquence? What devil do we need, when we have each other?

There is darkness all around. What light there is, is a will-o'-the-wisp and nothing more. Tycho Ceton has offered me a way out. Perhaps. What does it matter if I'm not the same afterwards, when I am as I am now? Tears of gratitude had already begun to stream down my cheeks when I gave him my answer. "Yes. A thousand times yes."

Her kiss. How I wish I could feel her against my lips again, if only for one last time.

PART TWO

The Lost Pocket Watch

SUMMER 1794

I see the land that sun forgot
By mountains hid, by cannon shot,
Watered by the plowman's tears,
For greed has left his gifts to rot
And elevated sinners' heirs.

—Carl Gustaf af Leopold, 1794

24

In the pubs and on the street corners, it is whispered that the end cannot be far away. Armfelt, loyal friend to the late king, has been driven into exile, but it is said he is using his time to plan his revenge. He travels from land to land, welcomed by all, gathering an army around his cause. Rumor has it he has been a guest of Catherine of Russia herself, in Petersburg, and spoken so eloquently of King Gustav's fallen crown that the empress has been driven to tears. Salvation is near, he'll soon be here, they whisper; at any moment Armfelt will come sailing around the bend at Skeppsholmen with the Russian navy in his wake. He will be rowed ashore without resistance, and Duke Karl, guardian of the crown prince, will see reason. The duke's only flaw has always been his weakness, and he will let Armfelt rule in his name, just as Baron Reuterholm has done these past two black years. In every pub where this story is told, other voices can be heard muttering ironic objections, when the candle stumps have started to gutter and the noises mute: yes, we certainly remember the days of King Gustav, and who in their right mind would not wish them back? Granted, we had to starve and send our sons to death, but never have plays been so well acted on our stages, never has French been spoken so flawlessly at the court.

Up in the palace, strange lights can be glimpsed by the windows: apparitions from another world, some say, others that it is simply flames lit under colored glass. The courtiers gossip: the baron is quaking in fear, though he spends his days in idleness like all other gentlemen at court, adorned like a peacock. In lieu of other measures, he has resorted to speaking with the dead. Séances are held each evening. Magnetists, spiritists, clairvoyants—all are welcomed to the palace after nightfall.

If the land is to be ruled from the other side, our ruination is assured, say the old ones, for the dead are jealous of the living, and want nothing more than the pleasure of their company.

....

Midnight approaches, the watchman in his steeple has stopped calling the hour, and the urchins who have thronged under the low ceiling have grown too many for the barkeeper to drive away. He knows that it is no coincidence that they have been tempted here this night. The City-between-the-Bridges holds few secrets that do not quickly come to light, and now the time has come to reveal his own. His pub stands without protection. No one will defend his wares. Individually, the children are timid and fearful, but one must be wary when they swarm together. Their numbers give them strength, and when they are together, a frenzy comes over them, stronger even than what the bottle offers. They are intent on mischief, with nothing to lose. Greedily they drain the dregs of tankard and cup. With a gesture of defeat, the barkeeper decides to purchase their goodwill, and exchanges their coins for a tankard to share, aware that the price for his generosity is yet to be set. Outside, the sticky heat that lingers in the alleys has started to dissipate, cooled by the night and fanned by the breeze that retreats out to sea from the darkening land. The summer sky remains bright. It will hardly have begun to darken before daybreak, the night nothing more than a blink between days that seem to last forever.

There are few other guests tonight. All but the hardest drinkers have long since staggered back to their sleeping quarters. The ones who remain are in poor shape and soon become the target of the youngsters' pranks. Leaning against the wall, there is also the large watchman, the one with the lumpy face that everyone recognizes but whose gaze they would never dare to meet during the day. He who once drank so copiously is sober now, they say, but sobriety hardly appears to have done him any favors. He has lost weight since winter, his cheeks are sunken, his eyes dull. As always, there is talk in the City-between-the-Bridges, one story contradicting the next, and which one holds the more truth is no easy task to determine. Some claim he has fallen into debt, will take money from anyone, toils every waking moment, but still has to use every coin he earns to keep the creditors at bay. For his part, he keeps his mouth shut, and no one dares ask him any questions. He has chosen to join the ranks of those that honest folk learn to look past, some shadow creature devoid of present and morrow, left with only a past, ripe with regret and painful memory.

Certainly he can fight still, but not tonight. The children creep ever closer. He sleeps deeply, every breath a drawling snore, his arms folded across his chest. All of the children know this kind of slumber: it is the sleep of the famished, when hunger causes the body to tremble, despite the warm air, and one has to hug one's limbs to one's middle in order to trick the belly into thinking it is full.

Now they make a bet. The watchman's wooden fist is well known and feared—who will have the courage to steal it? One of the smallest sees his chance to rise through the ranks, crawls closer, and carefully starts to unravel the left sleeve along the seam. The boy's nimble fingers expose scarred skin bound by leather straps and, holding his breath, he begins to loosen the buckles. Finally he loses patience, grips the tarnished wood, and yanks with all his weight. The tug-of-war only lasts for a moment until the leather slips from the arm and the boy falls backwards with his bounty. They make for the door with their trophy held high, screaming and laughing. Their escape makes no difference. Mickel Cardell hasn't budged an inch. He remains slumped for another hour or two in a fitful slumber until the cock crows and his cramps shake him awake. Then he staggers out, groping his way with his arm and stump through the labyrinth of alleys to the room for which he now owes several weeks' rent.

25

Summer grows searing, and what was at first merely a springtime soothing of winter's chill grows into a beast of its own. The heat rises in the houses, and once the stone walls have baked sufficiently, not even the night grants relief. The gutters turn rancid, and windows are kept closed to keep at bay the sickness that travels on tainted air. Damp timbers dry out, and the buildings groan as they shift position. Fear of fire grows rampant, enough to keep the stoves unlit and the smithy's forge dark. The heat begins to harvest its victims among those who haven't had sense enough to seek the well while they still had the strength. Lacerations swell and weep. The oldest succumb in their rented ovens; so do the youngest.

Cardell tries to sleep the summer away as best he can. He sweats the same as others do, but there is strength in him yet, and when he is overcome by thirst he drinks his fill at the pump. Sleep soothes the hunger that claws his belly, only relieved by the turnips traded with his neighbors for a couple of trips to the well with the yoke on his shoulders. His condition is known at the pubs, no one will offer him work anymore, and he avoids the only one of them that would show him mercy: the Scapegrace, where he suspects the girl Anna Stina would find him board enough, even to the point of bankruptcy, and the favor he had done her convert to debt. This last small piece of dignity is worth far more to him than any nourishment. And so he keeps to his bed, turns his face to the wall, and hugs his aching arm until sleep takes him.

He sleeps in his shirt on account of the lice, damp with sweat under the linen when he wakes. A look out of the window and the tower of Nikolai gives him the time, the hands of the clock wavy where the air trembles over scorched roof tiles. Evening, thank goodness. In groggy confusion, he gropes for water, and finds with a curse that his last bottle has overturned and every drop has spilled out. He pulls on his breeches.

....

The stairwell is worse than his own room. Broken windows have been replaced with rags and boards. All the rubbish that no one can be bothered to dispose of is abandoned on the stairs, the corners of which have served as privies for those whose need has been too great. Cardell has to pinch his nose as he starts down the steps in the vain hope that his soles will be spared the worst. It smells like an open grave. And all at once he knows why. Three steps down a ghost stands in his way. He loses his breath as suddenly as if he had been punched in the gut. He recognizes everything: the face as thin and pale as ever, the eyes and hair the same, always that handkerchief to cover the mouth and conceal the blood on the lips. Lame with terror, he stands frozen until he is addressed.

"Jean Michael Cardell?"

"Winge?"

But the voice is merely similar, and when the handkerchief is lowered, Cardell notices differences in the face. Alike enough to confuse another, but not him. Under the hard gaze of the watchman, the stranger fidgets with the fringed edge of his coat.

"By all means. Although not the one you think."

Cardell has enough presence of mind to wave his visitor down the stairs. Together they walk out into the alley.

"You almost gave me a stroke, for fuck's sake. Why hide in the stairwell instead of knocking on the door?"

The stranger's voice is hesitant, the words stammered forth with some effort.

"There was snoring. Rather than wake you up, I chose to wait."

"Well, if it is Mickel Cardell you're looking for, you've found him now."

"My name is Emil Winge. Cecil was my brother."

Cardell has trouble tearing his eyes from this Winge's face, and

Emil, ill at ease with this scrutiny, lets his gaze fall to the ground, where it rests until Cardell breaks the uncomfortable silence.

"Let's talk at the Brown Door. It's the one place that allows me any credit. Just a moment while I wash up."

Winge nods, and Cardell turns back towards the courtyard, where a cleft barrel holds water for the chickens. It looks clean enough, and he begins to wash himself. He holds the water in the cup of his hand, hoping to catch a glimpse of his reflection, but finds he is shaking too much.

26

The street they walk along is deserted. What people they see are gray shadows. At year's end, Reuterholm's most recent edict was read from the pulpits. A sumptuary law. Only the old remember the last one, half a man's age ago. Lace, embroidery, silk, colored fabrics, all will be forbidden in order to prevent Swedish currency from leaving the country in the pockets of foreign merchants. Color has been banished from the alleys.

Those who own the least are the easiest to deprive. The colorful fabrics that maids use to bind their hair—their only resort to vanity—have been replaced by unbleached linen, sweat stains the only pattern. The journeyman's inherited finery remains hanging in the wardrobe, a feast for moths, when his day off comes around. Dandies, who once paraded in garish coats and waistcoats, now only dare to wear them when the light is dim enough to dull their radiance, such bright colors reserved for those who enjoy a position high enough to stare down the city watch. It is as if all the inhabitants of the city have been robbed of what luster they once had and instead been uniformly dressed in gray. Sharp tongues have christened the year 1794 already: they've dubbed it the Iron Age.

Few patrons have made it to the Brown Door. Cardell gestures towards a table and benches, and feels a momentary loss of resolve when a stern look from the manager reminds him of debts that need to be settled before being allowed to grow. Nonetheless he brings over two pints of strong beer, albeit shamelessly watered down.

"I do beg your pardon. I should have knocked or at least come back later."

Winge takes several deep sips and Cardell notices how quickly the drink calms his agitated gaze, driving the stutter out of his speech and straightening his back. No candles are lit. They have to make do with what little light finds its way through the sooty glass.

"Don't fret about it. But damn it if the two of you don't look identical in dim light. For a moment I thought . . ."

He chokes down the words before the sentence is finished. Emil Winge doesn't seem to notice.

"It's been many years since I last saw Cecil, but all my life I have heard how much we both favor our mother."

Winge takes another sip before he goes on.

"Cecil was two years my senior. You knew him well, from what I gather. A policeman I asked sent me to a coffeehouse where I found a certain Blom, who gave me your name in turn."

"Sure I knew him, in a way. For a time."

"Did you attend the funeral?"

It is not a cherished memory. A dreary affair with only the minister, himself, and a handful of men from the Chamber of Police as witnesses. Cecil Winge had had to spend some time in the morgue until the gravedigger could get his spade to penetrate the frozen ground. Cardell gives a curt nod before emptying his tankard and waving for another round of the same. They wait in silence while the drink is poured, and only when his next drink is finished does Cardell pose his question.

"What's your business with me?"

Emil Winge already has his glass at his lips and seems determined to keep it there as long as possible rather than answer. When he puts it down, it is empty.

"I came to Stockholm to take care of Cecil's affairs. I have been to the ropemaker's, who kept his last possessions. One of these was noticeably absent: a pocket watch. It was a gift from our father. I was surprised to find it missing. It meant a great deal to Cecil, and it would not be like him to have lost it."

"I remember it well."

"Do you know what might have happened to it?"

Cardell takes his time as he weighs his answer.

"Your brother was involved in some strange matters in the evening of his life, and I had the privilege of being at his side. In the end, the only way for him to be successful in his dealings was to pawn the watch."

Emil Winge thoughtfully chews his lower lip as he considers what he has heard.

"Then I know where I should look. Thank you."

For a while it seems to Cardell that there are other questions swirling in the air, but Winge leaves them all unspoken. Cardell's head is spinning after having drunk so quickly in his dehydrated state. Once again he finds himself staring openly at this face that is both familiar and unknown. He shakes himself as if to break the enchantment.

"Sorry for the gawping. It's hard to grasp that there are two of you. Were."

He sees from Winge's wrinkled brow that the topic disturbs him. Winge waves one last time to the publican, drinks, puts coins on the table for the last tankard, and stands up.

"Three, in fact. Our sister came before us both. But as far as any resemblance is concerned, it is strictly confined to appearance. Me and my brother have never had much in common. For those who have made his acquaintance, mine quickly becomes a disappointment."

He rises in order to leave. Cardell empties his own tankard and wipes the foam away from his mouth.

"I can ask around for the watch, if you like. Where should I find you if I hear anything of interest?"

Emil Winge gives him the names of a street and a landlady, then steps out into the alley, steady on his feet with three tankards inside him, and leaves Cardell to say his farewells to an empty room.

"You certainly don't drink like your brother, that's for sure."

Cardell lingers for a moment with the creeping feeling that something has changed. At once he realizes what it is: his arm stump hasn't hurt him for the past hour; or if it has, he hasn't paid it any attention.

27

Emil Winge's room is one of the most private he has been able to find, rented from a widow with a large house and no income. The building is ancient, with thick stone walls anchored with wrought iron, and with barely more than two narrow openings to serve as windows. If anything, it reminds him of a fairy-tale dungeon where the noble hero languishes in his darkest hour. He is the only one on his floor, the other rooms being occupied only by turnips and onions, his only neighbors the merchant lackeys who come to drop off and pick up goods, and the rats who do what they can to gnaw holes in the sacks. Of all the rooms he considered, this he thought the best, hidden away from the city folk and their endless clamor. Public gatherings make him ill at ease. The door to the stairs is made of oak, clad in iron, and once he turns the key in the lock behind him, he feels calmer.

Intent on not letting the inebriation from the Brown Door go to waste and deprive him of purpose, he riffles through the stack of papers that have been left by Cecil Winge. The system is clear and easy: correspondence in one part, accounting in the next, each section chronologically ordered. His brother's aptitude for logic makes it easy to find what he is looking for. The pawnshop receipt is the last in its section. When he quickly eyes the rest of the receipts, he finds yet another one, a few years older, for the same watch. That Cecil would have pawned his Beurling in the face of death is one thing; that he would have done it once before surprises Emil. He takes a sip straight out of the bottle. With the warmth in his throat comes the feeling of indifference towards yet another of life's small mysteries that holds little promise of resolution.

For Emil Winge, the City-between-the-Bridges is unknown territory. Stockholm was Cecil's domain. He himself longs for Uppsala, for
the room he has had ever since he began his studies, which he hasn't paid
for in years since his landlady by now considers him part of the family.
The pawnshop ticket gives no clue to the name or address of the establishment, so he must search for it as best he can. He hesitates over yet
another drink. The smaller bell of Saint Nikolai tolls the half hour and
he decides to wait for the next whole one. The bottle is emptied through
regular mouthfuls. The third quarter hour is struck, and he soon walks
over to the door. He holds his hand still over the latch while he waits,
watching it turn to a sundial by the light from above. The shadows from
his fingertips crawl towards the handle as he counts the minutes. Then
the grand bell strikes, and as its toll reverberates he closes his eyes,
opens the door, and steps over the threshold.

The streets repulse him. They are so constricted that it seems impossible not to touch the arms, shoulders, or hips of the people encountered on the way, try as he might to avoid them. The cobblestones are
treacherous, and each time he isn't looking, brown puddles are lying in
wait. He hasn't gone but a block before his shoes are overflowing and
the seams bleeding every time he puts his foot down. It is evident that he
doesn't belong here, and whenever he betrays his weakness by a doubt-
ful glance or hesitant step, he inspires hostility in others.

"Out of the way, damn it!"

"Step aside, if you know what's good for you."

Each building is like a Tower of Babel, stones piled up far among the
clouds in praise of greed, and between the rooftops there is only the thin-
nest shard of sky. Even though it is midday, twilight seems constant in the
City-between-the-Bridges.

The pawnbrokers number beyond count, relegated to neither a spe-
cific street nor quarter, but scattered about in a way that seems completely random. Again and again, he loses his sense of direction in the
maze of alleys, and when he crosses a threshold, he encounters a face
that sent him on his way but moments ago, and now scowls at him with
ill-concealed irritation. Pocket watches abound—a trinket that changes

hands with ease once the owner falls on bad times. On their faces he reads Kock, Hovenschiöld, Lindmark, Ernst. Not a Beurling among them. No one can recall his brother's watch.

The sky opens wide when he emerges onto the slope flanking the palace. Afternoon strides towards evening. Emil Winge curses silently that he has misjudged his location once again, but a sudden clearing of the clouds calms him, and he breathes easier now that his view is no longer limited to the crowded alleyways. The hillside stretches down towards the water, the waves of which can be glimpsed through a lattice of masts where overlapping rigging makes such a tangle that it is hard to believe there can be any order at all.

He looks up at the clock face of the cathedral, and his thoughts circle back to the watch he is searching for. A masterpiece by Pehr Henrik Beurling, set with diamonds, the case engraved with two birds on a wall with Doric columns crowned by urns. A gift to Cecil on his graduation day, their father so proud the buttons on his waistcoat nearly popped. During the celebrations, the old man hadn't been able to resist charting out loud his eldest son's upwards course in life, somewhere between a dream and an estimate: first, a lawyer, then a judge and a lawmaker, and after that further upwards on wings of freshly won nobility. After his father had finished, his gaze had swept across the room, lingering only for a moment on Emil, who thought he perceived a twitch at the corner of his father's mouth, as if he had been reminded of something distasteful in the midst of his triumph.

A train of jackdaws pass so suddenly over Winge's head that their shadows cause him to take a hasty leap aside. Accompanied by the shrill laughter of a street urchin, he finds a place to rest by the castle walls. The sounds of a struggle come from two policemen dragging a man up the hill, on a steady course to a door on the opposite side. It strikes him that this must be Indebetou House, and that his brother must surely have crossed the very ground before him hundreds of times. Annoyed, he shifts his position without being able find much comfort. It is as if the building has grown taller at the same rate at which he has come to realize its significance. Now it looms over him like the palm of a hand raised above an encroaching fly. Here the men had greeted his brother with veneration and respect as recently as last year. Who was he by comparison? A nobody hardly worth their contempt. A source of shame for his father, and of interest to no one else.

Winge is sweaty; the salt stings his lice bites, more numerous than he is used to. He wonders if he's running a fever, feels his brow. His hip flask is as dry as the cobblestones themselves. He rises, and steers his course back through the City-between-the-Bridges, back to his room, his business as unfinished as when he began.

28

Yet another day that Cardell cannot identify by name draws to its end. He crosses the blue drawbridge at Polhem's Lock. Under him the water runs low, channeled hissing beneath his heels. He walks some distance up the hill and makes a turn at the first street wedged between the stone buildings.

Behind its walls, Maria churchyard lies silent and still, except for the occasional snores from those who have neither superstitions nor a roof of their own, and who have chosen to make their beds at the foot of the church. The tower cleaves the sky and the branches of the trees weave shadows over the tombstones, but here Cardell has no need of light: he knows where he is going.

The two graves lie very close to each other. The gravedigger was decent enough to move the corpse that Cecil Winge and he had finally given a name to. It came out of the earth barely more than a tiny bundle, like an infant in a swaddling of soil. In this way, sharing their soil, they await the Day of Judgment, Cecil Winge and Daniel Devall, each under a stone that bears his name.

The terror that comes over him so often, followed by a searing pain in his lost left arm, may be a product of fancy and beyond the help of medicine, but here he finds relief, as if the air over the graves were so full of memories that each breath gives comfort. When he lies down on the earth, he feels the crinkle of the dry grass, thirsty for dew that will not come. A moment's respite is all he requires, but sleep comes unbidden.

....

Hours go by. Around him, the city wakes. From the yards, the cocks tune up their coarse instruments. The ratchet of the pump can be heard incessantly when newly roused children come with yoke and buckets to fetch water. There is a clatter and clanging from the steel bars being traded at the scales by the Lock, and from the Russian Yard the sound of the eastern merchants starting to call out today's bargains. A man comes sauntering across the graveyard to take up his post in the tower, shaking his head at Cardell as he has done so many times that neither of them can put a number to them, and shortly thereafter the bell strikes the morning hour. Higher up and further away, Katarina Church replies and, from the other side of the Lock, the three other churches also bid this day welcome to the City-between-the-Bridges, and Cardell gets up and heads home.

"You've a visitor."

The mother of the large family that is squeezed into the room across from Cardell's narrow chamber calls out to him on the stairs and stops his ascent. His first thought is that Emil Winge must have forgotten something. The neighbor woman sticks her sharp nose out through a crack in the door to make herself more clearly heard over the noise of her children.

"I let her into your room to wait. Neither stairs nor yard is any place for a lady."

Cardell shrugs.

"If she's a thief, she'll soon find that she has more chance of dropping something of value than finding anything worth stealing."

He knocks on his own door before he steps over the threshold.

"Jean Michael Cardell?"

"Twice this year I have been asked that question, both in the same week."

He guesses her age at around forty. Her manner of dress is meticulous and proper, but worn, and of a kind seldom seen in the city. Sitting on the stool, she looks like a little old woman, but when she stands up she is taller than he expected, with a back as straight as a rod.

"My name is Margareta Colling."

....

Cardell has nothing to offer her, but manages to talk his way into getting a pot of burnt coffee from his neighbor in return for the assurance that this will be the last time. Cardell blows on the surface and takes a first sip.

"I used to detest this stuff but it grows on you. Just my luck that it will soon be banned."

To his relief, she leaves the offered cup untouched. She makes him uncomfortable. Her surface is smooth and controlled, a fortification of a kind that makes him wonder if what is concealed within needs to be restrained rather than defended.

"Do you mind if I get right to the point and tell you my story?"

Cardell waves her on, his mouth full.

"Last summer, my husband and I married off our daughter. It was in many ways a curious affair, attended by outsiders. We did not spend the night. When we returned the next day to greet the newlyweds and see the dower, the household was in grief. We were told our daughter was dead. During the night, she had left her wedding bed and gone for a stroll. A pack of wolves fell on her in the forest."

She allows the words to sink in. Cardell has the impression that her speech has been carefully rehearsed in order to keep it as short as possible to limit the pain it causes her.

"At first, they didn't want us to see her, but then they reluctantly showed me and my husband to the cellar where they had placed her, wrapped in a sheet that was more red than white. We each lifted a corner. And when I saw her, my thought was exactly what I had been told: Who but a pack of wolves could have caused her such injuries?"

Again a pause, long enough for Cardell to urge her on.

"And then?"

"Wolves haven't been seen in the forests around Three Roses for decades, Mr. Cardell, least of all in packs. Linnea Charlotta has had the run of the place her whole life. The truth is being kept from us."

Cardell is amazed by her self-possession. She does not betray the least bit of emotion. Her words are clear, her speech steady. The gaze that holds his is as hard as flint.

"What do you want with me, Mrs. Colling?"

"No one has wanted to help me in asking questions regarding my daughter's death. I came to Stockholm seeking justice. But even here, there is no help to be had. A secretary by the name of Blom gave me your name and said that you had provided assistance to the police before in matters that others had avoided."

"I have no hidden talents. What you see before you is no disguise to lull my enemies into a false sense of security. I am a lame soldier with hardly a penny to my name. The matter that Isak Blom refers to was resolved by another, who has long since mingled his dust with that of his forebears."

Margareta Colling nods to herself as if reflecting on what has been said. It takes a while before she speaks again.

"And what do you see, Cardell, when you look at me?"

Cardell doesn't know what to say.

"I shall tell you. A harmless little farmer's wife from the stables and sties who can hope for no better reward for her labors than pity. You know nothing of what it is like to be a woman, Cardell. We are expected to stifle our God-given sense and leave everything to men while busying ourselves with simple and worldly matters. You think that nothing goes on behind a forehead adorned with a bonnet. No thoughts of value are housed there, no dreams of anything but a quiet spot to crochet by the fire and to bring children into this world, one after another, preferably male, until age steals our beauty and deprives us of the only asset for which we are prized. Linnea Charlotta was my youngest. She was of another kind. I saw myself in her, such as I was before I conformed to everything the world demanded. She was wild, Cardell, and knew her own mind. Whenever my husband brought up the question of marriage, I shook my head: you can't lead that girl where you like. She will go her own way. And in my thoughts, I added: *as I should have done.*"

"Why are you telling me all this?"

"What I am trying to say, Mr. Cardell, is that I know better than anyone that one cannot judge a person by appearances alone."

"And this husband of yours, where is he?"

"To her father, Linnea Charlotta was life itself. After that cellar, I never again saw him sober. It did not take many days to realize what the drink was helping him prepare for. I found him in the stream, where he had sat down, the water no deeper than he could easily have stood up in. He had stuffed his pockets full of rocks. My husband is dead, my other daughters of an age, with sense enough to have left a home where there is no future and before misfortune attaches itself to them for good, and I am left alone. But do not make the mistake of thinking me weak. Had I been, I would have taken my place at Eskil's side."

She finally lowers her gaze.

"But it would be a lie to say that you are the first I have asked for help. The truth is that there is no one else for me to ask."

29

The coffeehouse, the Small Exchange, is full to bursting with all those who believe they can drink so much coffee over the summer that they won't miss it in the autumn. Already at the start of the year, the news was delivered from the pulpit: coffee will be banned once and for all, taking effect at the beginning of August. The reason given is that the import is bankrupting the kingdom, but few believe this explanation. Instead the decree is blamed on Reuterholm's irritability. The coffeehouses draw high as well as low, and everyone in between, who intermingle and compete in the art of mocking authority. The baron wants his people quiet and dutiful and therefore the black coffee beans must go. In the establishment of Gustav Adolf Sundberg, there has been a tradition since spring to read elegies in verse over that which is to come, where jest and despair go hand in hand.

Cardell elbows the other patrons out of the way, but not so fast as to miss the gossip along the way. On everyone's lips is the name Magdalena Rudenschöld, Armfelt's mistress, the one who remained loyal to him as he fled the country and who has been doing his bidding among the Gustavians. Since the new year she has been under lock and key at the palace, soon to be tried for treason.

The scandal provides everything the rabble could want, the abundance of details lavish: her love letters, as full of disdain towards the baron and duke as they are with sweet promises to her lover, especially tickling since it is well known that Duke Karl has, for many years, been unable to get within ten feet of Miss Rudenschöld without testing the seams in the crotch of his breeches. Bets are made as to her fate: there is no doubt that Baron Reuterholm wants her to lose her head, but others are doing what they can to lessen the severity of her punishment. Still others say that the eventual sentence will be irrelevant, since no Swede will live to hear it: greedy farmers have sold all the grain in the kingdom to Frenchmen in Copenhagen, and thus doomed the nation to death by starvation come winter.

....

By the time Isak Blom sees him coming, it is too late. Cardell places a heavy hand on the small secretary's shoulder and presses him back down onto the chair. A few meaningful looks are enough to remind Blom's companions about pressing matters elsewhere, and Cardell takes one of the empty seats. He pours all the remaining coffee into a single cup. Helpless, Blom plays along.

"Why, it has been a while, Cardell. I do hope your health is good."

Cardell drinks the lukewarm coffee with a grimace.

"A joke at my expense, was it, Blom? You did it to mock me."

Blom assumes an expression of innocence.

"Whatever do you mean?"

"You sent me that woman Colling as a prank. To my room that stinks of wood alcohol and rat shit. To remind me of how little I am without Winge."

Blom's face is contorted into something half frozen in terror and half an apologetic smile. Cardell stops his answer with a gesture.

"And you are right, of course."

Secretary Blom's expression changes to one of suspicion.

"You hold no grudge?"

"Your little antic serves to remind me that I've not always treated you with the respect that you deserve. I may have overreacted once or twice on earlier occasions. If you can forgive me, Blom, then surely we can make a new start, you and I?"

Cardell holds his hand out across the table and wraps it around Blom's chubby fingers. When Blom releases his grip to break free of the clasp, Cardell keeps him restrained, and when Blom tries to pull his arm away to stand up, he finds it impossible and has to remain seated.

"Now that old scores have been settled, brother Blom, I do have a question or two. Your time at the university overlapped with Winge's. Do you happen to recall a younger brother, an Emil?"

"Certainly."

"Well?"

Blom shrugs, and his fingers stop wriggling as he gives up any hope of getting his hand back.

"Cecil earned his law degree twice as fast as is customary, so I was still in the classroom after he left for Stockholm to begin his career. Therefore I remember very well the day that Emil Winge arrived. By way of Cecil's renown, Emil was highly anticipated, and he was impossible to mistake for anyone else since they look so similar. It was even said that the younger brother was the sharper of the two. Everyone expected greatness. When he first found his way into the library, it was an event that attracted an audience. He took some book off the shelf, stuck his nose in it, and turned the pages so quickly that people thought he was playing them for fools. In time, fewer and fewer questioned the critics, as nothing ever came of Emil Winge. He did not sit his exams, made no impression, and soon was hardly seen at all, and when he was, his behavior was increasingly strange. He adopted certain eccentricities. The phenomenon is not so unusual, you know, and I am sure that you have seen the same thing in the military. Young men leave home, test their wings, find they will not carry. They say that the disappointment over his youngest son gave Old Winge a stroke."

Cardell nods at what he has heard, thoughtful.

"If you would be so kind as to return my hand . . ."

"One more thing, Blom. As recently as last year, the police had a sum of money set aside for auxiliary personnel which made it possible for Police Chief Norlin to secure Cecil Winge's services. How does that fund stand, now that Magnus Ullholm is at the helm?"

"Everything in which our new chief hasn't yet shown any interest remains unchanged."

"Are you in a position to put my name on the salary list?"

Isak Blom makes a sound somewhere between a snort and a laugh.

"Why on earth? Is it your intention to pursue Mrs. Colling's case? Now you're the one pulling my leg."

Cardell shakes his head.

"I'm serious. Ullholm knew Winge's name but not mine. The small amount of money you administer would make it possible for me to at least make some inquiries. I don't ask much. I'm cheap labor and don't need a salary above the expenses I can't avoid."

Blom's fingers sporadically twitch in the viselike grip that keeps tightening. Cardell draws him closer.

"Blom, regardless of what you may think of me, you know that I am neither beggar nor thief. Hell, I may have reservations when it comes to you as well, but I'm inclined to believe that you conceal a righteous man somewhere in your spongy flesh. You met Margareta Colling yourself and you listened to her story. If my assistance is the only one on offer, is she not deserving of it? Or should the department's money stay where it is, awaiting the day when Ullholm finds the best way to embezzle it?"

"Colling struck me as an exceedingly honorable woman with a worthy cause. But her troubles, as terrible as they may be, appeared hopeless."

It takes half a minute of reflection before the feelings that struggle for mastery of Blom's face relax into resignation.

"All right then, Cardell, if I have your word that you will put each coin to good use."

Cardell gives him a nod and gives the tender hand an even firmer squeeze.

"Let's shake on it."

....

Cardell sweeps up and down the alleys that flow into West Street until he sees them, a bunch of street urchins who have gathered in a semicircle next to the wall of a building. Most of them are a couple of years shy of their tenth birthday, but the eldest may be fifteen. His face, marked with the blemishes that come with his age, towers above his companions. He has grabbed one of his lackeys by the collar and is holding him at arm's length, delivering slap after slap.

They are a remarkable mixture. A few are children who likely have homes of their own but are either permitted or at least not prevented from running about as their parents have better things to do. Others sleep rough, orphans, living hand to mouth. Parents or not, their poverty unites them, and its law is the only one they know. Any child with a solid pair of shoes and a freshly washed shirt would immediately have had to yield their riches to the rights of the stronger. Only those who own nothing of value go unmolested. Those who have had the misfortune of being born too pleasing to the eye, and who are unwilling to make money from their appearance, habitually smear their faces with dirt from the gutter in advance of the day when they can better defend themselves. Cardell seeks the leader's gaze and holds up a shilling between his thumb and index finger. The tall youth approaches like a skittish animal on guard for predators. Cardell lowers his voice so that their conversation will remain private.

"D'you know who I am?"

The boy nods.

"A week or so ago I nodded off at the pub and my wooden arm was stolen. It was either you lot or someone like you. It matters little to me. I want it back."

"Money first."

Cardell holds it out but yanks the coin out of reach when the young man makes his attempt.

"You'll have it, but first a word of warning. When the arm was stolen, I was asleep and harmless. Now I am quick and dangerous. And I'll make you a promise here and now: if you take my coin without delivering the goods, I'll find you. The City-between-the-Bridges is small, and it's only a matter of time before we meet again. I'll grab you by the ear and carry you up the steps to the Stock Exchange. There I'll put you over my lap, pull down your breeches, and give you a thrashing in front of anyone who cares to watch."

The boy swallows.

"You keep your shilling."

"If I made it sound like you had a choice, I didn't express myself clearly enough."

"I saw them toss your arm into the Flies' Meet."

A beloved topic of conversation in the City-between-the-Bridges is to muse about the true depth of the manure pile down by the quay, the pile that never seems to diminish, regardless of the barges that regularly transport so much of it that their decks sink almost below the waterline. Few guesses place it at under four fathoms. Cardell muses for a while.

"Let's say two shillings. Enough for a couple of square meals for the lot of you. But God help you if I hear that you searched less thoroughly than anyone else."

30

Cardell knocks noisily on the door with his reacquired left fist, deposited by his door earlier the same morning. The weight of it feels familiar and comforting. The quick wash in the gutter that the urchins had given it has not managed to erase the image of a cock and balls that someone has whittled across the wrist. He waits before he lets his hand tap out a tattoo again, with no result. When he puts his ear against the wooden door, he hears faint snores on the other side.

Widow Bergman takes some convincing before she is willing to unlock the door with her spare key. Only when Cardell mentions his connection with the police does she get her key ring and, obstinately slowly, eye each key in turn until she finds the right one.

The stench that greets Cardell when he cracks open the door is all too familiar. He has spent many hours in its company. This is the stench of the worst pubs, the ones whose owners are desperate enough to offer free rounds in the hopes that the patrons will disregard the fact that the floor has neither been swept nor scrubbed, and where everyone can do as he pleases. Where spills from a thousand tankards have drenched the sawdust on the floor, where those whose need grows too great will just step back to piss on the side of the barrel that serves as a table. Where the one who has drunk more than he should empties his stomach where chance would have it. Cardell obscures the view by shouldering the door open, to spare Mrs. Bergman the state of her tenant.

"My friend appears to have indulged in one too many refreshments. Let me take care of him and make sure he puts the room back in order. Does he owe you anything?"

"The room has been paid for till Sunday."

....

There are bottles everywhere. Emil Winge's labored breathing is the only sound that can be heard as he lies on the floor, so drunk as to have missed the bed by an arm's length. All the same he has been lucky, Cardell notes with the eye of experience, partly because his fall has spared his mattress everything that has run out of him in his unconscious state, and partly because he has landed on his belly and been spared death by suffocation. Cardell lifts a limp hand and lets it fall against the floor without any objection from its owner. He puts the empty bottles back into the basket in which they must have been brought in. The overflowing chamber pot he carries out onto the stairs, where there is a window large enough for him to empty the contents. With the floor cleared, he inches his hand under Emil Winge in order to move him onto the bed, and finds the effort less laborious than he feared. Winge is nothing but skin and bones. Cardell settles him on the pillow, wresting Winge's shirt over his head with some difficulty, dipping a rag in the water bucket and washing him clean of the worst of it. Then he gives the floor the same treatment. When he leaves the room, he takes the key from the inside of the door with him, and when he returns barely an hour later, he knocks at Mrs. Bergman's and places two coins in the palm already hovering in the air between them, guided by unfailing instinct.

"My friend wants to let you know he will be staying till month's end."

Back in the room, Cardell sets out everything he has brought on the table: bottles, water, whittled sticks for kindling, a tinderbox. Bread and cheese and a shoulder of smoked mutton, enough to last days. The hour approaches supper. The room is stale and dark. The glass in the window is not of the kind one can open, nor does it let much air out or light in.

His duties completed, Cardell sits down heavily in a worn armchair and unbuckles his wooden arm. He fills his cheek with tobacco and slowly starts to grind it between his teeth. From time to time he spits the juice into an empty bottle he has set aside. He waits.

....

It takes a considerable amount of time for Emil Winge to wake. Bloodshot eyes struggle open, followed by a whimper when the senses become aware of the condition of the body. Cardell gets up and puts a bottle under Winge's chin. He grabs it and drinks greedily. Cardell answers the disappointed expression before the question is asked.

"Small beer. It will serve to satisfy your thirst."

Emil Winge rubs his eyes and makes a face with each sip.

"Go back to sleep. Best way to lessen the pain."

....

Cardell waits, patiently. The light makes a skewed rectangle that slowly climbs the wall with the failing sun. Evening comes before Winge rouses once more. It is the change in breathing that first alerts Cardell. But Winge chooses to lie quietly in the darkness a long time before he says anything.

"Why are you here?"

Cardell spits his mouth clean.

"I came looking for you on a completely different errand from the one I found."

Winge's gaze sweeps across the room.

"There was no need for you to clean up after me."

"Someone had to, and I seemed the most likely candidate. Is it my turn to ask questions now?"

Shame falls over Winge's face.

"Be my guest."

"Did you drink all this yourself? Or was someone else here to help you?"

"All me, I'm afraid."

"Then you're thirsty again by now, I imagine."

Cardell reaches for yet another bottle of beer and hands it to Winge, who protests.

"Beer won't do, not by a long shot. Spirits, as strong as you can find."

Cardell puts in another wad of tobacco.

"This is what is on offer."

Winge gets out of bed and feels around for his shirt.

"I'll go out myself, then."

"You'll stay where you are."

It is fear that shines in Emil Winge's eyes when he goes to the door and finds the keyhole empty. Cardell pats his waistcoat pocket.

"I have it right here. Come and claim it if you dare."

Winge's voice is but a feeble whisper when he answers.

"I'll die."

Cardell leans forward.

"I've seen people like you before, in the war. In Finland, with my arm freshly shorn off, I was consigned to Lovisa. There were many of us in the tent camps, and the field medics were few and intent on returning home now that peace had been reached. After a while the spirits ran dry, and even though there were promises of a prompt delivery, none came. Many of my comrades had not been sober for years. The wounded who could walk were forced out of their beds by their thirst, and wandered off into the trees in the hopes of finding a farm or village where drink could be found. I never saw them again, but I don't doubt that they came to a quick end in the Finnish forest, stabbed by bandits in some thicket or surprised by the first frosty nights, yet with only drink on their minds, despite their skin blackening in the cold. Others couldn't leave their beds. I did what I could to assist the medics to ease their suffering. The kindest deed within reach was often to knock them out. Some died, certainly. Others got better. It takes a week to find out who's who. You'll manage the first day for sure. Then it'll get worse. But if you survive, Emil Winge, you'll have your life back. Dead or dead drunk, you aren't much use to anyone."

31

When Emil Winge finally wakes up, it is as if all fatigue has left him. His nausea seems greater than his body can contain, but there is also a restlessness, incited by a nagging fear of what is to come. Each time he draws breath, it is as if he is disturbing some beast slumbering in his belly, which responds by poking him in the side so hard that his stomach clenches. He can do nothing but wait out the one-armed watchman, who must surely rest eventually. Night comes and he feigns sleep with eyes half-closed until he hears snores come from the opposite side of the room. Slowly he lifts the blanket, turns his legs over the side of the bed with a prayer that the timber frame will remain silent, stands, and starts to tiptoe across the floor. Up close, he can see every feature in the sleeping face. Winge can't help but wonder what the watchman must have done to deserve such an appearance. The broad face didn't have many advantages to start with, and with age the lines have deepened. But more than anything else, it is a chronicle of violence. The nose is broken and badly healed, one of the eyebrows is almost bald with scar tissue. The temples and forehead are a grid of healed lacerations, some that snake further beyond the hairline. The ears are lined with lumps from old beatings, the cheekbones asymmetrical. And yet it is still a face to fear rather than to pity. He shivers and summons a trembling hand to search the waistcoat pockets, breathing through his mouth to be as quiet as possible. The tips of his fingers find iron and gingerly he pulls out the key and hurries to the door.

Emil uses both hands to fit the key in the hole and starts to turn carefully, with a silent prayer that the oil hasn't dried completely. The mechanism yields. The door has hardly started to swing open when the clang of glass against the floor shatters the silence. Cardell's living hand grabs him by the shoulder like a vise. The watchman must have been on his feet much faster than his heavy body should have allowed. Cardell's voice is a low growl.

"If you hadn't been in such a hurry right there at the end, you would have seen that I had leaned a bottle against the door."

He locks the door behind them while Emil backs up into the room. Cardell looks at him thoughtfully.

"You'll only try that trick once. Let's do this instead."

Cardell drops the key to the floor and pushes it under the door with his foot. Emil Winge responds in panic.

"Is it your intention that we should die here, me of thirst and you of hunger?"

Cardell waggles a loaf of bread at him.

"When we're done here, I'll break the door. I have compensated Widow Bergman enough to cover a new lock. Lie down now, try to sleep. You'll need every ounce of strength that you can muster."

....

The truth behind Cardell's words dawns on Emil Winge with growing horror. He was sure that the watchman had been exaggerating, or that the period of sickness had passed more quickly than anticipated, since the first day had already been the worst of his life. Molten lead roiled in his belly. The spasms bent him double over the chamber pot, and when the beer had run out, the bile dribbled yellow, searing his throat. Still, the day after is worse.

He would to do anything for a drink but the watchman doesn't respond to threat, pleading, bribe, or promise. When night comes the second time, Cardell starts to light his tapers. Each slender twig is lit with tinder, then gently placed in its holder, where the tiny flame warps the charred wood.

The smell of tar fills the room and Emil Winge sees something flit across his skin. He flinches, and tries to brush it off. When he lifts the blanket from his legs, he sees worms and beetles scatter in their hundreds. His skin bulges and swells as they dig their tunnels, and for the first time he screams aloud. The watchman wrings a rag dipped in water over his head.

"Whatever you see is only in your head."

Winge presses his eyes closed as hard as he can. He hears a creaking, squeaking sound and realizes that he is gnashing his teeth.

....

The fever comes later, and with it brief moments of respite when his consciousness can no longer bear the experience of the body. Cardell is at his side with his rag, feeding him bread soaked with beer that he rarely keeps down.

"What do you want with me?"

"You've asked me many times now."

"Maybe I'll remember the answer this time."

"I came to ask for your help, hoping that you would have as much of your brother inside as out. I found you incapable of giving assistance, even if you'd offered it. I'm making you well again. When we're done here, and you're sober, you can listen to my proposal and give me your answer. If you say no, we'll go our separate ways."

"You keep me here against my will. Why would I reward that with my help?"

"I have seen the bottle run errands for the reaper many times. Not a pretty sight. The way you drink, I give you another year, no more than five. I'm saving your life, against your will if needs be."

"I know nothing about matters of the kind my brother devoted himself to."

"Your brother was the smartest man I ever met. You are apples fallen from the same tree."

Winge shakes his head from side to side.

"Our resemblance tempts you into wishful thinking. I'm not my brother. Whatever he was to you, it is beyond my power."

The watchman breathes heavily and sits quietly for a long time. The taper burns down and goes out, and Emil Winge lies still, waiting in the embrace of darkness. But soon he hears the clang of steel against the flint and a new flame is lit, illuminating the watchman's face. His rough voice betrays no emotion.

"Well. You've one advantage that your brother lacked. What he had pulled him to the grave with no chance of reprieve. What you have can be treated."

Emil shivers, and pulls the blanket up to his chin. The waves of heat are so strong it feels as if he is being scalded. His voice betrays his fear.

"What's next?"

"The shakes. But they're still hours away."

....

Sleep comes to Emil Winge for a few hours. When he wakes, the nausea is no worse, but his heart beats faster and faster.

"Cardell?"

The watchman shifts position in the chair, likely awakened from his own slumber. The legs of the chair scrape against the floor as he pulls it closer to the bed.

"Present."

"I'm scared."

In the silence that follows, Winge's hand taps against the bed frame in a strange rhythm, never stopping. Winge tries to restrain it by force, to no avail.

"Cardell."

"Here it comes."

The hours go by. Again and again, Cardell offers the same quiet comfort.

"The worst is over now."

When the cock crows on the morning of the sixth day, those words are no longer a lie.

32

They stand in the alley, both of them, in the shade, squinting at the wash of the morning sun on the facade opposite. Never in his life has Cardell been tempted to call the stale air in the City-between-the-Bridges fresh, but the week spent in Widow Bergman's room has brought him as close as he's likely to get. He glances at Emil Winge and sees him drawing greedy breaths. Winge is paler and thinner, but Cardell senses a deeper change, one he has seen many times during the war. It is the look of someone who has come close to death and escaped with the knowledge that time is but a loan at steep interest. Emil Winge blinks in the light and looks around. He looks from rooftop to gutter until the goose pimples make him shiver.

"Everything is so sharp."

"More likely everything was fuzzy before. How are you feeling?"

A street vendor comes walking along the street, bent under his load. Cardell cuts the oily pleasantries short with a gruff gesture and gets a muttered curse in response. Further down the alley, a boy is running along with a piglet on a leash. Winge makes a face at the cacophony of the street.

"There is much I can't recall."

"What do you remember?"

"Uppsala. My room. How they all looked at me when I first arrived, so like my brother. Hopes and anticipation, envy and respect. First we were all of an age. I assume they graduated and went on, and others took their place. They looked much the same. The only one who grew older was me."

Lost in thought, Winge begins to bite a nail, but frowns at the taste and spits in the dirt. As if alarmed by a sudden noise, he throws his head to the side and takes a step back until the plaster of the wall behind him touches his back.

"Did you hear that?"

The babble of people from the Quayside, clinking glasses that betray the impending arrival of some traveling salesman from around the corner, the creak of wheels and thud of hooves against the cobblestones. Cardell can't hear any sounds remarkable enough to distinguish from the constant bustle of the city. His expression makes his puzzlement evident and Winge shakes his head.

"Can we go somewhere else, somewhere the buildings aren't so close together?"

They walk down the hill, where the land slopes to the water and the sky opens up above. Between moored ships, the water glitters under a gleaming sun, and Emil Winge straightens the back he has kept hunched in the shadow of the alleys. Cardell leads them up towards the church, where the crowd grows scarcer. He leans his back against the vacant stone plinth that dominates the open space.

"A widow sought me out the week before last. Colling by name. Her daughter's dead. She was told wolves were to blame, but Colling has reason to believe that they're not the kind with fur. No one will help. I've grudgingly been deputized by the police to aid in this affair."

He looks down before he continues.

"Last autumn your brother asked me for my help. He was alone, dying, and sensed that I had the kind of strength he lacked. I think he knew right away why my answer would be yes, and since he guessed my reasons, he chose to trust me completely. I have some strength left yet, but now I'm as alone as he was then, and this time around it is I who lack what he had. I can't see through you as your brother saw through me, but I need to trust you just as much."

Cardell fishes his purse out of his coat pocket and digs out a coin. The tender profile of the crown prince gazes towards a throne that is still two years away. He hands the coin to Winge, who responds with a confused look.

"You know my hopes, but the time for brute force is at an end. I'm asking you for help. I offer you the opportunity to right a wrong, and as long as you are by my side, you won't have to rely on your own conscience in order to keep the bottle at bay. There are more coins where this came from, and you are welcome to your half, but if my guess is correct, they will amount to fair compensation for the effort. The road will be long, dark, and arduous, the goal unknown, the risks not inconsiderable."

The bell of Saint Gertrud counts the third quarter of the hour.

"It is morning, almost ten o'clock. Meet me at the steps where the boats pull out, at four. If you want to go your own way, the coin will get you home and drunk enough to forget the past week. Get something to eat. But remember that if you have even a single drink ever again, you'll have been of use for the last time, not least to yourself."

....

Cardell turns his back and starts to walk towards the water. A bit further down, he turns left under an archway, and with each passing step the yellow buildings of the city slowly yield to sea and sky. The sun is in his eyes as he wanders south along the Quayside, ever closer to the sound of the rushing current. The lake water that has just taken its turn at the waterwheel leaps into the sea, frothing with newly won freedom. He passes the Customs House and sits down on the stone steps, to wait in the heat. A boat-woman calls out to him to move his fat arse unless he wants to get an oar between his cheeks, and out of habit he answers in kind. The bite of the straps gnaws his stump. The sounds of people fade away as Cardell loses himself in memories, aware of the fact that Emil Winge does not just carry one fate in his hands, but two. The hours go by, the sun heads west, until a shadow falls on his closed eyes, and someone sits down next to him. Cardell keeps his eyes closed and remains still for a moment. When he opens his eyes, Winge hands him half a loaf of bread with a hand that is still trembling with the effort it has cost him, then the change due.

"It was touch and go there for a while."

"What stopped you?"

Winge sighs and squints out between the ships' masts, out towards the wharf where the salt bay takes its leave of the City-between-the-Bridges.

"I came here to find my brother's watch. I intended to pawn it myself. It would have paid for all the bottles I could possibly have wished for. When I found it missing, I still needed to look for it, because if I could only find the right pawnshop, I could have written to my sister and asked her for the money to buy it back. And then, that money would have served the same purpose."

"And now?"

"If I help you first, will you help me afterwards? Will you help me find Cecil's Beurling?"

Cardell hesitates, kicking a stone in front of him over the edge of the quay and down into the water.

"Why do you still want it?"

"If I win back the watch by doing for you what my brother no longer can, then I will not only have regained it. I may also have earned it. Is that reason enough for you?"

Cardell nods.

"Yes. You have my word. Help me and I'll help you."

Emil Winge rubs his eyes in the sun reflected in the waves, and looks around as if for the first time.

"Cardell, what year is it now?"

"Do me a favor, will you? Call me Jean Michael."

33

They travel quickly and cheaply to make the trip as brief as possible, wedged among the goods on the back of wagons whose drivers pay little mind to the hour being early or late before setting out on the road. Emil Winge is restless, repeatedly changing position in order to find one where his back can rest comfortably, then swatting at the swarm of flies that harry their lumbering progress. Around them is only forest, occasionally thinning to pasture, where the farmer's axe has cleared the land for crops and for grazing.

"Let me try my hand at a summary, if not for your sake then for my own."

Winge takes a while to organize his thoughts before he continues.

"First we have to determine whether any crime has been committed. Can we take Mrs. Colling at her word, or has her sorrow given way to delusion? We might first of all do best to draw our own conclusions about the state of the wolf population around Three Roses."

Cardell has pulled down the brim of his tricorn over his eyes to shield his face from the pests, waving at those who venture too near with the long strand of grass tucked into the corner of his mouth. He grunts in response.

"The wolves are a fable. It'd take a lot for a pack of wolves to attack someone at this time of year, with the woods full of other prey. Such things only happen when the winter has starved all shame out of the beasts, if then."

"Then we should at least find out if the act did indeed take place in the forest or somewhere else, and if the site may yield any information."

"My thoughts exactly."

....

The landscape is dressed for summer, and each waving field of grain gives tentative promise of a passable harvest for the first time in years, as if it is nature's apology for the harsh winter that has just passed. For many, the mercy comes too late, and the leaves and flowers that are now offered in abundance only serve to decorate their graves; their wagon passes within view of homes that have been left derelict, and where the clouds of insects bear witness to those who died encased in ice only now being brought to light. The warped wheels complain loudly at each revolution of their axis, carrying them along a route that tortuously shies from hills and valleys and chooses the path of least resistance, regardless of how many twists and turns it may require. At the final inn they ask for directions, and proceed by foot.

....

Widow Colling comes out to meet them. As soon as they have stepped into the yard, she has already hoisted a bucket of water from the well for them to refresh themselves and wash the dust from their faces.

"I didn't think you would come."

Cardell takes another gulp.

"This is Emil Winge. He'll be assisting me in this matter."

He looks around a yard in disarray. Doors to the main dwelling and the outbuildings hang open, revealing the junk piled up inside them.

"What's going on?"

Mrs. Colling snorts.

"Am I to tend the farm on my own? The clerk of the estate had barely expressed his condolences before he posed the questions that led me to understand that I either had to surrender the tenancy or have it snatched from under me. The time allotted is at an end. I have a sister two counties over, and no other choice but to throw myself at her mercy and ask for some corner in which to sleep. I'm packing and sorting everything in the hope that I will get some sort of pittance for whatever I won't be able to bring with me."

The bitterness in her voice brokers no reply from Cardell or Winge.

"Well, we all have our crosses to bear. How would you like to begin?"

Cardell barely has time to open his mouth before Winge interrupts.

"The manor. We'd like to see Three Roses, inside and out."

She shrugs.

"I will show you onto the path."

....

She leads them through the forest to a clearing where the trees end. Three Roses can be seen on the other side of the field, a country house of the type that the nobility in the area like to call a castle, in a bluff that few city folk will ever take the trouble to call. For those who know Stockholm, it is more of a manor house, flanked on either side by freestanding outhouses that contain the kitchen and servants' quarters.

Mrs. Colling points out the way.

"Can you find your own way back? I'll go now to prepare supper for your return. I shall never again set my foot in Three Roses."

....

The maid who responds to Cardell's knock lets them wait a while before she returns with an uptight little man in her wake. His voice is stiff with irritation, and the look he gives them over the glasses balancing on the end of his nose is stern.

"Yes?"

"Jean Michael Cardell, Emil Winge. On official business from the Stockholm police."

"And the nature of said business?"

"Linnea Charlotta Colling."

"Dare I ask for papers to confirm this claim?"

Cardell frowns.

"That's usually the first question we get from someone who has something to conceal."

"You hardly have the air of people conducting police business."

"That someone doesn't look like they come from the police is rarely a disadvantage for the ones who work on behalf of the agency. We live in a world of deceptive appearances. You yourself, for another example, do not at first glance look foolish enough to question state officials with right on their side."

The color rises in the small man's face, but he hardly has time to draw breath before Cardell shows him the document that Isak Blom has prepared and marked with the correct seal.

"Here are the relevant papers. If you'd care to move of your own accord, I advise you to do so while there's time."

The man's dismissive attitude changes into perspiring servility as he steps aside.

"My apologies. The countryside is teeming with vagabonds, and I would not be doing my duty if I did not inquire as to the intentions of each visitor."

"And what is your position here, if I may ask?"

"I have been appointed to manage the estate in the owner's absence. Svenning is my name."

"Do you know the place of old?"

Svenning shakes his head. "No, not at all. I have been a bookkeeper all my life, but as a farmer's son I have assisted in similar matters elsewhere. I was brought here with the promise of a salary that exceeded my own. Old Three Roses passed away this spring, and as the only heir was abroad, the affairs have been managed, to the best of their abilities, by the local authorities. The son came home to marry, and I understand that some unfortunate events occurred of which I have been advised it would be best to remain ignorant. The previous foreman was fired, and the position was offered to me instead."

"Who is your employer?"

"The son, of course, the owner of the estate. Erik Three Roses."

Cardell absently scratches at a mosquito bite at his hairline.

"Now it is our turn to ask for papers."

"I have a contract, of course, which I'll fetch at once. All is in order. But I hazard to guess there are more pressing matters you would like to attend to?"

Cardell squints into the dim light of the foyer.

"The bridal bed. Show us the room where the bridal bed was prepared."

....

Cardell closes the door behind them when they have both crossed the threshold. The room is beautiful, dominated by a bed whose embroidered canopy is held aloft by four ornate posts. The furnishings are in keeping with the rest of the house: of good quality, passed down through the generations, maintained in the same condition as they were when originally obtained in an existence far from the constantly shifting fashions of the city. An oriental carpet, a floral-patterned wallpaper of repeated braided garlands. They walk to and fro amid the old-fashioned elegance of the room. Winge is the first to break the silence.

"Can you smell it?"

Cardell nods.

"Soap and water. But that doesn't tell you anything. They have scrubbed this room, but it would be just as natural to clean it in preparation for a wedding night as after a killing."

He falls to his knees with a sudden idea.

"Help me here."

Together they fold half the rug back, revealing a difference in color on the floorboards beneath. Cardell measures the fringed end of the rug against the area between light and dark wood.

"Another rug was here before. But is it because it became stained or because the old one was thought unsuitable for a bridal chamber?"

Cardell gets up on creaking knees while Winge nods thoughtfully. Together they scrutinize the rest of the room, but to no avail. Everything is clean and spotless, to the extent that flakes of soap are still visible in the cracks and crevices of the wood. Cardell is the first to call off the search and sinks heavily onto a chair, stuffing his cheek full of tobacco.

"Pointless."

Winge chews on a nail and glances up at the ceiling, where a chandelier hangs down from a stucco medallion on a chain wrapped in taffeta.

"Could you . . . ?"

Doubt silences him. Cardell gives him an impatient look.

"Spit it out. Whatever it is, it can hardly make the situation less hopeless."

"Could you ask someone to light the chandelier for us, Jean Michael?"

"It's the middle of the day. Isn't it light enough for you?"

Winge chooses to shrug rather than explain himself, and continues staring upwards until Cardell finally gets up with a sigh and leaves the room. When he returns after a couple of minutes it is in the company of the same maid who had first opened the door for them, now carrying a taper with a burning wick protected behind her cupped hand. One by one, she holds the flame against the candles of the chandelier, carefully, so as not to disturb the prisms of cut glass, while Winge clumsily loosens the ties on the curtains and pulls them across the windows. Cardell squints up at the sudden light.

"Not there, Jean Michael. Help me look along the walls. We are looking for a shadow that does not belong there."

Together they do a slow dance around the room. With a small cry, Winge spots what he is looking for: a stain on the wallpaper that trembles each time a breeze in the room sets the flames fluttering. Insect-like, as if something had stealthily hidden among the leaves of the wallpaper. He looks around.

"Help me to move the table."

They pull it over, and Winge climbs up to stand on the tabletop. Again and again, he seeks the line between flame and shadow, until he can put his hand in among the crystal and unhook the one he's looking for. Cardell offers his hand to help him down, and together they walk over to the window, where Winge can hold it up to the sun.

"She had red hair, Linnea Charlotta, like her mother?"

On one of the facets, a strand of hair has been trapped in a drop of congealed blood.

34

After his brief absence, Svenning interrupts them with the papers that have been requested. Winge studies the signatures in particular detail, Svenning's own alongside the other that should belong to Erik Three Roses but is not much more than a blot of ink struck through with some wavy lines.

"Did you sign this at the same time?"

"No, I signed it first, alone, two copies. Later I had one of them sent back to me, countersigned."

"You have never met face-to-face?"

Svenning shakes his head.

"Did you not find that strange?"

"Not really. If he weren't a busy man, he wouldn't have had need of my services. There was nothing for me to question."

Winge's one hand has made its way to a lock of hair at the nape of his neck, which he has started twirling.

"Tell me, what was your first task as newly appointed foreman here?"

"To appoint new staff."

"Everyone had been discharged?"

Svenning shrugs.

"So I would assume. To find replacements isn't difficult. Laborers of that sort come thirteen to the dozen and it's a buyer's market."

Cardell cuts in gruffly. "D'you have any idea where Erik Three Roses might be found?"

"No. For as long as my salary is paid, I see no reason to inquire as to his whereabouts."

....

The heat of the day lingers under the trees, though the sun has started to sink low, a red glow flickering through the branches. Flies and midges gleam as they swarm in and out of slanting beams. Cardell has unhooked his wooden arm and lets it hang over his shoulder by its straps.

"I have seen my fair share of bloodletting, and even so, I have trouble imagining how the hell there could have been stains all the way up there."

"And how goes your reasoning now?"

"Colling is right so far. Not only was her daughter murdered, but a great deal of effort has gone into concealing what happened. The room has been scrubbed clean, all those who must have been in the house at the time scattered to the four winds."

"There is only one person who should have been in the room at the same time as Linnea Charlotta, and that is the groom. The fact that he has disappeared does not speak in his favor, especially when the disappearance has been staged in such a way that it seems the tracks have intentionally been swept away. If we find Erik Three Roses, I dare wager we will also find her killer."

Cardell nods in agreement.

"I've heard of such things before, though never with as tragic an outcome. The bride and groom are both young, he as brash on the outside as tremulous inside, drunk to boot, and when he can't get it up, the disappointment sets in, so he takes to his fists and makes sure that she is the one to pay for his injured manhood."

"So does Occam's razor cut: it is the simplest explanation taking everything into account, and so the most plausible. But nevertheless, we still need to find Erik Three Roses."

....

The main room of the house is almost empty. Despite the warmth of the evening, there is a fire in the hearth, a fire that roars so that the flames stretch far up the chimney. The widow is burning those belongings that can neither be sold nor given away. She is sitting on a stool by the fireplace with a small axe, chopping up old chairs, tools broken beyond repair, and household items that have endured the wear and tear of generations until their weight has finally exceeded their worth.

The sweat has carved tracks through the soot in Margareta Colling's face. She stares into the hearth and keeps her gaze locked there, even though Winge and Cardell have stepped over the threshold.

"Well?"

Cardell sits down on the bench and puts his arm on the floor beside him.

"Do you know what became of the groom after the wedding?"

Colling breaks a cracked wooden platter over her knee and sets the pieces on the bonfire.

"I saw the carriage when it left the estate, and I ran after it to ask where he was going. I never saw Erik, and the driver was a Frenchman. He called out a few words in his own language and laughed, then took the road towards Stockholm, the same way you came."

"Can you recall what he said?"

"It is not a language I have mastered, but I have done my best to remember how it sounded."

She made a few attempts to relay the words as Emil Winge tried carefully to ascribe meaning to the sounds.

"Le ton beau des vivants?"

"Yes, that's how it sounded. Just like that. But if it is Erik you are after, you're barking up the wrong tree. He never killed my daughter."

Cardell leans forward.

"Why not?"

Colling turns sharply on her stool, her tone livid.

"That boy loved and respected Linnea Charlotta above all else, to the extent that he never even touched her when they had the run of the woods all summer, far from watching eyes, and even though she would likely have been willing. They were to be man and wife, and no obstacles were too great. I saw them reunite when he came home from his trip, and the love that shone in his eyes was of a kind I had never seen. For her sake, he had suffered greatly for many months. He would never have hurt a hair on her head."

Emil Winge stands at the door with his gaze on the woman's anguished features.

"Sometimes one strong emotion will transmute into another."

She shakes her head violently.

"He was a good boy. He only wished her well."

Cardell can't meet her eyes, and he turns away with an expression of distaste.

"And yet blood has splashed all the way up into the chandelier above his bridal bed."

Tears add new lines in the soot on her face.

"If Erik killed my daughter, there is no goodness in this world."

Neither of them is able to respond to her, and they can do nothing else but leave her to burn what remains of the life she once lived.

35

Sleep eludes Emil Winge, even though the night is cool and the wheels rock the wagon under him. He lies awake and stares at the stars cartwheeling across the sky. The unnamed thousands, impossible to reckon, revolve in the abyss between constellations whose names he recalls for the first time in years. He follows Virgo's left hand to Arcturus, from Boötes and on to Cor Caroli, and grunts when he remembers to which constellation the star belongs: Canes Venatici, the hounds of the hunt. Up at the reins, the driver allows himself to nod off; the horse knows the way. Cardell is snoring loudly at the other side of the wagon. If the sky stays so clear that the road is passable all night, they'll be back in Stockholm by daybreak.

He has not yet grown accustomed to the impressions that intrude on his newly restored senses. It must be well after midnight and a waning slice of moon is luminous in its ascent. The trees stand pale in its light. The sounds of the forest surround them, where an unseen tread snaps twigs among the shadows, making Winge feel increasingly ill at ease.

He tries to cling to the day that lies behind him, when he had an idea, the first one he can remember having in a long time, how it had borne fruit, and how Cardell gave him a look of a kind that was so unfamiliar that at first he couldn't interpret it. Gratitude, appreciation, respect.

He hears another sound now, and shivers as a chill caresses his back. A muted rhythm. The progress of the wheels over roots and stones can't conceal it, like the stride of someone in pursuit whose every step is heavy enough to shake the ground. He closes his eyes and puts his fingers in his ears. In time he calms, his heartbeat slows, and he dares to listen again, but can no longer hear it. He wonders how far his lead is this time, how long his reprieve will be. He wraps his arms around his knees, vainly trying to turn his thoughts to something else, forcing the night to pass. He inches closer to where the watchman lies, his sleeping form cradling his stump with his right hand. He hesitates before stretching out a finger and poking Cardell in the side. Cardell mutters in his sleep and snores on, and only when Winge repeats his maneuver a few more times does the watchman unfold his legs, sit up, and look around.

"Jean Michael? Can't you sleep either?"

Cardell grunts in reply, yawns, and scratches his stubble.

"If you are awake anyway, can't we talk a little together?"

"What about?" Cardell's rasping voice betrays his fatigue.

"The war, if you can stand it, or what you did before, or after. Reuterholm and Armfelt. The City-between-the-Bridges. Whatever you like."

All sleepiness has left Cardell's eyes by the time he looks at Winge, who recalls the offer he received on Castle Hill and how what Cardell had said must have twisted the truth, because those eyes are certainly sharp enough to see the nature of things. But Cardell shrugs all the same, shifts into a more comfortable position, and they converse until the blush of dawn is sifting through eastern branches, and Cardell gives him another look of the same kind, receives a nod in reply, leans more deeply into the sack behind him, and falls asleep once more.

....

Cardell wakes to morning light. He shakes his large body like a dog in the rain and rubs his eyes, one after the other, with his single hand. Ever since the stars dissolved, Winge has been sitting with his back against a bag of flour, pale, lids half-closed. Cardell reaches for the bottle of water they have between them, rinses his mouth, fills one palm, and rubs his face.

"Good morning, Jean Michael."

"Did you get any rest in the end?"

Winge shrugs.

"And you?"

"I'm used to resting when the opportunity presents itself. But sleeping on it has not made me any the wiser."

Winge pauses for a long time before he proceeds, uncertain how he should best dress his thoughts in words.

"I have been pondering the French driver's parting greeting. *Le ton beau des vivants* can be rendered in our language as something along the lines of *The beautiful song of the living*, as far as I know how to translate it. And Colling said their direction was towards Stockholm."

"That seems of little help."

"How would you assess her as a judge of character?"

Cardell thinks about it.

"When first we met, she said a thing or two to convince me that between the two of us, she was the more perceptive."

"Then consider for a moment that what she said about him is the truth. Before this point, Erik Three Roses had never shown a propensity for violence, and his deed on his wedding night came justifiably as a shock. A more hardened perpetrator might not have been so very troubled by his conscience, but Erik must have felt a deep contrition."

Cardell finds himself nodding appreciatively at the direction the logic is taking.

"Go on."

"My thought is that Three Roses set off for Stockholm in order to drown his sorrows, and that his driver's words should be interpreted in the sense that it is in the *noise of the living rabble* that we must look for him, at parties and ballrooms in the City-between-the-Bridges. A young nobleman, likely incognito, perhaps with a French servant in tow. Colling described him well: slim, fine-limbed, dark-haired, handsome."

Cardell smiles and shows a gap where there once were teeth.

"If that's where he is hiding out, our chances are good. There's no pub in the city at whose teat I haven't suckled."

36

In the City-between-the-Bridges, they shift their waking hours to the night. With dawn, Cardell collapses on the groaning frame of his bed, and Emil Winge returns to the chamber he is still renting, grateful to open his eyes on a room filled with light as the nightmares wake him. When twilight falls and the lanterns are lit, their work begins anew. They look for Erik Three Roses everywhere, along the streets where the pubs are crowded up against each other, from when the first hungover customers impatiently stomp in place by the door in the afternoon until the hustle and bustle dies down and they have to pry the drunkards from their heaps, limp in molten embraces or quarrels, sticking to each other by their secretions. With threats and bribes, Cardell secures the services of the street urchins, who spread the word and paint an even more vivid picture: a wife killer with the face of an angel is being hunted. One wouldn't think it of him but for the sorrow in his eyes. He is young, hardly a grown man. He drinks to forget.

Often the description is answered. The pubs are too numerous to be counted, each filled to the brim. One in a hundred guests appears to be a nobleman on the run, some exiled second son, an unwanted bastard who vainly flaunts his parentage, a wastrel who has squandered his inheritance. Some are drunk and morose, others in a frenzy of self-destruction, woozy at the tables where the swindlers are playing faro and divesting them of their last coins. Each a leading man in his own tragedy, but none of them with the blood of a bride on their hands, and none bearing the name Three Roses. Cardell and Winge search high as well as low: they wait on the square outside the Stock Exchange as the last cadence of a ball dies away, and when people start to stream down the stairs, they intercept counts as well as lackeys. Summer wilts around them. Each day is shorter than the one before, the night hours multiply. The month changes and August is over, and those who call September a summer month are proven wrong yet again. In its daily shifts from sea to land, the wind grows ever colder. The warm stones of the city cool in the evening, and a shirt is no longer sufficient to meet the once sweltering gloom of the alleys. And so comes autumn, with its stranglehold on all that lives, and the oppressive heat of summer is forgotten, forgiven. The herald of winter promises imminent hardship. Last year's was a killer, perhaps this one will be even worse? People remember last year's graves, and fret over those still above ground.

....

The linden trees in the graveyard of Maria parish shed red leaves on him the day that Emil Winge stands at his brother's grave for the first time. The dawn is pale and raw. He is alone; Cardell left to rest until the pubs open their doors anew.

The new day drives the dew off the ground. The fog lies over the Southern Isle, partitioning a space for him apart from the waking city. Here it is just him and the grave, a few feet of earth to separate the living from the dead. Cecil's grave is humble in its simplicity. Cecil Winge, 1764–1793. For Cecil, time has stopped. In a little more than a year, Emil will be the elder of the two. The thought is so absurd that he can hardly restrain a guffaw. With it, he hears something else behind him, a small sound that betrays the presence of another, and he turns on his heel.

"Emil."

Another face he hasn't seen in years, but from her, time itself seems to have shied. His sister is just as he remembers her. Beautiful; blond hair; her skin translucent, as ever, carefully shielded from the sun. She stands close enough to touch shoulders had she wanted. He had forgotten how quietly she could move. She never tired of such games when they were children: she, Cecil, himself. She would tiptoe up behind him soundlessly, and whenever his attention was elsewhere, her cool palms would close over his eyes, her clear laugh by his ear.

"Hedvig. The years have been kind to you."

"How I wish I could say the same to you, little brother."

He snorts at the sympathy he reads in her wrinkled brow.

"Yes, it is remarkable. I have seen spirits used to preserve dead creatures in glass jars, but if you pour the same liquid into a person, the effect is quite the reverse. But such was the price of a cure for my disease, far better than the one you gave me."

"Don't let us quarrel, now that fate has brought us together."

For the thousandth time in his life he has reason to reflect on how her appearance differs from her person. She is still trim and fine-limbed, with a face as if chiseled by a sculptor in praise of unattainable beauty. He recalls a never-wavering line of youths kneeling before this face, all without exception dispatched on their way to piece together the shards of their shattered hearts. He was never surprised. Who could have been good enough for her? At a glance she would solve equations that had presented him and Cecil with hours of resistance. The brothers were close in competition and friendship, but she, the eldest, stood aloof. To measure her strength to theirs was beneath her dignity, and if one of them was spurred to challenge it, they soon learned their place. She was also the first to leave. He remembers her fight with their father, even if few words found their way through the closed door to which he had so urgently pressed his ear. Afterwards, anyone who let her name slip from their lips got a taste of the cane. Hedvig Winge caresses Cecil's gravestone with alabaster fingers.

"When did you see him last, Emil?"

"Cecil came to my room in Uppsala, to ask why I was still there, and why I hadn't taken any of my exams. At first I didn't recognize him and refused to let him cross the threshold. I had dragged a chest of drawers in front of the door, which I was hardly able to move afterwards. I told him the truth, that the clause in our father's will that guaranteed me an annuity from his estate for each year I spent at university had been a mistake. We quarreled. I shouted at him."

"You and Cecil were always so close."

The memory of pain is a stab to his chest. When the three of them were children, sent to bed without supper as a punishment for some offense against the many rules of the house, and lying in their cots within reach of each other, they would seek comfort by holding hands until sleep came to them in turn. He was in the middle, and always the last awake: first one grip loosened, then the other.

"Both of you deserted me, but it was Cecil's farewell that stung the most. For two long years after you and Cecil left, I remained alone in that house, forced to submit to Father and his labyrinthine games. However much I tried to appease him, however quickly I reached the center, it was never good enough for Father. But I can hardly blame him. First there was you, then Cecil came along, and finally me, the runt of the litter, a disappointment who would never grow to fill his siblings' shoes. You know, when I first came to Uppsala, I could never show my face without hearing stories about Cecil and his triumphs: *Cecil Winge once completed an examination in under a quarter of an hour . . . When the professors stumbled over their Latin quotations, Cecil Winge corrected them from memory . . .*"

"How did you part?"

"He told me he was getting married. He asked if I needed anything. He asked me if I was drinking, and I answered no, which at the time was no lie. Finally he gave up, and left me in peace, but warned me that while he had failed to knock some sense into me, *you* would try all the harder. I was foolish enough to laugh in his face."

Hedvig turned her face away from the accusation in his eyes.

"What brings you to Stockholm, Emil?"

Anger seeps out of him as quickly as it has arisen. He sighs and lets his shoulders fall, shutting his eyes and pulling his fingers through his hair.

"I'm assisting the police in some matter."

"How is it going?"

His silence is answer enough.

"Perhaps I can help?"

Emil seeks her gaze to see if she is serious, and to his surprise sees there the feeling he was least expecting: regret. And yet his reply is a bitter hiss.

"You, help me? As if I didn't know your help better than anyone. The last time I saw you was when you left me in Uppsala at the Oxenstierna. I shouted your name through the bars and leaded glass while you turned away so you wouldn't have to watch. You put me in the madhouse, Hedvig. Do you know what the unfortunate call such places, sister?"

Emil turns his back to her in order to leave. Her reply is hardly more than a whisper.

"I go to church at the Knights' Isle on Sundays. Should you change your mind, you will find me there, *mon frère*."

With a gesture of irritation, he swats the words away as if they were flies at his ear. By the gate, he almost bumps into the bell ringer, but he pays no attention to the quizzical eye that follows him out.

37

The room at Goose Alley is growing chilly as the shadows chase the rays of afternoon sun out of the window. Cardell guesses the time from their angle among the ceiling beams and is proven correct when Saint Gertrud chimes the hour and a quarter. He has slept late. Drafts of air rush up from between the floorboards, and it is time to get going again. Tonight their journey will take them along the Rill, all the way to the Bog and to Pretty Klara, a public house of ill repute in a desolate and unfortunate neighborhood where no decent person would be seen dead. And sure enough he soon hears steps on the stairs, shortly followed by the sounds of Emil Winge at the door. The footfalls alone tell Cardell that something has happened. They betray movements of another sort to the ones he has seen from Emil Winge during this dismal summer, increasingly melancholy and subdued, quick only when he has backed away from something in alarm. Soon he has crossed the threshold, panting from the stairs and flushed by his news.

"A memory made me aware of something I should have thought of a long time ago."

"Well?"

"The French driver. Let us assume that what was shouted was not *Le ton beau des vivants*. What he instead said was *Le tombeau des vivants*. I assign no blame to the widow: the sounds are the same, especially for anyone who doesn't speak French, but if I had known better from the first, we would have been spared a great deal of effort."

Cardell throws out his arms, a gesture that for a moment allows himself to forget he only has the one.

"Do me a favor and speak as if to a normal person."

"I think Erik Three Roses is in Dane's Bay."

"The madhouse?"

"Either that or the hospital. They're next door to each other."

"And how do you know all this, all of a sudden?"

"The words don't refer to some 'beautiful song of the living.' *Le tombeau des vivants* can instead be understood as a deprecatory phrase for places like Dane's Bay."

"Namely?"

"The *tomb* of the living."

....

They walk over the Red Lock, where the current has begun to calm in anticipation of winter, past Ironmonger's Square and the marketplace, along the quay under the cliff. On the side facing the rocks, boards and ballast lie piled on top of each other. Sheltered by the cliff, a sailor has started a fire over which sits a steaming cauldron. Others are lined up on their way to the shack that leans against the rock, where some opportunist publican has set up an establishment in the hopes that the sailors' thirst will exceed their desire to walk all the way to the Lynx at Sutthoff bridge. They tread the stairs that climb the wall, catching their breath on the rickety platform halfway up. Fewer ships than ever dare the waves of the inlet. Commerce is scarce. Few bother to sail all the way to Stockholm anymore, and those who do are met by a city where their goods have been declared illegal.

At the far slopes of the ridge they pass Ersta, and then they stare right down into the abyss of the shipyard, at the bottom of which the workers can be seen scurrying like ants through mud, pressed down under the weight of their burdens. The isthmus narrows and they can see water on both sides. At the tollgate, Cardell announces their intention soon to return. All they have to do is follow the millstream north to bring the hospital within sight. In its grounds, the half-naked branches of the trees grope at the wind. The leaves tumble through the air until the wind deserts them in the hollow through which the stream trickles. Winge and Cardell follow its path past a poorly raked gravel yard, where the stream tunnels under the foundations of the building itself.

At the entrance, a woman in an apron answers their knock, nods at the name they give, and ushers them in.

A large chapel fills the entire middle of the building. There are stairs on either side, and they are shown one floor up, past open doors where beds are crowded together, and then on to a corridor. She opens a door and gestures them in with a muttered confirmation. "Erik Three Roses."

There he is, sitting on his bed with his hands in his lap, as if lifted straight out of Margareta Colling's description, albeit marked by his suffering. The handsome face that still shows more of the boy than the man is pale and gaunt, his body thin, his hair limp. He shows no reaction as they walk in until Emil Winge addresses him.

"Erik Three Roses?"

The boy stares dully in front of him, and although he makes a small attempt to lift his head, his gaze remains fixed on the same spot.

"This is Jean Michael Cardell, on official police business. My name is Emil Winge. We have come to ask you a few questions about Linnea Charlotta Colling."

A spasm of pain comes over the boy's face as if he has been struck. His voice is thick and the words sound as if formed with a swollen tongue.

"I killed her."

Cardell steps forward. He can't keep the anger out of his voice.

"But why, for the love of God?"

Three Roses looks down into his lap, astonished, then shakes his head.

"I don't know."

He stares at his palms for a while, before lifting them up to his visitors, his eyes now tightly closed.

"See!"

His hands shake. They are spotless.

After an hour of plying him with questions they are none the wiser. Sometimes it is as if Erik Three Roses is answering a different query. On other occasions, he doesn't answer at all, lost in thought and seemingly oblivious to his visitors. When his attention returns, he no longer knows who he is talking to, and the introductions must be repeated. When Cardell's patience wears thin, he stomps out, thumping his wooden hand on the door frame on his way, muttering curses to blacken the air in his wake.

Emil Winge remains for a while until he too grows tired of repeating the same thing over and over. He finds Cardell in the corridor, leaning against the wall as if bracing himself against his anger. In one of the rooms they find the same woman who showed them in. Winge takes her aside.

"Is he always like that?"

She shrugs.

"I just see him at mealtimes, but I can't remember him any different."

"Is he given anything apart from normal food and drink?"

She nods.

"Oh yes. He is well cared for. His curative is paid for in advance."

"May I see it?"

She leads them to a storage room, opening the heavy door with a key she wears on a chain around her neck. She follows a row of bottles on a shelf with her finger until she stops at one with Three Roses's name, with the dosage written on the label. Emil Winge lifts the cork, smells first, and then carefully dips a finger that he brushes over his tongue. He shakes his head at Cardell, who interprets the meaning of his gesture and takes the woman by the arm.

"Listen carefully to me now. Erik Three Roses shouldn't be given anything more than the same food and drink you give your other patients. No drops, whether these or anything else. I speak on the authority of the police. We will return . . ."

He turns his gaze to Winge, who holds up two fingers.

". . . the day after tomorrow. At this point, Three Roses should be more capable of speaking for himself, and if not, we will know that our instructions have been ignored, in which case any responsible party will be held to account."

....

Cardell spits against the building wall after they have exited the front door.

"It's not an easy thing to believe when you see him."

Emil Winge nods in agreement.

"That was also my first thought. But if all murderers betrayed their intentions by mere appearances, the world would be a simpler place than it is."

"So what now?"

"The bottle contained thebaica, a poppy extract. It dulls pain at the cost of confusion. I both believe and hope that it is these drops that make him as he is, and that his speech will be clearer when it has left his body."

"It's just as well you have experience with these things."

Winge suppresses a shiver, recalling a narrow room with straps holding him down against his will, the sickly-sweet drops being poured into a mouth forced open: a lifetime's worth of enduring humiliation.

38

It's been a long time since Cardell had a day off, and now that it has arrived he doesn't know what to do with it. He sits for a long time on the bed, listening to the deathwatch beetle ticking away in the damp timber of the walls. Lice and hunger finally drive him out of bed. He pours water into a bowl and splashes his face and hair. Once his morning toilet is completed, he fixes his wooden arm between the bed and wall, guides the stump into place, and tightens the straps. As always, the skin stings under the grip of the leather, but after a while it dulls, and the feeling dissipates. He pulls on his coat and sets off down the stairs.

During the night, a quiet rain has washed over the city, and the light of a pale and distant sun, robbed of the ability to warm, shimmers on all the wet surfaces. Cardell grunts at the sight. Life has taught him not to hold a high opinion of the City-between-the-Bridges, and each time it surprises him by revealing its beauty, he becomes uneasy, as if it were a trick, a beguiling act that only serves to conceal an intrigue. Nonetheless he pauses on the step to study the play of light over rooftops and buildings. He pads his mouth full of tobacco and chews for a while, and when the herb's gratifying tingle begins to spread through his body he knows immediately where he wants to go. He heads right, down the sloping cobblestones, towards the Lock.

....

The Scapegrace is more of a pub than an inn, but it belongs to the better of its kind, and someone has proudly hung a sign over the door to prove it. On it can be seen the painted image of a monkey in mid-jump;

not a beautiful sight, but easy enough to recognize, and so it serves its purpose. Cardell has not been here all year. After Cecil Winge's burial there were many distractions, and he found comfort in knowing that the girl Anna Stina—now Lovisa Ulrika, ever since taking the place of the publican's daughter—had found a secure home, one he did not find any reason to disturb with his miserable presence. He counts the months on his fingers. The girl was pregnant when he last saw her. She must be a mother by now, by a long chalk. A sudden worry hits him when the thought comes. Half of all newborns have hardly been welcomed into the world before they bid it farewell. Life is fragile. Cardell, who has never asked higher powers for anything for himself, listens with surprise as some kind of prayer slips over his lips.

....

Cardell has to knock more than a couple of times before someone slides the latch back on the door and cracks it open. He doesn't recall having seen the face before, but the pub employees turn over frequently: it's a thin man with a frightened face.

"I'm looking for the lady of the house, Lovisa Ulrika Blix."

The man opens his mouth as if to say something, but decides otherwise. The door opens, and with some mumbled words he is asked to wait. The taproom lies empty, but it isn't time yet to welcome the day's guests. The fireplace is filled with ashes. The last time he was here, it was clear that the girl had wisely managed the coins he had given her as a belated dowry from the boy Blix, her nominal husband. Benches and tables had been sanded smooth of splinters, the floor scrubbed, the whitewashed walls shone. Now it is as if all Stockholm has returned with renewed hunger, that all-consuming chaos she had temporarily managed to drive from her door. The furnishings bear marks of neglect, broken and stained without repair. Hay lies strewn on the floor to absorb all the spillages, but the rancid heaps have been left unattended and permeate the air with their stench. There are rat droppings by the walls where the vermin dart from hole to crack. Cardell senses ruin. Did the girl never recover from her labor? Has the fever raged here?

....

A woman he has never seen before, not unlike Anna Stina but also not her, comes down the stairs along the far wall. The disdain in her gaze, when he meets it, is plain to see.

"If you are looking for Lovisa Ulrika, you have come to the right place. But I have never had the name Blix, even for as briefly as the one you are looking for has called herself Lovisa Ulrika. My name is my own again, and the cuckoo has long since been pushed out of her nest. If you're one of hers, you'd best be on your way before I send my man for the police."

Cardell bites his lip hard as his thoughts go to Anna Stina's plight on the Scar. For a few moments he stands silent, weighing which way will best lead him to what he needs to know. A wave of rage causes his left arm to twitch. He surprises himself by lowering his voice and forcing himself through clenched teeth to adopt as persuasive a tone as he is able.

"Ma'am, you'll have to excuse my mistake over the name. God knows it ain't easy to keep track of who's who in this town. I'm with the city watch, as you see by my garb. The girl Anna Stina is sought for whoring, and since this is on her list of known places of residence, I thought it best to follow up."

She snorts at him.

"It's no wonder you're so inefficient, when one hand doesn't know what the other's up to. I've already spoken to one of your colleagues, and my answer hasn't changed: if she isn't in the workhouse already, then that slut is hiding in whatever gutter she crawled out of. The city isn't large, and I don't know how it can take so long for the police to find a single girl."

Few know the truth of those words better than he.

39

A cool rain falls over Emil Winge and Mickel Cardell as they walk back to Dane's Bay Hospital, by a now familiar route. From time to time the wind picks up, and the salty gusts from the water tear at every strip of cloth that isn't secured with stitches, buttons, or clasps. The wheel tracks in the road are slowly filling with brown water until it finally spills over, leaving their leather soles without refuge. For a time, the sound of their progress grows irregular as they vainly measure their steps between dry spots, but soon the wetness of their feet makes the point moot, and the march resumes at a regular pace. Cardell maintains a grumpy silence, and for Emil Winge it becomes clear that it is something more than the weather and boots that is rubbing him up the wrong way. Time and again, Winge sends him a sidelong glance, only to find him wearing the same sour face, frowning in thought. Only once they are out of sight of the tollgate does he find the courage to ask.

"Jean Michael, what's wrong? Our chances are better than ever before. Three Roses will be clearheaded by now, and we'll finally get to hear the whole story, straight from the horse's mouth."

Cardell pauses, sweeps his hat from his head, and scratches angrily at his forehead, where his exertions have caused the sweat to run.

"It's about a girl. No, nothing like that, I'm too old for her, and for . . . many other things besides. She helped your brother and me with the missing piece of a puzzle. I went to look her up yesterday, but she's nowhere to be found. When last I saw her, she was with child. She should have been delivered of it by now. Where she has gone, I have no idea, but I sense trouble. Stockholm is no place for a young mother with a babe in her arms."

Cardell turns his back to the wind and squints at the buildings of the city, as if what he is looking for could more easily be spotted from a distance. When he turns back again he meets Winge's eyes and is brought up short by the disappointment he glimpses there. He wipes the rain off his face.

"I beg your pardon. You're right, and it's a poor way to repay your sharp mind for me to go moping around like this. Our business does for the first time look promising, and that's thanks to you. If I let my thoughts wander for a moment, then don't take it as anything but proof of my confidence in you."

He sets off again and gives Winge a clap on the shoulder, strong enough to make him stumble sideways. Winge hurries to keep pace.

"I wish I could help you. Will you describe her to me, so I might recognize her if I see her?"

Cardell does his best to oblige.

....

In Erik Three Roses's room, the bed has been stripped to its slats, the mattress confiscated. What few possessions there once were, are nowhere to be seen. In shocked silence, Cardell and Winge each cross the threshold and survey the empty space. Cardell is the first to express their feeling in words.

"What the fuck?"

Winge stays put while Cardell circles all four corners of the room, as if to assure himself that no explanation has been concealed among the sparse furnishings. Their confused silence is interrupted by a knocking on the wall, and they follow the sound to the room next door. Here the situation is reversed. The room bears traces of long-term occupancy, and half sitting in the bed is a man in shirtsleeves. A curtain hangs in front of the window, and it's only when their eyes have grown accustomed to the dim light that they can see how the sheets have been arranged to hide the dropsied man's swollen belly and legs.

"Joakim Ersson is my name. A merchant once, before this malady laid waste to me."

Cardell gives him a nod in greeting.

"Cardell and Winge. We extend our hopes of a speedy recovery."

Ersson pats his thigh and chuckles with bitterness.

"Every day they come here and drain me of a whole pitcher of mucus, to no avail. If I could only find any demand for the stuff, my fortune would be made. Here are deep resources, let me tell you."

"We are looking for Erik Three Roses."

The merchant nods.

"He isn't here any longer."

"No? Then where?"

"They have taken him to the madhouse."

Cardell's voice is a shocked roar.

"What the hell for?"

An expression close to despondency flickers across the merchant's face.

"They saw no other way. The boy was no longer himself, not even compared to how he was before. Once they drain me, I can sometimes walk a few steps, and more often than not those take me to Three Roses's room. The drops he receives make him groggy, and he'll rarely speak to me. But I can banter enough for two and at least I always felt myself in the company of a fellow human being, but now . . ."

"What happened?"

"There were visitors. Two unfamiliar voices alongside that of Three Roses. They talked for some time. Then they did something, and I don't quite know what. I heard some noises I can't explain, and then there was a smell like that of roasted meat, and then they left Three Roses alone. When I finally managed to drag my miserable body over to him some hours later, he was lying in his bed and he . . ."

Ersson's heavy lips begins to tremble, before the corners of his mouth curl into an involuntary grimace.

"I was already here the day Three Roses arrived. You gentlemen can see that I will never be well enough to return to any normal life, but that boy was young, with his whole life before him. I always hoped that Three Roses would recover. So few of us can afford any hope of such a thing. In lieu of any triumphs of my own, I told myself I would at least have the chance to witness his."

The tears begin to roll down the merchant's plump cheeks, and his nose starts to run. Ersson conceals his face in a corner of the sheet. His words emerge muffled from the cloth.

"They did something to his head. There were stains all over the floor. The bandages weren't enough to stanch the blood, his whole pillow was stained red. And Three Roses . . . there was only an empty shell left of him."

....

On the cliff by the sea, the lunatics are restless. The guard who shows Winge and Cardell the way through the corridors, resounding with derision and despair, sends them an occasional apologetic glance over his shoulder.

"They are too many, the overcrowding has got too bad, and if any of them start acting up it'll spread like wildfire through the entire building before you know it."

They walk up a flight of stairs, across a courtyard and onwards through the large building, before a guard unlocks a heavy oak door and shows them into a corridor flanked by doors with hatches at eye level.

"Here's our new arrival."

He opens a hatch and peers in, making a face at the smells and gesturing them to see for themselves while he steps aside to scratch a stye on his eye. Cardell blinks to force his eyes to make sense of the gloom. There is hay on the floor, an overturned chamber pot, four men, naked or in rags, tightly crowded together to shield themselves from the light they have learned to fear. He curses profusely as he makes room for Winge to have a look. Cardell shakes his wooden fist at the lock.

"Open up and let him out. And get him something to cover himself with."

The four lunatics meekly back away, and Cardell stands wide-legged in the middle of the room as if to keep them at bay in the corner. The room is chilly. Three Roses is sitting on the floor with his legs bent in front of him and his hands resting on the floor, motionless, without any noticeable reaction to the changing light or the visitors who now lay their hands on him and try to get him to his feet. His limbs appear palsied. Shaking and limping, he allows himself to be led across the floor. Winge whispers the few words that come to him, their blandishments meaningless. He places his hands gently on Three Roses's shoulders in order to get him to sit on the bench under the barred window. The boy stinks worse than the rest of the cell. Excrement and urine have run down his legs, dried, and caused his skin to break out in a bright red rash. His lips are blue. Around the boy's head is a soiled bandage, adorned as if with an obscene rose where the wound has bled through.

The guard returns with an oversized linen shirt, and when Winge has carefully pulled it over Three Roses's head and threaded his arms through, he points to the bandage.

"What can you tell me about his injury?"

The guard shakes his head so hard it sends the lice flying.

"Nothing, sir, he arrived here in that state."

Erik Three Roses doesn't move a muscle as Winge palpates his head with light fingers, loosening the knot that keeps the bandage in place and starting to unwind it. Underneath, the long hair is shorn away, and parts of the skull have been shaved. The wound itself is as small as a shilling. It is at the top of his forehead, ringed by clusters of lice that have drowned at their feast. The blackened crust cracks where it has caught in the fabric bandage and lets out a thin stream of blood and fluid. Winge sits staring at it before kneeling in front of Three Roses, his hands on his cheeks in an attempt to get him to meet his gaze. He only finds emptiness there. The swelling from the injury has spread to the forehead, where a dark engorged bruise now hangs down over the eyes, forcing a squint. One eye is crossed inward, inert as marble. The mouth hangs open and as saliva pools under the tongue, it overflows the corner of his mouth. Cardell turns towards the guard.

"Wash him up and give him a room of his own."

The protest is almost on the man's lips before Cardell beats him to it.

"I don't care how cramped you are. Do as I say, even if it must be your own. He won't be any trouble, and if the door lacks a lock, so what, given the state he's in."

He shifts his gaze to Winge, who whispers in response.

"An empty shell."

....

Outside, the evening wind whistles by the corners of the madhouse. Headwind on the trip out, headwind on the way back. The waves lick the shore. When the sunset wind starts blowing out to sea, Cardell is usually the first to head inside, but now he tolerates its gusts with equanimity, happy to let the blasts air the madhouse out of his clothes. On the opposite shore, the shadows of the shipyards blend into a greater darkness. Beyond the islets, the flag is lowered on the fortress guarding the inlet, and further inside the bay, the City-between-the-Bridges waits for its lanterns to be lit. A delayed vessel is making its way towards the harbor, its lanterns twinkling, in hope of docking while there is still some light. Only when they have left the tollgate behind them and found shelter from the wind under the ridge does Cardell open his mouth.

"What now? What should we do?"

Winge jerks at the words, interrupted from the same line of thought. He hesitates for a moment before shaking his head.

"Please give me time to think, Jean Michael."

On the other side of the Lock they part ways, each to a different alley, Cardell in his heavy boots, Winge with rapid steps, avoiding the flickering overtures from the shadows when the gusts start to set the lanterns in motion.

40

Seagulls in their hundreds circle the pale sky, ever watchful for an opportunity to dive earthward at unguarded fish or else to steal the prey from their fellow's more successful beak. The street vendors occupy great half barrels, insulated with hay against the cold, which line the stone bridge and the square, waiting to sell perch and pike to those who will soon pour out of the church after mass, their counterweights hollowed and stuffed with cork, for come winter every shilling counts. Emil Winge crosses the stone bridge, past the gray walls of the mausoleum, to find himself a place from which he can observe the church gate. He is not alone. Wretches and beggars of all kinds, who have managed to slink across the bridge before their way was barred, now emerge from cover and wait impatiently for the generosity that God's words may have awakened in the penitent. Each one is practicing their most mournful face, carefully arranging their clothing so as to most enhance their defects. The wait is short; high above, the bells ring in mourning of this week's dead. The doors open and people start to pour out over the threshold. Emil cranes his neck to make himself taller than he is, so as to see and to be seen. The church doors open flush to the ground, there are no steps to better display the blessed as they emerge, one by one. And yet there is no mistaking her, and as if she were expecting him, her gaze is drawn to his. Winge can't tell if she is unaccompanied, but she gingerly steps aside and waits where she is until the crowd has thinned enough for her to approach with ease.

She wears a dress of somber shades, a black shawl over her hair, in contrast to all those who have chosen to dress in vivid colors merely to show that they stand above the sumptuary law. She greets him with a simple nod, with no need to ask why he has come, and follows him back across the bridge.

Outside the establishment where he had been planning to take her, the line reaches out of the door and down the street, for many have found that communion did little to quench their thirst.

In the arcade under the pillars, he instead finds a stone bench, and invites her to sit. The wind shifts, bringing the smell of stabled horses from the northeast.

"It is not for my own sake that I seek your aid."

She leaves her reply unspoken. He answers the question all the same.

"Someone that our brother held in high regard has asked for my assistance: one Jean Michael Cardell. You wouldn't believe it when you see him, but he is a good man. The war swallowed him up and spat him out, short of an arm. Even so, he wants what is best. It is for his sake. He deserves better than what I can give him alone."

She only nods.

"Why don't you start from the beginning?"

She listens for a long time without interrupting, thoughtfully shaking pinches of snuff from a pouch and drawing them up her nose. She sneezes into her handkerchief.

"Well, little brother, I see two possibilities here. Maybe Three Roses has been the architect of his own misfortune from beginning to end. For reasons we will never know, he did away with his newly wedded wife and, with the help of others, has ever since engineered the punishment he felt himself deserving of."

"And the second?"

"Conspiracy, of course."

"How can I discover which?"

She begins to walk to and fro in front of the bench, her hands behind her back, just as she used to do in those moments when, stirred by assiduous pleas, she relented and helped him with the homework their father had assigned.

"My thoughts go first and foremost to the money, a factor you have hitherto overlooked. Although he was the second son of the house, Three Roses was the sole beneficiary of his father's will. Who controls those assets now that he himself is indisposed? The one who has the most to gain by a tragedy is often its author."

"Where do I start?"

"The foreman at Three Roses, this Svenning. I have no reason to believe him guilty of any crime on his own behalf, but you should find out how his salary is paid. The signature on the contract he showed you—what did it look like?"

"Illegible."

"Just the one signature, no more?"

Emil shakes his head, and Hedvig gives him a half-smile in return.

"So the document has not been signed in the presence of witnesses. If I were you, I would begin to pull on this thread and see what unravels. Only after this should you and your friend allow yourselves to grow despondent. Now go and write to Svenning. Demand an immediate answer."

For a while they consider various turns of phrase before the draft letter is completed, and Hedvig, who has been walking back and forth with her hands behind her back, stops and stands quietly.

"This matter is important to you, isn't it, Emil?"

"Yes."

"I understand that it is tempting for you to follow in Cecil's footsteps. You have your own reasons to see this matter through. But it would be naive to believe any less of others."

"What do you mean?"

"This Cardell."

She shifts position, as if to better prepare herself for her speech.

"You say the war laid him waste. I think our late sibling gave him back his dignity, for a while. Then Cardell finds you, and no one can deny that you are alike, you and Cecil. I hazard a guess that Cardell sees the possibility of reliving the past. You'd do well to keep in mind that his greatest loyalty isn't to you, but to a ghost that haunts his memories. There's danger there. His actions spring from the heart, which is generally both a deceitful and unpredictable organ. Watch how you go."

She sits down next to him, right up close.

"And will you tell him about me? That the help he receives comes from more corners than he could have anticipated?"

Hedvig responds before he can.

"I am in your debt, Emil, deeper than I can ever repay. If his appreciation means something to you, then by all means keep it to yourself, and with my blessing."

Emil sits still, quieted by a feeling he remembers from his childhood: to converse with someone who knows him as well as he knows himself and from whom no secret is worth keeping. Instead it is Hedvig who rises, takes a few steps past the columns, and comes to rest, staring down at the current. When she speaks again, it is on a new subject.

"Emil, your disorder, when it last started—what did you first notice of it?"

He turns away and closes his eyes. The memories come all too easily.

"I saw things that did not exist."

"In what way?"

"I woke one morning certain that I was being observed. Father was sitting on my bed, his face ashen. He had a stack of papers on his lap, all of the letters I had received from my professors conveying their reprimands, warnings, and complaints. He was furious, and if he had only had the strength, I think he would have used the cane on me, worse than ever. He wanted to know what I had to say in my defense, why I did not exert myself more, how I could manage to repay so poorly all the efforts that he had gone to in order to prepare me for my studies. He threw Cecil's successes in my face, each one proof of how well his child-rearing methods had borne fruit in more fertile soil. I had no excuses to offer him, and when he became more enraged, I started to cry and pulled the blankets over my head until he stopped."

"And?"

"It was only then that I remembered that Father had already been dead for weeks, although I had not managed to get back in time for the funeral."

She stands silently for a while, her gaze downturned. Emil waits.

"And later? Did it get worse?"

Emil chuckles.

"You will think me facetious, sister dear, but I will tell you anyway and risk your ridicule. Cecil gave me a book once, on my name day. I was seven years old, eight maybe. It was Plutarch, the story of how Theseus braves Daedalus's maze and finds the Minotaur in its center. For Cecil it was a joke, a way to make fun of Father's labyrinthine games, but I was too young to understand the humor. I did not know how many nights I would wake in soaking sheets from nightmares of the Minotaur, with his terrible bull's head on a man's shoulders. A merciless man-eater. Shortly after my encounter with Father, I started to hear the Minotaur, his heavy steps on the other side of the wall that could as well have belonged to the labyrinth in Knossos. Stalking me. Each time I heard the sound, it appeared closer than before."

"Surely you don't believe in fairy tales?"

Emil wrinkles his brow.

"No, Hedvig. Not here, in broad daylight. I believe that my disease has chosen a form lifted from my childhood memories, the most terrifying image it could find. But ask me in the night if I hear the beast approach with steps that shake the ground, when I am alone and there is no one to help, and in that moment my answer will be different."

"Do you hear them now?"

"Yes. Sometimes."

He wonders if what he really means is clear to read in his face. Sometimes they are stronger, sometimes weaker, but he always hears them.

If she senses the lie, she is tactful enough to leave it alone, and he goes on.

"Mania. That's what the doctor said. Chronic phantasmagoria. An inability to separate reality from fiction. Delusions of persecution. They had seen things like this before, and each case was unique. But no one ever recovered. Once out of the madhouse, I sought my own way to ease the suffering and found that only intoxication offered respite."

Emil can feel her warmth at his shoulder. He can't remember when she last touched him. Her voice is soothing, one she used so many times so long ago to lull him to sleep when his anxiety kept him awake.

"If you need my advice again, put a piece of paper in the corner where West Street meets Tailor's Alley, next to Nikolai Church. I walk past there every afternoon."

She puts a hand on his cheek.

"Theseus defeated the Minotaur. Ariadne's thread showed him the way out of the maze. Maybe you too must first face your fears to be free of them."

"Who's believing in fairy tales now?"

41

Cardell is on the prowl, and before evening he's had a dozen sightings of her, stalking the same alleys where he had seen her so many times before. Time and again he runs up to some girl with Anna Stina's straight hair sticking out from under her kerchief, puts an arm around her shoulder, and spins her around with a strength he forgets in his eagerness, only to have to excuse himself sheepishly a moment later. She is everywhere, but it is never her.

Night comes, and smoke from the impure oil in the lanterns spreads everywhere, a reek so pungent that many quip it is easier to traverse the maze of alleys by smelling one's way from lantern to lantern than to try to see by the little light they provide. Cardell needs neither one nor the other. He knows every nook and cranny in the City-between-the-Bridges, by night or day. A boisterous hubbub can be heard from every establishment, and each time a new customer reveals a pub by cracking open the door, loud cries admonish the newcomer to quickly close it behind him to keep the night chill at bay. Wherever Cardell goes, they laugh at him.

"Last time it was a young fellow who had killed his wife, now some runaway whore. What'll it be tomorrow?"

Not even those he bothers to give a reason to regret their words have any answers to his questions.

....

Even though the memory of his army years is fading, Cardell often finds himself waking at the hour when reveille is bugled or drummed. Usually he turns over and falls back to sleep, but this morning he gets up, gives himself a shake, and begins his ablutions. He sharpens his razor on the sole of his boot and wets his face, after which he laboriously begins to shave. It is an undertaking he rarely bothers to do with any care: his chin and cheeks are marked by so many scars and bumps that the strands of hair have many places to hide from the blade. The water is cold, the soap miserly, and the edge could be sharper, but finally the mirror shows two ruddy, stinging cheeks, bare and smooth. From the chest under the bed he takes out his watchman's uniform in its entirety, including gaiters and bandolier, and gives the jacket a once-over with his brush to chase off the lint. He sets off down the stairs and out onto the street in time to encounter the waste women's wheelbarrow, only to hear their taunting laughter follow him as he ducks down an alley to avoid the splashing of night soil. He passes Polhem's Lock and turns west.

Once past the bridge, he imagines he can sense the presence of the workhouse before he sees its outline, squatting in a hollow in the center of the island known as the Scar. He rarely sets foot here, at the heart of the watchmen's thankless labor. The soot and dirt of the windows go safe from mops and buckets behind their narrow bars, but in the rooms behind them he can sense the women, already hunched over their spinning wheels for hours. In silent desperation, they toil their lives away. He gives himself a shake to clear his head and announces himself at the gate.

"Cardell. My number is twenty-four. I need to speak to the custodian."

The watchman peers back at him.

"Hybinett's down with a cold. If you're lucky, I might be able to find Pettersson. Or unlucky, more like it."

It isn't often that Cardell meets his match in size, but Petter Pettersson is an ox of a man, as wide as he is tall. Although the uniform has been let out with cloth that doesn't have quite the same shade of blue, its seams groan each time he stretches. The sour smell of yesterday's drink hangs over him. His red eyes squint suspiciously at Cardell as he explains his business. Pettersson leans back and considers the words he has just heard.

"You wish to confirm that Anna Stina Knapp is here, in order to be able to stop looking for her?"

Pettersson lifts a bottle to his mouth, bites the cork and spits it across the floor, then takes a couple of long swigs. With a raised eyebrow, he holds it out to Cardell, who shakes his head.

"I know that name all right."

The custodian leans across the table that separates them.

"The name Cardell also rings a bell."

Pettersson empties the bottle before he goes on.

"Cardell, I hear, isn't one of us. Cardell thinks he is too good for our work, but doesn't mind pocketing the salary. One can't help wondering why you took the trouble to dust off all your loaned finery just to come here and ask me about a runaway wench that I thought I was alone in knowing by name."

Pettersson holds up his hand, strong enough to lift half an anchor, before Cardell has a chance to respond. He knows his lie is transparent, and his assumptions about the ignorance of his colleagues were a mistake. Now he can't do anything except curse his own stupidity.

"Your inquiry, as you have presented it to me, Cardell, is no more than the worst kind of drivel. As far as the authorities are concerned, Knapp is long dead, and no one cares about the fact that the remains that were found last summer in the cellar clearly belonged to someone else, so long as all the numbers eventually tally. But I know better, and apparently so do you. No, Cardell, there is something more personal at stake here, of the kind I can only guess."

Pettersson's eyes narrow as he deliberately sizes up Cardell with the stern expression of an interrogator.

"You'll pardon the fact that I am thinking aloud, Cardell, as I am a little hungover. The last time little Knapp was here, you saw no reason to come and ask for her. Therefore you must have made her acquaintance after she slipped out, however that may have happened. Therefore she must be somewhere at large in the City-between-the-Bridges. Isn't that right? She surely fell back into hawking her mouth and her mouse on street corners. Perhaps you were one of those who bought her services, and who now long for more of the same?"

In an unguarded moment, some appealing memory drops the mask from Pettersson's face and a dreamy expression spreads across his ugly visage.

"She has something special, that girl, doesn't she, that Anna Stina?"

Cardell feels his cheeks grow hot and the rage simmers inside, but he is unable to do more than remain sitting while Pettersson's face breaks out into a mocking grin.

"I'd given up hope of ever seeing her again, since I thought she'd fled the city and settled somewhere far beyond my reach, but now here you come blowing life into old dreams. I owe you my thanks, Twenty-Four Cardell! Now I feel as if it were yesterday she stood in front of me, trembling with respect for the rod. You've restored my purpose in life. I'll renew my own search. If the girl is to be found in the city, it's just a question of time. Hey, if you find her first, bring her here once you've had your fill, and I'll throw in a small finder's fee for your trouble."

Pettersson lifts one cheek from its seat and breaks wind with a blissful sigh.

"Now do me a favor and get the fuck off my island, Cardell. There's nothing more for you here."

Cardell has no choice but to do as he has been told, accompanied by the jeers of Pettersson's comrades. One recurring thought haunts him as he makes his way back through the old stone houses and hovels of Maria parish: what was bad before, he has made worse. He has to find her, and quickly. Everything else will have to wait.

42

The address Svenning gave him in his prompt reply has led Emil Winge to an alley on the slopes leading down towards the Quay-side, where the cobblestones are so slippery with mud that a handful of men are having a tough time pushing a cart of firewood up the hill. A knock on the door two floors up sees him shown into a small but well-ordered office. A bundle of twigs is crackling in the tiled stove. The man who opens for him and who has now returned to his place at the desk bears the name Pallinder, sits bareheaded, and has hung his lamb's-wool wig over the back of his chair. On the table, alongside various bits and pieces and writing implements, there is a cut-crystal decanter and two monographed glasses. The man's body has been molded into a rounded form by his sedentary work, with rosy cheeks and a pair of reading spectacles perched on the tip of his nose, over which he peers at Winge with an apologetic smile.

"Well then, Mr. Winge?"

The mention of his name causes Winge to hesitate.

"You were expecting me?"

"Of course. I imagine that we received our respective messages from Svenning at the same time. He did, however, lead me to believe that I could expect two visitors."

Twice he has sought Cardell since yesterday, his knocks on the door of his room unanswered.

"My colleague has business elsewhere."

"All right then, to the point, as simple as it is. Yes, after what Svenning has already explained in writing, it would be foolish of me to deny that I pay his salary on behalf of another. But you surely understand that I put my patron's interests first, and thatI am free to divulge neither name nor other details to any third party."

"You have seen my papers, issued from the Chamber of Police."

Winge curses silently that he is unable to utter the words without stammering, like a pupil before an examiner, certain of failure. He can see for himself how every repeated syllable is like a puff from the bellows of Pallinder's self-esteem.

"Of course, but I have never seen anything like it before, and I can't help noting that the name on the document does not correspond to the one you have given me as your own."

"I have Cardell's permission to act on each of our behalfs, as well as on that of the police."

"Never before have the police thought it wise to question that which counts as standard practice in my profession. I don't lack for confidants close to the police chief, and I would greatly appreciate a confirmation of your authority by means of my own sources before we continue this conversation."

Winge remains quiet, changing position in the chair and vainly searching for the words he needs to prosecute his cause. Hopelessness descends upon him. It spreads its weight on his neck and forces his shoulders forward and his head down, all the while with Pallinder waiting him out, patient as a lizard, peering over his spectacles. Winge is about to stand and leave, with a final glance at Pallinder to offer a delusory promise of his return, when he sees that the little man's hands are trembling on the table before him.

He searches for Pallinder's gaze once more, and now catches it there in flight, something unmistakable to him, swiftly concealed but momentarily unguarded. Pallinder quickly pulls his hands from the tabletop into his lap in the hope of undoing the damage they've caused, while Winge allows himself to sink back into the chair he was about to vacate.

"Mr. Pallinder, would you offer me a drink in parting?"

Pallinder can hardly deny him, fumbling bravely for the glasses, but he can't manage to bring his hands under control. He spills brandy on the table, puts the decanter down, then rubs his face with ink-stained fingers. They both sit quietly, each unsure of the next step. Emil weaves his fingers together in his lap and takes a deep breath.

"Fear." Emil can feel his voice carry better now, over more stable ground. "It is no pleasant feeling. A palsy of the mind. An enemy within that puts one at odds with one's own thoughts. I imagine that few have had the opportunity to make its acquaintance better than I. I was an anxious child, beset with nightmares, untrusting. I grew older, but scarcely less afraid. No one outpaces their shadow. And never does it feel worse than when alone. But there are two of us here, now. Perhaps we can help each other feel better."

Pallinder lifts one of the overfilled glasses from its puddle and tosses the contents as far back in the throat as he can manage. He makes a face.

"What about you, Winge? Nothing for you? For fear, this is also a kind of curative, if only for a short time."

"I'm afraid I can't hold my drink."

"Who the hell can?"

Pallinder downs Winge's drink. He unhooks the gilded stems from his ears and sets the glasses on the table.

"Do I speak openly under your assurance that you won't pass my words on?"

Winge nods in the affirmative. Pallinder pours himself another drink. Each time the glass stopper is pulled out, a sweet scent is released as of boiled pears, not unpleasant. He takes the glass with him as he stands up and walks to the window, staring vacantly down into the alley.

"Forgive me if I have trouble finding quite how to say this. Never in my life have I chosen words when numbers have been closer to hand. I beg your indulgence if I express myself clumsily."

"I'll hardly cast the first stone in punishment for that sin."

Pallinder clears his throat, steadying himself against the windowsill.

"I'm sure you've noticed how the economy fares around us. Show me a business that has been left untouched. You understand that I must be grateful for every client I am able to keep. In this case, it is a contract that has been passed down through the generations; I was of service to the father, and tradition dictates that I therefore continue to be of service to the son, as many documents already bear my seal, and every fortune develops its peculiarities over time. I would have wished myself shot of him, but as if the grave were not deep enough already, the king himself went and got himself killed. Things went from bad to worse, and the shameful truth is that I would hardly have been able to afford it. But he is of another sort; even the finest tree bears rotten branches. There's no telling how you will be received if you impose yourself on him. From your current position, you can't see the whole picture, nor guess the consequences that may strike not only those of us who are closest to the matter, but also others who are far less deserving of harm."

Winge frowns.

"I appreciate your confidence, but an explanation of such a general nature is not easy to follow."

Pallinder dabs his sweaty cheeks with the arm of his shirt.

"No. No, I can hear how this all sounds. And I have not given you any reason to harbor elevated thoughts about my motivations, but let me for all our sakes utter a simple plea: Would it not be easier to point the wakeful eye of the police somewhere else, just this once? Stockholm certainly has no lack of other crimes worth the avenging."

"Nor can you see the whole picture, Mr. Pallinder. If I could lend you my eyes, you might be less wedded to your hesitations. A girl is dead, the deed done with enough violence to stain a chandelier. A boy has had his skull pierced and sits shaking in his own filth, awaiting a death that could rarely have met with a warmer welcome. Whoever your client is, he has something to do with all this that needs to come to light, and if he is innocent it should serve his interests just as much as ours."

Pallinder lowers his voice, nods dejectedly, and retreats to his desk once more.

"Yes. Perhaps. As I said, this is not a client I would have chosen of my own accord."

Conflicting emotions battle in Pallinder's swollen face as he reflects further.

"If there is nothing I can do to dissuade you, don't you think we should still be able to come to an agreement that will satisfy both parties? Allow me to contact my patron myself and convey your business. If I know him correctly, he will soon come to you of his own accord, if you'll provide me with an address. In this way you will spare me from betraying the confidence with which I have been entrusted."

As Winge tries to weigh the pros and cons, he sees how more blood leaves Pallinder's face and senses that there is more at stake for him than the prospect of a reprimand and lost income. Emil wonders if the combined might of the police force instills more fear than this nameless client. He sighs and gives his answer, aware that a string can be tightened to serve its purpose, but becomes useless if stretched past its breaking point.

"All right, Mr. Pallinder, but if I do not have my answer by supper tomorrow you can expect me here again, likely in the company of one who I suspect will be less accommodating."

Pallinder releases the breath he must have been holding this whole time and reaches for the decanter he appears intent on emptying. His relief is so palpable that the room feels freshly aired.

"Your courtesy will not be forgotten for as long as my practice endures."

Pallinder's voice stops Winge on the threshold, the effects of the spirits he has been drinking since their meeting began for the first time audible.

"Mr. Winge? A warning, as down payment. Handle this one with care. And not just for his sake."

43

For two hours, Emil Winge has been waiting at the street corner where Hedvig asked him to post his note, increasingly nervous as the sun sinks lower below the rooftops.

She comes with the afternoon from the direction of the Quayside, just as she promised, following him silently to the Small Exchange, where they find a private corner. Hedvig raises an eyebrow.

"I have received a message from a certain Tycho Ceton. He introduces himself as the guardian of Erik Three Roses."

"What else does he write?"

"He wants to meet me tonight. He expressly asks that I come alone."

Emil lays the small letter with its broken seal in front of Hedvig and she lifts it up to the light in order to read it more easily. Emil waits for her comments.

"There, of all places? And at that time of day?"

"Yes. Hedvig, Jean Michael is still nowhere to be found, and if I could only reach him, I would ask him to at least follow me at a distance. But time is short. Instead I ask the same of you."

"I would hardly be able to come to your aid if this Ceton has any tricks up his sleeve."

"No. But if things were to go badly, you could let Jean Michael know of my fate and . . ."

His voice breaks and he has to clear his throat before continuing.

"The bookkeeper Pallinder warned me. Simply the knowledge of your presence would give me the courage I otherwise lack."

She pauses before giving him a nod.

"So be it."

"Tonight then, half an hour before midnight?"

"Yes."

"Keep to the shadows. He can on no account be allowed to notice your presence."

....

The night has darkened Ironmonger's Square, the edges of which are marked by the faint light from the lanterns on the corners. Time and again the flames flicker and crackle as impurities in the oil are drawn up through the wick. When Emil Winge crosses the cobblestones, the outline of the well can be seen against an opening between the buildings, its lines grotesque enough to trick the eye, made unfamiliar in the absence of light. All at once his heart is in his throat, and whatever courage he has gathered for this late meeting is immediately exhausted. He waits for a while in the shadows, the darkness both a terror and an ally, until he has assured himself that the only sounds that disturb the hour are the rowdy noise from Bagge's Row and the shuffling gait of someone who cannot be seen, every other step marked by the strike of a crutch against the stones. He reminds himself of Hedvig's presence somewhere in the alleys in front of him, approaching from the Quayside in order not to attract any suspicion in case she is discovered. When he has calmed himself, he staggers on across the unseen ground and keeps his steps short so as not to trip over any rubbish that has been left on the square. Above him, the gilded grape clusters from the sign of the Golden Peace glitter. And now, before him, a waiting figure, outlined only by the lantern he bears in his hand.

"Mr. Winge?"

"Mr. Ceton?"

They greet each other with a bow, and Ceton raises his lantern to more easily let them see each other's faces. Winge can't refrain from making a noisy inhalation when he sees Ceton's scarred cheek. The edges of the wound gleam wet in the light from the lantern. Ceton's own gaze is one of curiosity.

"My apologies for this odd meeting place. I have some business here tonight. It may amuse you as well, and in this way we can marry duty to pleasure."

Ceton pulls open the door and shows Winge in.

"I gave the doorman a couple of shillings to leave it open for us."

The establishment is dark, closed for the evening a few hours since, even though the smell of the guests lingers, and will remain until the maids begin to scour the floor at sunrise. Ceton continues with his lantern, down the stairs where the arched ceiling of the cellar carries the weight of the building. Uneven bricks make a pattern over thick walls, white-washed here and there to lighten the room. Ceton lifts the lantern, and when Winge follows him around a corner he realizes that they are not alone. The room is full, but the behavior of the group is strange, uncanny, and soon he realizes that not one of them is moving at all. Only the flick-ering of the flame gifts them the illusion of life. Ceton turns towards him.

"Wax mannequins, all of them. Perhaps you have read about the business at one of the booksellers'? The scandal has not gone unno-ticed by the newspapers."

Winge shakes his head and moves deeper into the room. Before him is a woman in a magnificent dress, her features so lifelike it is as if she were holding her breath as a joke. Ceton walks closer in order to see her better.

"Marie Antoinette, here a head taller than at present. And see there her husband."

Ceton moves slowly from figure to figure.

"The maker's name is Kurze, a German who travels from city to city in order to show his art. Here in Stockholm, however, his good fortune de-serted him. The exhibition is closed already, tomorrow they will start pack-ing for departure. And see! Here we have the reason for it, in all his glory."

The bust of a man with a high forehead and a proud face sits atop a pil-lar. When Emil Winge passes the point where the wax maker has directed its artificial gaze, it is as if the thing alights with sudden life and looks directly at him. He shivers, and Ceton chuckles.

"The late King Gustav himself. It didn't take long for our nervous Baron Reuterholm to send Police Chief Ullholm here to shut down the show. The bust is considered so lifelike that it alone could incite the people to rebellion. But that is not the reason I have come. Look over here."

A drapery conceals an alcove and Ceton moves it aside so Winge can enter. He allows the curtain to fall behind them and holds an arm in front of the lantern as if to let the room keep its secret yet a moment longer. Winge peers through the darkness, and slowly the shadows take form in front of his eyes. A figure prone on a stretcher.

"Are you ready?"

Ceton lets his arm fall, and the light streams out, suddenly blinding in this confined space. On a low table lies a man, naked and covered in sores. His arms and legs have been removed from his torso; only the head remains. The small stumps have stiffened in their futile battle, the eyes are wide open in terror and confusion, the mouth a shocked *o*. Ceton laughs at Winge's expression.

"There, there, it isn't real. Kurze doesn't show it to everyone. Nonetheless we stand before his masterpiece. Do you know who this is?"

Winge shakes his head, stretching out a hand to graze the blood that every sense tells him must still be warm and wet, but yet only meets dry wax.

"Allow me to introduce Monsieur Robert-François Damiens, the one who lunged at Louis of France in fifty-seven with a knife that would hardly have been able to sharpen a quill. The king received a scratch on his chest, hardly noticeable, but thought his last moment had come and called the queen to his deathbed in order to confess the names of all the ladies of the court whom he had bedded during their marriage. Then he was given a bandage and returned to health. Ah, Winge, Damien's execution was a party for the masses, of that you can be sure. Four hours they let him languish on the rack. His feet were crushed, his genitals removed with a red-hot pliers, the hand that had held the weapon reduced to ash over a brazier. Chest, arms, and thighs were slit, and molten lead was poured into the wounds. They bound his limbs to horses, one by one. Unaccustomed as the steeds were to the task, they toiled for an hour before someone took a saw to his shoulders and hips. Thus he lost first one arm and then the other, next his legs, and finally his executioners managed to make him what we see here, a bloody lump with a wobbly head, still clinging to life beyond all reason, only capable of groaning and staring at the crucifix that his confessor held out for him to kiss. The people enjoyed themselves royally, and up at a window, Casanova himself fondled a companion under her skirt."

Ceton turns the lantern to and fro in order to prevent any detail of the modeler's art from hiding in the shadows.

"A send-off like no other, don't you think, Mr. Winge? In Paris they have dispatched thousands with a machine solely invented for the purpose, each condemned to a nameless death robbed of value. But Damiens here? Thanks to Kurze, he may still give us pleasure today. Even his last words have been preserved for posterity. Do you know what he said that morning in his cell as they came to lead him to the slaughter?"

Winge shakes his head.

"The day will be hard."

Ceton laughs, and lifts his handkerchief from his pocket to wipe the corner of his mouth, then takes a step back. Winge clears his throat and seizes the moment.

"Erik Three Roses . . ."

"Please excuse me. I have accomplished what I came for and I thank you for your patience. Yes, Erik Three Roses. You are working on behalf of the police, I believe, and I assume that it is Widow Colling, mother of the bride, who has raised questions about the tragic fate that befell her daughter. There is one thing I need to clear up right away. The boy is innocent. His temper may flare when provoked, but he is no murderer."

"Colling has it on good authority that no wolves have been seen in the forests around Three Roses for many years."

Ceton nods in agreement.

"Nor are wolves to be blamed for what happened."

"What makes you so sure?"

The light plays tricks as the lantern sways, and just as it gives the wax mannequins the appearance of movement, Winge cannot be certain if Ceton is smiling or not.

"I would like to explain the whole business, as I see it, to you and your companion—Cardell, if Pallinder has provided me with the right name—if you would do me the favor of sharing my table tomorrow at Horn Hill, on the King's Isle. You will have to excuse the trouble of this evening, if the sight of Kurze's talents has not served as apology enough. I wanted to meet you alone before I extended you an invitation, and you do not disappoint. I can see that you are not a man who is driven by ambition or vanity. Knowing that such is the case, there is something I would like to confide . . ."

He stops himself, and puts his head to the side as a scraping sound is heard from the room next door.

"Did you hear that, Mr. Winge? I do believe that someone has followed us in. Surely it can't have been you who has invited any unwanted party, even though I specifically asked for privacy? Such behavior would change the situation completely, I'm afraid."

Ceton pulls the curtain aside and raises the lantern to cast light into the room outside. The shadows of the mannequins dance along the walls, contorted to strange proportions, while Ceton walks along the rows and turns his head from side to side. Hedvig stands completely still, her head turned towards the floor, one of two ladies-in-waiting preventing the lace on Catherine the Great's train being sullied by the floor. For a second, Ceton's eyes fall directly on his sister, and Emil has time to think that the smallest intake of breath would be enough to give her away. But she remains still. Along the wall behind them, Emil catches sight of something scuttling towards the safety of its hiding place. Ceton turns on his heels and shrugs.

"A rat—the rest only some passing fancy."

44

As Cardell looks back at him, Emil Winge reads something new in his features, something he at first doesn't know how to express. To his consternation, he realizes that it is admiration, an awareness bordering on pride, that Cardell has been right in his choice of partner. A tone in his voice that his brother must have been familiar with to the point of boredom, now directed at him for the first time.

"You've certainly not been idle without me."

Winge's thoughts go to Hedvig, and all at once the praise feels undeserved. Embarrassed, Winge averts his eyes and looks over at the bridge spanning the canal, past the road that stretches towards the King's Isle.

"So far we have no idea where this road will lead us."

They begin to walk side by side over damp boards and, rather than answer more questions, Winge poses one of his own.

"What about you, Jean Michael? Where have you been?"

Now it is Cardell's turn to answer vaguely, in a voice clearly marked by fatigue.

"I'm sorry. I had some personal matters that couldn't wait. I haven't been back to the room since we last saw each other and I had but an hour to sleep before you knocked. It's nothing to do with this matter. But damn it, Emil, if my absence has spurred you to such accomplishments, then I should leave you alone more often."

....

They cross the bridge and follow the road that starts where the glassblowers ply their trade on the left, the Seraphim Hospital on the right, forming a gateway to the King's Isle. These establishments mark the edge of the city:

beyond are gardens and fields whose harvest has been reaped weeks since, and now lie fallow awaiting the frosty nights. They follow the path between the ditches for a while longer. Behind them they can see the brooding colossus of the orphanage, and when the wind changes and blows straight in their faces, it brings gusts from the niter beds: a foul wind bearing a flatulent reek as of rotten eggs. Even further away stand row upon row of trees, on land that neither city nor farmer has had the energy to tame. Beyond the forest, a view of the water opens up as the island starts to slope towards the shore. Rows of linden trees flank their path, their knotted trunks standing to attention, leading them into an apple orchard, lovingly pruned to allow the fruit to be picked with minimal effort. On one side, the land is divided into square sections, each dedicated to a particular crop. It is late morning, and the clouds have scattered, letting forth a pale autumn sun still capable of granting a little warmth. In front of them rises a whitewashed manor house, with wings stretching east and west, surrounded by outbuildings and stables. A flock of sheep bleats in the distance, driven down along a meadow by a group of boys in bright blue caps. The view across the smooth waters beyond is breathtaking and stops them in their tracks.

"And the man said nothing about what it was he wanted to tell us?"

"Only that we are welcome to share his dinner, during which he is eager to shed light on the misfortune that befell Erik Three Roses and his young bride."

Cardell spits tobacco into the grass and clears his throat loudly. Winge gazes over the landscape before them.

"Jean Michael, do you know what place this is?"

Cardell shrugs.

"A manor house like many others, it would seem. The gentry built these places to escape the city, but Stockholm spreads like gangrene and has forced most to retreat further. The houses are sold and turned to manufactories and the like. The name of this one I've not heard before."

....

A man with a shiny bald pate and a red velvet coat waves them on from his station between the columns by the front door, greeting them with a smile as they get closer.

"Mr. Cardell and Mr. Winge, I presume? Rudstedt is my name. Welcome to Horn Hill. I'd dearly like to show you around at once but I am afraid that Mr. Ceton would like to save this diversion for a later time. First, your meal awaits, and if it disappoints, you must have discerning palates indeed. Joakim! Klara Fina!"

He claps his hands, and a girl and boy, nine or ten years old, and both in long white shirts, come running with quick steps.

They bow and curtsy, assume their places at the side of each guest, and take each by the hand. The boy to the left of Cardell can't mask his exclamation of surprise. Cardell grabs him by the shoulder and spins him to the other side.

"You'll do best to choose the right hand, if you must."

The children lead them through a beautiful room with painted walls before they, in a silent but practiced maneuver, let go and run ahead to open the two half doors at the end. Beyond the threshold, an atrium extends all the way up to the ceiling. White walls guide the light down through the skylight, and in the middle of the floor is a table set with lighted candelabras. Ceton rises from his seat and approaches them with open arms, impeccably dressed, with silver clasps on his shoes and breeches. He indicates the two empty chairs.

"Welcome, gentlemen, welcome. Would you like to sit and share a meal before we continue the rest of the evening's activities?"

The children who accompanied them pull out the two chairs, and they hardly have time to sit down before the girl fills their glasses with red wine from an ornate decanter. Ceton raises his own glass and allows his gaze to shift from Cardell to Winge.

"Your health."

They drink the toast, Winge without bringing the glass to his mouth. Cardell, on the other hand, recognizes the taste of wine from the Rhine, of a kind that vastly surpasses all he has earlier tasted, but not even this can restrain his impatience a moment longer. As Ceton leans his head back, the red wine gushes from the tear at the corner of his mouth, down across shoulder and chest. He pays no attention to it, but Cardell shivers and looks away.

"What is this house? Is it your residence?"

Tycho Ceton shakes his head.

"No. I am no less a visitor than yourself, although I can't deny bearing responsibility for the activities. Horn Hill is an orphanage, and although it goes against my nature to boast, I would say that it lacks a rival not only in this city but in the entire realm."

The food is carried out from the kitchen on silver trays by children in white. A pheasant, decoratively presented within its plumage, along with turnips, carrots, and a rich sauce. Ceton watches as the bird is carved and served.

"The children do all the cooking, under supervision of course. Please, enjoy."

The meat is tender and juicy, the vegetables swimming in molten butter. They eat for a while in silence before Emil Winge pushes his untouched glass of wine away and wrinkles his brow. His voice is hesitant and the words falter.

"You claim to be the guardian of Erik Three Roses?"

Ceton nods in agreement.

"All of the necessary documents to prove that point can be supplied, should you insist. But please note that this would only ever happen with my express agreement. You say that you have been sent from the police, and Pallinder assures me that your papers are more or less in order, but you are hardly acting with Police Chief Ullholm's knowledge."

Cardell clears his throat loudly.

"What makes you say that?"

"Ullholm is the lapdog of the establishment. Cases like this do not interest him. Not in general, and absolutely not in particular. But this doesn't really matter. I am prepared to be of service nonetheless."

Ceton continues his dinner during the silence that has had time to settle before Winge makes a new attempt to snatch at the thread that he has lost.

"And Three Roses? What is it that has befallen him? Do you know anything about the procedure that has deprived him of his senses?"

Ceton takes a thoughtful bite of his food before setting his cutlery aside. He takes a rolled cheroot out of an engraved case and lights it on a candle while he inhales. He keeps his lips closed as he allows the smoke to seep out of the wound in his cheek.

"On Saint Barthélemy, where I languished until summer last, during the many months that went by before I first encountered Three Roses and his cousin, I made merry with the slaves that I acquired. One of them stuck out from the crowd, and although I never managed to ascertain his background, it would not surprise me to learn that he was a chieftain of his people, perhaps even the ruler of a province. From the beginning, I could sense a gleam of intelligence in his eyes, and although he was as obedient as his fellows, he could not help revealing that he was far from defeated. He was attentive and bided his time. Long after the rest were gone, he still gave me pleasure. Together we played a game, the rules of which we made up as we went along, and it was yet another testament to his intelligence that we could understand each other so well despite lacking a common language, left only to gestures and signs. He had, of course, seen and heard the fate that had befallen his kin, but I left him to understand that he could buy himself a longer life for a price. He tried to offer me many things, we haggled back and forth, and finally agreed that one day was worth the value of one finger. At first he chose the smallest digit on his left hand, which he managed to sever with the use of his teeth alone, presenting it to me barely an hour later. We continued in this way as the days went by, and new rent became due, and when only his thumbs and index fingers remained, he offered other things to me, but made me understand that he would need to negotiate the use of tools as he could not with his teeth reach the parts in question. The strength of his will never failed to impress me, and even though he did not win much else in this game, he did win my respect. I should, of course, confess that the game was as rigged as ever a game of faro at the inns, and that the loose plank in his cell that he so patiently worked on with a sliver of bone each night had been prepared on my orders to inspire hope. His dreams of escape were never more than a chimera. When he became aware of this, which naturally could not be kept from him forever, something was extinguished in him, and there was nothing left for me to do than to let him go the same way as the rest, even though he showed a notable resistance in this matter before Louis and I could finally throw him on top of the pile in the hole that would turn out to become such a source of nourishment for my flowering frangipani, the likes of which could soon not be found on the entire island."

Ceton blows out a series of smoke rings, remarkably asymmetrical in shape like the mouth from which they originate, each one dissolving into mist as it wafts over the flames of the candelabras.

"I have troubled you with this anecdote because the sight of you both has brought the memory of this man to mind. You can hardly be distinguished from the rabble on the street but there is something of the same spirit about you, so determined and diligent, despite the odds weighing so heavily against you."

Winge shifts his plate aside in order to rest his elbows on the table and lean forward.

"It was you, then—Linnea Charlotta, Erik, all of it?"

"Of course it was me."

Anxiously, Winge leans even further forward, as if to block Cardell's nearest route to Ceton.

"Why confess this to us now?"

"Ask your companion for yet a little more patience and I will tell you. Over coffee, if you would like. I hope you will overlook the fact that, against all regulations, we allow ourselves to indulge in the black gold here at Horn Hill."

The children come in with a silver coffeepot and fill three delicate china cups. Ceton drinks eagerly, and black stains mingle with the red already on his coat.

"Do you know, most people appear not to have any difficulties in calling a good deed by its name when they see it. They apparently have the ability to distinguish good from evil. But if it costs them the smallest little thing to do what is right, they'll prefer to do what is wrong or to let matters be. At least as long as their choices remain clandestine, and there is no witness about to praise virtue or call out sin."

He gestures with his hand as if to include the entire room.

"We already have an orphanage here in Stockholm, supported by the city itself. It is not much more than a place for the manufacture of children's corpses. I have used the estate of Erik Three Roses to found Horn Hill. The credit for the entire undertaking I have gifted to the city fathers, and, as it costs them nothing, they are happy to bask in its glory.

People think they pay out of their own pockets to grant guttersnipes a future, and wherever they go, people point in wonder and whisper, *There goes a good man, one who puts others before himself.* Thanks to their example, many others also want to count themselves among the bene-factors of Horn Hill, and I gladly let them borrow the same feathers. Well-dressed gentlemen come here discreetly in their barouches to show the place to their mistresses, who, in the way of women, carry a weak-ness for goodness and will happily open their legs for these undoubtedly righteous men before the day is done. Without me, these lies would not be possible. Therefore, I enjoy their protection, and with the blessing of the establishment, not even my own worst enemies can touch me. The money, around which everyone's existence appears to revolve, only in-terests me to the extent that it can allow me to live the life I want."

Winge looks around with doubt in his eyes and imitates Ceton's sweeping gesture.

"When Catherine the Great was to visit Potemkin's newly conquered regions, it is said that he constructed facades of bustling, prosperous vil-lages along her way in order to deceive her into thinking that everything was well when in fact poverty was rampant."

"Ah, but you do not see the whole beauty of my plan. I see your line of reasoning: How ill must these poor vulnerable children fare in the care of a monster like Tycho Ceton, when the lights are snuffed out and the visitors go home? But the fact is that Horn Hill is no charade. Therein lies the beauty. This house is exactly what it seems. And why? Well, because I have been expecting people like you. People who have found some pretext to hunt me down, and who will not let themselves be dismissed. People who do not have much to lose, but who still stand aloof from bribes. The exceptions to prove the rule. And lo, here you are."

Ceton claps his hands and calls to the girl, who is obediently wait-ing by the wall.

"Please, Klara Fina. Would you be so kind as to join us for a moment?"

The girl curtsies, takes a few quick steps, and stops by the edge of the table.

"Mr. Ceton?"

"Let it be Tycho. For tonight."

"Tycho."

"Would you please tell our guests about your life before you came to live with us here at Horn Hill? Come now, no judgment will be passed here."

She looks down and blushes.

"In the daytime, I slept wherever I could find a spot, and in the evening I went up to the castle under the western wall where the ones who want their whores very young know they are to be found."

Ceton leans over and dries a tear from her cheek with a corner of his handkerchief. He turns to the boy, who is still standing behind Emil Winge.

"And how about you, Joakim?"

"I stole what I could, by guile from those who weren't paying attention, and by force from those who were weak. The days when hunger got the better of me, I went to the castle like Klara Fina and did as she did."

Ceton throws his arms out.

"Here we give these children a lease on life, not for the moment alone, but also with hope for tomorrow. When they aren't attending to their duties in the kitchen and garden, we teach them to read and count, and should they find something that they are particular suited to among all the crafts that they are given the opportunity to test, we help them secure apprenticeships within the same profession when they are old enough. No one so much as touches a hair on their heads, I least of all. After we have finished our repast, you are free to go wherever you like here at Horn Hill. Speak to the children. And then ask yourselves the question: What fate would await these children if not for Tycho Ceton? Each blow aimed at him would strike them all the harder. You want to see me punished for Linnea Charlotta's broken body and for Erik Three Roses's scorched mind. But the small crime you are solving can only be addressed with the price of a far greater evil. With the same fists that would put me in irons, you would force Joakim, Klara Fina, and hundreds of foster children on their knees before yet another night walker's unbuttoned trousers in the shadow of the castle walls, soon forcing them to swallow what will likely be their only nourishment that day. Is that not the plain truth?"

He turns once more to the boy.

"Joakim, would you be so kind as to run and fetch the folder that is lying on the desk in the office?"

The boy takes off running. Ceton slurps his coffee to the dregs.

"It would perhaps amuse you to read an excerpt of Erik's own words while we conclude our meal . . . maybe from the time our paths crossed? I asked him to write down his memories of the whole affair while he languished in Dane's Bay, for the sake of my entertainment. And this is the other reason I have looked forward to receiving guests such as yourselves: in your powerlessness, I may show you all that I have achieved without having to conceal anything. Long have I felt as if I were Sergel, the master sculptor, and yet forced to hide my masterpiece under sheets in a shuttered studio. After all, what is art without the admirers it deserves?"

45

E mil Winge's gaze flits across the lines, growing increasingly pale as he passes each page he finishes to Cardell, who can't manage quite the same pace. As the unread pile on his side of the table grows, the watchman simply lets his gaze cross the pages in the hope that he will pick up a couple of words that would allow him to grasp a larger meaning. Before the hour is up, Winge has started again, leafing through the pages in search of particular passages to scrutinize. When the first of Ceton's cheroots has turned to ash, he lights another, leaning back against the chair with his legs crossed, his gaze alternating between his guests.

Time goes by, and the tense silence is more than Cardell can stand. It is only with considerable effort that he retains control over himself, but he has to turn away from the table. His breathing is heavy and he feels a shooting pain in his left arm. His voice betrays his emotions.

"What did you do to Three Roses?"

"Personally, I didn't touch a hair on his head. It has always been my preference to be an observer while others act. But I arranged the wedding, of course, sent the invitations. I offered Erik my *pastilles de serail*, in sufficient quantities for him to collapse onto his wedding bed, dead to the world. When the other guests had bade us farewell, the young couple's chamber was breached, and turns taken at them, for each according to his pleasure. Poor Erik wasn't much entertainment, for obvious reasons, as pretty as he was, but his wife provided better sport, and thereby, I imagine, a more satisfying conquest. Erik's surgery took place on my advice, of course, as my access to Three Roses's fortune is eased considerably the longer he lives and the more cooperative he remains."

Emil Winge is unable to meet Ceton's gaze as he begins to pose his questions. Instead he allows his gaze to rest in his own lap.

"These guests of which you speak. Who were they?"

"Before I left for Saint Barthélemy, I belonged to a society that to some extent shares my interests. We no longer see eye to eye, and this spurred my trip. The bacchanal came as a peace offering from my side."

"And did it fall on fertile ground?"

He shrugs.

"Enough to call a truce, if not to mend all bonds of friendship that had broken beyond repair."

Winge's voice has decreased to something hardly louder than a meek whisper.

"Johan Axel Schildt—what became of him?"

Ceton laughs, so that a flake of tobacco lands on his trousers, which he brushes away with care as the rings on his fingers catch the light.

"Ah, that's delicacy! Did you not sense his presence in the text? He returns for a final farewell, although Erik himself neither recognized him nor understood what he was trying to say. They met briefly on the Carenage before Schildt said goodbye to Saint Barthélemy for good."

He blows a cloud of smoke through his cheek.

"We locked his jaw with a bridle, shaved his head, and smeared him with tar until his skin was dark enough not to draw attention. We were surprised it worked, but even his best friend wouldn't have recognized him when we were done: *quod erat demonstrandum*. He got some incredulous looks at the slave auction, but he still went to the lowest bidder."

Ceton nods to himself as he lets the words sink in. Cardell wipes his face with his hand, and when he speaks, the anger has left a voice that is hardly more than a gruff whisper.

"Why all this?"

Again, Ceton shrugs.

"I live as nature fashioned me. What should a bee do with its stinger other than sting? Don't you do the same, in your own way?"

"What the hell is wrong with you?"

Ceton sinks into thought for a while, his gaze turned inward. When he answers, the levity has left his voice.

"Von Rosenstein's beautiful speech to the Academy appeared in bookshops last year. He delivered it in eighty-nine, and praised our era as the Great Enlightenment. Four short years went by before the text was ready for printing, and see what fruits his so-called Enlightenment bore in that short time! Down on the continent, they have rid themselves of the superstitions that once oppressed all. The God of the Testaments has been dealt a mortal blow, next we will question the monarchs who rule in His name, and the blood of the unpopular, whether innocent or guilty, will still run the same color in the gutter. Everyone will seize the day to avenge wrongs with the axes that have long been ground in silence; *bellum omnium contra omnes.* I don't doubt that they meant well, our great thinkers, but all they have accomplished, when they overturned the despots of yesterday, is to give mankind a new excuse to show itself as it is, and always has been. As governed by laws of nature as any animals in the forest, where force rules uninhibited and the strong prey on the weak at every turn. Look at Paris. Executioners everywhere. Where now are the *Encyclopédistes?* They were all hurried to their graves before they could list Madame Guillotine under the correct letter. Such philosophers call Rosenstein and Kellgren men of the Enlightenment! Such titles are misplaced. What delights won't the future have in store for such as me, who find pleasure in the slaughter they've made into a righteous duty on the altar of progress? The century to come awaits me with open arms."

"How was that an answer to my question?"

Ceton raises an eyebrow.

"Excuse me, I thought it was obvious. What I am trying to say is that there isn't anything wrong with me. I am simply the man of the future, born too early."

"What about such as us, then?"

Cardell growls his response, and it makes Ceton laugh.

"Let's be honest, now that our conversation has grown so intimate. No age has welcomed people like you with any degree of enthusiasm."

He grinds the cheroot down in his coffee cup, where it meets the dregs with a sizzle; then he gets up from the table and starts to walk across the room.

"And so I leave you, gentlemen. Look around to your hearts' content. I doubt that we will have reason to meet again."

With one hand on the door handle, he pauses.

"Three Roses says in his story that my disfigured face made it difficult for him to determine if I was smiling or not. The truth is that I smile almost all the time. What is there to stop me?"

46

As they leave the estate behind, each remains silent, absorbed in his own thoughts. The sun sets behind them, and their own lengthening shadows direct them back to the City-between-the-Bridges. Cardell still sees before him the faces of the children he met before finally leaving Horn Hill, so different from the ones he is used to in the city. Neither worn, nor dirty, nor covered in blemishes and sores, nor dressed in torn rags, but with cheeks that have become rounded and rosy from care and nourishment, and clad in shirts laundered white as snow. Gratitude in their voices, in their eyes hope.

He was surprised at how easy they were to talk to, and only realized afterwards what the difference was. In the City-between-the-Bridges, in Maria and Katarina parishes, for example, the children all learn to stay out of the reach of adults, as they know from experience that danger lurks in every touch. Those who address them will notice that they always remain half-turned away, feet arranged for swift flight. But not so at Horn Hill. When he sat down to speak to a boy the same age as Klara Fina, a little girl of around five crawled onto his lap of her own accord, seeking warmth and closeness, and a few moments later the child had fallen asleep, her ear nestled against his chest. She woke with a smile, to a world that remained the same as when she last saw it, took her friends by their hands, and walked on to her next adventure. Never had he heard children laugh so freely, play with such abandon.

....

In the night, the Minotaur disturbs Winge's slumber. He stands barefoot on the red Cretan soil, in the wasteland out of sight of Knossos, and before him rise the walls of the labyrinth. No sun illuminates the landscape of his nightmare, but still he is able to peer through the darkness. He wonders where the others are, the rest of the seven young men and seven young women who have been sent here to be sacrificed, but there is only himself. He knows that he has no choice, and so begins to walk towards the entrance that Daedalus built.

He sleeps long into the day, feeling safe only when the night is lifting, and by midday, on his way from Ironmonger's Square, where he has bought himself a bite to eat, he climbs back up the steep alleys. Clouds veil the sun. From the square rises the sound of people busy with their own affairs, words exchanged in a dozen languages, flattery and insults mixed into babble. The City-between-the-Bridges always mocks him. The ebb and flow of people make a remarkable pattern among streets and alleys, governed by some unseen force, the nature of which he has never been able to grasp. Often he has to push his way through the throng in order to take a single step in the right direction, but when he rounds two corners he finds himself alone, and the city quiet as the grave. The stretch outside his door is something in between: a forlorn crossroads in the midst of the hubbub, a place between places, past which everyone hurries but at which no one has any reason to stay. On his step, his hand fumbling in his pocket for the key he has been lent, he is stopped by a voice he knows well, albeit hoarser than before. He turns around, and the sight causes him to step back as if from an impending blow. A mirror seems raised before him.

"Cecil?"

There his brother stands, pale and thin, his hair black and tied with a ribbon, a cane in one hand and a handkerchief in the other. Cecil waits patiently for the shock to abate. He lets Emil sink down on the step to release the weight from his trembling knees.

"Cecil, I have stood at your grave, what . . ."

"I beg your pardon for the surprise. I would not have come if I could have avoided it. I have made this journey not for your sake, nor my own, but for Jean Michael."

He suppresses a cough with his handkerchief.

"My consumption may have forced me to seek a different climate, but I am not without connections in the City-between-the-Bridges. Your activities have not gone unnoticed. What are you doing, Emil? Is this some sort of revenge?"

"I . . ."

"I came to Uppsala to help you, a long time ago. If you had listened to me then, this could all have been avoided. After me and Hedvig, Father felt he had perfected his strange theories of child-rearing, and you were the youngest, intended to serve as his crowning achievement, the one he was given the longest time to polish to perfection. Nothing came of it. Father took to his grave a broken man. Now look at you, Emil. You cannot change what has been. Whatever gifts you once had you have frittered away. I do not intend to waste my time blaming you for the choices you made, but I simply cannot watch you lead Jean Michael astray with your erroneous conclusions. Must he be sacrificed at the altar of your broken self-confidence? What you are doing is selfish."

"He was the one who came to me."

Cecil brushes the step free of gravel and sits down next to him. In front of them, two men hurry by with a cart, one in front with the handle in his fist, the other behind it to push, and with terrible curses each time the wheels slip in the mud and spray his breeches.

"Jean Michael and I, we were like two sides of a coin. He was strong where I was weak, and where he was slow I was all the faster. We both had our own reasons for seeking justice. Together we became more than the sum of our parts. We accomplished all we set our minds to. But what are you to Jean Michael, Emil?"

Emil buries his face in his hands.

"A consolation prize."

Cecil nods.

"Jean Michael isn't your friend, Emil. He merely wishes you could be like me, but of that you are incapable. He deserves better. This can only end badly."

"What do you want me to do?"

"Go home while there is still time. Return to your bottle if you so wish. There at least practice made perfect."

Emil chews his nails until he feels a sudden jolt of pain and tastes blood on his tongue.

"As long as there is a way forward, he'll stop kneading his stump. The pain dissipates or else he forgets it."

"And in misfortune?"

Emil remembers the expression well: each time the flame of hope flutters, Cardell clenches his jaw until his teeth squeak. His lips tighten to a white line as his right hand seeks the tender spot where flesh meets wood.

"Will you stay in my place, Cecil, if I do as you want? You should never have left him, and whoever stands by him, the battle he wages is a worthy one."

Cecil sits quietly for a while, his hands clasped around the handle of the cane and his chin resting on its top.

"Circumstances prevent me from assisting him this time. My condition . . ."

Silence falls once more, and when Emil's gaze once again dares seek out his brother's face, he can't believe his eyes.

"Cecil, are you crying?"

He receives no answer.

"Everyone thinks that you're dead. Why . . ."

But the tear on his brother's cheek appears to wander upwards, and when Emil draws closer, he sees that it is a worm, white and segmented, patiently making its way towards the safety of the corner of the eye. The collar he believed had a red pattern is simply stained with the dried remains of bloody mucus. Cecil's skin is pale and mottled. Eyes that once burned a dark blue are now milky, swollen, and writhing with the fellows of that worm that will soon find their way home. Cecil turns his face away, as if to hide his shame.

"You . . ."

When Emil stretches out to touch his brother's shoulder, there is nothing there except dust caught in a ray of sun. In the labyrinth of his confusion, the dead return to life. Emil wraps his arms around himself as if to quell a chill, his heart a quaking drum and his breath quick enough to make his ears pop. He shakes his head to assure himself that he is still in the city. He can't tell for sure. There are endless angles everywhere, and hidden paths where the steps of a monster sound ever closer in greedy anticipation, unhurried in the knowledge that the outcome of the hunt is inevitable. He listens for a long time before he can distinguish the thundering steps from the beating of his own heart.

47

Emil climbs Cardell's staircase, where the evening light conjures ghostly beams from each narrow window, all the way up to Cardell's room. He finds the watchman lost in silent ponderings, his forehead in his hand. Only when Emil stands waiting inside the threshold does he look up.

"Come in and close the door, you are letting out what little heat there is."

"I won't be staying."

Cardell senses from his tone that the words hold a meaning beyond the moment.

"What do you mean?"

"I leave for Uppsala in the morning. Everything has been taken care of. I have been by the Scorched Plot and arranged for transportation. Tonight I'm packing my trunk."

Cardell is up on his feet. The blood rushes to his face.

"What the hell for?"

"Can't you see that our labors will bear no fruit? Ceton is in the right. Evil is often simple and banal, but when it's not, how then can we help, you and I, on our own?"

"There must be something."

Emil shakes his head.

"I have no more to offer. I am going home."

Cardell's eyes narrow with a sudden suspicion, and he takes a step closer.

"Something's up. You're so scared you're shaking just standing there. It isn't because of Tycho Ceton. What's happened? Surely we know each other well enough for you to tell me the truth."

Cardell holds out his hand to usher Emil in, but Emil sinks back as from an assailant. Inside, Winge's fear strikes a spark on the shame he feels. He hears his voice lower to a malicious whisper, each poisonous syllable clawing its way through the air.

"I'll give you the truth you crave. There is no *we* anymore, not after tonight. Look at us. I'm a drunkard forced into a sobriety whose every moment I already regret, and you a cripple who has taken your dead friend's little brother hostage in your loneliness. But I am not Cecil, and now the dream is at an end."

The words come to Emil as if of themselves, and he does nothing to stop them.

"You think he was your friend. Never in my life have I heard that Cecil made a friend. He was most comfortable with his own accomplished self, in sole majesty, the better to sit in judgment of others. He certainly never suffered any pangs of loneliness. He used you because it suited his purpose. Cecil was weak and dying, and he did not choose you because he saw anything special in you, Cardell, he chose you because no one else wanted to help him. And you're so grateful to have been used that you're still mourning his death. It's pathetic."

....

Each word is a spear to the gut, hitting hardest where they come so close to the truth. Cardell has no response to offer. His left arm throbs at his side, forever trapped under the anchor chain of which nothing remains but a rusty scar at the bottom of the Gulf of Finland. Only when Winge turns around, to hurry back the way he has come, does he hear Cardell's answer as a muted rattle.

"Wait a moment."

Cardell steadies himself with his right arm and lets both knees sink to the floor. One of the floorboards is loose, and with a practiced grip he lifts it up and takes out the bundle hidden underneath. He sits heavily on the bed, placing the bundle on the blanket and unfolding it until its treasure is revealed and he can wind a golden chain around his fingers and hold it out to Winge.

"Your payment, as promised."

Emil takes it in his hand; it is Cecil Winge's pocket watch. Beurling, Stockholm. Arabic numerals around the circumference, diamonds in between. On the back, two birds under a wall with urns. The key, with its carved laurel wreath, attached to the chain. They exchange a look full of all that is best left unsaid before Emil slips the watch into his pocket and disappears down the stairs.

....

Mickel Cardell sits hunched as the shadows rise around him, rocking back and forth while he tries to soothe his severed arm. Then a scraping at the door interrupts his train of thought. He staggers across the floor, hopeful for a moment that Emil Winge has returned in order to take back his caustic words. When he opens the door, he doesn't know at first who he is looking at. A famished shadow, worn and tattered. Only after a few moments does recognition sink in, with a force as from his days in the artillery when he stood next to the cannons as the powder flared and the cannonballs flew.

"My God, what has happened to you—what is the matter?"

She is staring at him wide-eyed, she whom he has been trying to find for days. Never before has he seen even a hint of supplication in that face, not from her who has withstood suffering to make his own pale in comparison. To find naked supplication there now makes the sight worse. Her voice is hoarse through cracked lips.

"I need your help, Mickel. There is no one else."

PART THREE

Will-o'-the-Wisp

SPRING 1794

I'm motherless, beset with blight,
Great my need and woe;
Were I to freeze to death tonight
No heart would heed or know.

—Anna Maria Lenngren, 1794

48

Johan Kristofer Blix's dower, the purse that the watchman Cardell had given her for no other reason than that right should be right, has come in handy. She who once answered to the name Anna Stina Knapp and is now called Lovisa Ulrika Blix has used every shilling wisely, and the pub, the Scapegrace, has flourished under her care. Gone are the overturned barrels that used to serve as tables, now replaced with planed boards set on robust trestles, surrounded with benches where patrons can stretch their tired legs. Neighborhood boys and girls come in after ten o'clock each night to sweep and clean. The floors are scrubbed daily, the tables wiped and scoured, and the reputation of the pub has risen accordingly.

The first time she went to the man who passes for her father, Karl Tulip, the Flowerman as he is called, and told him about her aspirations for the future, she saw his eyes run with pride and hope. The pub is the only thing he has to show for a lifetime of toil, and it appears to be a part of him as much as he of it. Now he mirrors the renaissance of the Scapegrace. Once Anna Stina had brought order to the run-down establishment, attention turned to the host himself.

He protested at first, accustomed to thriftiness in order to safeguard the meager takings, and only with reluctance did he let himself be convinced that the waistcoat he has worn over the same shirt for years was no longer worthy of the establishment he represents. New clothes, new shoes. Even though he assured her his rags could serve for another couple of years, she can see how good he feels in the new ones, which appear to mold his worn body back to its former glory. His back straightens in its white shirt, his legs stretch in the blue breeches. Finally, Anna Stina convinced him to stop wearing the wig that has concealed his bald head for years, and has carefully taken the scissors to the white tufts that still cling to his temples. At first he was embarrassed, fearing the ridicule of his regulars, but their greetings were hearty, and when the lice found themselves deprived of their old hiding places, they abandoned Karl Tulip entirely in order to find better hunting grounds.

When Anna Stina first arrived, she attended to those things that others had neglected, and did not shirk at the most laborious tasks: the crust of dirt that had been allowed to thicken and dry in layer upon layer over the years, the waste barrel in the outhouse that had been overflowing for several months, at first because the dung fetcher's fee was left unpaid, and thereafter because the effort of the task was greater than the value of the payment. Tulip himself suggested to wait until winter, when the frozen waste could be hacked away and loaded onto a cart without the reek being overpowering, but tasks of this kind did not faze Anna Stina. She had seen worse. The floor was cleaned, the yard raked, the leaky barrel's hoop replaced.

After a while she noticed that her care was needed in other areas as well. Karl Tulip, whose drunkenness was seldom far behind that of his customers, had not managed his accounts. Each evening's profits were gathered in a box whose key was often misplaced and therefore could rarely withstand the nimble fingers of patrons who felt deserving of a discount. The expenses had never been totaled or written down. Anna Stina does what she can and finds to her surprise that the principle isn't harder than when she walked her basket in Maria parish: profit and loss must be lined up against each other, and when the latter exceeds the former, measures need to be taken. She halts the worst of it quickly by stopping the petty thefts, and by making sure that the Scapegrace closes at the hour the city has appointed, there is no longer any need to provide free drinks to the city watch. With the holes in the pub's strongbox mended, she begins to think about ways to grow the income.

This turns out to be easier than she would ever have imagined, and perhaps it is because too few women manage pubs, and men apparently are unable to see what is in front of them. A clean and tidy pub attracts more customers, since not even the ones who make the biggest messes relish the sight of their excretions. When she can afford it, they purchase better wares, and soon everyone knows that the best beer on the block is served at the Scapegrace, and that the barrels are not refilled with water as soon as the bottom comes within sight. Crowds gather at the counter and tables grow bigger, and when their number becomes a problem, they can afford to raise their prices somewhat. In the yard, they begin to keep hens, and along one wall they make space for some pigs. With the kitchen slops they buy the goodwill of the guttersnipes, and the children repay their debt by keeping their own away from the pub during opening hours. At the Scapegrace, pocket watches and purses go unaccosted, even if the owners have drunk themselves senseless. Without Anna Stina having given it a thought, the clientele begins to change.

Together, they prepare for winter, although he is too old and she too young. A chimney sweep tackles the fireplace and they carry in enough bundles of firewood to last them until spring. When the cold arrives, they have what they need to keep the main room warm, and this without the smoke settling like fog in the room and prompting tears and coughs. Tallow candles are replaced with wax ones. The pub's regulars, many of them old drinking companions of Karl Tulip, and who rarely missed an opportunity to drink on credit, are seen less frequently, replaced by more affluent folk.

....

The child she carries grows ever bigger inside. She is amazed at the changes in her body, once so familiar. The skin is stretched taut over a belly that soon grows large enough to hide her feet. She isn't sure how much time is left before the little one is ready, but it can't be long. One day she gets on her knees next to the scouring pail in order to take on a stain that others haven't managed to scrub out and realizes her belly reaches the floor. And yet it continues to grow, and inside her she feels hour by hour this life flourish. The child kicks and wriggles as if it wants nothing more than to leave the safety of its first home, but still it hides from the light of day and remains secure in its warm darkness. She starts to waddle under the weight.

Karl Tulip longs for his grandchild. He is always on his feet before Anna Stina, and after she wakes up he sits on the side of her bed with a candle, wearing an expression of concern and anticipation in equal measure.

"How're you feeling today? Should I get the midwife?"

Somewhere Anna Stina knows that Tulip is much more shrewd than people give him credit for. She is no daughter of his, and he knows it as surely as she knows he is not her father. Sometimes he looks at her kindly with a spark of acknowledgment of their shared secret as he gently chides her.

"You used to eat with your left hand, Lovisa."

She smiles back with feigned surprise.

"Of course, Father dear, I don't know what's got into me today."

They will laugh together afterwards, without either of them feeling the need to address their arrangement in so many words. She is the daughter he has chosen for himself, and he the father she never had.

49

Anna Stina has often told Karl Tulip not to overexert himself and take on too much, especially as she is able to help less with each passing day, and sometimes has to go up to her room to rest. But the old man is stubborn, and perhaps it is a rejection of age itself, a need to prove all that of which he is still capable. She has lost count of the number of times he has shifted a keg of beer on his own despite her asking him to accept help, and answered her reprimands with a grin of equal pride and contrition.

She becomes aware that she has been sleeping longer than normal for her afternoon nap and wakes with a feeling of concern. Steadying herself against the wall, she makes her way down the stairs.

"Father?"

No one answers. The Scapegrace is empty, with a couple of hours still left before opening time. All seems in order. A window is open to let the mopped floors dry, and outside in the courtyard a bird is singing, its trills resounding between the buildings. The neighbor's girl is out there rifling the hens' nests, gathering each egg one on top of the other in her apron.

"Have you seen my father?"

She gives her head a shake. Anna Stina can do nothing but wait, a knot of unease tightening in her gut. It is not like him to go out on long errands; in fact, it is as if he were tethered to the Scapegrace with a rope whose strength draws him back all the faster, the further he strays.

"What about Nils?"

The girl responds by saying that her older brother, who helps with a range of duties, is sick, but hoping to get back on his feet soon. Anna Stina sits at the chopping block and spends her time splitting the wood into kindling.

....

They bring him on a stretcher, hastily improvised out of two poles and a rope. When she hears the knock on the door she lets them in, pointing up the stairs when the two strangers harshly ask where they should carry him. She interprets their meaningful glances on the way out to indicate that they would like some recompense for their troubles and she hurries to her kitty. An older gentleman stays a little longer, his hat in his hand.

"He collapsed down by the well just as he was lifting his buckets. Someone recognized him as the owner of the Scapegrace and we carried him here."

Anna Stina understands what must have happened. The boy Nils was not around and, rather than wait, Tulip took the yoke and buckets himself and set off to the square for water. The weight proved too much for him. She pats his forehead with a rag that she has dipped in the last drops of water in the bowl. He is awake but does not appear able to see.

His eyes flit back and forth without finding focus. His face seems altered. On the right side, the corner of his mouth hangs far down towards the jaw, one eyebrow sunk over the eye. She discovers after a while that the palsy appears to have affected all of one side of his body, from head to toe. Only on the left side, life clings yet. His foot is jerking, his hand groping the air while everything else is perfectly still. The weight of the lame half confines him to his back, helpless as an overturned beetle. Again and again he tries to speak, but all that comes out is a wailing cry in which no words can be discerned.

....

She sends the neighbor's girl with a message for the doctor, and when he turns out to be otherwise occupied, she lets the girl stand out front in order to be able to distinguish him from the horde of thirsty customers who have gathered to beat on the door that should have opened a long time ago. Eventually he arrives, in his black coat, his bag at his side. He hardly needs to touch the sick man in order to confirm the diagnosis with a sigh.

"Tulip has had a stroke."

She doesn't need to ask any questions. He has heard them all too often before and he gets there first.

"It's not clear what may have caused it. Everything and nothing. Life itself. The only thing I can say with any certainty is that it goes with age and debauchery. Now there is nothing else to do but wait, because science knows no cure. Some of those with stroke improve, others don't. Time alone will give judgment. But you should be grateful that your father has been granted the mercy of reaching an age advanced enough to be vulnerable to stroke. All too many end their days far younger and far worse."

He takes his farewell with a glance at her large belly.

"One takes his leave and makes way for the next. Such is the way of the world. You will do best in procuring help for your father since that one looks ready to come any day now."

Anna Stina hands him the hat and coat she has been holding in her lap.

"I will find someone."

....

And yet her belly keeps growing. It feels as if she is going to split open at any moment. She finds a man who has driven his own pub into ruin to help her run the business, and even though she knows that he steals the greater part of the kitty and mishandles the rest, it yields more profit than letting the Scapegrace close its doors. Her own time she spends nursing Tulip. He cannot suffer a mug to his lips without choking. Instead she gives him a wet rag to suck. It is a comfort to her that the thin gruel that is all he manages to get down appears to be nourishment enough.

Every morning she looks for the glimmer of the man she knew in the eyes that have been deprived of their sight, finding nothing. This lack of knowledge is worst, not knowing if he is still in there, trapped in a body that no longer serves him, or if his consciousness has already fled and left his body adrift. He has become a grotesque infant. She makes a nappy for him from two old shirts, tied around his hips and legs to more easily keep the bed clean. How he can separate night from day she doesn't know, but it is when the night is the darkest that his anxiety peaks. She makes a place for herself beside him and her warmth seems a comfort, enough for a couple of hours' sleep. To wash and feed him is all she has energy for, as the life growing inside her also needs its share, and increasingly she falls into slumber at any time of the day.

....

Three weeks go by and Karl Tulip appears neither better nor worse. Day to day he remains the same, if increasingly thin. The Scapegrace is under siege from all the forces that were there before her arrival, and they conspire to return the pub to what it once was: dirty and unkempt, unprofitable and disreputable. She does everything in her power to keep them at bay, but the odds are stacked against her. And so one Wednesday morning when she is lying with aching hips in the bed she has had brought into the room that earlier belonged to Tulip alone, she hears a noise on the stairs, and soon there is a small gathering of people before her. A woman is at the front of the pack, tall, with flashing eyes.

"So this is how she looks, the imposter."

By her side stands a man who does not even reach her shoulder, but who is broad and stout, with a large moustache. Others stand further back. A few faces she knows by name, men she has become acquainted with from the bar. Anna Stina blinks the sleep out of her eyes and rolls with some effort into a position that allows her to get to her feet.

"Who are you? What do you want?"

The woman's voice trembles with indignation.

"You ask me my name? Fitting indeed, since that is the very thing I've come to reclaim. I'm Lovisa Ulrika, Karl Tulip's daughter. The only one."

The man at Lovisa Ulrika's side smirks at the emotions that wash over Anna Stina. She gives the woman before her an imploring look.

"Will you speak to me alone? Please?"

Lovisa Ulrika reflects for a moment before she curtly nods to her husband, who ushers the others out through the bedroom door and closes it behind him.

"Well?"

"It is my time soon. I beg you to let me stay until the child is delivered. Then I will leave and you will never lay eyes on me again."

Lovisa Ulrika is silent for longer than Anna Stina can stand.

"I only ask this one thing. Have you no children yourself?"

Perhaps it is these words that tip the scales. The expression that had wavered between mercy and resentment stiffens into indifference.

"None that have been allowed to live, even though they had an honest woman for a mother and not a tramp like you. You'll find no sympathy here. Get out of my house. You may keep the clothes you are wearing, but if you so much as glance at anything else I will send my husband for the police."

....

She encounters one of the former regulars at the Scapegrace on the stairs on her way down, one of those who had always been closest to Karl Tulip and whom she had seen at his side in merriment many times. He gives her a look of reproach.

"As long as the old man was happy and contented, there was no harm in it. Now that he is at death's door, it's a different matter. It's not right that a stranger should inherit from him. What could we do but send for his real daughter?"

Behind her in the room she hears a shrill cry intensify in strength, Karl Tulip's wordless howl for the warmth that has left his side.

50

It takes her three slow blocks before she has to seek the support of a wall and rest against the rough plaster, leaning until her belly is supported by her thighs, giving the small of her back some relief. She has not walked this far for a week or more, but she will have to go further still, for there can be no return. Panic robs each breath and forces her to draw air more rapidly. The security she has worked so hard to gather around her has been torn away with a single blow. She lets herself sink to the ground, her forehead to her knees, wound around her center of burgeoning life. The air is mild, and summer is soon to come, but the stones are cold and spread a chill through her that only consoles by reminding her of a greater danger. She owns nothing but the clothes on her back. A dress, a blouse, a slip, a piece of cloth to keep her hair out of her face. City-between-the-Bridges is not a place where any weakness is forgiven. If someone even notices her where she sits, it is only as an obstacle to be circumvented, cursing.

She gathers her thoughts against the feelings that threaten to overwhelm her. Then she stands up, leaning heavily against the stone, seeking some purchase, and starts to waddle along the street again, northward. Her thoughts first go to the public lying-in hospital, but something about it scares her. Even though they will deliver young mothers without asking their names, she knows she may still be wanted. Those places attract fallen women, and more than once she has seen watchmen lurk by the square in the hopes that their prey will waddle straight into their arms. She doesn't want to take that risk.

....

It takes her hours to reach the King's Isle at her glacial pace, although she is hurrying as best she can, worried that the doors will shut before she arrives. She knows the way and counts the steps. Past the Royal Mint, across the bridge to the Islet of the Holy Ghost over the current between city and mainland. The water thunders under her feet, a perpetual break where the lake water surges out into the sea with all the ferocity a spring flood can muster. She walks along the road to the left past the crowds of harbor folk around the Red Sheds, and then over the long jetty that cuts through Klara Lake. The afternoon is calm, the water still. The sun blinds her, but she can already feel the day cooling off with the promise of a night when she will freeze. Around her, the people of the city pass in both directions, busy with their own concerns. Man and nature are united in their indifference towards her, and within herself she feels an old rage answer, a smoldering furnace that more than anything helped keep her alive behind the walls of the workhouse.

....

Anna Stina arrives at the outer door of the Seraphim Hospital as evening falls. The place is as Kristofer Blix described it, with its coat of arms proudly hung over an arch in the outer wall, next to a chestnut tree. Of everything he told her about, she remembers this place as the only one where he was shown some measure of mercy. No one questions her as she walks through the garden across crushed stone, nor when she pushes open the crack in the main door of the building enough to slip her belly through. Inside the corridor, nurses hurry to and fro. When one of them finally gives her a questioning look, she clears her throat and says a silent prayer that she has remembered the name correctly.

"Professor Hagström?"

The woman purses her lips and shakes her head.

"The professor is abroad and we don't expect his return before midsummer. And you should know better than to come here in your condition. The heat is coming and the fever is spreading and nowhere will you catch it more easily than here."

Hopelessness must be easy to read in Anna Stina's face because when she remains standing without knowing what to do next, the woman's stern face softens.

"Well, wait here. I can see well enough what brings you here."

Anna Stina waits where she has been left, worried that the smallest change in her stance will be enough to upset the scales where life and death hang in equilibrium. It does not take long before a young man comes walking towards her. He wipes his hands on a stained apron and gives her a short nod by way of introduction.

"Will you please come this way?"

She follows him through a door that opens onto a corridor where, after having opened several doors on the left only to find the rooms occupied, he finally finds an empty one. He signals to her to sit on a bench by the window where the light is best.

"May I ask you to lift your blouse and slip? I need to examine you more closely."

She does as he says and he gets down on his knees in front of her. His fingers are gentle as he squeezes and palpates her belly and he is attentive to the places where pain and discomfort might be located. Once he has completed his examination, he places a kind of funnel against her stomach and puts his ear to it. He changes its position several times and nods slowly as if confirming a guess. Finally, he gestures for her to restore her clothing and sits down on a stool across from her.

"I understand why you have come."

She doesn't know what to say, simply waiting for him to go on.

"Luckily, I am well qualified to assist you, and what is even better is that I can do so at no fee whatsoever. We keep two beds here for those who have the need without being able to pay, and one is vacant."

He puts his hands behind his back and turns to the window, where the light is starting to fade.

"In view of your age, I assume that it is your first birth?"

She nods in assent and lets him continue.

"Your hips are too narrow and from what I can tell from your belly, they are arranged in quite a jumble. I can't see how the birth can have a successful outcome, either for you or for them."

"Them?"

He interrupts his train of thought.

"You carry twins. I assumed you knew."

It sounds so obvious when he says it. Of course it is the beating of two hearts she has heard inside her, two sets of limbs that have caused her belly to grow far bigger than others she has seen.

"In your case there is only one course of action. We must wait, and do so with great patience. We take no lives here at the Seraphim, so we must let nature take her course. Once the fetuses are still, we can remove them from the uterus safely. With a hook and a special kind of scissors we can dismember them in the womb and remove the parts one by one with the help of tongs."

When she remains silent, he stands somewhat at a loss, rubbing his hands.

"Would you like me to show you my instruments?"

51

Nausea at the proposition she has just refused threatens to rise in her throat when she leaves the Seraphim Hospital. Again she drags her feet across the bridge, back whence she came. The sky glows pale, but the land lies in shadow and the path across, over empty boards, frightens her. She never allows her hand to lose its grip on the railing, lost to her sight, no longer distinguishable from the black water of the bay hissing all around her. Nor can she see where she puts her feet; each step is an act of blind faith. She slows down, fatigue, too, affecting her. Surely the bridge wasn't this long before? When she reaches solid ground on the other side, she has to go on without any support. No lanterns light up this distant shore. A nameless rooftop hovers against a deep blue sky; beyond, she can make out the church spire. She staggers over to the rough logs of the wall and allows herself to sink down to seek what warmth is to be had where the timber meets the ground.

It takes her two long days to cross these lands, that stretch out north of the city, fading into wilderness, all the while slowly swaying, as if in a feverish daze. Her feet chafe in shoes that were never made for such a march. She can think of nothing except escape, to leave people and their dwellings behind at any cost. When they aim to hurt, they do so with ease, and when they try to help, the outcome is the same. The further she goes, the sparser the settlements. By the church she finds a drink of water, and from there she sets her course towards a further spire, the one marking the final city parish. In the shadow of the hills, the Bog stretches out like a sore on the landscape. It is hard to tell where firm ground ends and the water begins. An open stretch foams in the middle, circled by floating debris where tufts of grass and reed have gained a foothold. All around, the ground is muddy, every hut and house in the vicinity subsided, slanted at drunken angles. Few would willingly choose to build their home on shores like these. The residents scurry between unlicensed pubs and mischief, shying from the gaze of the righteous, and their children play on the Bog and laugh each time one of them misjudges a wrong step and sinks their leg in the muck. Around the lake, fenced enclosures are positioned to gather waste to be hauled away, but the wood is long since rotten, the nails rusted, the structures on the verge of collapse. Boards hug the shore to make for safer footing, and Anna Stina makes her way across. Before her there is only the outlying forest of the Great Shade by Lill-Jans. Then nothing.

Evening overtakes her as the final houses give way to the trees. The Shade lives up to its name. Sections of the boundary fence have fallen over, offering no resistance to her passage. Beyond is a fence of another kind, far more effective, of bushes and brambles where thorns claw at her. Then the ground clears, bare under the canopies of the centuries-old oaks. She stands among the pillars of this otherworldly ballroom. At first the silence is oppressive, but then her ears meet sounds of a kind to which she isn't accustomed, low but insistent. High above, a wind tousles the canopies but never reaches her, and everywhere she can sense the movement of unseen creatures traversing a vast carpet of last year's dead leaves. By the huge trunks, the warmth of the day lingers. She doesn't know what she is looking for. Her world is a confusion of exhaustion and pain, but still she lurches on. A long time has gone by since last she ate. Her belly is both full and empty. Her midriff contracts in a throbbing spasm. It soon recurs, and again, increasing in intensity.

....

At first Anna Stina doesn't know if she is hallucinating. There's a glimmer between the trees, although night has long since fallen. She steers her course towards the light and when she has climbed to the top of a hollow, she sees the fire, carefully encircled by a ring of stones. At first the fire blinds her, and it takes her a while to see that the camp is not deserted. There is a girl next to the fire, right in front of her, no older than she. She must have jumped up when the uninvited guest appeared. She looks as if sprung from the forest itself, a creature of bark, moss, and root. Next to her, a piece of cloth is laid out, and on it a few simple possessions. A sooty and warped copper kettle, a collection of small bags, a bottle stopped with a bit of fabric, a well-worn knife. Anna Stina crawls the final distance. When she is close enough to feel the heat, she curls up, meets the girl's gaze through the flames, and sees there the same wariness as of some wild beast, but no malice, and she closes her eyes and lets her consciousness dissolve into the void.

....

Anna Stina can't tell how long a reprieve she has been granted, an hour's or a minute's. She wakes, the darkness the same. The girl is still there, staring at her with her knees pulled up under her chin. Their eyes meet for a brief moment until the girl looks away and speaks in a hoarse, unpracticed whisper.

"The child. I think it wants to come out."

She nods to show her what she means, and Anna Stina sees that her waters have broken while she slept, a trickle hissing angrily against the stones around the fire.

"Lisa is my name. Lisa Forlorn they call me, those who know."

Anna Stina wants to answer with her own name, but a contraction stabs her belly and all that comes out is a gasp. Lisa stands up, uncertain, shifting her weight from side to side before grabbing a jug from the ground and disappearing between the trees.

....

Lisa hasn't been gone long when the pain wells up again. It takes Anna Stina's breath away and her legs tense in response, hard enough to lift her hips off the ground. Just as she thinks she has reached an unpassable limit, the inner grip tightens even more, and the scream that comes from her lips will not be stopped. The contractions come more quickly. Around her, the world fades away before an unstoppable force that must find outlet, indifferent and merciless to all in its path.

Lisa is by her side again. Over the curve of her belly, Anna Stina sees a pale and worried face. What she at first thought was mere dirt is a birthmark that, seen up close, glows red, an uneven stain that snakes across Lisa's face as if it had spilled from her scalp, around one eye and down across her cheek. Her limbs and body are thin, but with a sinewy quality indicating a hardship met with strength. It is impossible to determine the color of her hair where it pokes out from under her kerchief. She shares colors with the trees and the ground, faded shades of brown, green, and gray. Her eyes are a clear blue. She could almost have been called beautiful, Anna Stina reflected, if you looked beyond her face to the whole of her. Darkness goes light. Light becomes darkness again. All is agony and bewilderment, and her only comfort is that the enormity of what she feels no longer leaves any room for fear. She passes in and out of consciousness, awakened only when the rhythm of her suffering quickens. They can't get out, they can't get out. Her belly is a cage to them, a cage of flesh and bone.

52

Lisa Forlorn walks to and fro, muttering to herself in a language that others no longer understand. She listens to the laboring girl whose name she doesn't know, who raves in a high voice in her brief periods of stupor. She speaks to the living and the dead. A mother she loves but who is no longer alive, an unknown father who seems shaped by wishful thinking and excused by sentiment. The father of her own unborn child, whose name she curses. Lisa claps her hands to her ears before this stream of unasked knowledge. The troubles of others are nothing to her; she has renounced all duties and asks for nothing in return. The forest provides everything she needs. She longingly turns her head to the desolate safety of the deep forest, and a voice inside tells her to run, to gather together what few possessions are hers into the bag and abandon the girl to her fate. But a conscience she thought long since smothered roots her to the spot, and without being able to put her feelings into words, she knows that her escape would gnaw her insides for the rest of her life. Never again would she sit in peace by her fire. Through the flames she would sense a ghost with a swollen belly, and be forever haunted by the one she had doomed to certain death by her betrayal.

It has been a night and half a day since the waters broke, and yet the child will not come. Lisa knows that something isn't right, and that the problem is beyond her powers. She knows what she has to do but can't work up the courage, and curses herself for her cowardice. Only when afternoon sets in does the girl's suffering finally overcome her own resistance. She leans down, awkward and unaccustomed to another's presence, to whisper in her ear.

"I will soon be back. I'll return with help. Wait for me. Try to hold out a little longer."

....

She sets off quickly through the undergrowth on sure feet. Her unease turns to nausea once the first storehouses and farms meet her on the meadows, marking the outskirts of the city. Soon she can glimpse people in the distance, small figures busy with their work. She slides the shawl down to her shoulders to reveal her face and show her birthmark, the ugliness that is her only defense against unwanted attention, lowers her gaze, and hurries past, ready at any moment to bite the hand that stops her to ask her business, ever counting with her eyes the steps to the nearest escape route. The only looks she gets are of open disgust, and for that she is grateful. She moves further in towards the City-between-the-Bridges, the distance between the houses shorter with each step, the people more numerous, and an ever stronger howl inside her tells her she needs to turn, get away, get back to the wasteland where she belongs before it is too late. She still has strength enough not to listen. Part of her wishes the other girl was dead already, a simple, quick death that would leave her without guilt, knowing that she did what she could without it costing her anything.

53

Age has stitched its cloak over Hedda Dahl, one seam at a time, day by day. She is old and gray now, an elderly lady of some seventy years, and every morning she is struck by the cruelty of life, giving her an abundance of what she used to lack, but only after it has robbed her of the ability to enjoy it. It is ten years since a gallstone felled her husband, a master tailor who had held a burghership for thirty years. In accordance with the rules of the guild, she was allowed to keep his workshop open with the aid of the journeymen, and soon found an aptitude for business which her husband never had. She does well enough to keep the poorhouse at bay on this side of the grave, but her failing sight no coin can redeem. Every morning when she opens her eyes she is afraid of the moment when the world will be extinguished for good. It is still vaguely visible, like some benighted chamber where the glow of a forgotten candle spills in from the next room.

When the last of their children left to set up their own home, a great restlessness came over her, all of forty years old. Without the children to look after and be proud of, her domestic duties were no longer enough to satisfy her. When she had baked, pickled, juiced, and salted, when she had overseen the laundry and brewed beer and hung the meat, she still had energy to spare. She wanted more, now that she saw her life pass its zenith without really having accomplished more than caring for others. A thought came to her, and when she went to her husband to talk it over, she was confident enough to get her way.

Hedda Dahl was going to be a midwife. Her age was right, she herself had borne seven children, and she was no dimwit. All was confirmed with approval by the court midwife Båll herself, who accepted her with a nod.

From that moment, all spare time was spent furthering herself in the craft she had chosen. The demands were high; many couldn't cope. She was required not only to read well, far beyond the eternal recitation of the catechism, but also to use writing implements. Every evening she followed some elder sister in the profession to assist at delivery. In the anatomy theater of the City Hall, a surgeon laid bare all the secrets of the human body to her and her fellow sisters. A woman who had died in childbirth was opened, and they were shown the child who had never seen the light of day still curled up in its place. Although her stomach turned over, she has since made use of the memory countless times when feeling a swollen waist to try to establish the position of the child. Together with a handful of others, she finally went all the way to Wrangel Palace to be examined before the royal physician Schulzenheim himself, who had been ennobled after variolating the crown prince for smallpox. Her qualifications were deemed of the highest order: a good head, great determination, and ability. She laid two fingers on the Bible and swore her oath by God and the Gospel, to serve both low and mighty, rich and poor, night or day.

For twenty years she served the north of Stockholm as a midwife with those same words close to her heart. This was the best time in her life. She gained appreciation and respect, and every day her deft fingers granted young people a joy beyond words. She was embraced by teary fathers, and young mothers kissed her hand. All too often now, she dwells on what went wrong. No single thing, but a series of events, a conspiracy of circumstance. What is true is that she grew older and her sight was already starting to fail; true, too, that younger women, ingratiating and obliging, started to take over her work. Many of the young wives preferred someone closer to their own age, someone in whom they found it easier to confide, and old Hedda Dahl was rejected. They still called her in for the hardest cases, and when others had fallen short. Often the time to help was already past when she crossed the threshold, and soon people took her mere arrival as a harbinger of death. She was the last to hear the names they called her. Hellish Hedda. Hedda Hereafter. Death Dahl. Soon her assistance went entirely unwanted.

All that was now offered her was to provide her expertise to the courts to try to establish the evidence of recent birth in cases of young women who stood accused of infanticide. Only once did she testify under oath, and the truth she was not able to withhold sent the unfortunate mother past the Sconce to kneel before the headsman. The girl was guilty, of course, but not a day goes by without Hedda wishing that she could retract her words and instead confirm a late miscarriage. So Hedda Dahl had done her last work as a midwife. All that remained was to nurse a growing bitterness in a steadily darkening world. But still the sign hangs above her door, the tiny infant's body stamped in copper that proclaims her craft. Even had she the heart to take it down, she no longer has the eyes. The last time she paid any attention to it was because someone had chalked an angel's wings on the child's back.

She sits as she usually does on the edge of her bed, lost in thought. Part of the curse of her old age is that she sleeps less, but doesn't have much with which to occupy the extra time. The maid that helps her has gone home; dusk approaches. It is a time of day she dreads, and her thoughts are drawn to the places she wants most to avoid. It takes a while before she becomes aware that the scraping sounds she hears are coming from her own door. She rises with some effort and starts to feel her way through the room with hands outstretched. From the bed to the doorpost, from the doorpost to the table, along the wall to the hall. She doesn't much want to open for a stranger at such an hour, but does so anyway, rather than test the strength of her voice through the wood. Outside everything is a blurry darkness.

"Yes?"

No answer comes. There is no one there. A childish prank. That happens. At least they haven't peed on her door this time in order to trick her into walking barefoot into the puddle. Then she hears her guest breathe quickly, agitatedly, in front of her. Shallow breaths. Most likely a woman. She waits.

"I saw your sign."

The voice is high-pitched, but also rough as it continues.

"There is a girl in need. The child won't come."

"There are others to help. I'm sure it is one of them you are looking for. You'll find Susanna Alfvars three streets over, level with the well.

Lotta Riga lives up the hill towards the Observatory, a cottage in the yard behind the merchant Petters."

She hears her caller's weight shift doubtfully from foot to foot.

"I don't know my way around here. And there is no time. If it's not too late already it won't be long now."

Hedda Dahl hasn't attended a birth for years. The same feeling fills her as when she stepped before the magistrate to swear her oath, nervous and frightened at the prospect of a task of which she fears she will not be worthy, despite her training. Her thoughts go to the oath itself, and the words she said give her strength now as they did then. She has given her word, well aware of how it has bound her to a duty greater than herself.

"Where?"

"Up in the forest. In the Shade."

"How far?"

"No more than a mile and a half. But there will be no path at the end."

"Under the bed, all the way in, there is a bag made of linen. Will you get it for me?"

She smells her guest as a shadow passes. Moss and spruce fir. The once so familiar cloth handle is gently pressed into her hand, and the weight of the bag is comforting. Inside there is still needle and thread, a syringe for enemas, oil for her hands and fingers. Hedda Dahl steps over her threshold. When did she last do so? It has been a long time. She ends up standing on her own doorstep with surprise over what she has just forgotten.

"I can't see. You'll have to show me the way."

She stretches out her hand in her gray fog, feeling her fingers tremble, betraying the fear that still claws at her inside. For a few long moments the arm hangs untouched. Then she feels a hand in hers, one she has trouble squaring with the young voice she has heard, ridged with calluses, the skin rough, but small and fragile like that of a child's when she tightens her grip around it.

54

The girl is raving weakly; she can hear it already from a distance. That's never a good sign. Hedda Dahl lets herself be helped onto her knees right next to her, panting from the exertion, her feet teeming with bleeding blisters. At once she knows it is twins—such a swollen belly would not have been possible otherwise. She sighs heavily as she measures the girl's hips with a knowing grip. Narrow, oh so narrow. Young. She fumbles in the bag beside her and searches the interior, chooses the bottle, and pours oil onto her hands. The girl is limp and beyond hearing, and without knowing in which direction to speak, Hedda tells her guide, "Hold her knees apart." The help she has asked for comes without question, and she demonstrates with small pushes the posture she is looking for.

The cervix is three shillings dilated as it should be, ready to give birth. The contractions are not coming quickly enough. They must have subsided as the strength has been sapped from the body for no purpose. She lets her fingers probe further in, searching for a problem, gets the umbilical cord around two fingers, and feels it pulsing with life. One child at least is still alive, impatiently waiting. Behind the cord her fingertips graze what she had feared but least of all wanted to find. It is an arm she feels. The first twin is resting on its side, pressed up to the opening like a cork in a bottle, with its sibling close behind. Her fingers move along the tiny limb in the hope of establishing the child's position. Now she feels a hand. She feels a grip on her index finger.

At this point she would have been oath-bound to send for a doctor or surgeon. They would have given the mother laudanum for the pain, awaited the inevitable, and dismembered the first child with scissors, puncturing the crown of the sibling's head and letting it come after, both sacrificed to save their mother's life. Here there is no help to be had, and these two have to get out some other way if all three lives are not to go to waste. She has never been particularly religious, but still the old prayer comes now, the words that the more devout midwives say when they feel the need.

"May God bless the work of my hands and by His mercy assist me in this time of need."

Her next words go to the girl who brought her here.

"Your name?"

"Lisa."

"Have you means to boil any water? Is there any cloth we can use?"

"I have a kettle. There's water in the brook. Of linen I have hardly any except what I wear on my body."

Hedda sends the girl for water as she removes her own blouse. When Lisa returns, she demands the same of her. She oils her hands again, places herself where she needs to be, and starts to turn the infant. The craft she once mastered is coming back to her more strongly by the second. It is a sixth sense that allows her to see through membrane and skin by touch alone. She knows that in her prime she had the best of hands, though few can appreciate the art to its fullest extent when their progeny has just come into the world. Memories of the old grips return, how to fold her fingers to allow the hand to shift without hurting the mother. Even so the girl screams, because for this kind of pain there is nothing to be done. Hedda has her right hand inside, allowing it to glide over the baby's head and down the neck. Her left is at the cervix for support. She puts more power into her grip, a mild but determined shove. If the child doesn't want to, all hope is lost. She lets her arm glide further in and says a silent prayer that the girl won't tear more than she must, happy for her sake that she herself has grown thinner in her old age. The child resists, and she senses the obstinate will of the unborn, until something shifts, and the tiny body suddenly assents. She pulls out the arm but lets the fingers stay at the opening of the cervix, waiting for the girl's body to recover and the contractions to begin anew. She leans over to the girl's face.

"You must push now. You hear me? The child is on the threshold but it needs your help. When the pain comes next time, you need to push, push with all your might."

A half hour goes by before Hedda turns over her shoulder.

"Set a twig between her teeth and hold her by the arms. The child is coming."

"She is too strong, I can't hold her."

"Put your back into it!"

And then she comes, the firstborn girl, in a single moment when life is partitioned from death, as fleeting as the blink of an eye. Her flesh is fine, the baby girl fully developed and big. Hedda's movements are automatic as with a finger she clears the mouth of mucus and brings forth the first breath with a slap on the buttocks. Then comes the cry. She calls Lisa over.

"Swaddle her and hold her in your arms."

Hedda can feel her hesitation.

"Stop dawdling. I need my hands free. There's another on the way."

A little boy soon follows his sister.

....

As the mother sleeps, Hedda washes her clean, sprinkling her blouse with hot water and folding it into a pillow to place between the girl's legs. The other shirt she makes into a warm compress around the belly. When the kettle has cooled off enough, she starts washing her own hands. Her body aches from the exertion. She knows that she is only allowed to baptize under the most dire of circumstances, when the children are not expected to live long enough to be brought to the church and a minister. These newborns are both healthy, but who else will minister to their souls here in the wilderness? She turns in the direction where she can hear three kinds of breaths.

"Lisa, will you go back to the stream and fetch me a small bowl of water? It needs to be clean, perfectly clean. You can give me the little ones until then."

Lisa obeys without a word and leaves Hedda Dahl with a child in each arm. The weight of them is comforting. Lisa returns very soon.

"Take them and hold them out, one after the other, so that I can reach. Someone must serve as sponsor too, and there is no one else here, so if you have always wanted to be a godmother, I congratulate you."

"I don't believe in God."

"Then you'll have no objection to listening to some superstitions."

She recites the words as she cups her hand and sheds water over a furrowed brow.

"In the name of the Father, the Son, and the Holy Ghost."

The Lord's Prayer. The Lord's Blessing. The mother makes a soft sound, still half-unconscious, and Hedda leans closer. She nods.

"I christen you Maja and Karl."

It is done.

....

The mother is still sleeping when Hedda takes her leave. She allows Lisa to escort her as far as the tollgate. In the middle of the day this is close enough for her to find her way back, the streets that were once familiar still where they have always been. As they are about to part, she puts her hand on the girl's arm and turns her so they stand face-to-face.

"I heard you packing. But you can't leave her."

"When can I?"

"Not until she is strong enough to mind herself and her little ones. You will know when. Not before the end of the summer. Give me your word."

After some moments of hesitation, she feels the nod through her arm but presses the hand in rebuke until the answer becomes audible.

"Yes."

....

Hedda Dahl goes on alone through the outskirts of the city in broad daylight, very different now than she was when she left. The twilight of her life appears brighter than before, the sorrows of yesterday all now given coherent meaning. The other infants died so that these two should live. With this hard-won insight, there is much she can understand and forgive. She hears the shocked intakes of breath from those she encounters on the street, feels them staring. She is not wearing her blouse, is walking bare-breasted, unashamed. Sure in her knowledge that they have been wrong before, their looks no longer concern her.

55

"Your clothes are in the stream, under some stones, getting rinsed. Here is neither swan's down nor silk covers, but you can have my old blanket."

Anna Stina doesn't know if what she has experienced can be called sleep, and doesn't know if the words wake her up or only recall her to a reality she has momentarily forgotten. They lie one on either arm, her two beautiful children, still wrinkled and rosy. The boy is sleeping peacefully, but the girl is awake, and struggling with eyelids that don't want to open fully, in order to catch a glimpse of the world in which she has arrived. Her lips gasp for a breast and then find what they seek even though there isn't much milk to be had yet. She makes do nonetheless. Anna Stina can't get enough of looking at them. Every little part and each little movement appear as a miracle to her. Shallow breaths, but strong. A sudden glimpse of blue in a squinting eye. From one day to the next she belongs to another age, one where the fear she feels for her own sake will never again approach the one she feels for them. Lisa Forlorn sits on the other side of the fire and turns three dace over the embers, each speared on a sharpened branch.

"It'll be a day or two. Then you'll be back on your feet."

"I don't know how I will ever be able to thank you."

Anna Stina's voice is hoarse. Her screams still sting in the back of her throat. Lisa takes the spit from the heat and holds one out to her.

"Of everyone around the fire last night, I did the least."

....

Lisa Forlorn's prediction proves true. Anna Stina's strength returns faster than she would have expected. The food is simple but nourishing. Fish of different kinds, in which she soon realizes that each part has its value. The flesh of the dace and bream tastes good, although it is shot through with needle-thin bones, and the skin is tasty when it has been toasted to a crisp. Whatever is left can be saved and simmered to a thin soup. In the evenings and mornings when the coolness of the night is either approaching or lingering, they boil tea made of wild strawberry leaves and eat the tiny berries. Lisa Forlorn only speaks when signs and motions will not suffice, and since Anna Stina is quick to understand, they need but few words. Lisa shows her a creel she has woven of hazel saplings, and lets her see how it is best baited with remains of the latest catch. Anna Stina is led past the places where the wild strawberries and raspberries grow and where the undergrowth will shortly yield lingonberries and blueberries. From an unknown spring deeper in the forest, a fresh stream runs down into the bitter brackish water of Owl's Bay.

Whenever they leave camp, they each carry a child, Lisa with some reluctance at first but in silent agreement that it is the only way. They often change. Both of the children want their mother and complain when the breast is out of reach. The milk comes steadily now, out of a swelling bosom that has quickly learned to adjust to the need. Every evening Lisa counts her possessions, sorting them with care and putting them in the order that she wants to pack them. Every time Anna Stina is sure that she will wake up and find Lisa's spot empty. Every morning she is still there.

....

As evening comes, they sit together on each side of the fire with the children in a peaceful slumber. While they are awake, the children keep silence at bay. But no longer. Anna Stina returns again and again to Lisa's face, where she sits crouched by the fire, poking every branch into the best position with a stick, in a linen shirt that will always bear the stains of Anna Stina's blood.

"Have you never wanted children?"

Lisa doesn't look away from the fire.

"I've nothing against children. But they come at too steep a price. A man. Someone who runs at the first opportunity. Or even worse: one who stays."

Lisa's gaze falls to the bundle of cloth where brother and sister are lying tightly next to each other, at ease in their shared warmth. She lifts her hand and holds it by the side of her face.

"When I was younger, I thought that the red mark I carried with me into the world was a curse. It singled me out. People saw that I was different and kept their distance, and those who were looking for company would rather choose another. Now that I am older, I know that it's the other way around. It's a blessing, for the very same reasons. As a child, I cried myself to sleep over having been born deformed. Now I give thanks every day."

And later, when they are both lying down to sleep, her voice comes unseen, like a whisper out of dying embers.

"I had a child once. He died inside me. He never got the chance to draw breath."

56

I t isn't long before they learn that each child has a particular character, young as they are. Maja is calm. She rarely complains and shows
you what she wants, even if her needs are simple enough. Milk, sleep,
warmth, a change of swaddling. Anna Stina imagines that she can already read a wisdom in her gaze, which is steady and inquisitive. Often
it turns in the same direction to wherever Anna Stina's own attention
goes, as if with some dawning comprehension of the connectedness of
things. Already Anna Stina thinks she can see traces of the one who has
given Maja her name, her own mother, Maja Knapp, and although she
soon grows accustomed to the similarity, she never stops being amazed
that it is possible, that someone thought lost can return to the world in
such a way. Even the hair matches. The compact, soft down on her little
head is the same as her grandmother's, darker than Anna Stina's own.

The boy, Karl, is slighter, more anxious. He is easily agitated and
quick to vent his feelings. He doesn't particularly resemble his sister,
nor can Anna Stina see much of herself in him. She wonders if what she
finds unfamiliar in his face is in reality the first glimpse she has had of
her unknown father, whose name she never learned, or if it is the boy's
own sire who has marked him thus. He is less endowed with hair than
his sister, and his strands are lighter. He is as close to tears as to laughter,
and mother and sister both tend to catch his mood. When he laughs it is
an irresistible, bubbling sound, a joyous gurgling that paints the entire
forest in cheerier colors. She quickly notices how ticklish he is, how the
tips of her fingers barely have to touch the soft flesh under his chin or at
his navel for him to start writhing in merriment.

As different as they are, they always want to be together, as close as they can get. They can't even stand the separation of the blanket she uses to swaddle them, but struggle with combined forces against her until they lie skin against skin, secure and satisfied only in the heat from each other. She watches over their sleep, her gaze lingering over their peaceful faces and reflecting on the bond of blood that ties them together. Mother Maja always emphasized its importance with a superstitious conviction.

Nothing binds like blood, Anna. Remember that.

Sometimes, when her temper was short and she was of an age, Anna Stina would talk back. *Where's my father, then? What happened to the bonds of blood that should have kept him here with us?*

Maja Knapp was never in the habit of letting someone wait for an answer. Nor this time.

Your father set off the moment I started to show. If he had but seen you with his own eyes he would never have been able to disavow his responsibility.

In her and Mother Maja's crowded neighborhood, she must have babysat hundreds of times. Children in the city are born pale and sickly, anaemic and pitiable. Early on, she learned to see children's lives as feeble flames in a capricious breeze, so vulnerable that you hardly dared count them among the living until they had seen their third year. The countless funerals spoke for themselves. Every other grave that is dug, and more, spares the gravedigger's back with its small size.

Even though forest-born, Maja and Karl are of a different sort. They are rosy and strong, and from week to week they gain an increasingly healthy weight. In them she sees something else, something she hasn't seen in children before: a pure life force with a strength that exceeds their tender bodies, fierce and impatient. Nor are they troubled by disease. She remembers the children in Maria and Katarina who were constantly embattled by all kinds of diseases, all runny noses and hacking coughs. Her twins keep healthy. Their strength increases with each passing day. Maja is the first to lift her head, the first to stretch her legs upwards until she rolls to her side. Her brother is quick to copy, masters the same abilities with tiny squeals of undisguised joy.

....

The forest favors them, as does the summer. The heat lingers. Even when the rainstorms whip the branches and leaves, the canopy doesn't let much water through. When the sky is cloudless and the sunshine sears the roofs of the city, the trees give her children a cool shade and strew the moss with billowing pools of light. Lisa baits her trap each morning while the children are still asleep. Each morning the creel is bursting with life, more than enough to feed them all. Soon the raspberry bushes hunch under their burden, not long after the undergrowth comes aglow with blueberries. On the other side of the hill there are ferns whose roots she gathers and rubs clean. She is attentive to the arrival of dusk, watchful as the days grow shorter. But summer endures.

Lisa teaches Anna Stina to find her bearings. To the north there is Owl's Bay, joined to the salt water by a narrow strait, bridged to allow a road to cross. From time to time, travelers or carriages come this way, fine folk on their way out to Fisherman's Rest to enjoy the day. Further north they are building, and in the early mornings, carts come laden with timber and stone, pulled by oxen. If the wind is just right, she can hear the blows of the hammers. When she dares to venture further in the same direction, she has seen workers swarm like ants over a newly raised frame that promises to be a grand building to tickle some gentleman's vanity. They remain far enough away never to bother her and she does not return.

She wills them never to end, these summer days. She doesn't ask for more company. But mushrooms start to sprout on the forest floor, and the nights grow cooler. She and Lisa have moved their beds closer to each other, with the children between them. One night when the blanket has slid off her, she wakes in the early hours of the night and gets up to gather stones from the fire for warmth. That is when she sees them for the first time, tiny lights through the trees. The glow flickers for about an hour until it dies away. She sits completely still, keeping watch. In the morning she asks about it.

"What is it that shines among the trees at night?"

"It's the will-o'-the-wisp, nothing more. Don't go there."

57

Her curiosity gets the better of her. It is to the dance floor of the will-o'-the-wisps that Anna Stina goes when it is her turn to collect berries, while Lisa watches the children whom hunger has not yet awakened. There is a clearing there. The trees open and embrace a round area clad in tall grass that remains green even though everything else has yellowed. A summer meadow in a hiding place behind trees, full of flowers that still stand despite the ebbing season. It is beautiful enough to take her breath away.

She does not see them at first, concealed as they are by swaying stalks. There are small graves strewn everywhere, marked by simple sticks or scratched stones. Mementoes are mixed in with withered bouquets: a doll, a carved horse. At once she knows where she is. This is a place where young mothers come with children who are not welcomed in hallowed ground, unchristened and brought forth into the world out of wedlock. Trampled grass leads her to the freshly dug ground of the previous night, where a wreath has been laid alongside a rag doll cat.

She turns away, knowing that this warning has come just in time, just as she had started to toy with the idea of spending the winter in the Great Shade, tempted by the summer that will come again in only a few months' time. When the night frost comes creeping, yesterday's paradise will turn into a death trap. Around her the dew clings to the grass, but it is tears of the same kind she has heard told of beasts in strange lands that, it is said, cry as they devour their prey. Of course the flowers grow stronger and more beautiful here than elsewhere. Would the forest itself be here if not for the fact that it could lure its guests to stay longer than they should? Its gifts are conditional. When she lifts her gaze to the trees, they are not the same, now only endlessly patient predators. Their protective branches are also greedy claws stretching out for her and her little ones. Here in the meadow of the tiny dead is where their rent falls due. They cannot stay.

....

When Anna Stina returns with far too few berries, she sees from Lisa's eyes that she knows where she has been. To her surprise, she sees shame rather than disapproval.

"The child you bore, does he also lie there? Is that why you come in the summer?"

Lisa turns her face away.

"The surgeon said that he fell apart the moment he came out of me. As gray as spoiled meat, he said. I never got to see him. They gave me a little bundle that I never dared to open. But in my heart he looks just like yours. Pretty and well formed. But dead all the same."

58

Autumn comes insidiously to the Great Shade. The days grow shorter, and on each tree and bush the leaves start to change color until Anna Stina can lift her gaze and see more yellow than green. Still it is the air that best heralds the turn of the season. In the evening, the forest cools quickly. Time becomes harder to tell. The beams of light that once fell straight through the foliage fade by midday, and as the wind blows in from the city to let her count the chimes from the church bells, she often thinks she has miscounted, until the light fails, each day earlier than the day before. When storms ravage the foliage, the forest floor is also scorched with whirling gusts of wind, stinging cold. Each day they take advantage of the final gifts that summer's bounty has to offer. The branches of the wild apple tree hang heavy with fruit to pick and dry. There is a multitude of chanterelles. The fish still bite in Owl's Bay, but Lisa smells the air with a worried look.

"Come with me."

They each carry a child, going deeper into the forest where a hidden path leads on under beard lichen and decomposing oak. They haven't got far when Lisa stops short and peers in between the trees towards a low hill. She takes a few more steps and finds what she is looking for. She shifts a bunch of dry sticks to reveal some planks that have been tied together. These can be moved, and when she has lifted them out of the way, she gestures for Anna Stina to come. It is a burrow that stretches half a dozen feet into the hill. Thick roots serve as beams to keep the roof up. The floor is hard enough to make its surface feel like stone.

"Did you make this?"

Lisa shakes her head.

"I prefer to sleep where the only way an intruder can enter is not the way I need to escape. I don't know whose it is. But I don't think whoever made it will need it anymore and I don't think anyone else knows about it. I found it years ago, and nothing has changed."

Anna Stina creeps closer as Lisa stretches to tug on one of the logs that have been buried in the earth to help carry the structure's weight. It doesn't budge.

"In the summer I don't need the shelter anyway. But now it's getting cold, and soon there'll be no more food."

Only now does Anna Stina understand why Lisa has brought her here.

"You're leaving."

She receives no answer but silence, and that speaks clearly enough.

"Can't I go with you?"

Lisa looks up out of her own thoughts, furrows her brow, and shakes her head.

"Why not?"

"There are rules to follow for those who live as I do. You have broken them already. You mustn't have any ties from which you can't disentangle yourself in the time it takes to stand up and swing the bundle that contains everything you own over your shoulder. You must avoid the company of others. Women are bad. They might be all right individually but never more than that. Their intentions are never easy to interpret. Often they are malicious. Men are easier but more dangerous. They want what is yours and there are no lies they won't tell to get it. If they are denied, they'll use force. In the same moment that a price is set on their enjoyment, they're off, and are nowhere to be found, leaving you alone to pay. But children are worst. They burden you. Soon these will be too heavy for you to carry and will anchor your life, and you'll never shed that chain. Already they weigh too much. Once you work out the best way to carry them both, I will be long gone, and you'll never catch up with me."

"But if you help me?"

"If there was only the one, maybe. With two it can't be done. You have to find another place for them."

"Where?"

She follows Lisa's gaze through the trees, where the City-between-the-Bridges can be glimpsed, amid pillars of smoke and sharp spires.

59

Anna Stina knows of only one place where she can find anything resembling help, but the road is long and she has to prepare carefully. She will have to get back before the darkness hides the forest paths she has otherwise learned so well. She wakes in the night, blows on the embers to warm her flat stones, and winds them tightly in cloth to let them give warmth to Lisa and the children for as long as possible. She is quiet enough not to rouse them. The dawning day is overcast. The clouds are light, and appear to carry no threat of rain. She squeezes her bosom as hard as she can to empty each drop of milk into a jug for Lisa to let the children suck through a rag. She kisses Maja and Karl goodbye. Then she hurries away through the forest, down to the road. She takes the long way around the customs gate, crossing the sloping northern city outskirts. Soon she is back in the City-between-the-Bridges.

After a summer in the forest, the city is an assault on all her senses. She can't believe that this is the same place she has spent her life. Her stomach turns when the wind off the lake reminds her of the Flies' Meet and forces her to breathe through her mouth. People are everywhere, all is movement, chaos. The crowding in the alleys is great, and farmhands and paupers and gentlemen are always on the verge of coming to blows over keeping their shoes out of the gutters. Cattle are led forward, forcing the pedestrians even further to the side. In the crowd, clever hands find their way into pockets, purses are cut, sharp elbows are aimed at strangers' chests, walking sticks prick at unshielded shins, all to the accompaniment of colorful curses.

"Hey, watch where you're going!"

"Punch 'im in the face!"

"Dog's pizzle!"

"Scamp!"

"Stop, thief!"

When the bells strike the hour from three directions she has to cover her ears with her hands, and when she chooses a different path to escape the throng she is taken for what she is not. A youth in a striped coat, his hat cocked at a jaunty angle, catches her against a wall and clinks his purse as he blinks and whispers in her ear.

"Top of the morning, little sister. A few moments on your back behind the corner and your reward will be two shillings in the hand and a spoonful of pearl jam. I'm not picky, we can do it between the thighs if you insist."

She slips away and hurries on towards Polhem's Lock.

....

Anna Stina only knows the name of the street, but can't be sure which door is the right one. The building yields no clue, and when she feels how time is starting to run out she picks one at random. After several knocks, a woman opens. When she hears who is being sought, she looks Anna Stina up and down. Her eyes are hard.

"Word to the wise. I'd think twice before you get involved with the likes of 'im."

"If there was any other way, I would take it."

The woman nods. Something softens in the stern face, and she dips her head to gesture to the other side of the street.

"Then look for a door as black as the soul of its owner. But you should know that I've lived here many a year and rarely seen any cross that threshold of their own accord. Most are brought kicking and screaming."

Anna Stina curtsies in thanks to a door that is already closed. She quickly finds what she is looking for in the direction the woman indicated. A door is opened a crack to reveal a coarse-looking face.

"Well?"

"I am here to find Dülitz."

"Fuck off, little girl, before I come out to slap you."

"Tell him the widow of Kristofer Blix is here to see him."

....

The boy never described the room to her, nor the man behind the desk who now receives her without even bothering to lift his gaze from his papers. He carries life's first traces of old age but still radiates power. The hair has left the crown of his head and what remains around his temples and the back of the neck is trimmed short and tends towards gray. He is lavishly dressed without being gaudy, in a shirt and waistcoat, a piece of silk tied at his neck. A ruby pins his cravat, gleaming in the light of the candles as he gathers his papers into a pile and turns to her. His eyes are a light blue and betray no emotion.

"I had until this moment been under the impression that my business with the young Mr. Blix was at an end. The fact that you call yourself his widow hardly indicates the opposite."

She is reminded of the day when she was called before Elias Lysander on accusations of whoring. The scene is similar. Before her is a man with might on his side, a lackey waiting in the wings. But it is also different. This man frightens her far more, even though she has come of her own accord. She shakes her head.

"I don't come on Kristofer's behalf, but for my own sake."

Dülitz raises an eyebrow, an action that would have been invisible if the light on the table hadn't filled each line in his face with shadow, rendering his expressions grotesque and exaggerated.

"Kristofer told me what you do. You weigh a person's qualities and abilities and find a buyer for him. You gain power over your goods by acquiring their debts. I want the same thing for myself, but not through force of debt, but of free will and with a fee in return."

"Then look for work like everyone else."

"There is nothing to be had for the likes of me."

"All women have been granted gifts for which men are prepared to pay. You to a greater extent than many. All you have to do is stand at the corner, and you will soon see that an income comes staggering along of its own free will."

She meets his gaze.

"No."

He lets the silence last and lets her go on.

"I have no one left. Kristofer is dead, in part because of you. He left his clothes on the shore to tread onto day-old ice until it could no longer bear his weight."

Dülitz chuckles, a dry and crackling sound.

"You say that you know who I am and what I do. And still you come here with an appeal to my sympathy?"

"I would not have come if I didn't think I had something of value that you could sell."

He leans back and gives her a thoughtful look. She senses a glint of scorn that soon hardens into something malign.

"So show me."

Anna Stina takes a deep breath and advances until she is standing right in front of the desk. She steels herself for a moment, then locks her eyes with his and holds out her left hand until it is right above the flame of the candle. If this act surprises Dülitz, he masks it well. He follows her hand with his gaze, but the ice-blue eyes quickly return to a scrutiny of her face.

The pain doesn't set in gradually, as she had thought it would, but instantly, like grabbing the handle of a red-hot kettle. The scorching flame bites her hand and its teeth are terrible. The walls of the world collapse around her and shrink to a single trembling point where fire meets flesh.

She needs all her will to keep her eyes glued to Dülitz's indifferent face. She can't allow herself to look away. In her thoughts she searches for Karl and Maja, but not even there does she find purchase. The pain controls her completely and is converted into images in her head. She sees her skin bubble and blacken, the fat melt with a crackling sound, only finally to burst open. The fire burns a hole, and underneath, flesh and bone are laid bare, blackening. Her blood hisses while the fire greedily digs its way up. Time slows down. Only agony persists.

It takes a while before she becomes aware that something has happened, and when she returns to her senses, Dülitz has moved her arm from the heat of the flame. Her hand stings, but when she sees her palm she only finds a few blisters and an angry red hue.

"Point taken. There is no reason for you to damage your hand for good."

He turns to his servant.

"Ottoson, bring out a chair for Widow Blix and see that Ehrling comes with a balm for the wound."

....

As she sits down with her hand in a rag dipped in cold well water, he takes out a ledger and turns to a blank page.

"Name?"

"Anna Stina Blix."

"Tell me what you can do."

She does her best and realizes it isn't much. She thinks about everything she has gone through, tells her story, and wonders at how much a single year can age a person, but in the stream of memories she has trouble identifying any abilities of the kind that a man like Dülitz can turn to profit. She notices this in him as well, not from his unmoving face but from the notations his goose-quill pen makes on the paper; few and far between. There is not much to say about Anna Stina Blix, née Knapp. A body on its path to decay like all the others, no good for anything but renting out for a bedding while youth lingers. Finally he puts the pen down entirely, even though her hesitant words continue. When she has no more to say, he sits there, aloof and detached.

"Is that all?"

She doesn't know what to do other than nod. The covers of his ledger bang when he shuts them again. She knows that she will leave unsatisfied. She should have known better than to allow herself to be seduced by such a vain hope. She stands to leave, the shame over her own stupidity a yoke on her shoulders and the burning left hand an additional reminder of it.

"Do you know the inn at Fisherman's Rest? When you hear the bells of the city call to mass you will know it is Sunday. Should I want anything from you, I will send one of my men in the morning to tie a red ribbon at the corner of the house. If you go down to the shores of the bay you will see it from there. If you do, come back here again."

60

"I saw you this morning after you drank from your cup. What was it you were doing?"

Lisa stops short for a moment at Anna Stina's question.

"I was reading the leaves. I met a woman a long time ago who showed me how."

"And what did you see?"

She shrugs.

"A hard winter here in the north, one that I'll barely manage to avoid. A danger that awaits me in Tiveden."

"Won't you read the leaves again for me and my children?"

Lisa hesitates, then shrugs again and pushes the kettle onto the embers until the water that is left starts to simmer. She nods to Anna Stina.

"You have to prepare the drink yourself. Otherwise I can't see anything."

They exchange places. Lisa soothes the boy, who wakes when he senses his mother's absence, putting a hand on his chest. Anna Stina strews the dry strawberry leaves over the bottom of the mug and pours boiling water on them. She blows on the surface until the water cools, then slurps slowly until only the dregs remain on the bottom. Lisa stretches out her hand, Anna Stina hands her the vessel, and Lisa gets up and walks a few steps away with her back turned, while she reads what the leaves have to say. She takes her time before crouching to clean out the mug with a twig.

"Your children will grow up strong and healthy. You will be with them. You will be happy together."

"Why are you crying?"

"A gust of wind came through the trees and blew dust in my eye."

The wind is still under the treetops and the lie is much too simple.

"What did you see in the leaves?" Lisa Forlorn dries her cheeks and shakes her head.

"I saw what I just told you. It is mere jealousy for all the happiness that will be yours and not mine."

They sit by the fire far into the night before they go to bed. Lisa's hand finds hers across the calm breaths of the children, and thus, hand in hand, sleep comes to them.

61

Lisa Forlorn wakes when the night is darkest. Before sleeping, she drank far more water from the stream than she needed to, sip after sip just to fill her stomach enough to wake her before dawn. She could have spared herself the trouble, because she hasn't slept a wink, has simply lain still and tried to get her fill of listening to peaceful breaths. Silently she slips out from under the blanket, tucking it around Karl, who has been lying next to her and who now turns to find his way closer to his mother. Lisa hurries away between the trees and squats behind the overturned tree they have selected for this purpose. She shivers as cold air raises goose pimples on bare legs, happy when she can hitch her skirt around her waist again. Back at the fireside, all is in order, her possessions ready to be packed in her bundle, everything that jingles safely wrapped in a muffling cloth. She doesn't want to say goodbye. She isn't sure that she has the strength.

They first called her Forlorn to make her an object of ridicule, the ones who had taken pains to make sure she didn't make any friends, those who found a value of their own in the devaluing of others. At first it made her ashamed, but that was a long time ago. Their name for her she has made her own, but it came at a high cost. Even for one such as her it is hard to break bonds that have always existed. It may be that her stained cheek was never caressed, but even a slap may be preferable to being alone. But practice makes perfect. Old pain is forgotten now, all that hurt her before numb under a bandage of time passed. But this summer will be hard to forget. Much is left undone. She must start again, learn to live again without company, master the art of solitude once more.

She comforts herself with the thought that her departure is also for their sake. In Anna Stina's company, the temptation would have become too great to rely on their combined strength, to gull herself that they have the fortitude to wait out winter and receive summer as their prize as the season changed. She knows how it would have ended. One day one of them would have stepped through the snowy crust and caught her foot in some badger's den, broken their shin, and suddenly four mouths would have needed feeding by one. None would ever have escaped alive out of the Great Shade, and Lisa, who knows better than anyone what a winter in the wild means, would have borne the guilt. Her selfishness would have doomed them all.

She walks towards the meadow and gathers some of the toys that have been left on the graves. A cat made of knotted rags for Karl, for Maja a carved horse. For both of them, a stuffed ball, a wooden man with a rounded base. She returns with her arms full and places the gifts where the children will find them the moment they wake up.

She strokes her godchildren on the cheek before she leaves, and the kiss she places on Anna Stina's forehead makes her mumble something and turn anxiously in her sleep, groping with her arm until she senses the warmth from the hot stone that Lisa Forlorn has put in her own place. Only when Lisa is a mile or so away does she realize that she has forgotten to take leave of her son's grave, reminded that only fresh wounds will cover old scars.

62

Anna Stina can't view Lisa's departure as a betrayal; she is much too deep in her debt. It's not only the children who wake up to gifts: carefully lined up in a row are all of those objects that Lisa can do without, and without which Anna Stina would not be able to manage. When the last ember in the hearth goes out, she breaks up the ring of stones and sweeps earth over the black mark of the fire. When no trace remains of their camp, she carries her children to the burrow.

The branches of the forest trees still sometimes offer fruit, and the fish still bite. She gathers extra when she can, to build her store, but soon finds that there are others who want the hoard she accumulates. One morning Anna Stina finds a rat in the pile of apples she has built against the wall of the burrow. It steps clumsily among the fruit and makes a mess of her order, and hisses in rage at her when she hits at it with a branch. Anna Stina realizes that she can't keep her stores in the same place where she lets her children sleep. Maja and Karl are still ignorant of what lies ahead. They have never tasted need. Dread gnaws at her.

Amazed, she watches how their interactions increase day by day. More and more often they roll over onto their sides in order to look into each other's faces and find joy there. She leads and he follows. When Maja moves, Karl does the same. A wave becomes a clasp of hands and they grab each other. With cooing and babbling, they pose questions and give answers. Laughter and whining are shared alike. They can no longer be separated without wails, not even when she nurses them; she finds a position where she can accommodate both. She sings to them, songs whose words and melody have bided their time, dormant in her consciousness since the cradle was hers, and that now return to her of their own accord.

Every morning she listens for the bells, and when Sunday comes, she blocks the opening of the burrow with branches and rolls a heavy rock up the hill to secure them. Behind this, her little ones are safe from the fox. She hurries down to the shores of the bay, but no red ribbon flutters on the side of the inn.

....

The next day, for the first time since she arrived in the Great Shade, she hears the sound of a stranger's footfall. Heavy steps crunch over twigs and leaves on the ground, hands sweep branches aside, and curses abound when they spring back and give a slap in return. It is a man who is coming. What else? Loud and unabashed, he proceeds as if he were doing battle with the forest itself, as if it should have had the sense to see him for who he is and show him the respect that he deserves. His kind disgusts her. She wraps her hand around the handle of her pitiful little knife, the only tool she has to defend herself with, pleased that the fear she feels can so easily be converted into rage. Suddenly she knows who it is: Ehrling, Dülitz's man, whose curses are uttered in broad dialect. When she reveals herself, he rests his hands on his knees and wipes his shiny forehead with a sigh of relief. He pays no attention to the shiny little blade she grips between white knuckles.

"Thank the devil. Master wants you. It's urgent."

He refreshes himself from a flask before waving with his hand in the direction he believes to be the right one.

"He's waiting at the tollgate himself, there's not a minute to lose."

....

Dülitz is waiting for her in the hastily erected and ramshackle building that serves as a pub for those in need of a drink to fortify themselves on their way either in or out of the city. Over his fine clothing he wears a cloak, and on his head a hat that droops far down over his eyes. The room is almost empty, and when Ottoson gives the barkeeper a knowing look, he drives the remaining patrons away with the excuse that it is closing time.

"Mrs. Blix. It turns out that something in your unique possession has suddenly become a sought-after commodity."

He invites her to sit.

"I fancy that our affairs in the city do not reach you in your country estate?"

"No."

"Nor is there much you need to know. In a week's time, the twenty-third of this month, there will be a flogging in front of the Hall of Nobles. A scaffold has been built. A woman will be brought in, she will be tied to the whipping post, and then she will taste the lash. You are to go there and pay careful attention to that woman's face so you would be able to pick her out if you were to see her again. This is the conclusion of an affair that has occupied the entire realm for the past year and, with the exception of enterprising housebreakers and our most notorious drunkards, the entire city will be thronging the square. It will not be easy to get close enough to her to get a good look."

She nods.

"After the provost has completed his task, the offender will be led to a wagon, which will rattle off to the place where she will serve the remainder of her punishment, at least until our young monarch comes of age. This is a notable prisoner, intended for a gilded cage, and they are currently furnishing an old rectory for her to serve out her time in comfort. But the refurbishment is not yet ready, and until then she is being detained in temporary quarters. The moon is a waxing crescent now and on its way into the next quarter. On the twenty-fifth it will be a new moon and the sky will be as black as the grave. Do you know what they call it in the City-between-the-Bridges?"

Of course she does.

"The Night of Thieves."

"You will make your way to the rooms that have been prepared for her. You will give her this to read, and wait until she has composed a reply. You will take that reply with you, and present it to me."

Dülitz pushes an envelope across the table, secured with a shiny seal. Anna Stina can't hide her confusion.

"You said there was something that only I had and that someone needed. This assignment sounds like one that many others would be far better suited for."

Dülitz smiles faintly and shakes his head.

"Believe it or not, you are the only one who knows a secret way into the workhouse on the Scar. That is where they will be keeping her, in a suite hastily furnished for the occasion. You crawled through the foundation, through a hole in the cellar of the old building. You have to make your way back in the same way. And back out again, if you can't find a swifter route."

The memory comes back to her all too quickly. The rough embrace of the stone around her chest, her lungs empty and her next breath impossible. The tunnel that became Alma Gustafsdotter's lonely grave. The air leaves her as if the rock has already exerted its grip, greedy for another chance to catch the one who got away. Dülitz anticipates her answer.

"I understand your hesitation. If you fail, you are in the hands of the watchmen once more, and the nightmare from which you believed you had awakened starts all over again, possibly worse than before. I'll cut your anguish short, Anna Stina Knapp, because you don't have any choice. I'm sure you think badly of me, but let me assure you my employer in this matter is worse by far. This is a matter bigger than both you and I, and in order to pursue it they can justify the misfortune of many a young girl, in particular ones whose disappearance will prompt no query. These are people devoid of any scruple, as only those with higher purpose can be. I informed them that you might be difficult to convince, and was given the answer that if you wouldn't make your way into the workhouse of your own accord you will be brought there on a leash and left at the mercy of the watchmen."

She finds his words have the cruel ring of truth; it is a relief not to have to choose. She meets his gaze steadily, without betraying her feelings.

"The building is full of locked doors I can't get through."

The swift answer silences Dülitz for a moment, and only with a visible effort does he check himself. He takes a ring of keys from his pocket.

"This is a key ring of the kind that unscrupulous men like in order not to have to break their way in. The locks are old and of a familiar kind. Where one doesn't fit, another will."

He leans forward and steeples his fingers on the table as his expression changes to something more apprehensive. His earlier instructions were delivered in a harsh voice, and to her surprise, Anna Stina finds that the mood has changed and that he is now speaking to her as if they were equals.

"There is still the matter of agreeing on the price of your services."

"Two hundred. That was my dowry from Kristofer, money I used to improve the home from which I was thrown out and called an imposter."

He sinks back in the chair with a frown.

"You sell yourself cheaply. The employer I mentioned and for whom I speak would be willing to give you more. If you give me a tenth for my troubles, I will make sure that they pay you the highest sum possible."

In the end she shows the only power she still has, the only one she has ever known: the power to refuse. For each coin she rejects, she buys back her self-respect.

"No. That two hundred is what is owed me by the world. More than that and I will be the one who is in debt. I need no more."

He looks at her for a long time before he acquiesces to her decision.

"May good fortune be ever at your side."

63

Anna Stina feeds Maja and Karl until the milk inside them makes a clucking sound as she rocks their contented bodies to sleep. A hot stone, round and smooth and wrapped in the blanket, gives them warmth. She sets the burrow's cover of woven branches into place, testing their strength one by one, and strews the top with leaves to conceal the entrance. She studies the position of the sun. Three hours, four at most, then she has to be back. A final, anxious look at the opening that can no longer be distinguished from the rest of the hill, and then she hurries away towards the City-between-the-Bridges in the knowledge that every moment counts.

....

The crowds are already great on the bridges over the Stream, and as she tries to make her way over to the Knights' Isle she has reason to be thankful for her slender body, slipping easily between elbows and hips. From his stone plinth the bronze image of a king of old gazes out indifferently over the hustle and bustle. At the bridge, members of the Royal Dragoons are standing to attention alongside the guns that have been rolled into place to bar the flow of people. She passes by unnoticed. On the other side of the water, it is as if the ground has been raised and covered in human heads of all kinds. Not a cobblestone can be seen for the throng. As she turns around, she can see how street urchins have climbed onto the roofs to straddle the ridges for a better view. The square itself is packed to bursting, from those who have been pressed up against the church to those shoving each other in panic to avoid being pushed into the canal or over the railing of the bridge. From time to time, screams and splashes bear witness to the fact that not everyone succeeds, followed by laughter and hilarity from fishermen who have rowed over in their boats to save the drowning from their fate at the price of the contents of their pockets.

The alleys continue to empty people out into the crowd, so many of them that Anna Stina can't believe the city can accommodate them all. In the middle of the square, the scaffold looms over the masses. On the steps of its wooden structure, the provost waits, hooded. Beside the pillory also stands a gold-decorated officer with his hands behind his back. He looks out across the heads of the people as he restlessly shifts his weight from one foot to the other. Around the platform, the guardsmen stand in a group, each one carrying a long pole, soon to be collectively presented as a living fence to keep the crowd at bay.

The people are of a different kind than Anna Stina is used to, the atmosphere different to the public punishments she has witnessed before growing old enough to choose not to attend. It's not only the mercurial mob here, excited to forget their daily toil by satisfying a shared bloodlust. It's as if all of Stockholm has come out. High and low are both in attendance. Every window in the palace wings lining the square is packed with gentlefolk leaning out as far as they dare to catch a better view, and those who can't get in have arranged their carriages so as not to jostle with commoners. There are as many women as men.

An unrest spreads through the crowd, like water disturbed by a tossed pebble. The cart has been spotted, but the woman in black and brown that is seen at the gate of the courthouse eschews the transportation and strides out of the gate herself, walks down the stairs, and on towards the scaffold. The guardsmen link their poles to make a chain, pushing at the throng with all their might. A path is cleared sufficient for the condemned to walk across the square with an officer on each side, to the pillory.

Anna Stina begins to make her way forward, closer and closer, ducking under elbows and dancing past knees. She needs to reach the front to be able to see. The voices of the people murmur around her. A man in a handsome coat and embroidered waistcoat whispers theatrically to a companion, "Shall we have Paris in Stockholm now? The aristocracy sent to the scaffold for the amusement of the mob. Hell! Dark times indeed, my brother. I've never thought well of little Reuterholm, but not even I ever accused him of being a Jacobin."

A little while later she passes a fat man in stained clothing who prompts laughter from his peers by shouting at the prisoner.

"Malla! Malla Rudenschöld! When'll it be my turn? In all of Stockholm, it is only Duke Karl and me who haven't fucked you yet!"

A small group of women point the finger.

"Harlot!"

Another, a few rows closer, hears the exclamation and hisses in her companion's ear.

"Shh! If she had had the sense to be more of a whore she would have been free as a bird. Had it been me, I'd have spread my legs for the duke, closed my eyes, and pretended that it was Armfelt I was squeezing between my thighs."

Rumors are flying from lips all around Anna Stina. Someone claims that Baron Reuterholm demanded the death penalty but was forced to see reason at the last moment. In revenge, he has made sure that the rods with which Magdalena Rudenschöld will soon be flogged have been soaking in brine all night.

"Traitor! Serves you right for selling out your motherland!"

"Russian whore!"

"Now it's time to taste a different kind of rod!"

She makes her way closer. Like a ghost, she glides through the crowd until she stops an arm's length from the array of pikes. Any closer, and all she'll see is the sweaty face of an infantryman. Only a couple of feet away, Rudenschöld is led up to the scaffold.

As if a single entity, movement ripples through the crowd. It sways back and forth. Sudden pushes from one side force everyone to stagger forward and back in order to stay on their feet. Anna Stina finds herself leaning on a servant-girl her own age, brightly dressed, in open disobedience of the sumptuary law, in a dotted calico jacket with French sleeves and blue trim over a cotton skirt in red and white. When Anna Stina looks around she finds others like her, others who have realized that there is safety in numbers and that the watchmen on this day have better things to do than chastise the well-dressed. Their eyes meet as they are knocked together shoulder to shoulder. Anna Stina leans closer to make her voice heard above the din of the people.

"Who is she? What has she done?"

The young woman blinks at her in surprise, and giggles.

"What're you talking about? Have you been living under a rock?"

Before Anna Stina has time to answer, the young woman leans closer and cups her hands confidingly over Anna Stina's ear, happy to have found someone for whom the story has not been told to death.

"You know Armfelt? Old King Gustav's best friend, the most handsome man in the realm. Until last year, Malla Rudenschöld was the most celebrated lady at court, and both Duke Karl and Armfelt competed for her favor. Of course she chose Armfelt—who wouldn't? Well, Armfelt is exiled, trying to muster allies to put an end to the tyranny of Reuterholm. Now they say that Malla has been his confidante in Stockholm, and that she has done everything she can to further his cause."

The girl cranes her neck to get a better view of Rudenschöld's labored way up the stairs.

"You know, when Reuterholm's men broke into Armfelt's estate, they found more than a thousand of Malla's love letters in a rosewood chest bound with red velvet. A thousand! Can you believe it? And he saved them all, to read them over and over. Some of the best ones have been printed as broadsheets. Isn't it romantic?"

The young woman's look of anticipation changes into open disappointment when Magdalena Rudenschöld can finally be seen in her entirety on the platform.

"I thought she'd be more beautiful. To think that Armfelt would fall for someone like that."

The young woman hushes Anna Stina even though she is the only one speaking.

"They're starting."

....

Anna Stina has never seen anything like it. In her experience, the kind of people who gather around the scaffold are of one mind, all spite and excitement. The mood on this square is different; a hesitation, an ambivalence. A young officer with a weak chin and receding hairline can barely conceal his emotion as he leads Malla Rudenschöld up to the pillory to leave her in the charge of the provost. The latter hesitates as he approaches her with a chain and neck iron to fetter her to the pillory, and when she shrinks from his touch, he stops altogether. Instead of locking the iron around her neck, he stands confused. No one comes to his aid. Maybe he had been expecting the applause of the audience at this moment. Finally he takes a step back and leaves his prisoner unbound. Everything stands still. The silence is unbroken. Sweltering, like the calm before a storm.

Magdalena Rudenschöld stands there in brown clothes and a black coat, a garb completely different from the kind she has worn for balls and at court. Her hair is blond, cut short and combed to hang down on either side. Her skin is pale from the months spent in confinement. For close to half an hour, she just stands there, mostly with her eyes downcast, but sometimes looking out at the crowd of thousands. Twice she is given a drink of water. No one touches her, there are no whipping rods to be seen. Finally she sways, her legs can no longer bear her weight, and she sinks down on the planks without a sound. The nearest officers hurry over, fan her face, and lead her back to the wagon she had refused before. It trundles off, accompanied by the curses with which the driver and the city guardsmen try to force people to step aside. The crowd draws Anna Stina with it, and she has no other choice but to follow it slowly towards the Lock. In the distance, she can see a flock of guttersnipes and chimney sweeps' apprentices running out into the street in front of the wagon and beginning to march as if on parade: one a drum major with a broom held high, the others hung with wood shavings for decoration. The policemen who are following the procession turn a blind eye. Slightly behind Anna Stina, a man who has been watching the same events over the shoulder of a friend, leans forward.

"Doesn't Reuterholm understand how clear it is that he has bribed both the police and the beggar children from the state's coffers? If the man had had an ounce of sense he could have staged a more believable performance."

His friend spits in the gutter.

"I don't know about you, but as a subject of the realm, I have a hard time taking it as a compliment that the highest man in the land is an imbecile."

"God help this poor bloody country."

64

Anna Stina quickly hurries on to attend to her second piece of business in the City-between-the-Bridges. He's no longer resident in the neighborhood where Anna Stina first tries to find him, but more than one knows where he's moved. Mickel Cardell is the kind of man that draws attention, and he has been seen not far away, around the Pandora quarter at Tailor's Alley. Once there, people know exactly where to look. A girl in the yard is herding geese with a stick and points her to the right entrance. She can hear his heavy footsteps across the floor when he comes to answer her knock.

The door opens, light spills out into the stairwell. The light behind him at first means she can only see a dark outline against the illuminated room. At first nothing, but when he recognizes her, he hears a quick intake of breath.

"My God, what has happened to you—what is the matter?"

Now she can see him too, and her own surprise is no less. It's less than a year since last they laid eyes on each other, but he has been badly marked in the time that has passed. The eyes that were mournful before carry greater sorrows now, the back more bowed under unseen burdens, his face prematurely gray, his hair is a tousled mess. She looks down rather than let him catch his reflection in her eyes.

"I need your help, Mickel. There is no one else."

He steps aside and lets her in with a mumbled apology over the state of the room. She needn't tell him much. What can she say that he can't read with a look? Cardell seems to appreciate not having to offer his confidences in exchange. He anticipates her before she has time to explain why she has come.

"If it's money you need, you're welcome to share what I have, but I'm afraid it isn't much. If you give me time, I may be able to find some more. If it's a roof over your head, then take my bed as long as you need. A blanket on the floor is enough for me."

She shakes her head, ashamed that Lisa Forlorn's warning returns to her and makes her ask herself how virtuous a man's motives can be behind such an offer.

"I don't need anything like that."

"What then?"

"The moon is waning with each night, and the day after tomorrow it will be dark. That is the night I need your help. From the tollgate by the Great Shade, you will see a large oak a little way down the road, one that towers above its neighbors. Will you meet me there in the afternoon, as the clock strikes three?"

"What do you want me to do?"

"I have an errand, one that will take longer than I dare leave my little ones. Someone has to watch them until I return."

Cardell opens his mouth and closes it again. His eyes blink in astonishment. His face appears to gain more furrows.

"I don't have much practice as a babysitter. Can't you take my other arm instead?"

"All they need is for you to be there."

"There are two of them? What if they start screaming?"

"Sing to them, or tell them a story. Comfort them as best you can, or let them cry themselves tired. The only thing I ask is that you keep the fox at bay."

He gives her a gruff nod and follows her to the door. She can sense the words concealed by his silence. She isn't sure she wants to hear them, and quickens her step. And yet they come, when she is halfway out the door.

"Your well-being was a comfort to me, when last we met. Of all that happened to me last year, you were the only one who gave me hope, and the gods know I need it now more than ever. I promise you that fox will be sorry if he appears."

She doesn't want to turn and meet his gaze in the way his words deserve, and so doesn't show the blush of shame sweeping over her face for that very reason. She can do no other. A feeling eats away at her; she has asked for his help already, but the less she partakes of his goodwill, the fewer terms he'll set.

65

Dawn drives away the rain of the early hours, and by midday the sky is a pale blue. Anna Stina walks to the tollgate in good time, and from the edge of the forest she hears the steeple at Johannes sound the third quarter of the hour. Cardell is already there, restlessly circling the trunk of the oak. They look sprung from the same carpenter's bench, coarse, rough, and heavy, but she notices that Cardell's jacket has been brushed clean, that his shoes have been greased and rubbed to a sheen, that his cheeks are shaven. He sees her come and nods curtly, and she waves him over onto the forest path that she alone now knows. At the burrow, she shows him everything he needs—where there is water for cleaning and where there are fresh rags to change them, the carved horse, and the rag doll cat, where to find the pile of branches outside from which to feed the fire. She dips a cloth in milk and lets Maja have a taste, but she cries inconsolably knowing that her mother has more to offer.

"You'll do better than me. From you, she won't expect anything else."

Cardell nods. She gathers what little she needs—the letter, the keys—and kisses Maja and Karl goodbye.

"If all goes well, I will be back at dawn, or mid-morning at the latest."

Both the little ones watch gravely as their mother turns her back. They examine their new guardian with concern. Cardell stares at them, and puts his arms, one of wood, the other flesh, on his hips.

"At Viborg I rowed past the promontory under fire from fifty Russian frigates. I can handle you, wee ones. Courage, damn it!"

Their wails rise almost as soon as Anna Stina begins hurrying away between the trees, and she hears Cardell mutter grimly to himself.

"The day will be hard."

She increases her speed until the heartrending sound of her children's tears can no longer affect her decisiveness. Down the slope, out of the forest. After a while she sees the light flash in stained windowpanes, and the reek of the Bog assaults her nose. She has a long way to go still, and the quicker her pace, the better. Through the Northern Isle, past Cat's Bay, and on over the bridges to the city.

66

She pauses at the drawbridge of the Lock and picks a place. Anna Stina has to wait for twilight, and she would rather do that here where the crowds are greater and she has a smaller risk of running into someone who knows her of old. She pulls her shawl down over her face and finds herself a spot near the mill houses where she can see the clock face of Saint Gertrud high up in her tower.

The Night of Thieves is coming, darkest of the month, and it promises to be the worst in a long time, because the city is still brimming with people from the countryside who have traveled in to witness the public flogging. Outside each pub door, the line curls far down the block. Many a proprietor has found the promise of a quick profit irresistible enough to break the rules and open for business early. In her hiding place behind a barrel, Anna Stina curls together more tightly as the noise from the alleys worsens. Booming male voices echo as if in competition, slurred with strong spirits. Some are singing, others are merry, and yet others wild with rage. Darkness falls, and no sooner has a lantern been lit before some young men stand on each other's shoulders to blow out the flame again: an old tradition.

During the Night of Thieves, light is banished from the city, and everyone unable to defend themselves fair game. In narrow passageways, where pickpockets have lain in wait, the shrill, mocking laughter of the perpetrator mingles with the victim's indignant howl. Fights break out for the sake of honor or enjoyment, with the sound of panting breaths, fists on flesh, and fast feet that scrape across the cobblestones seeking some fatal advantage. Somewhere a woman cries for help, likely a young woman from the country who has made the mistake of wandering into a dark alley where

someone waiting can now have their way without risk. If she had had her
wits about her, she would have done as the daughters of the city have all
been taught: better to pose as a prostitute under the protection of some
pimp or madam from the brothels on Bagge's Row so you at least gain a
few coins for your trouble. The city watch hear, but shrug their shoulders,
themselves drunk and indifferent to the scenes fitfully thrown into shadow
by the glow of their clay pipes. It is the Night of Thieves, and those who
are foolish enough to seek its pleasures have to play by its rules, with only
themselves to blame. Madness rules Stockholm; to resist it would be futile.

....

The church tower slowly merges into the darkening background. The
bell strikes eight, and she begins to walk down the road towards her destination. Across the Lock, and then she is back in Maria parish, her childhood neighborhood. No one has missed her. Everything is as it was. The
night may have dulled the yellow stone houses, but their storeys are des-
perately many and the families squeeze together by the hundreds under
the tiled roofs. The wings of the mills do what they can to harness the
evening breeze and sweep lazily through the air up on the hill. Somewhere behind them roils the quagmire of Larder Lake. The working day
is at an end, the last of the pig iron clatters by the scales, and sailors who
have begun the evening's debauchery before finishing the unloading of
their wares argue as overturning barrels threaten life and limb. The trun-
cated tower of Maria church cleaves the starry night. She has no time to
linger here, hurrying along Horn's Street.

Only when she meets the hillock that marks the end of the road does
her rising panic make itself known. The gradient forces her to curve, and
she knows where this slope leads. Below it is the Bridge of Sighs, spanning
the narrow strait, and beyond is the workhouse itself, unmoved by her
fate, patiently awaiting her return, eager for another chance to bar each
exit behind her. The watchmen pass by here often, and she will have to
take care. There is no one down by the shores. The lake water flows by
languidly. The bell from Maria strikes a farewell to evening. The water
lies black, as does the bridge. She hears no one, sees no one, wondering if
it would be best to run or walk, and decides on the latter. Under her feet,

the creaking of the boards sounds like the booming of great guns. In a pond under the bridge, a trapped fish splashes its tail and makes her jump. Then she is on the other side, and sets foot for the first time in a year on the barren soil of the Scar. Somewhere in front of her lies the inspector's villa, from which forgotten arias will no longer be sung in a cracked voice echoing across the water, for Hans Björkman left his position last year, followed in turn by Pastor Neander, each one in his own season. She takes the left-hand path into the overgrown vegetable garden, and finds a place among the blackcurrants to await the far side of midnight, with a heart beating so loud she is sure it will reveal her hiding place to any passerby.

Few enter her line of sight. Weary hooves drag a wagon along the road, causing the planks of the bridge to creak. Two men, side by side, watchmen surely, saunter back to their quarters after the city's enjoyments. She leaves her hiding place and starts to creep closer, bent double. Soon it is close, towering above, its outline bloated and shapeless. The workhouse. The wings hug the bloodstained well of the yard, around which Petter Pettersson and Master Erik request the pleasure of the prisoners' last dance. Only a window or two are illuminated in the manor house at the back.

Soon she is close enough to stretch out her hand and touch its wall. Plastered stone, stained a bright saffron-yellow by the sun, now as black as everything else. Anna Stina makes an attempt to feel the malice from the house through her palm, some kind of muted pulse that throbs in its very foundations, but there is nothing. What evil there is, is the work of men, surrounded by dumb, dead stone that has perhaps seen worse and will see worse again, but lacks language to bear witness. From inside, nothing can be heard.

Anna Stina's memories of the night when she last saw the walls of the workhouse are blurred. She remembers the sight of stars as she crawled the last inches through the tunnel, but that gives her no clue as to where the opening is. She remembers the breeze off the water, one that swept over her, fresh and cool, and took away some of the unease that had followed her out. The side that faces the bay, is her guess. She feels her way around the corner and starts crawling along the foundation with one hand on the stone, searching for a gap. She senses it already from a distance and when she gets closer sees a sliver of black on black. A musty smell hovers around the hole. She lets her fingers trace the edges and the hairs stand up on her neck when she realizes how small it is. The gate to some miniature hell. Not large enough for Alma Gustafsdotter, who found her grave in its midst. But large enough, once, for her to win her own freedom.

The night is warmer than it has been for days, and for this small mercy she is grateful as she removes all her clothes. Naked, she gathers them into a bundle, takes a strap of the skirt and ties it around her foot to drag it behind her. She hides her shoes in a tuft of grass and does as she did last time: lies down on her back with her arms over her head.

Heels and shoulders, the back of the head, and backside all become the feet of a human worm that slithers along under the earth, an inch at a time. She feels the stony embrace of rough darkness around her entire body, ever tighter the further in she goes. It will get worse, she knows. At a snail's pace, she labors forward to the passage that cost Alma her life, the center of the foundations where the stone above has slipped out of position and subsided. She hits her head against it when it comes, lies still for a moment to gather her courage for the final exertion that will either press her past this point or allow the stone to suffocate her with a grip she will never escape. She turns her head to the side so far her neck hurts, pushes with all her might, exhales the last bit of air from her lungs. Then she comes to a stop, the stone at chest level, the tunnel the full width of her body. She tries to draw a breath but there is hardly any room, and in the darkness, stars and colors dance in her sight. In a panic, she starts to squirm to and fro, harder and harder in a last vain rage against death. Last time, the stone was smeared with the lubricant of Alma Gustafsdotter's decayed corpse, but it is rough and unyielding now, long since licked clean by rats and vermin. And now, to her horror, Anna Stina realizes that her body, gaunt as it is, is not the same as it was last year. She has grown, and is too large now to make her way either forward or back.

67

A rat comes from inside the cellar, drawn by her sound and smell, and she screams when she feels its nose at the tips of her fingers. Her yell is enough to scare it off, but she knows that the respite is temporary. She is warm and fresh, quite different from the salt, hard meat, and rotten turnips in the cellar barrels. Soon the rat will return, at first alone in its greed but soon enough with others that have sniffed out its secret. The hands she has stretched out in the hole are her only defense: if she lets even a single one of them get past, her face will be at the mercy of teeth and claws.

Outside, time may pass, but under the earth, it stands frozen. All she can do is to try to control her breathing. Her skin goes numb where the stone holds its grip and where the ground is sharp. Now the rat is heading back on soft paws that nonetheless echo in the black silence of the tunnel. Closer and closer. She hits at it with her hand and scares it off again, alone once more.

Crying hurts too much. Each time her body shakes in a sob she awakens pain all around her, edges and protrusions finding new purchase on her body. She lies still, awaiting the end that appears as distant as it does inevitable. She wonders how long death intends to wait before it shows her clemency. Perhaps she can help it on its way, let a rat find its way in, squeeze its hairy body between jaw and shoulder and keep it there until its teeth finds her throat.

Paws in the distance, scrabbling and turning.

....

Reality is not what it was. Everything is black and devoid of meaning; if she lies still enough she no longer perceives any limits at all, no sense of where her flesh ends and the stone begins. She blinks to see if her eyes are open or closed. Colors emerge out of the darkness. She sees green, like the leaves in summer, silver gray, like a winding stream over shiny stones, and brown, like the forest floor through which it has carved its path.

Maja has a little boat made of bark. She leans over a bubbling brook with a body that no longer belongs to a child but a young girl. Her legs have grown long, her knees stick out all the way to her ears when she crouches. Karl stands behind her, waiting, a little shorter and with doubt in his eyes. "Mother has told us to stay away from the water." Maja snorts at him over her shoulder, shrugging a plait out of her face in order to better launch her vessel with the current. "Don't be a baby. If we're to drown here we'd have to lie down on our faces." She resembles her grandmother. Karl's blue eyes have the same hue as her own. Then Maja lets go of the boat. It rocks from side to side before it balances, the twig keel setting it straight as the current takes hold. Laughing, they both set off barefoot across roots and stones to follow it downstream, Maja first and Karl at her heels. When Anna Stina hurries to follow them, she wonders if this is the same future that Lisa Forlorn saw in her tea leaves.

....

The sight is snatched away as a finger suddenly burns. The rat has drawn blood, and where the lower teeth have slipped on the nail, the sharp upper teeth have cut into the top of the finger. She screams and jerks her hand, managing to clench her fist around the front feet of the rat. It gives a piercing shriek and wriggles free, away now, but with the memory of her taste on its tongue.

Anna Stina tries to conjure up the images again, but in vain. All she sees are two defenseless infants left with one who is barely able to care for them for a single day. What she left for them to eat is likely gone already. Far away, her children are crying. A sob she can't contain causes the stone to bite her sides.

Something is happening, something strange. Suddenly she is warm, and when she feels the walls again their grip is not the same. Rivulets of liquid are spilling over her. She doesn't understand, but her heels dig deep and she gropes along the rough walls for purchase, empties her lungs of air, and presses forward. She suddenly inches forward, which allows her to take a deeper breath. Then another, and another, and when she picks up the smell she knows what it is that has saved her. Mother's milk has started streaming out of the neglected bosom pressed against the rock, and this is what has allowed her to escape its jaws.

68

Where the tunnel ends, one darkness turns into another, just as familiar and just as foul. Here is where they must have found what remained of Alma Gustafsdotter after Anna Stina shifted her remains, and the unnamed body which probably allowed them to account for her own disappearance, but the watchmen have done no more than they had to. The endless night in the cellar is full of sour odors from long-neglected barrels, from sacks whose cloth has ripped and granted access to the unseen vermin of the earth. Her feet bump into all manner of objects strewn across the floor. Small insect legs crawl across her bare skin, interrupted in their feast, and flies startled into the air bounce against her face and arms. Other recollections of this place, long repressed, invade her senses. She can't linger, but hurries in the direction where she knows the stairwell is and waits for a few moments, her ear to the door. It is quiet. The workhouse is sleeping.

The stairs take her up to the ground floor of the old manor. The rooms are dark. Not even from above, from the watchmen's chambers, can anything other than a chorus of snores be heard. On the right hand there is a door, locked. She lies down to peek under it, and can neither see nor hear anything. She has wound the keys in cloth so that their clinking does not betray her, and the third one she tries turns the lock with some effort. Dülitz was right. The locks are old, uncomplicated. Beyond is a messy office where worn ledgers lean heavily against each other, their bindings askew. The air is dry, as is often the case where papers are kept, and it smells of dust. Another door, a new key, behind it the next stairwell, and on the other side of the hall are the rooms Dülitz mentioned as the new prisoner's temporary residence. Neander's old offices. As she fits the keys into the lock, she encounters resistance for the first time, then realizes that the door is already unlocked. She lets it glide open. The crack throws light onto the stone floor. Someone is awake.

She is sitting in a nightgown with her back to the door, staring into a gilded mirror as she combs her hair. It is her, the one from the scaffold. She turns her head back and forth with the air of an expert, perhaps searching for the remains of a beauty that a year in prison has robbed her of, stretching her neck to smooth the lines there. Anna Stina doesn't know how best to break the silence but loses the initiative as their eyes meet in the mirror.

"Why are you disturbing me? Don't you know what time it is?"

Magdalena Rudenschöld turns and fixes Anna Stina with a look of consternation.

"What is this? They lie to my face. The chief of police himself swore on his mother's grave that I would never have to mix with any of the prisoners. Isn't it bad enough that they have placed me among whores and loose women only to humiliate me? Have you come to steal, my girl, or simply to brag to your miserable friends that you have met Malla Rudenschöld?"

Anna Stina gropes around in the folds of her skirt for the letter.

"I have been sent with a message."

Magdalena Rudenschöld stands suddenly and snatches the paper out of her outstretched hand. Gingerly she slits its side with a nail and reads greedily, before holding the page against the flame of the candle and tossing it into the fireplace. She reveals her teeth in a spiteful smile, returning to the table and removing the lid of an inkwell. The quill dances over the page and a few mumbled words escape as she writes her reply. The view over Rudenschöld's curved shoulder allows her to divine its contents: names, written one after the other in a long list.

"Retribution is still within reach, my sweet Gustaf. When we have retaken all that is ours, we shall give them what they deserve, and we shall drown out their pleas for mercy with the kisses of our reunion. As a queen, I shall be beloved of all."

Once she has laid down her pen, she folds the corners of her note and drops wax over the flap.

"Take this now and carry it back quickly, do you hear? It won't do to stop at the pub, however great your thirst."

Anna Stina lets her gaze sweep over the windows in the hope of finding a way out, but each of them is barred. Magdalena Rudenschöld raises her chin impatiently until a thought lifts the corners of her mouth.

"Of course. You want *un souvenir*. You are far from the only one. They have sold all my possessions and those that are on my side bought them for a fortune, to wear my old jewels openly as a sign of loyalty. Well, my little rag doll, if we had met under different circumstances I would willingly have signed a piece of paper for you to show your friends, but that would imperil our secret."

She looks around and lights up as her eyes land on the dressing table. Turning towards Anna Stina, she raises a conspiratorial finger, rises, and lifts up a distinctively cut bottle, holding it up so that its many facets catch the light, and waves Anna Stina close with a gesture: Rudenschöld shows her how to hold her arm, lifts the crystal stopper, and splashes an oily liquid over her skin with practiced ease.

"If you put your hand under their noses, no one will doubt where you have been. The duchess herself sent me this bottle, all the way from Paris, where the perfumeries have been forced into bankruptcy and each drop that remains commands a king's ransom. Can you smell it? Lavender, cassia, bergamot, and, underneath, the finest ambergris. We call it honey water. This scent drove my Gustaf crazy."

She takes Anna Stina's confusion for mute admiration and hurries her to the door with an indulgent smile befitting a future queen. This time she locks the door once it is shut.

69

Once she has crept back to the cellar door, Anna Stina realizes her mistake. She has allowed it to swing shut behind her and she sees now that its lock is of a different kind. The others may be old and worn, but this one is new, its shiny metal still free of the ugly scratches a drunkard makes when trying to fit a key to a lock. She curses herself for her inattention. Even if Björkman and his watchmen had never found the drainage hole through the foundations of the building, they would know that something in the cellar wasn't right. Two girls had disappeared that way. A new lock on the door and a stricter circulation of its key would have neutralized that problem.

Now the mousetrap has closed around her. The keys Dülitz gave her won't even fit the hole. With her back to the wall, she sinks down on her heels to think. Her eyes are drawn to the stairs that wind upwards, where the rumble of the watchmen's sleep echoes in the stairwell. She takes one step at a time, listening carefully on every landing.

The watchmen's dormitory both sounds and smells like a pigsty. She counts eight narrow beds, of which five are occupied. Their snores are such as to make even the windowpanes rattle. On a table there are empty glasses and bottles. The air is thick with sweat, sour wine, and flatulence. As she takes a step across the threshold, the one closest to her sits up in his bed, his back as straight as a pitchfork, and stares at her.

"Fuck off, Nyblom, it's my night off. Get someone else to take over your shift."

Just as suddenly, he falls back onto his straw mattress, into a sleep as deep as before, and leaves her standing with her heart in her mouth. As she creeps closer, a few more muttered words come from the same bed.

"Hey, Nyblom? You look like shit."

She goes from bed to bed and stares down at the pillows. Often she only sees a mop of hair and has to wait until the head moves or tiptoe to the other side in order to see it. At the far end she finds the face she last saw in the glow of a clay pipe on the stairs of the cellar that she is now unable to access. Jonatan Löf, the father of her children. He lies with his mouth open, panting in the stale air of this room heated by so many bodies, a strand of drool at the corner of his mouth. She searches his face for some likeness to her children. Yes, he has passed his features to Karl. That much is clear. She leaves the room.

....

Morning is approaching, but not so quickly that she doesn't have time to consider her options. She sees only one, and that is to mingle with the rest of the female prisoners. In the morning there is an assembly in the courtyard for roll call. Anyone missing will be discovered, but no one expects to find one girl too many. Likely as not, no one will notice. Of those who are considered trustworthy and who have so little time left to serve that they will soon be given their freedom, there is always one group sent outside to work in the garden, or even to go to the city for firewood and other necessities. If she can join them and be let outside the door, she will be able to avoid discovery.

From out in the yard she can follow the light of a lantern at a slow pace past the leaded windows of the building, and when the night watchman is at a safe distance, she dashes across the stones to the section of the workhouse where she once slept. She unlocks it, slips in, and finds a place next to the wall, hidden from view from the door by the spinning wheels that have been gathered in the middle of the room. As she waits, she drops off into restless slumber.

....

When the morning bell tolls the day's beginning, the routine is familiar. She is on her feet as if no time has passed since her own days in the workhouse. While the women make up the beds, she walks to and fro between them and tries to appear as busy as they are. No one has time to pay her any attention. After a few minutes, the key is turned in the lock, the door opens, and a gruff voice orders them out to the courtyard for roll call. A subdued row of women hurries out, and she is right in the middle.

It takes a while for them to arrange themselves. The watchmen are irritated. Now she sees men of a different kind to the ones she remembers from last year, and it takes her a while to realize that they are in fact the same, that it is her own perception that has changed. Once she only felt fear. Now she sees a motley crew of a kind she would never have allowed to cross the threshold of the Scapegrace, human wrecks marked by the war, one with a lame foot, the other half-blind, in uniforms so worn and ill-fitting that they look like caricatures of soldiers. Each of them stinks of alcohol and tobacco. The only ones who aren't hungover are those who have already had time to have a few over breakfast, swaying as they stand. With a great deal of effort, they force the women into formation, in dormitory order, and begin calling out names. Misunderstandings and mispronunciations slow the process, and in the confusion Anna Stina makes her way to the group of women who have already gathered to pick up baskets for gardening, those who are given some breakfast bread out in the meadows. Several of them look her up and down with restrained surprise, more than one lets her gaze linger at her bare feet, but in the prison everyone learns to mind their own business, and each look soon gives way to indifference.

A watchman stands in front of them, ready to show them out, the large gate key spinning around his finger, while the rest are led away to eat. One of them lingers: an old woman, her face in ruins, limbs so thin and crooked that she looks like a squashed spider. She stays in her spot and stares at Anna Stina, blinking slowly. When one of the watchmen shouts at her to hurry up, she holds out a crooked finger and points.

"That one. She shouldn't be here."

When the watchman grabs the woman by the ear and twists it to force her to follow along, she holds her ground. Unused to resistance, the watchman is unsure of what to do next. From a deep-seated instinct for self-preservation, the other women back away from the one who has been pointed out. The outstretched finger jabs at the air.

"Her! She shouldn't be here!"

The small group is starting to attract attention. More watchmen walk over to curse their colleague and ask about the reason for the delay. The old woman raises her voice to a howl.

"That's Anna Stina Knapp. She's the girl who disappeared. She's back, I don't know how."

At least one of them finds the name familiar.

"They didn't take in any new prisoners late last night, did they?"

There are shrugs in response. The man who spoke rubs an unshaven chin and spits tobacco into the gravel.

"Get Pettersson."

"Wake that devil at this hour? Get him yourself."

Under mumbled protest, the youngest of them is dispatched. In the silence, the old woman makes her voice as ingratiating as she can when she addresses the watchman who has taken command.

"Surely I deserve something small as a reward?"

He shoots her a look of undisguised contempt.

"You've had it already."

She shakes her head, puzzled, and the watchman holds his fist in front of her nose.

"Your reward is that I didn't punch you in the mouth the same moment you started yammering without having been asked to."

One among them laughs more heartily than the others.

"Don't you know who she is, Söderhjelm? You must be the only one. We call her Ersson-on-her-Knees. She hasn't spun any yarn since Pettersson invited her to dance on the same day she arrived. Instead she has to support herself with the only means she still has at her disposal. The funny thing is you would have done her a favor by hitting her. If you'd knocked out those buck teeth she might have been able to raise her fee from a crumb to a crust."

Söderhjelm smiles mirthlessly.

"I'll leave that to you whoremongers. You know as well as everyone else that I stopped a bullet with my groin in the war, and I can't say I've ever been as happy about that as the moment I laid eyes on Ersson here."

There is a great deal of merriment, and Anna Stina draws a breath, doubting what her eyes are telling her. The person standing there is the Dragon, Karin Ersson, the woman who betrayed her, the same age as she is, transported here on the same wagon last year. The last of her hair that hasn't been ripped from her skull is lanky and gray-white, her skin a grid of wrinkles and scars, her body so thin that the skin sags over her bones. As if she was in on the joke and not its butt, she gives Anna Stina a malicious grin.

"Anna Stina Knapp."

It is Petter Pettersson who is speaking, and Anna Stina knows she is lost.

70

S he stands by the well and slowly backs up until she feels its mortar on her back. She glances down: she has seen many a newcomer creep close to the edge in the hope of escape that way, as the thought dawns in them that half a minute spent on their heads at the bottom of a watery grave seems a better future than disconsolate years of famine at the spinning wheel. Without exception, their expressions of terrified anticipation change to relieved disappointment. Inside, there is a net of heavy ropes rigged low and out of reach, allowing the pipes of the pump to pass by, but sufficient to dissuade thoughts of suicide. Pettersson closes the distance between them, and before she has time to think further, his hand is around her neck and his small bloodshot eyes are right in her face. His breathing is heavy, and in his eyes she sees something that approaches devotion, and that frightens her more than anger or desire could ever have done. The fingers that meet around her neck do not squeeze, the grip instead feeling more like a confirmation of what his eyes are telling him. He is trembling. Then he lets go, blinks a couple of times, and issues an order to his subordinates in a harsh whisper.

"Put her in solitary. I'll see to her myself once the morning duties are done."

Two men grab her by the arms and lead her away, accompanied by the mumbling of the prisoners. Assured hands search her, and Rudenschöld's letter and Dülitz's keys are both soon confiscated. A brusque shove, and then she is alone again.

The tiny space lacks windows. The floor is not large enough to fully stretch out in. It is intended in equal measure for confinement and punishment. They drag hysterics here until their rage has subsided in futile violence against the stone walls, or allow those who need a reminder about the prison rules to spend an uncomfortable night until hunger and fear have underscored the advantages of obedience. The walls are marked by previous occupants, the floor saturated with a sharp stench of urine, since there is no chamber pot and each guest only has the four corners to choose from. A broken fingernail is wedged between two stones. Pettersson takes his time. Anna Stina can't tell exactly, but it must be afternoon already.

....

Down in the prison yard, Petter Pettersson feels his large chest brimming with excitement. His good mood makes him benevolent this day. The slaps he delivers for various transgressions are halfhearted; sometimes he makes do with the threat alone. All seems well in the best of all worlds. Inspector Björkman has been gone since last year, exchanging positions with the county clerk in Savolax, one Bengt Krook. Rumors of Björkman's diligence have already circulated around the Baltic; he never set foot in his posting, instead contracting out his duties and now raising his salary to reward his idleness. Krook is a man of the same kind, who leaves the daily routine to the guards in order to be able to enjoy his new life in the capital, with constant visits to the cavalry master in Årsta. As for Pettersson, he has not held back this past year. No time has been wasted in making all of the changes he has found suitable. With Master Erik in his power, he can invite the women to dance with him as often as he likes, and has no need to invent reasons to justify the punishment.

The girl from last year, the one who got away, has eaten away at him, even before Cardell, Watchman Number Twenty-Four, came by with his strange inquiry to remind him. Anna Stina Knapp. In his dreams he has seen her furtive looks, her quiet plotting. She pretended to be like the others, cowed and docile, but he saw through the charade. He had marked her out for the next dance, played out each step in his head. He had even waited longer than strictly necessary, as he has found that a self-imposed patience yields twice the results once the dance is under way. Then she was gone, from one night to the next, and left him with a gnawing desire that no one else could satisfy. The circumstances forced him to play along and pretend to acknowledge that the corpse in the cellar, which anyone could see had been there for at least a year, was that of the girl Anna Stina, all to protect Björkman from accusations of neglect.

Now she is back. And how he has longed for this. He lets her wait, safely in his power at last, behind lock and key. He delegates his tasks to a subordinate, and instead goes to the bathhouse to wash. He wants everything to be perfect. He lathers himself up from head to toe, washing the dirt from his hair and doing the rounds with a lice comb. Once he is clean, he wrinkles his nose at the smell of his uniform and selects a fresh shirt. Only when everything is in order does he fetch the key to the cell.

....

The sight that meets Petter Pettersson when he makes his way to the one in solitary is always the same. The girls in that cell always do everything in their power to get away from the door. In vain, they make themselves as small as they can, crouching with their faces towards the wall in one of the piss-drenched corners, like so many mussels that yield their meat to a quick kick in the small of the back. But not this one, and he inwardly rejoices at how she presents herself. Anna Stina Knapp is different. Why else would he lust for her above all others? Now she stands in the middle of the floor as if it were the most natural thing in the world, meeting his gaze as if they were equals, causing him to pause at the threshold. She takes the opportunity to speak first.

"I have a deal to offer you."

It takes Pettersson a few moments to collect himself enough to reply. He throws out his hand.

"As this meeting room surely indicates, your opportunities to negotiate are somewhat limited."

He is irritated by how his voice sounds. Like a boy recently come of age reading aloud before the priest, suddenly catching his breath in his throat. He coughs. If she has noticed, she doesn't let on.

"I can buy my freedom. Your guards took a letter out of my blouse. To the right buyer, it is worth a fortune. I will give you half to let me go."

Pettersson stands silent for a moment, deep in thought.

"You've been to see her, haven't you? Rudenschöld. Her scent is strong enough to sting your nose."

Unwilling to confess, Anna Stina remains quiet as Pettersson continues to think out loud.

"Last year you escaped. How, I don't know. Someone has paid you for your knowledge. You entered the same way, to seek her out. Do you even know what you've mixed yourself up in? You're playing with fire."

He reaches a hand inside his jacket and holds out Magdalena Rudenschöld's letter, still unopened.

"What's in it?"

She shakes her head.

"I don't know."

"You named a sum."

"Two hundred daler. Half is yours."

Pettersson's mind spins at the very thought. He has rarely seen one such coin on top of another. One hundred would be enough to buy him all he has ever wanted: well-fitting clothes, for once, lice-free walls, and a position far from the muck of the city. But the vision recedes when he looks at Anna Stina Knapp with her defiant face, her freckles that glow as she blushes, and the tender skin that lies revealed where her shirt has been torn. He knows that his answer must be different to the one she wants to hear.

"I'm a simple man. I ask but for little. Your money is not what I want."

His answer silences her, forces her to stare at the stone floor. But then she looks straight at him, through him, and he feels a dizzying sensation in his gut.

"You want me to dance for you."

"Yes."

At first he can't manage to get a sound out of his dry throat, and must repeat himself.

"Yes."

She stands without speaking for a moment, and when she does speak it is with a low voice that is nonetheless full of conviction.

"If we can come to an agreement, I will dance better than anyone you have ever brought to the well, you and Master Erik. Have you counted the turns? Can you remember who did the most?"

The recollection causes his lips to twitch. A thrilling sensation runs up his back, a tickling caress that rises from his manhood.

"She was a tiny little thing. Dark curls. Quiet, timid, pale. I counted a little over sixty laps. One would never have believed it from looking at her."

"I'll do eighty."

He feels the hairs stand up on his log-shaped arms, his nipples scraping against his linen shirt.

"Eighty?"

"Eighty, at least, and after that as many more as I can manage. I'll be the best you've ever had. My screams will be louder, my pleas more heartrending, without ever giving in. Because you want the terror too, don't you? You'll have it. It is here, I am afraid of you. I only hide it for the moment. But you'll never get what you want without paying the price."

"And what if I don't agree?"

"Then I will lie down on the flagstones until it is over, without moving an inch. I will lie there and take every blow while I chew my own tongue, swallow my own blood, until my veins are empty and my stomach full, all to make it as quick as can be. You'll never get me to take a single step or make a single sound, however much you want it, and however hard you hit."

He can see that she is serious and finds, to his surprise, that he believes she is as good as her word. He sees strength enough to deny him all that he yearns for. It is the only currency she holds to which he ascribes any value, and it is enough to force a negotiation.

"So what is it you want?"

"Give me back the letter, and a week's respite. I have given birth to two children, twins. Without me, they have no one. For the money I've been promised, I can secure their future. Let me go and give me a week, and then I will return to you. I swear it on my life's blood, on their lives, by all that I have ever held sacred. Look me in the eyes and you will see that I am not lying."

Pettersson has started to sweat, and scratches himself around the collar to lessen the itching.

"That's what you say now, and if you are lying, you do it well. But all good liars believe what they say in the heat of the moment. Later is another matter."

Pettersson weighs the letter in his hand.

"The lives of your children, do you value them more highly than your own?"

"Yes."

"Two hundred daler. With such an inheritance, the little ones will do well."

She sees his forehead furrow as he reflects. Then he dampens his lips with his tongue and tucks the letter inside his jacket.

"I'll make you a counteroffer. I'll keep the letter as an insurance that you will keep your promise. You have a week to see to your children. Then you will come back and pay your debt. Afterwards, I'll make sure the letter gets to wherever it is you want it."

Anna Stina tries in vain to find a better way. She sorts through her friends in her head and finds no one that passes the test, no one to whom she is not already too deeply indebted. Of blood ties, only one remains. Mother Maja's words come to her: *Nothing binds like blood, Anna. If your father had but seen you with his own eyes he would never have been able to disavow his responsibility.* Little Karl has his father's face. She fixes Pettersson with her gaze and clutches at the last remaining straw.

"When I return, I will give you a name and a place. Give the letter to the watchman Jonatan Löf to carry, and tell him that the money he receives is for the twins, Maja and Karl, to buy them a better world than ours. He'll be told later where they are to be found."

Pettersson spits back the name he has just heard.

"Löf? What on earth for?"

"He is the children's father. He took me by force, but they are his nonetheless. Will you make sure he fulfills his responsibility if his own conscience is not enough?"

"I will. If you dance a hundred turns around the well for me and Master Erik."

She nods because there is nothing else for her to do. He spits into his fist, a gobbet of brown tobacco juice. Across the threshold of the cell, they shake hands, hers so small it is lost in his.

"I swear by the lives of my children."

"And I before God and the devil."

On his way out, he can't help seeking reassurance that he didn't mishear, with a voice that is hardly more than a whisper.

"A hundred laps?"

"A hundred."

PART FOUR

The Minotaur
AUTUMN 1794

Is life truly worth living?
No, I'll that claim deny,
For look now with misgiving
Where our joint path must lie:
There sits a still and empty skull,
Its shining locks reduced to null,
With darkened sockets, black and dull,
Observing, unforgiving.
                    —Carl Michael Bellman, 1794

71

It is early evening still, with the long night ahead of him, the last he must spend in the City-between-the-Bridges. His words of farewell to Cardell still sear his tongue. A scratch at his door; he opens for Hedvig.

"I saw your note on the corner. What do you want?"

He returns to the pile of papers he has sorted to pack in his trunk, but not quickly enough to prevent her ever-watchful gaze from seeking out the gold chain that now decorates his waistcoat. He lifts the watch from his pocket and holds it out to her.

"Jean Michael had it, this whole time. He must have got it from the pawnshop last winter, just after Cecil's death. God only knows what it must have cost him. Every penny of his wages, and more besides, for months on end. For him, Cecil's memory was worth the hunger it cost."

The tireless brass pulse of the watch counts out each moment. Hedvig studies it for a long time, as if to assure herself that every last detail concurs with her memory.

"Do you want it? Take it. You have more right to it than I do."

He unhooks the chain from his buttonhole, places the watch on the table, and resumes his packing, all of his possessions strewn in disarray across the bed, ready to be swept into the trunk. A comb that lacks some teeth; some bread, and a bottle of well water for the road; travel documents at the ready. The stack of papers Cecil left behind in his room in the Meadowland. The leather pouch of tiny tools required for clock repairs. He feels Hedvig's eyes burn into his back. He only manages to pretend being busy for a few minutes before he gives up and sits down in front of her with sunken shoulders, his hands in his lap. He lowers his chin before the worry in her face.

"So you are leaving us. Why this sudden change of heart, Emil? What has happened?"

The mere memory is enough to make his lungs pump with rapid and shallow breaths.

"I thought I saw him, Hedvig, this morning. Cecil came to me in the street, in the middle of the day. As real as you are now. The apparitions are coming. My disease has grown too strong. I must go home. I should never have come."

"Back to your old quarters, then. For what? To wait out your life? Will you start drinking again?"

"Better that than this. Your doctors in the Oxenstierna madhouse had no cures. No medicine would work. They took my clothes away, and put me in a dark chamber with a hatch in the ceiling through which a bucket of ice water would come pouring when I least expected it, so as to shock my body back to health. After a while I realized they were only keeping me as a curiosity. A line of students came for daily visits to stare at me through a hole in the door. Escape was my only chance to keep what little sanity still remained, and once I was out, only the drinking helped. Maybe it will help again. The price may be high, but the illness is worse. I never want to see Cecil in the street again. He said terrible things. All of them true."

In his rage at his lack of self-control, he blinks a tear down his cheek. She allows him to calm down before she answers. It takes a while, but finally his thin shoulders stop shaking and his breaths slow down.

"You shouldn't mistake the vision conjured by your ailment for our brother."

"Whatever I saw was made up of memories, what else? If Cecil had been there and alive, he would have said the same thing, word for word."

Hedvig shakes her head.

"No. You're being unfair, or else bitterness has clouded your memories."

"Prove it."

"Your escape from the tomb of the living, Emil, how did it happen?"

"I stole a key."

"From whom? And how?"

"I don't recall."

"Did it simply appear in your cell one evening, just as the lights were being doused for the night? And were the corridors empty as if by coincidence, all the way out to the square, unlit by either moonlight or lanterns?"

"What are you trying to say, Hedvig?"

"Perhaps you had help, little brother, from someone who knew that a helping hand would be swept aside if you only knew to whom it belonged."

Emil feels the blood rush to his temples and drum an increasingly rapid rhythm in his forehead.

"Cecil? Are you saying that Cecil helped me escape? But how? Where would he have found the money to buy my liberty?"

He goes to the bed and pulls out the brown-paper parcel of his brother's documents, leafing quickly through them until he finds what he is looking for, then follows the text with his finger until he finds the date that coincides all too well to leave any room for doubt. For a moment, his sight darkens.

"I saw the receipt before, but not the date. He pawned his watch twice. The first time was to pay my way out of the madhouse."

"When I found you, you were in a terrible state, Emil. You were no longer among us, saw things beyond our sight, spoke only to phantoms. Perhaps the treatment would have alleviated your suffering if you had but stayed long enough for it to take effect. Cecil chose another way, but I don't doubt that his reasons were the same as mine. To him, you may still have a debt to pay."

Emil puts the receipt back where he found it and covers his face with his hands.

"Too late now."

He feels her hand on his shoulder, cool in its comfort.

"Is it?"

She leaves him alone in a silence broken only by the anxious ticking of the watch.

72

The children are crying, and Mickel Cardell can do nothing about it. The mother they so long for has disappeared beyond the edge of the forest, and the man she has left in her place is someone they have never seen before. He reaches for their toys, a carved horse and a rag doll cat, and dangles them in front of their tiny faces in the hope of distracting them. To no avail. They scream worse than before, as if chastising him for having tried to minimize the gravity of their mother's absence. Tears roll down bright-red cheeks.

In a panic, Cardell takes a few lumbering dance steps, but they are unimpressed, and he can't help but glance around to make sure that no concealed observer has seen him. Cardell tells himself that they will have to cry themselves tired, and lets them sit next to the opening of the burrow while he moves away to the other side of the ring of stones that forms the fireplace outside.

He does what he can to think of other things, but finds the task impossible. He puts his right index finger in his ear and tries to block the other one with his wooden fist, but the cries still come through. Although the air is cool, he notices that he is sticky with sweat under his shirt, and wonders if he has brought a fever from the city. But no. It is the children. With a half-muffled curse, he goes back and gets on his knees in front of them and tries to speak in the voice that he imagines the children most want to hear.

"If only you'll be good, I'll show you something you've never seen before."

He holds out both arms in front of them and stealthily slips his right hand inside the arm of his coat. He loosens the leather straps that hold the wood in place, bends as if to pick up Karl's cloth cat, and lets the stump fall out of its sleeve. The wooden fist lands on the ground with a thump and Cardell feigns surprise. Maja stops crying and studies him with an inscrutable face. Her brother, who has kept his eyes shut, also closes his mouth when he realizes that something new has happened. Cardell hurries to pick up his arm to repeat his routine. He does it again. And again. And again. When they grow tired of it, they wriggle over to examine the strange object that has given them such entertainment, and find that the carved fist only needs a little push to roll away across the smooth dirt. In amazement, they follow it, laboriously, on their bellies, but with indomitable patience.

....

Slender flames dance from the embers and cast their light into the burrow as the sun goes down. Inside, Cardell sits with his back to the rough wall. The children have crawled up next to him almost immediately and he clumsily helps them with his one hand, carefully, as if the slightest touch could hurt. Karl soon finds Cardell's little finger and pops it in his mouth, calm and contented now. The girl is more curious, reaching for his face, and he nudges her closer with his stump so that she can satisfy her curiosity. Smooth hands graze his bumpy scars; she feels his nose that juts out at an unfamiliar angle and the uneven cheekbones. Maja lets out a gurgling laugh. Soon night is upon them. Both curl up tightly towards Cardell's warmth and he folds them in his arms and settles in. Still they are restless, and don't want to sleep, unused to their mother's absence and the strange man who has taken her place.

"Should I sing for you?"

Cardell clears his throat and searches for a note to begin on.

"I know a lovely rose, as white as lily petals . . ."

His gravelly voice is ill-suited to singing; the key is off and the words to the old lullaby forgotten. Nonetheless he feels their attention shift; they have stopped squirming, and the stage is his. The dimness of the burrow hides his blush.

"It'll have to be a story, then. But I know so few. The one about the ghost of the Indebetou and the one-armed watchman is ill-suited for the ears of innocent children."

He thinks for a while as he rests his gaze on their faces. He can glimpse their mother there.

"Right then, what the hell."

He shifts around until he is lying comfortably with his one arm outstretched so that they can both use it as a pillow. They find their places as if they have never had another bed. The boy clutches his rag doll cat in his little arms. Cardell knows that they are too young to understand his words but they still listen wide-eyed through the dusk.

"Once upon a time, there was a handsome young prince, and Gustav was his name. His father was a foreigner, fetched from faraway lands when the old king died childless, and there was no head to be found in all the land where the crown might sit well. The people wanted a king, but they didn't want to give him any power, and the new monarch bowed to the will of the people, sat idle on his throne, and let them rule themselves. But the young prince saw injustice everywhere, and when the day came for him to ascend the throne, he stepped in front of the royal guards and asked them to swear loyalty to him and no one else. The soldiers were righteous men, for no others are ever allowed to wear beautiful uniforms, and in the young prince they saw the promise of a better tomorrow. They laid their weapons at his feet and fell on their knees. The prince was carried through the city to show everyone his pure, just face, and in all those who saw him, hope was reborn. All day they toasted and celebrated him. Newly crowned, he took a wife, a lovely princess from Denmark. The young couple only had eyes for each other, and it was not long before their love bore fruit. A son was born whom they loved so dearly that their hearts would have burst had they had another. When the enemy threatened King Gustav's borders with malice and mighty weapons, he commanded a navy to defend the kingdom so that his subjects would be able to live on as free and happy as before. All saw that the king's cause was just, and everywhere men flocked to his banner. The war cost them dearly, but his subjects stood by their king. The enemy trembled before King Gustav, who, despite his peaceful nature, possessed both brilliance on the battlefield and courage in his heart, and a glorious victory was won. And King Gustav cared for those among his gallant troops who were wounded so badly they could not resume their peacetime occupations, and he arranged for them to be garlanded and praised wherever they went, and they were so well compensated for their service that they soon only remembered their injuries when their gratitude overflowed. And when peace was won and the kingdom happy once again, the people decided to honor their beloved regent with a masked ball."

He can't see anything any longer but he can hear from the children's breathing that they have fallen asleep to the sound of his voice.

"Let's end the story there."

And sleep comes to him also, uneasy with unfamiliar responsibilities.

73

Consciousness slowly returns to Cardell, and the moment after, he breaks out in a cold sweat when he finds his arms empty and the children gone. The dampness of dew hangs in the air, morning glows red, and when he blinks his eyes he can see that she has returned and that she is nursing her little ones. He stares stupidly for a second before he has the sense to turn away and leave them in peace. He rubs the sleep from his eyes, rises with some effort, and shuffles out on stiff legs. By the time Anna Stina follows, he has managed to coax a few sparks to take hold of some birch bark, and modest flames have started driving the dampness out of the sodden wood that hisses in protest.

"Thank you for staying."

Out in the light he can see her more clearly. She is dirty, and her clothes have been ripped to shreds. He answers with a curt nod.

"I'll fetch water."

She points out the way for him, and when he returns with a full pot and his socks wet, she soaks birch leaves in a mug to wash herself and lets the rest simmer full of spruce fir. A few mushroom caps toasted on the stones makes a frugal breakfast. Cardell tastes them with trepidation before he shrugs and eats what he is given. Around them the trees are already half in autumn garb. She huddles closer to the fire. He can see that she is cold, though she conceals it well.

"You can't stay here much longer."

"Nor will I need to."

She has circles under her eyes and sounds despondent, and he senses something worse than lack of sleep.

"You won't tell me where you've been?"

She shakes her head.

"Did it go well, the thing you had to do?"

He looks away and answers his own question.

"Forget it. I've eyes of my own to see."

Her silence tells him he is right. Inside the burrow, the children are chasing his wooden arm, which rolls across the dirt floor each time they lose their grip, sending them into peals of laughter and forcing them to start their hunt anew.

"What can I do? You know you only need to ask."

She sits quietly as if she hasn't heard, her eyes on the children, and finally he gets up, fumbling with the last bit of water to rub his mug as clean as possible. When he goes to put it back next to hers, it slips from his grip and he does something he has done a hundred times before with the same result: he stretches out the arm with the stump to catch what he has dropped with a hand that is no longer there, knowing that he could have caught his mistake if only he had been whole. Instead, the clay cup tumbles through the empty air and cracks in two when it hits the ground with a mute thud. Both do the same thing at the same time, crouching down to pick up the pieces and choosing the same one. Cardell grips a sharp edge with fingers that have grown numb in the cold and only when Anna Stina lets out a cry does he see that he has cut himself.

The memory of a similar moment gives them pause. The last time they were this close there was also a blade between them: one they both gripped, he to save and she to kill. Cardell seeks her gaze, and when he finds it he can't bear to let go of it again. As if pulled by forces beyond his will, he leans closer, as much to his own astonishment as hers. A heartbeat's hesitation, then she flinches and backs away, violently enough to burn her hand on the embers behind her when she seeks something to steady herself on. It is a mercy for him as her grimace of pain replaces the distaste that was there before. She shouts and rolls back, out of his reach. They stand, each with a smarting hand, their breath making white plumes as they wish for this moment to leave and a better one to come. To no avail.

Cardell rises heavily to his feet and backs away to give her more space, putting the fire between them for her own comfort. He searches for words to apologize but all he finds are curses at his own stupidity. With a sigh, Cardell presses his hat on his head and mutters his good-bye down at the fire.

"Well, I'll return from where I came. You know how to find me, Anna. Don't hesitate if the need grows too great."

He turns to the burrow and waves farewell to the twins with his stained hand.

"Goodbye then, Maja and Karl. Be good to your mother now, and to each other."

Cardell steals a glance at Anna Stina only because he knows it will be his last. The momentary impulse that he could not restrain has told her that his help is conditional. Now she'll never want it again. He can see it on her: shoulders pulled high, not against the cold, but against him. Her eyes are those of a hunted animal.

....

Cardell trudges down towards the tollgate and beyond without paying any attention to the guard who calls out, on, further on through Norrmalm towards the trio of church spires that marks the City-between-the-Bridges. He stops next to the Bog. He chooses the most unassuming establishment he can see, a hovel so dilapidated that the wind has free passage between the boards. No sign indicates business, only a door that hangs askew on broken hinges and a steady stream of vagrants who walk in with thirsty expressions and out again with stains on their shirts. After the first sip of beer, he roars at the proprietor.

"There is more foam in sludge from the lake, and damn my eyes if that shitty water won't taste better as well."

He drinks quart upon quart, going to the tap himself to fill up as soon as he glimpses the bottom of his tankard. He is awkward at first but soon gets the hang of it. The day goes by and his intoxication grows to a rumbling chaos in which he has trouble remaining on his feet. Her last look still stings his skin. He allows his hate to wash over everything that makes him a man. Muscles and ugliness, a form molded only to inflict violence on others. He belongs to a kind that has had their way with such as her since time immemorial, and rarely has it been anything good. He is as powerless to change as anyone else. Quietly at his table, he waits for the scum from the outskirts of the city, fresh from a late bed or a sloppy day's work. He hides his left arm behind his back, and when they are numerous and drunk enough to meet his challenge, he saunters over to the largest and most confident, placing himself so close that a spark could have jumped between the tips of their noses, and hisses the most effective invitation to a fight that he can think of in his current state.

"What the fuck're you staring at?"

They step out into the yard once the squabble has made them exchange words neither can take back, and the rabble make a circle around them. They cheer at the spectacle—such entertainment without a fee!—and the bets are quickly made. They pat their chosen winner on the shoulder and whisper bloodthirsty advice in his ear.

Cardell meets the first punch with his forehead and feels his eyebrow burst like an overripe blister. He laughs.

"I do believe a little maid just fanned me with a feather."

The next one strikes him on the cheek and his skin immediately swells to a tight bag of blood.

"I can get caresses like these in Bagge's Row but only for a fee."

He takes a jab to the ear and feels the warmth trickle down his neck.

"I got one just like it from your mother because I only had the stamina to last half the night."

His chest booms like a drum under the rain of blows. After a while, his cracked lips lose the ability to shape any audible insults, but they are no longer needed. The meaning is clear.

They don't know him, and for a long time they think him a trickster who has let a friend put money on him and takes the punches only to better the odds. Only after a long time do they realize that the fight only has one participant, and the crowd's delight turns to resentment when all betting is ruled invalid, based on an unwritten rule of the street. Carousing dampens to muttering, only interrupted by a few crunching blows.

Eventually they leave the yard one by one or in small groups. A few linger, their mouths agape at how much beating the stranger can take without his knees buckling. When the bloody fists bouncing in front of Cardell are finally lowered, they reveal a look of disgust. All stare at him as if he were an abomination.

....

Finally Cardell becomes aware that not even his opponent is still there, and he stands alone in a cooling puddle. He raises the blunt stump of his left arm, taking a swing at the empty air and sending a thought to the wooden arm that is still with the children who found it such a joy.

74

Cardell limps home in the early morning. His face has stiffened into a mask of dried blood, enough to scare off the few morning wanderers he meets in the alleys. Even the waste collectors, who are used to others shying from them like the plague, turn away so violently that the barrel they are carrying between them lurches and splashes their legs. Cardell's tongue waggles a loose tooth back and forth, and crusted wounds crackle as he opens his mouth to poke at it with a pointed finger. He pushes it back until the root gives way, and spits it into the gutter. On his staircase, he has to bend over and catch his breath every couple of steps, tender ribs smarting.

Emil Winge sits on his threshold, curled up against the wall with his arms around his legs, his head on his knees, fast asleep. Each exhalation is given form by the cold air. Cardell rests against the wall and Winge opens his eyes and looks straight at him.

It takes a while before his silent horror gives way to recognition. Cardell sees the mouth move, hears the buzzing of questions over the ringing in his ears, but doesn't have the energy to listen or understand. All the energy he still possesses he now uses to shove Winge aside, open the door, and, on trembling legs, stagger the last few steps to the comfort of his bed. Cardell is out in the same moment that his head hits the mattress.

....

He wakes from the ache in his face and has to lift his hand to use thumb and forefinger to force open eyelids that have been glued shut by blood and swelling. Winge sits on the edge of the bed with a bowl in his lap and washes his forehead with a bit of cloth.

"Does it hurt?"

"Only when I laugh."

"What happened?"

"Nothing in particular. It was my name day. Tradition bids me to indulge myself with an annual fight as a pleasant distraction."

Cardell hears himself lisp with lips thick as steaks.

"I have been to the Raven and convinced an apprentice apothecary to drop in. He examined you, and gave me instructions for further care."

"From what I remember, we did not part in the best of terms. Why this sudden benevolence?"

Winge dabs at a cut on Cardell's forehead. Cardell smells the vinegar the second before the cut burns and he swats the hand away with a hiss.

"Stop messing around and leave me in peace, for God's sake."

Winge looks away with a sigh, walks to the window with the bowl, and empties its contents outside. He sets it down, clasps his hands behind his back, and begins speaking, his back turned to Cardell.

"When we last saw each other I said much that I now wish had been left unsaid. I chose my words to hurt you. I have come to ask your pardon."

"What's changed in these few hours?"

"Of all my siblings, I am the youngest, and the one who had to make do with any wits still left to inherit. I have spoken to my sister. She has helped me understand much that I did not grasp earlier. My memories of Cecil are colored by feelings that have grown without grounds and that have not been pruned by reality for many a year."

Cardell runs his fingertips over his ravaged face.

"When I met your brother for the first time, a year ago in Maria graveyard, I also said some words intended to cause pain that I soon had reason to regret. What I said was true, of course, as true as what you said to me. How could it hurt otherwise? That time the roles were reversed and I went to Winge to apologize. He accepted it without hesitation. On the other hand, he needed my help. Just as I need yours. Who can say what is honestly meant under such circumstances?"

Winge turns and shakes his head.

"Whatever kind of forgiveness you extend to me is up to you. I am here to beg for it regardless."

"Help me to cut a plug of tobacco and you can have your forgiveness in exchange."

Cardell pulls a whistling breath between clenched teeth as the juice stings his lacerated gums and cracked lips.

"So what now? Will you take your absolution with you back to Uppsala and water it with wine, or will you stay and help me flog this dead horse?"

"I'll stay, if you still want me to."

"Tell your sister that I owe her a drink then, in the event that she has a better tolerance for such things than her siblings."

Cardell grimaces as he leans over the spittoon and lets the juice spill over lips that have trouble moving.

"But the odds are as high as ever, and the chances of us succeeding are no better than they were. Your sister didn't happen to tell you what we should do next?"

Winge starts to walk around the room, back and forth, his hands clasped behind his back.

"It is true that the situation looks grave. But, Jean Michael, we can hardly claim to know all of the circumstances. About this Ceton, we know nothing more than what he himself has admitted. There may be chinks in his armor yet, and only once we see the situation in its entirety can we say with certainty if the whole appears as hopeless as its parts."

Cardell leans forward to say something but only manages a low groan when his breath catches on a cracked rib. Winge still nods, as if the sound has conveyed meaning.

"We are taking a terrible risk, Jean Michael. Ceton's warning leaves no room for doubt. I don't like to imagine what he would do with his orphans in order to make an example if he finds out that we are still sniffing at his heels. We can only continue with the greatest possible care. Are we in agreement?"

"Widow Colling will hardly be the last one that devil renders childless if he is allowed to continue. The risk is worth taking. We'll proceed with caution. But how?"

As if someone could overhear, Winge leans closer and lowers his voice.

"When we were at dinner, I glimpsed a ring on Ceton's left hand.

Tycho Ceton has a wife, and if it is a happy marriage, I'll eat my hat. Perhaps Mrs. Ceton knows more, and she may be willing to tell us. If we can find her. How quickly can you be back on your feet?"

Cardell stretches in his bed to test his limbs.

"I took most of the blows to the head, and luckily that is the part I can most spare. But if you'll give me one day for the swelling to go down, Stockholm's streets will be forever in your debt. Can you hand me that sliver of mirror by the window?"

Cardell examines his mask of red and black with the eyes of an expert.

"Well, fuck me if that goon didn't punch my nose straight again."

75

Down by the Quayside, Winge finds Pallinder's office vacant. The door is locked and when he bends down to look in through the keyhole, he sees that the shelves of folders and ledgers have been rifled and left with large gaps. A gentleman on his way to the neighboring door gives him a curious look and lowers his voice in a companionable whisper.

"Have you come to collect some debts?"

When Emil shakes his head, the man gives a neighing laugh.

"I met Rudolf Pallinder the other day on his way down the stairs with his arms full of papers, pale as a ghost and eyes like a bolting cow, and thought to myself that here we have a man with the soldiers at his heels who is at risk of being hauled to debtors' prison at any moment."

"I do come from the police, but on a completely different matter."

"Well, to judge by his haste, I would be surprised if he was still to be found within the borders of this kingdom."

The man takes out a snuffbox from his waistcoat pocket and offers it to Winge, who declines. The man empties some out into the depression between thumb and forefinger and draws it up into his nose, before sneezing loudly.

"Well, damn it, when one's own business falters it is nonetheless a comfort that others are in a bigger pickle."

....

For better or worse, Emil visits the churches in order, Gertrud the closest, Nikolai next to the castle wall, and Franciskus out on its islet. The church books are a tangled affair. He has neither year nor date to look for as he searches for banns or marriages, the writing difficult to decipher and the many gaps in the records telling of sloppy and hasty work. The ministers have much to attend to and are of little help.

When he can, he chooses routes where the sky lies open. He takes the long way around, by way of the Quayside and the quay under Lion Hill, and even past the defile where the Flies' Meet proves worthy of its name, and the public latrines reek. He walks wherever the City-between-the-Bridges meets the water to determine how to get to where he wants by way of as few alleys as possible. He hurries towards home but feels fear growing into nausea. The steps carry him towards light and company, and soon he stands with his heart in his throat in front of a coffeehouse where he finds an empty corner and stays, forgotten by the world but safe for the moment. People are still talking about Rudenschöld and Armfelt, asking who among the exile's loyal followers will be betrayed next and whether this time Reuterholm will be able to entrust them to the executioner's blade or if he will once more make do with imprisonment. A group of gentlemen next to him have congregated after the end of the working day and each calls for a cup of chocolate.

"And don't skimp on the cacao, because it needs to keep me going all night long!"

They are headed towards Bagge's Row and soon start talking about the relative advantages and disadvantages of the various ladies of the night, and who is the most experienced in the arts of lovemaking.

"The Little Lamb."

"The German Well, for heaven's sake."

"Either you don't know the difference between wine and water, my brother, or else you have never bedded the Rose of Sharon."

"Let us not squabble but go to peruse the light brigade this instant. If everyone's tastes were the same, the wait would be longer than any man's patience would allow."

They laugh at the truth of the last speaker's words and leave a stained table behind and Emil Winge with a hopeful thought.

....

Cardell resists every attempt to rouse him.

"Jean Michael? The account by Three Roses made it clear that Tycho

Ceton was known and banned from every brothel in Gustavia. Perhaps the case is the same here in Stockholm?"

Cardell cracks his eye, revealing a sliver of white between blue-black folds, and grunts in answer before the pupil rolls up and he turns over on his side. Then he gives a loud snore and Winge's attempt to shake life into him could just as well have been applied to the pile of firewood. Winge chews his thumbnail until his teeth draw blood.

"Alone, then, or not at all."

....

He takes the stairs down to Cutter's Alley and walks up the hill to the square. The city lies dark, but in the pubs the night remains young. The footsteps of the Minotaur rumble among the houses, still far away in the distance. Many lanterns still hang unlit along the facades, and none of them would anyway have been bright enough to reach the well in the middle of the square. Even so, Winge prefers the open air, bending over a little to let the urn at the top of the well form an outline against the darkening sky, and hurries on. One of the waist-high railings that prevent carriages from getting too close to the pump lies hidden by the shadows and strikes him on the knee before he can lean in towards the damp stone and take a handful of water to rinse his face. Lights are being lit at the Stock Exchange. A few candles cast a flickering light through sooty windowpanes, the ballroom floor is being swept clean, and the black spire of the cathedral looms over the eaves. Men and women concealed by the shadows pass by at a distance, accompanied by laughter and snatches of conversation. He hurries away, towards the dockside. Bagge's Row can be heard from afar, before he rounds the corner.

The light is different here. The lanterns are partly masked to grant anonymity to the visitors who keep to the middle of the street. Instead the light spills upwards, the better to light up the pride of each house. The ladies of the night parade in the windows. One is sitting high up on the ledge with a clay pipe in her mouth, dangling bare legs over a certain death. She fans the folds of her petticoat for those who wish to see what is underneath. Others lean out to yell promises of certain talents, or let outrageous shadows play against closed windows to emphasize their nakedness without allowing closer inspection. Down on the cobblestones, the desperation and concomitant audacity is far greater. He sees a drunken woman come swaying along with a breast in each hand which she mutely offers to everyone she sees. Vacant eyes bear witness to a ravaged life, above a mouth that remains blankly open in a toothless grin. The madams stand outside the doors of the brothels, announcing the qualities of their establishment. Reuterholm's sumptuary law has little effect on those who are already deemed guilty in the eyes of the law, but who still operate their business in response to general demand and the averted eyes of the city watch. The colors of their clothing are bright enough to light up the dusk. Everywhere, men are on their way in or out: journeymen enjoying their day off, well-to-do burghers alone or in groups, crowds of young men, alongside individual sinners hiding their faces in handkerchiefs. Unified by desire, the distance between the estates is reduced to nothing.

A heavy-set woman, her face smeared with gray-white paste, grabs at Winge's coat sleeve as he tries to push past. She is wearing a gray coat with a blue collar and red slippers, and is carrying in her hand a parasol of a brilliant shade of green. She has hardly begun to recite the attractions of her establishment when she is interrupted by a gaunt man who staggers over with a bottle in one hand and his hat in the other.

"Your filthy whores have given me the French pox, madame."

He is slurring his words and turns his head this way and that in search of an audience. He drops both hat and bottle, and unties his trousers at the waist, taking his member in his hand to display its weeping sores. His voice cracks as he roars, echoing through the alley.

"Beware, good people, of the girls at the Lizard!"

The madam raises her voice to a scream so that her answer won't be lost.

"You're mistaken, good sir! All my girls obediently spread their legs for the doctor on Saturdays."

The man's trousers have slid down to his knees, and he is close to toppling over in his rage.

"Disease! Disease! Stay away if you don't want your nose to rot away and your cock to fall off!"

The woman decides to change strategy, takes a step closer, and lowers her voice to a soothing tone.

"There now, why don't you calm down? If you lack the funds for some mercury and a week at the spa, I'm sure we have some to spare."

He gives her a shove.

"Fuck off, witch. Don't you realize that you have taken my life? All of my possessions belong to my wife and when she sees how my manhood has moldered away, she'll lock me out forever."

When he begins to repeat his shouted warnings to passersby, the madam gestures back towards her stairs. A burly man with murder in his gaze steps out briskly, grabs the plaintiff under the arm, and leads him under protest into a side alley as he loosens a cudgel from his belt. The screams die down before the blows, and when the thug returns, his thighs dyed red where he has dried his hands, the woman grabs him by the collar and whispers in his ear.

"Find out who gave him a good time and make sure she gets the hell out of here."

From the shadows of the side alley only a racking sob can be heard, and Winge hurries on in the certainty that he has nothing to learn in Bagge's Row.

....

He walks against the flow of people, who all appear to be going in the opposite direction. The walls close around him and the anxiety creeps in, but the more energy he puts into making a path for himself, the more he is rewarded in kind. A shoulder bangs hard into his own, an elbow jabs into his side. As his panic flares, he feels a hand in his.

"Is your name Winge?"

He turns to a woman a few years older than himself. She has a mild face, prematurely aged by her profession. Her words have the lilt of an Eastern accent.

"I saw you from my window, along with the troublemaker and Little Platen, the one with the green parasol. My name is Johanna. They call me the Flower of Finland."

"How do you know my name?"

"Calm down, I can't hear what you are saying."

"How do you know my name?"

"You have a brother, do you not? Older? You are very much alike. For a moment, I thought that you were him. I want to ask you what has become of him."

"Cecil's dead."

He hears a sharp intake of breath and watches her turn away.

"Oh."

"Was he often your guest?"

"Does that surprise you?"

At first, Emil doesn't know what to say, unsure of what etiquette this kind of conversation requires. Finally he gives her a curt nod.

"Every day now, I learn things about my brother that I did not imagine of him. Why are you crying?"

"I meet many men in my line of work. Good men, bad men. Men who do what they must and are gone in ten minutes without even asking my name. Men who want to let themselves be seduced, as if someone had forced them to my room to let me have my way with them. Men who fight, men who cry, men who only want someone who listens. You're all different, only your desire is the same. Cecil was the only one for whom I felt affection. He chose me because I looked like the wife whom he missed. All he wanted was that I play a charade, to hold him in a certain way as he fell asleep and lull him into dreams. Wear her scent. He got what he came for in those few moments between wakefulness and sleep when he imagined that things were as they had been before. He never asked for more than this. He gave me money so that I would pretend to be someone else. In the morning, as he whispered her name with a smile on his lips, he showed me a world that will never be mine. I came to love him for it, and because he never treated me as if I were someone less worthy than him."

She looks at him with reddened eyes.

"Don't you want to follow me in? I can give you the same thing. You look like you need it just as much as your brother."

He shakes his head.

"I have nothing to pay you with."

"There is no need. If you only let me hold you."

"Perhaps another time."

"It has to be tonight."

"Why?"

"Little Platen has sent her henchman after me to let me know I need to be out of the house before the cock crows."

76

A dying flame clings to its wick. The tallow smokes, the candle soon to be a pool to drown the fire. The small hours of the night are called out from the church towers one by one.

"Emil?"

Her hand is on his chest, his head on her arm. He lies staring up into the ether.

"I'm awake."

"The night is almost over. Soon I must go."

Neither of them moves. He can feel her gaze on his cheek, concerned.

"Your dreams must be terrible. You call out in your sleep, and sometimes you speak in a language I don't understand."

"It's probably Greek."

"When I took your hand out in the street it was as if you were seeing things that didn't exist. What is the matter?"

"I am losing my mind, slowly but surely. It has happened to me once before. The process appears somewhat slower this time, but is otherwise the same."

"Is there nothing that helps?"

"The only thing that helps me makes it impossible for me to do what I must."

She ponders this for a while. The flame flickers in the draft.

"Such is the world. Every medicine hides a poison and all paths are lined with traps. It is like some . . ."

Someone slams a door at the other end of the house and she pauses. The light goes out and he finishes her sentence.

"Labyrinth."

....

They dress in the gray light of approaching dawn, each in their own corner of the room, strangers once and now strangers again. Johanna begins to fill a cloth bag with a few possessions. She crosses the room and turns her back to him as she gets close, sweeping her long hair to the side, and when Emil understands what is wanted, he clumsily begins adjusting her corset.

"What brought you to Bagge's Row last night? You didn't come here for the same reason as everyone else."

"Do you know someone called Ceton, by any chance? Tycho Ceton."

"I don't recognize that name."

"He has a scar from the left corner of his mouth up over his cheek, an old wound that makes it look as if he is smiling, that has never healed properly and that still weeps. But perhaps he was uninjured when he came here, if he did."

The corset is pulled tight and he ties a bow at the top where the ends meet.

"I know of whom you speak. We have other names for him."

"Did you see him before or after his injury?"

She opens the door and peeks out. The house is still sleeping. The snores of customers who have stayed mingle in the corridor. When the door is closed again she sits down on the edge of the bed.

"Both. I have never been with him myself or anywhere near him. But the girls will talk. Such is our only power, to laugh at our clients behind their backs, highlight their flaws, act out their ridiculous attempts at love-making, make fun of their grimaces as the little death comes to them. Everyone who pays the agreed price may do as he pleases, for the most part, and he leaves here carefree, in the knowledge that he has paid in full for his pleasure. But there is a limit to what is tolerated, even for us. Not that our madam cares about us other than as wares to hawk, but even if we are simply meat to her, meat can spoil and then it can no longer be sold. There are those who enjoy beating us and inflicting pain, and as long as the bruises can be covered with makeup, all is well. Most of us get used to it. For those who want to go further, there are some more seasoned, often older ones, those who have been here so long they hardly feel anything anymore and are as good as dead inside. They are willing to go along with it if the price is right and enough to cover the cost of spirits for the duration of their convalescence. But if a man like the one you speak of asks for a young girl, one who has recently arrived from the country, or a maid who has lost her position, or whose parents have recently died, then she can be ruined for good. Nothing that her madam threatens her with thereafter will have any effect, no slaps about the face, or even wine—she will become as stiff as a board at the mere thought of being alone with a man, and all that remains is to put her out into the street, she who had the potential to be able to pull in a small fortune in a single night."

"And Ceton?"

"At first there was no scar. A handsome man, even, someone the inexperienced girls willingly led to their bedroom before learning that appearances make no odds. I was told he was of the kind who watches rather than acts himself, and sometimes he had another man with him, sometimes he wanted to give instructions to two girls. His whims stayed within limits then, if barely. On those occasions when an injury occurred, he paid so well and conveyed his apologies so eloquently that exceptions were made. He was gone for a while, then returned with his cheek torn up, and then he was different, worse. Soon there was not a single establishment in Bagge's Row that would take his business. He hasn't shown himself here since."

"Do you know if he is married?"

"It was always said that it was his wife who cut him, and there was no one who didn't think that woman a saint. They say that he keeps her locked up as punishment, but who can tell if a rumor like that is based on fact? The last time he was here he carried on in such a way that he could not make up for it with the contents of his purse alone. When such things happen, Little Platen sends one of her men home with the perpetrator to make sure he makes good on the debt. She may remember where the house is."

"I will speak to her."

She follows him down the stairs and out, her knapsack on her shoulder, and points out the right way for him, which is opposite to hers.

"Farewell, then. And Emil? You spoke with your brother in your sleep, as if he were still alive. If you see him again, will you please send him my regards and let him know I miss him?"

77

However hard Winge tries, Cardell cannot be awakened. He is lying in bed with his back towards the room, arms crossed over his battered chest, snoring like thunder. Now and again, his breathing is interrupted by a groan when some pain makes itself known, but without disturbing his sleep. Neither coughing nor nudging helps, and when Winge uses both hands to push Cardell in the back, he might as well have been trying to rouse an ox. The man who is waiting at the door, stocky, dusky-complexioned, and completely bald, indicates his impatience by clearing his throat, and although it makes him uncomfortable, Winge has no choice but to help himself to Cardell's purse that is tucked inside the lining of his trousers and counts out the price that has been demanded.

"Thirty shillings."

The man casts a quick glance at Cardell's unconscious form and then assesses Winge's thin frame as if to remind himself that the border between a negotiation and robbery can become blurred according to the circumstances.

"Let's make it an even daler, shall we?"

Cardell's room has neither a fireplace nor tiled stove, and is heated only on those occasions when a fire has been made elsewhere in the house. Winge has had to knock at the room next door to ask for a bit of coal, and with it he writes a hasty message on the inside of the door for Cardell to read when he finally regains his senses. Winge takes a couple of shillings out of the purse, then walks down the stairs. At the threshold, he stops for a moment with closed eyes as he tries to summon the courage that remains elusive. Then he sets off.

....

There is a commotion in the alleyways: he encounters people returning from the other side of the Lock where a large public event has been held. Today's scaffold was raised in honor of Ehrenström, who, like Magdalena Rudenschöld, was one of Armfelt's loyalists, whose head was to be severed from his body there to save the audience a walk through the Sconce. When the blow fell towards the bared neck, the executioner struck the pillory instead, with the announcement that Ehrenström had been pardoned at the last moment to live out the rest of his days in penance and contrition in the dungeons of Karlsten fortress. The hotly debated topic of the day is whether the condemned had been told in advance of his salvation, and if he otherwise would have shown such equanimity before death. The Estates side with their already established sympathies, where Reuterholm's supporters argue that the public would have been exposed to both wailing and wet trousers if no one had informed the prisoner, while the Gustavians claim that Ehrenström's chest has always held the heart of a lion. The fact that the spectacle is yet more evidence of weakness by the wavering regency government is something few can be bothered to dispute.

He makes his way past the throng, over the blue drawbridge across the Lock and up the hill above the square. It is the third time he's seen the same streets that day, since Little Platen's thug showed him the way to the house that is Tycho Ceton's and escorted him all the way back in order to be paid. At a stall on Postmaster's Hill, Winge exchanges his coins for some apples and hard tack, and tucks the bundle inside his coat. The wind surprises him from his right-hand side, with a gust from the Larder that forces him to hold his nose and struggle to keep his stomach from turning. He hurries away to where the ground starts sloping down to Hammarby Lake.

....

The building he is looking for is a stone manor house on the outskirts of Katarina parish, within sight of the workshops by Children's Lea. The main house stands behind a wall where vines grow thick and where a few brave roses remain to mourn the summer that has passed. Inside the gate, there is a garden that is still lush, as if its southern exposure has made the season last longer here than elsewhere, a rural idyll so close to the City-between-the-Bridges. On the other side of the road, a hundred feet away, Winge finds the place he has already picked out in the shade of a knotty linden tree growing on a small mound that both shields him from view and affords him a clear sight over the wall and gate. He flattens the high grass to sit on and makes himself comfortable.

A long afternoon turns to evening and night as he waits, constantly looking in the same direction, afraid to miss something vital if his attention is allowed to flag even for a moment. The lights behind the windows are extinguished, and the overcast sky turns the night to pitch. For many hours, his world is only sound, touch, and smell. He can hear how the Minotaur gropes among the vegetation for him, but not in the right place. Maybe the beast can't see in the dark either.

By morning he sees that he was mistaken: the sounds he has heard are only that of a vagrant, who has come lurching along and finally fallen asleep in the ditch into which he has tumbled. The man wakes up in the morning, expressing sounds of surprise at his situation and doing a strange dance to bring warmth back into his frozen limbs, before trotting back into the city to minister to his hangover with the only medicine on offer. Winge eats his apples and crunches on the hard bread. By mid-morning there is a light rain, and he crouches closer to the tree trunk to seek shelter from the branches, in vain as the water seeps down the bark. In this way, the first day goes by of the three he has assigned himself.

78

"Is that the smell of coffee?"

Winge's appearance in the doorway is a pitiful sight, as pale as a drowned man with sodden clothes to match, stained with dirt, his hair full of straw. In answer, Cardell merely points to a copper pot on the table.

"I sent the neighbor's girl down to the quay to buy this for me from the people who sell it under the counter, and had her carry the bag back under her skirt. There's a cup or two left, though it's lukewarm and a bit cloudy. The ban on coffee may be the worst act Reuterholm has inflicted on his poor nation, but in this very room tyranny has been vanquished, and my head has lost a pound in weight."

"It is said that Voltaire never drank less than sixty cups a day."

"Lucky that Reuterholm never had a head for reading, because in that case the bean would have been outlawed a long time ago. I have yet to hear of any regime that wants its subjects to be other than stupid and compliant."

Winge uses his thumb to dry the edge of Cardell's empty mug, the only one to be found in the room, and pours out what is left, careful not to disturb the dregs. He lets the bitter liquid roll across his tongue and drown the lingering taste and smell of the street. Cardell gives him a reproachful look.

"If you had written where you were going, I would have been able to come and relieve you."

"I wasn't sure I would find you in any better state even now."

"I'm always happy to exceed expectations, low as they may be. So, how were you rewarded for your troubles?"

Winge downs his cup, slowly swallowing the last sip and licking his lips.

"Yes, there are people in the house. A maid who every morning takes her basket into the city to buy bread, vegetables, and meat, enough for several people. There is no reason to assume that Ceton keeps a staff simply to populate the house, so I assume that food is being purchased for the wife who is never to be seen. In the evening, there is only one light in any of the rooms. And each morning a man comes by with a horse and cart and leaves big bunches of flowers."

"What about the grinning bastard himself?"

"The routine has been the same ever since I took up my post. He has arrived in a barouche each day around dinnertime, stays for an hour or two, and leaves the house in fresh evening clothes, not to return until the same time the following day. His nights are spent elsewhere."

"What are your thoughts?"

Emil has lifted the lid of the kettle in order to press his knuckles into the dregs and thereby extract the last few drops but without getting much for his troubles.

"The rumors on Bagge's Row said that Ceton keeps his wife locked up. I suggest that we do what we can to get in through the door and hope that we encounter a wife who will be sympathetic to our cause."

Cardell shifts his weight on the bed, testing his legs, making a growling sound as broken ribs and torn muscle take exception to the shift.

"Jean Michael, are you in any condition to accompany me?"

Cardell shoots him a poisonous look.

"Don't be silly. As long as there is a way forward, I'll be fine. There is only one way to handle pain, and that is to ignore it. I have learned as much through dearly bought experience. The swelling has gone down enough to shave, I'll have you know. I suggest you do the same before we go. The knife is sharp, and there is water in the pitcher by the window. If we are going to rely on our charm alone to make our way inside, I fear my once so comely appearance will no longer be a guarantee of success."

79

Winge is astonished at how quickly Cardell's heavy body appears to have recovered. After limping along for a few quarters, his ailments seem to lessen, his hefty muscles primed once more to do their duty as blood rushes back to them. The walk has not lasted an hour before they reach their goal and can watch the ocher plaster of the mansion glow golden in the rays of the westering sun. Cardell spits out his plug of tobacco and scrapes impatiently at the cut leaves with the heel of his boot.

"Must I feed you your lines? Every time I have stood alongside a Winge outside an ominous-looking building, the suggestion is that we should knock on the door and announce our arrival."

"I was just about to say exactly that. I simply dread what we are going to find."

They pass through the gate, walking along the flagstone path. The answer to Winge's knock is a long time coming, and when it does, it is in the form of a frightened voice through the door.

"We don't want anything. Please leave us be."

Only when Cardell mentions Police Chief Ullholm himself does door separate from frame in a narrow cleft. It is a young woman who has opened the door, a servant to judge by her dress. Her hair is knotted at her neck and hidden under a shawl. Her face is pale and her expression alarmed. Winge adopts a soothing tone.

"We have come to call on Mrs. Ceton."

The young woman draws her breath as if he has asked for the impossible. She shakes her head.

"The missus doesn't see anyone."

Cardell pushes the door out of her grip with the foot he has teased over the threshold and steps inside.

"Go on now and let your mistress know that someone is here to see her, and that she can either make whatever preparations she feels are needed or receive us as she is. We'll wait here, but if it takes too long we'll find our own way."

She flees into the house and leaves them in the hall. On the floor, the dust lies thick enough to show trodden paths where the inhabitants of the house have walked from room to room. No candles have yet been lit. The portraits crowding the walls only show ghostly black-and-white figures, and of the furniture, only bulging forms can be discerned, but their wait is brief: the maid returns and waves them on without a word. The corridor bends, and at the door on the right she lets them pass into a room where two chairs have been placed next to each other. The room is elegantly furnished, the walls clad in a wallpaper with garlands of flowers and laurel wreaths braided in a pattern. Portraits and landscapes hang on silk ribbons from the crown molding. Two large windows have been opened to air the room, and whenever a faint breeze puffs towards the house, the white curtains flow into the room. Everywhere are roses—in vases, on flower stands, some even in copper kettles that would otherwise be more at home in the kitchen. The smell is overwhelming, overwhelming in its sweetness. Still, it is not sufficient to conceal what it is intended to: decay, as if of a dead rat under the floorboards. There is a canopy bed with its curtains drawn, thin white drapes that only allow them to sense the outline of the figure lying within. Although the bed is intended for two, she fills it completely by herself. Winge can see the mound of swelling flesh billow in time to her panting breaths.

"Mrs. Ceton?"

A giggle comes from the other side of the veils, as high as a little girl's.

"You ask for me and not for my husband. But no doubt he is the object of your affairs."

Cardell feels the hairs rise on his arm at the sound. Her voice seems too high to come from such a body. But there is something else there too, a slurring as if her tongue and lips were unable to form the words completely. Each sentence is followed by a clearing of her throat and a snuffling sound.

"Do you wish my husband ill?"

Winge's answer comes without hesitation.

"Indeed."

"A long time I've waited for someone like you. But it would be a lie to say that your appearance matches my expectations."

She pauses, completely still. Not the least movement can be sensed. Then the sparkling tone of a bell can be heard from the bed. In a moment, the door opens slightly, and the maid shows her face.

"Ma'am?"

"Sweet Gustava, would you be so kind as to stand here on the floor in front of the bed?"

The maid curtsies and hurries to her assigned spot.

"How long have I been under your care?"

"I have been in the house six months now, ma'am."

"You do a fine job in changing my bedding and washing my bedsores, but heaven knows you're not the brightest of sparks, are you, Gustava? Still, the time you have been here has perhaps been long enough for you to guess how I have ended up in this condition?"

Gustava squirms as if stuck with a pin and doesn't dare to say a word.

"He fills you with terror, my husband, isn't that right?"

The maid has chosen a spot on the floor between her feet to rest her gaze on, her hands clasped in front of her and now softly weeping.

"As he should. Tycho pays you far more than you deserve, and demands your loyalty in return. If the police had not been mentioned, you would rather have obeyed his order about never letting in a guest. I am sure you want to make apologies on his behalf. But look at these two men. If you ever say a single thing to my husband about this visit, they will hurt you so badly that my suffering will seem like a delightful evening in King's Park by comparison. That the big one is a watchman, you can see yourself by his uniform. He will take you to the women's workhouse, and if you haven't prostituted yourself before, you will find more teachers there than the most eager pupil could wish for. You are nice enough to look at, and the other convicts will queue up for the pleasure of feeling your tongue between their thighs, and won't leave you alone until they all limp away bandy-legged with their blisters. Do you understand what I'm saying, sweet Gustava? That's right, just nod, and then hurry over here to wipe my chin."

The girl darts over and carefully pulls aside the drapery to do as she has been told, then flees amid heavy sobs. Wet footsteps follow her from the puddle she leaves behind, its smell lost in the scent of roses.

"Do I shock you? You should know better. I am Tycho's wife and I deserve to carry his name."

Cardell squints in vain to get a better look at her while Winge clears his throat and asks his question.

"Do you know where your husband is now, Mrs. Ceton?"

"You have seen how he looks. That is my doing. Tycho Ceton is not an easy man to get close to, but I stole a razor once and bided my time until the moment came. Now I laugh at him each time the pus spills out of the corner of his mouth and forces him to pull out one of his silk hand-kerchiefs, or when the tip of his tongue runs across the wound as if it were fresh. He must taste it always, and that is a joy to me. Tycho begrudges me even this meager consolation, and I have to pretend otherwise when he visits me. For he is certainly back again, and we are man and wife once more, even though he thought me dead a long time ago."

"He has been out of the country and only recently returned?"

"Dear Tycho returned last year. How I had missed him. The last time I saw him his head was stuck in a noose from which he only narrowly escaped. I thought him secure somewhere on the far side of the world. But then he came home, and even better, managed with only a couple of moves to outplay all his enemies into a draw. With his orphanage, he has made himself untouchable, to the point that it would cost more than it would benefit the Furies to go after him. Instead they bide their time and pretend to be appeased by his little offering—the poor little Three Roses and his pretty wife. He keeps nothing from me, you know. To a great extent, Tycho is still the little boy who longed for the praise of an absent mother, and now when I can no longer be a wife to him, I fill that role instead, and listen mildly as he unburdens himself. I rejoice at his fortune. It gives me the opportunity to assist in his downfall. Fate has a reckoning in store for him to which I can contribute. That is why you are here, I take it? I have long hoped for this."

Cardell is the one who answers her, curt and direct like a soldier.

"A mother asked me to investigate the circumstances of her daughter's death. Your husband stands responsible."

She laughs.

"What a coincidence. I am also the daughter of a mother. I am so happy that I had only to wait in this bed for six years before the servants of justice found their way here, if not to interview me as a victim but a witness. But the police are hesitant to take on Tycho. His allies are too powerful. To a certain extent you must be acting of your own accord."

Their silence is an admission. The sounds of sobbing issue from the darkness before she finds her voice again.

"Do you know, I lie here wrapped in the softest sheets woven from silk, but after all this time it is like resting on sharpened sticks. But I have found God here. The maids read to me. Not of the God of the New Testament, for what is the suffering of God's Son compared to mine? If He could forgive, it is only because He was not tormented enough. As if I wouldn't exchange my years in this room for a few hours on the cross without a second thought! Nay, it is the God of the older texts that is mine. The one who drowned the world when it did not show Him sufficient honor. The one who suffocated the firstborn sons of Egypt. He who sent His bears to maul the forty-two children who had taunted the prophet Elisha. He who demanded an eye for an eye and a tooth for a tooth. Such is a God worthy of humans."

The childish laughter comes again and Cardell shivers.

"I have bedsores. They fester. I'm sure you can smell it through the roses. I am washed every day and my dressings are changed, but the wounds won't heal. My skin is worn as thin as silk and breaks at the slightest touch. My suffering is soon at an end, and even if my God sends me to hell, I know it will seem like the fields of Elysium compared to my time in this place."

She pauses.

"You. The large one. Will you step closer to the window so I may see you the better?"

Cardell gets up with some hesitation and does as he has been told.

"You have been in a fight. Was it of your own making?"

Cardell nods, and for several moments all that can be heard is Mrs. Ceton's wearied breathing, before she clears her throat and continues to speak.

"And it is justice that you seek, whatever that word may mean in a world such as ours? You should know that you can hardly count on any help, not even if you back Tycho into a corner holding a signed and witnessed confession."

She appears to consider this herself. Cardell feels her gaze linger over his mangled features.

"Earlier this week my husband came to me, and after we had spoken for a while he retreated to entertain a guest in the room next door. The walls are thin, and it seems that my hearing only grows sharper with each year. Tycho has arranged a meeting with a representative of the order to which he once belonged, to negotiate a permanent end to hostilities. If you are able to eavesdrop on that conversation it might help your case considerably. Do you know the Capricorn Palace on the Knights' Isle? They will meet at midnight in the wing where the surgeons do their business. Come in good time. Find the only room still lit. Do not be shocked by the nature of the place. Gentlemen of this kind have the habit of choosing unusual rendezvous. I do, however, believe that you will be able to use its shape to your advantage and find a hiding place where you will be able to see without being seen."

Cardell begins to move to the door, happy that the spell that had kept him still has been broken, but Emil Winge remains in his seat.

"Mrs. Ceton, what ails you?"

"My back is broken. The only thing I can do is move my head."

"His doing?"

"The squabbles of marriage that once occupied us went too far. First his face, then my back. Tycho prided himself on his looks, and I was the one who cut short his joyful days before the mirror. One can certainly understand his consternation, and this was his response. It did not turn out as he planned. I am fat now, but for a little while I still had my youthful body, slender and enticing, if immobile—and do you know, he made an attempt to rekindle the nightly pleasures of love, mainly to emphasize my powerlessness. My limbs may be useless, but I know him all too well, and so while his servant did everything that he was told, and Tycho sat beside him to watch, I lay here and hissed to my husband all those things I know that he fears most, until his own manhood wilted in the chair and he had to shuffle off to satisfy himself elsewhere. Since then, whenever he has wanted to hurt me, it has been my turn to laugh, because whatever he does, I feel nothing. He has never been a subtle creature; simple brutality is enough for him, and I am beyond its reach."

"Mrs. Ceton, is there anything we can do for you?"

"Your pity is wasted on me. There must be plenty of other miserable souls who seek it. This bed where I have languished will soon be my deathbed, and we don't want to arouse Tycho's suspicions by my sudden absence. I shall be dead soon enough, and patience is a virtue I have been given much opportunity to cultivate."

Winge is halfway to the door, but when Cardell follows him, she stops him.

"Watchman! I have seen you. Would you like to see me also before you go?"

Cardell thinks this offer over, and then nods. He crosses the room to the side of the bed and parts the curtain, forcing his eyelids to stay open and pinching his nose with this thumb and index finger. She laughs again.

"Send in Gustava on your way out. I have soiled myself and need changing."

....

Outside the gate, Cardell bends over with his elbow against his knee, and draws deep breaths. Winge turns his back until Cardell spits his mouth clean.

"Jean Michael . . ."

"Don't ask, not ever. Go back and look yourself if you are curious."

"How did she ring her bell?"

"It was sewn to her ear."

80

Light streams from the Capricorn Palace where candelabras have been placed on each windowsill. Through the archway to the courtyard, they can see the shadow of the crowd. There is a party, and the exertions of the ball have tempted the guests outside to cool off, despite the raw evening air. From inside there comes the sound of a fiddle and oboe, and loud voices and scattered laughter carry across the flagstones. The wood used for Rudenschöld's scaffold is still stacked nearby, waiting to be carried off. Winge and Cardell continue across the square towards the palace, the eastern annex of which frames a triangular garden. The structure is separated from the rest of the building, and the Collegium Medicum has hung its crest over the door. They can pick out the anatomical theater by its tall windows, and through them the flicker of candlelight. The door is unlocked and, in the hallways, the smell of vinegar is heavy in the air. They pause at the threshold, listening for any sound of movement from inside, before Cardell takes the lead down the corridor.

....

Along the walls of the anatomical theater, seating is arranged in steep tiers all the way up to the ceiling, rising in octagons to give an unimpeded view to as many as possible. Sconces hang in pairs on all sides around the table at the center of the room. Only one is lit, and on the table rests a woman's body, in an embroidered dress, pale and still. The few possessions of which she has already been relieved have been placed on the floor by the table: a cap, two shoes with red bands, a pair of sky-blue stockings. Winge and Cardell both pause at the double doors and take in the scene before them.

"What the hell is this? Is there to be an anatomical lecture as well?"

Winge takes his watch out of his waistcoat pocket and angles it towards the light until he can read the time. It is just past the stroke of midnight. Behind them comes a rattling at the entrance, followed by footsteps on the stone floor, and a voice. Cardell gives Winge a push into the room and whispers in his ear.

"Get up to the stands and stay low. There, up top, where it's dark enough for us both to see and hear."

Winge does as he's told and whispers his reply over his shoulder.

"Remember, Jean Michael, under no circumstances can we reveal our presence."

Cardell nods in answer and leads the way with quick steps as Winge gently lets the doors close behind them. It doesn't take long before they are flung open again.

....

The man at the front is a youth in his twenties, tall and lanky, with an apron over one arm and a case in the other, and the manner of one who has not yet become accustomed to the rapid growth of his limbs. His clothes are worn and poorly paired, with a pale-yellow coat over a stained waistcoat and two mismatched clasps at the knees of his breeches. He speaks incessantly, with a voice that is nasal and eager, still characterized by the treble of youth. When he sees the corpse, he interrupts himself with a gleeful yelp.

"Just as you said, Mr. Ceton! I hardly dared believe that it was true. You've no idea how hard it is for us students to procure necessary specimens on which to practice our craft. I can't understand how our professors expect us to be able to learn technique by observation alone. You have my eternal gratitude."

Ceton walks behind him, his hands clasped on his back, dressed as if he has just come from the ball on the other side of the square. The shadows play across his mutilated face.

"On the contrary, I am the one who should thank you, Nyberg. It seems equally impossible to gain entrance to a demonstration where one is not forced to crowd in with the rabble who are only drawn by the sensational aspects. I count myself lucky that you were willing to let me attend a more private event."

Nyberg lifts one of the lit candles from the sconce and transfers the flame to the rest, before hanging up his coat, wrapping the apron around his middle, and starting to roll up his sleeves.

"And the corpse? Prudence bids me ask your assurance that it was obtained by honest means."

"Don't worry on that account. She has no family who will ask any questions. My man Jarrick brought her in earlier, as we arranged. I assume you have your own routines as far as disposal is concerned?"

Nyberg places his case on a bench, opens the lid, lets his hand glide over rows of shiny steel, and gives a curt nod.

"Our night porter usually handles that matter, and will come before dawn to clean and transport the remains for burial. I have promised to treat him to an evening out for any additional inconvenience."

He loosens the fastening that keeps one of the knives in its place and tests its edge against his thumbnail before he spits on the whetstone and sharpens it some more. Ceton takes the opportunity to sit on the lowest tier.

"Will you be so kind as to explain each cut, Nyberg, just as your professors would have done if this were a formal lesson? I fear my knowledge of human anatomy leaves much to be desired, though my curiosity is substantial."

"Certainly, Mr. Ceton. Please let me know if you have any questions as the work progresses. I shall begin by opening the abdomen to reveal the chest cavity, and will thereafter ease the ribs open by saw and hook so that we may view the larger organs."

Ceton clears his throat and wipes the corner of his mouth clean before continuing.

"If you have no objections, Nyberg, I would prefer that we begin with something less drastic. Say, exposing the nerves and musculature of an arm or a leg?"

Nyberg gives Ceton an understanding smile.

"Ah, you would like to begin on a smaller scale? You'll have to excuse me, Mr. Ceton. We students spend so much time in each other's company that we tend to assume everybody is as familiar with the inside of a human being as we are, and so rush right to the heart of the matter, so to speak. Of course we can proceed more gradually if you so wish."

He tests the knife again to his satisfaction, then loosens the straps from the rest of his instruments, which he places on the bench in front of him in the order in which he intends to use them. He first selects a pair of scissors.

"I will begin by removing her clothes. Would you like me to keep her midriff covered for now? In our lectures, my friends sometimes find it distracting."

"Not on my account."

....

Nyberg has hardly started cutting the dress before the scissors slip out of his hand and clatter to the floor as he takes a startled step back.

"Mr. Ceton! There has been a terrible mistake. This woman is yet living. She is still warm and her lungs are drawing air, if only slightly. Will you hurry after some water while I try to get some life back into her?"

Ceton remains seated and crosses his legs.

"There has been no mistake, Nyberg. I thought it would be more interesting this way. If you have misgivings with regard to her life, let me assure you the dose of laudanum she has been given is far greater than anyone can accommodate and survive, and whatever you do, this hour will be her last. My man has secured her with thin leather straps, but that is mainly to show me his thoroughness: she is no longer able to move and surely can't feel anything either. Her death is inevitable, and you will remain free of guilt. This I swear on my father's grave."

Nyberg stares at Ceton for a moment before returning to the bench to put away his instruments.

"I have been gravely mistaken in you, Ceton. You are mad. Know you nothing of the Hippocratic Oath? My craft is intended to save life and nothing else. I will go to inform the city watch what is afoot here, and will not hesitate to provide a witness account to your detriment."

"My man has instructions to wait for me by your own door, Nyberg, behind which your beautiful Ulla and little Ulrika sleep so sweetly. Please remain calm: Jarrick will keep himself outside the threshold until the strike of four. If I have not returned by then to inform him that everything has turned out to my satisfaction, he has been given leave to break the lock and go inside, and how he should like to have his way then is not to be fathomed."

....

Winge has kept his eyes on Cardell ever since he first started to suspect the worst, and when the watchman now makes an attempt to get up from his hiding place, he puts his hands on Cardell's shoulders with as much weight as he can. Under his fingers, Cardell's body trembles with barely restrained rage. Winge puts his lips to Cardell's ear and tries to give his whispered words all the conviction he can muster.

"Jean Michael, you can do nothing. Kill Ceton here and you will seal the fate of the children, just as he has said."

Only his grip stops Cardell from giving them away, but it is not enough. In his desperation, he instead grabs the watchman by both ears, but when he is not able to turn Cardell's head, he has to move himself to get the eye contact that he seeks.

"You heard him. The woman is almost dead already. If you lay a hand on him, all of our efforts have been in vain. Can't you see that?"

There is still no glint of understanding in Cardell's bloodshot eyes, the enlarged pupils shifting their color towards black. Emil grasps at the last argument he can find.

"Jean Michael. Cecil would not have wanted to see you a murderer."

The crisis passes. Cardell's grimace of bloodlust relaxes, and resignation takes its place as reason returns. Emil is given an assenting nod.

....

Nyberg stands quietly on the floor. His face has taken on the white color of his shirt. Ceton lets him stammer out a mixture of pleas and protestations, promises and threats, before he silences him with a gesture.

"Hush now, little man. There is no one here except you and me, and no higher power to see or judge. Nature itself is indifferent. It would look on without the slightest objection if our entire race were to perish in suffering and misery. The woman lying there will soon join the many thousands of dead over whose graves we pass every day, and no one will ever ask after her. Don't you carve meat at your table each night to eat yourself and to serve to others? Is this really so different? When we leave this room, your memories will be the only connection between you and what has transpired here. So forget about it. Devote yourself to your wife and daughter instead, and be a loving husband and father if that pleases you. Let this have been a dream and nothing more."

Ceton pauses to wipe his chin.

"Time is ticking by, Nyberg. Now set to work. The right leg first, or what say you? Do not forget to describe your work, as you have promised me."

Nyberg's words can hardly be heard.

"*Quadriceps femoris* . . ."

"Will you be so kind as to press the rag further down her throat? I do believe she is about to wake and I don't want her cries to be a distraction to you."

"But you said laudanum . . . that she was beyond saving."

"Only very drunk, I fear. But even if what I said before was a lie, then it is the truth now, thanks to your cutting, don't you agree? Her life is bleeding out of her and it will soon be over. Come now, the rag, please. Hear how she cries."

Nyberg does as instructed.

"I hope you will excuse me, Nyberg, if I make myself a little more comfortable?"

Ceton unbuttons his trousers and lets them fall to his knees. From his place up in the stands, Cardell sees Ceton's hand bob up and down in a regular rhythm as he leans his head back against the back of the chair, to the sounds of Nyberg's sobs and the woman's increasingly faint moans. Saliva leaks down onto his shirt, but he takes no notice.

81

Emil Winge walks along the Quayside in the direction of the Stream, and only turns when he comes within earshot of the river that thunders ceaselessly towards the unfinished arches of the bridge. The castle is darkly silhouetted against the sea, from which a raw wind is buffeting the buildings that form the city's wall against the archipelago. Once he is past Lion Hill, he turns, and takes the same way back along the quay, where the remains of the Michaelmas market still linger in the form of some stubborn shopkeepers.

Shielded from the wind by a heap of sacks, a few sailors are playing cards on the cobblestones, with pebbles placed on the upturned cards to keep them from blowing away. Those who are not crouched in order to play their hand are jumping up and down on the spot and stamping their feet to keep warm, each with their shoulders hiked up to their ears and their fists under their armpits. Winge walks forward aimlessly and halts each time he risks getting in the way of a porter or errand boy. The stone pavement is still unfamiliar to him here; hewn granite seems always to lie in wait to trip up the inattentive passerby. His sister walks at his side, less bothered by the weather and wind.

"Thank heavens your friend saw reason."

"Jean Michael is no fool. He may be blustery of manner, but that's all. There is such rage inside him. His injuries pain him. When he doesn't wear his wooden fist, he sometimes makes gestures as if his missing hand were still there. I think he can still sense it, if such a thing were possible."

"What happened after that?"

"Her suffering was brief, too short for Ceton's taste. Perhaps the student had the presence of mind to puncture some larger artery for mercy's sake.

They both left, leaving what remained for the porter to dispose of. We let a few minutes go by, and then we left as well. What else could we do?"

Hedvig shakes her head and lets the breeze gently pull her fringe to the side as she looks Emil in the eyes.

"Mrs. Ceton deceived you. She read Cardell correctly in your meeting. It can't have been hard. You say that his face is roughed up, which confirms his predilection for violence. She showed herself to him in order to increase his hatred for her husband, and then she sent you into her trap under false assumptions. She hoped to make Cardell her husband's killer."

"But why? Her help would have been able to further our case and give her justice."

"For one reason or other, she does not believe your investigation will meet with success. Perhaps she believes the Chamber of Police itself will throttle it in its cradle the moment they become aware of it, regardless of any breakthroughs. Perhaps she did not think much of either of you—a crippled watchman and a lapsed student who is frightened by sounds no one else can hear. Mrs. Ceton does not concern herself at all with the children at Horn Hill, and she is not in fear of damnation."

Emil nods at words that ring true.

"Let's hope she has misjudged us."

He sits down on a pile of wood and gazes out, frowning to protect his eyes against the gusts. The clouds are thin enough to allow pale beams of light to sift through and glisten on the waves as they roll in around the headland. The ships lie in rows, tethered to the roadstead and to each other, their masts rocking to and fro. He sighs.

"Hedvig, I don't know what to do. My thoughts go round and round, so quickly that I have trouble pinning any single one of them down."

She sits next to him.

"Ceton stands and falls with Horn Hill. That protection must be removed. Perhaps it can be bought from under him?"

"How?"

"If the running of the orphanage can be secured some other way, Ceton will be superfluous and your way to him will lie open. You and your friend have pursued the problem as if it were a question of assigning blame. It seems to me rather a question of money."

"We have even less money than ears willing to hear our evidence. Horn Hill must cost more than the Crown spends on the whole of Indebetou House and all its staff."

He is on his feet again. His hands start moving of their own accord to help sort his various ideas.

"Unless . . ."

Hedvig nods him on.

"Go on."

"Erik Three Roses. Ceton controls his inheritance. Perhaps Three Roses's condition may be improved upon. Perhaps he can be made to sign new documents. It was at Dane's Bay the trail started and it is to Dane's Bay I must return."

Emil is already on his way when she stops him. Her grip on his arm causes him to twist a half turn until they stand face-to-face. Once again he is struck by how lightly the years have affected her.

"Hedvig, I must hurry. My stupidity has already cost us too much time."

She lays her cool hand on his cheek.

"Do you remember when Father locked you in the cellar in the evening, those times you did not manage to do the labyrinth game fast enough? Cecil and I could do nothing but listen to your sobs because Father guarded the door well and never let us help you. Once I was grown, I was the one who had you locked up, and when I think about that I feel shame, so much shame my heart aches in my chest. If you have forgiven Cecil, can't you also forgive me?"

"You only wanted what's best for me."

"*Facilis descensus Averno.*"

"Virgil?"

"I hurt you. I ask your forgiveness."

Tears spill down her cheeks and render her unable to speak for a moment. In his heart, Emil finds that forgiveness has long been granted and that the words needed to confirm it leave him like a bird alighting upon a branch.

"Without your help, I would not have managed, and my debt to our brother would have gone unpaid. Yes. Yes, I forgive you."

"You know that I have always been fondest of you out of everyone, dear Emil. Cecil and I both."

If she has ever embraced him before, he can't remember when. Unused to it as he is, he is at first stiff until some inherent but long-forgotten gift shows him how best to nestle his body against hers, cheek against throat, his arms around her back, and he at last closes his eyes and feels a peace that he has sought for as long as he can remember.

82

Maja and Karl are heavier than Anna Stina can believe, but still the burden feels natural. They each find a place to perch above her hip bones, as if the weeks in the forest have shrunk her waist in preparation to give them room. When she forms the blanket into a sling that runs between their legs and up over her shoulders, they sit snugly, and she only needs her arms to steady their backs. Over her shoulder she tosses a sack, the contents of which cut into her back at every step.

When she emerges from the edge of the forest, she sets her sights on the roof of the Observatory and the soundless wings of the windmill. The roads on the outskirts of Stockholm are rarely worse than now, saturated with the autumn downpours without any hard freeze to give footing. Soon the mud paints her brown up to her knees. The city sneaks up on her unnoticed when the wooden houses that recently appeared strewn about at random begin to align in rows, making streets straight enough to be bestowed names of their own. She rounds the hill until she can see the spire of the church, and asks a woman with a stool in one hand and a pail in the other for directions. She only has a few more blocks to go, and it does not take long before she arrives. The outside of the building runs the length of the entire quarter, three storeys high and crowned with a penthouse floor. She has to walk back and forth to find the right entrance, takes the street down towards the water, and follows a baker's cart in under the archway.

The Common Orphanage hugs the courtyard on three sides. Behind the wall, she sees an extensive garden that follows the sloping ground all the way down to the marshy shore meadows of Foundling Bay, behind which the water rises and falls in the same gray color as the sky. Down from the smithy by the water, she can hear the heavy breath of bellows and the clanging of hammer and anvil, and outside the building there are newly sewn sails hung to dry in the wind.

"Have you come to drop them off?"

A stout woman, with red, chapped hands from laundering or baking, has stepped out of the entrance and stands on the stairs with her hands on her hips to examine her guest. Anna Stina curtsies.

"May I look around first?"

The woman tilts her head to one side.

"Are you implying that the orphanage may provide less care than what they're used to?"

The woman answers her own question before Anna Stina has the chance.

"Well, I wouldn't chide a mother for wanting to see how her children will be cared for, even if she is leaving them to others. Ebba is my name, I am matron here. Go and take a look around, and come back to me when you're ready for the registration."

The housekeeper sizes up the little ones with a stern look.

"Two of them, huh?"

Anna Stina nods.

"If I leave them, will they be allowed to stay together?"

Ebba purses her lips and crosses her arms.

"If you insist on that, we'll do our best. But I warn you: in that way they may grow old in this house, if the fever spares them. Well. I have other business to attend to."

Anna Stina curtsies again, and while the matron hurries on, she walks up the stairs and goes inside. Behind the baking room and kitchen there is a dining hall for the boys and girls, next to it classrooms in each of which teetering piles of catechisms and hymnals flank a single black Bible on their bookshelves. There is a pervasive smell of vinegar in the rooms, albeit too weak to conceal what it has been intended to do. You can still sense the presence of crowded bodies, their dirt and sweat. Of the children, she sees nothing.

In the dunce's corner, someone has drawn the crude outline of a donkey. When she encounters locked doors, she turns and goes out the same way she came in.

....

Out in the courtyard, a man in a worn wig is arguing with the baker by his cart about the price of his wares. The baker has crossed his arms and refuses to listen to the arguments, even though the man takes two loaves and bangs them together like logs of firewood. Only after his customer reaches into the middle of the bread pile and pulls out a loaf spotted with mold, emitting a victorious yelp, does the baker see reason.

"Five loaves for a penny, then, just because I am so fond of the little ones."

Some distance away in the courtyard she sees what must be one of the orphans, although he is older than the others she has seen. Twelve years, perhaps eleven. He wears a surcoat and a black scarf. He has outgrown his blue shirt, and it leaves a gap showing his stomach and back. He is barefoot despite the cold, holding a broom in front of him, slowly rocking back and forth, pushing wet hay and pig dung in front of him. His mouth is open and his tongue hangs swollen over his lip as he makes his way closer to the baker's cart. In an unguarded moment, he lets a hand shoot out, snatches a piece of bread, and hides it under his shirt. For a brief second his eyes come alive with watchfulness before he continues slowly on with the same expressionless face, humming tonelessly. She follows him around the corner.

"I have berries if you'd like some."

The boy rocks back and forth, his jaw moving in an agitated way in feigned confusion.

"I saw you. I won't tell."

He lets his eyes scan the surroundings before he shrugs, wipes his chin, and drops his act.

"I imagine you want some bread in exchange."

His voice is still unbroken. Her mouth waters at the thought. It has been months since she last had baked bread.

"If you like, we could share."

She turns around and shows him the bag she is carrying. He evaluates its size and jerks his head in the direction of the coach house.

"Not here. Over there, behind the dung heap. You go first, I'll come after. Utterström is still arguing with the rascal baker and if he catches sight of me, things will go badly."

It takes him a good while to shuffle his way across the courtyard. Behind the coach house there is an old crate being used as a bench. Anna Stina fumbles with the string of her bag until the boy reaches out and puts Karl on his lap. They share berries and bread. He never takes his eyes off her, chewing and swallowing as quickly as he can. She also eats, and the taste is strange and good, even though each bite has to be moistened in the mouth for a long time before it can be swallowed.

"I can see you have a question."

"Why are there so few children here?"

"They don't want us to stay. We are given to others, to be raised, as they call it."

She pours out more berries for him as she awaits his explanation. He tears off some bread between his thumb and index finger and gives it to Karl to taste. Karl smacks his lips and lets his tongue struggle with the unfamiliar mass, and the emotions playing across his face end in comical distaste. The boy laughs.

"Three times they put me in the cart along with a handful of others. They drive us into the country, to villages far away, and try to find someone willing to give us shelter. Where the farms are dilapidated and the peasants grind bark into their flour is where they are most likely to take us. We are most welcomed by those who need someone to work for no payment other than a piece of bread and a stack of hay to sleep in, and for each child they receive eight daler a year. The girls go first. Then the best of the boys. Each time I have had to go back alone."

"Why do you play the fool?"

"Sometimes the kids who've escaped or been rejected walk all the way back to Stockholm, and when I see them, they are worse off than if they had stayed. Those foster parents who have already dug the grave before they wave for the orphanage cart to stop, those who work a pretty girl or boy to the bone, what do you think they would do with someone like me? If they think I'm simple, and that the effort of putting me to work is greater than the reward, they'll let me stay here, at least for a few more years. Only those they can't place anywhere get to stay here. The simpletons, the maimed, the ugly. It isn't good, but it's better than the alternative."

"And how is it here, for those of you who stay?"

He sighs.

"Soup every day, watery and thin, cooked turnips and carrots, and meat so salty that a girl had to be saved from the well after she reached for water without permission. You learn to sift it between your teeth to catch the copper flakes that loosen from the kettle they never scour, because if you swallow you'll throw everything up, and might just as well have saved yourself the trouble. We recite the catechism every morning until we know the words by heart, helped by the cane, and the teacher calls that learning. Everyone who lives long enough is put to work."

"What kind of work?"

The boy points up to the second storey of the wing.

"Go up and see for yourself."

She stands up to go in the direction that his hand is pointing, and when he hands her Karl he leans closer.

"You know, they hardly see me any longer, and when they speak, they don't pay any attention to me, any more than they would have done if a horse or pig had been caught eavesdropping. When Utterström was new to the house, they showed him around, and he was all questions. The first morning he was here, the watchmen came by with two infants they had found in the street and shortly thereafter a mother limped in to give up her baby, just like you. Utterström asked how the house could afford them all. The gentleman who was showing him around answered that the costs were far lower than they seemed, because of every five admitted, only one will see the end of the first year. The little ones come here to die. The orphanage is the finest angel maker the city has ever seen. If you want a different fate for yours, take them as far away from here as you are able. Well, mustn't tarry. That pig shit won't sweep itself back and forth across the yard all day."

"I wish you luck."

"Wish in one hand, shit in the other, see which fills up first. But perhaps we'll meet again."

"Or perhaps not."

Anna Stina lifts her children to her hips and walks towards the wing. She hears the sound already in the stairwell, one she knows well and will never forget. The chorus of groaning wood pumped in repetitive motion, under whispering wool and the crackle of the carder. She doesn't need to see to know, but does so anyway. Three unlit wooden chandeliers in the ceiling, spinning wheels in long rows, a child hunched over each.

Out on the street, she first looks to the left, where the forest awaits beyond the houses of the city, soon to be robbed of harvest and fruit, famine its only promise. She turns her head to the right, towards the City-between-the-Bridges. Three churches stand in a row, Nikolai and Gertrud, and Katarina on the hill beyond. Maja gurgles happily. Karl nods off into sleep and Anna Stina puts a hand behind his neck to keep his head upright. There's only one way to go. Yet she hesitates for a long time. Mickel Cardell's wooden fist bumps against the small of her back as she follows the lead of the spires.

83

Fallen leaves blow gently back and forth across the hospital courtyard until some capricious gust sweeps them into the brook that trickles lazily from the lake out into the bay. Everything is bare and desolate; the weather now is too harsh for the ailing to do anything but wait behind their walls for spring. Cardell pushes his hips forward with his hands against the small of his back, still stiff despite the walk to Dane's Bay; he has had to sleep on the floor, and the planks have had their effect. When Cardell and Winge approach the hospital building, a man comes walking around the corner. When he sees them, he gives a little cry of astonishment.

"My apologies. We were hardly expecting guests on a day like this."

He is short, clad in a gray coat, with an over-large wig that appears more like a bonnet than anything else. His eyes are watchful as he sizes up the two men, before he finally chooses to address Cardell with a gesture to Winge, whose gaze nervously flickers towards the asylum a little further back on the cliff.

"Have you come to find a place for your companion?"

Cardell frowns and snorts.

"What are you talking about? We are here to see Erik Three Roses, one of your patients in the asylum."

The man reddens somewhat and gives a shrill laugh.

"Gentlemen, you will have to excuse me. Out here, hallucinations are so common they are infectious. My name is Näsström, neighborhood physician in Katarina, but I come here to assist as often as time allows, as God only knows the help is sorely needed. I know very well the one you are talking about."

He joins them in their walk, the yellow plaster of the madhouse sharply outlined against the black of the sea cliffs. Winge clasps his hands behind his back and walks alongside him.

"Do you know anything about his condition? Has there been any sign of improvement?"

Näsström gives him a regretful look.

"It was you who made sure he was afforded better quarters, I take it? That was a good deed. The boy shares a better room now, where a barrier has been installed to protect him from the others, as sadly he is not yet in any position to defend himself."

He continues down the slope and gestures at the ground to warn them of the treachery underfoot, soil churned into mud by rain and damp sea air.

"I have been given to understand that the condition in which you first found Three Roses was no credit to our institution, and I do want to underscore that the boy's situation is now much improved. I have been away from my duties for a while as I was dealing with personal matters, and when I returned I was alarmed at the terrible state in which the place has been allowed to deteriorate. Filth and mismanagement, routines no longer observed, the lunatics left to their own devices. You can now be sure that the boy has daily visits and that all of his needs are met the moment they are discovered."

Once at their destination, Näsström puts his weight against the door to force it open and shows Cardell and Winge in with an outstretched arm.

"Does he communicate at all?"

Näsström shakes his head at Winge's question and points out the way to the stairs.

"I have spent some time with the boy. He spends his waking hours in the position in which he is placed, unmoving except for a slow rocking that is probably caused by the body's humors and the beating of the heart. From time to time he hums to himself but with no melody to speak of."

The corridor to which Näsström leads them is a different one to last time, and when he opens the door to let them in they see that the window is at least no longer covered and lets in the light. A poorly constructed wooden wall with a locked hatch in the center divides the room into two parts. On the other side, they can hear dragging steps moving back and forth along its entire length, as well as heavy breaths and occasional murmurs. Erik Three Roses sits on a chair by the window, turned away. His hair has grown back in a thick stubble, through which the angry scar on his scalp gleams red. They become aware that the seat of the chair has a hole and that a chamber pot has been placed underneath. A long shirt covers Three Roses's bare lower body. The head rests against the back of the chair, eyes half-closed, his gaze vacant. When they draw closer, they hear a monotonous sound, a faint humming. Näsström kneels by the chair and examines Three Roses's face.

"We must not give up hope, gentlemen, and show Erik patience. He is still young, and the body has a remarkable ability to recover as long as it senses a future worth the effort. His wound is closed and clean, and perhaps the healing process may in time reach deep enough to restore what ails him, if we can only show him all the tenderness and respect that he deserves as a human being. You should know, as true as my name is Näsström, that love can effect miracles beyond the reach of science. Well, I will leave you in peace."

....

Winge waits until the physician's steps have died away before sitting down on the side of the bed. The face before him is worn and pale. He seeks Three Roses's gaze, but his eyes don't seem to be able to focus on his and only stare vacantly straight ahead. The boy has lost more weight. In the places where the damp linen shirt is stuck to his chest with sweat, each rib can be counted.

"Erik?"

The breaths are shallow and cause a gurgling each time the lungs are filled. Winge places a hand on his bony shoulder and gives it a careful shake.

"Erik, you must listen to me. Tycho Ceton has given you papers to sign, either in person or by way of a mediator, or both. Isn't that true? Where are they, Erik?"

He tries to rephrase his words, to make them shorter or simpler, as if language contains some hidden key to wake the boy from his daze.

But to no avail. Cardell, who has been walking in tight circles around the room, points under the bed.

"There's a chest. I believe it's the same I remember from his room at the hospital."

They move it with combined force and find it unlocked. Inside lies all that remains of the Erik Three Roses who would have been able to answer their questions. A jacket and a pair of trousers that have been relieved of their buckles by some nimble-fingered employee, a pen and a dried-up inkwell. Under these, a pile of correspondence that Winge grabs with trembling hands. When he has flicked through the pages, he crosses the floor to hold a few of them at an angle to the light, one by one. Cardell watches these activities with a furrowed brow.

"What the hell is going on?"

Winge waves him over and holds up the pages.

"See here. This is the letter that Three Roses's cousin Schildt supposedly sent him after his departure to join the fight for liberation on Hispaniola. Hold them to the light, Jean Michael. Can you see? On each and every one of them you can read the impression of the earlier text."

Cardell squints at it with irritation and without understanding what he is looking at.

"What about it?"

"Schildt wrote them all at the same time, one after the other, as the pages lay in a pile. Doubtlessly forced to do so by Ceton, before they stained his skin and sold him into slavery. From time to time, Ceton could present Erik with the latest letter as proof that Schildt was still alive and that the story about his flight was anything but a lie."

Cardell shakes his head and spits before withdrawing to give Winge space to continue his search, standing still all the while, and searching Erik Three Roses's limp face for some remaining sliver of humanity. He is given plenty of time. Nevertheless, he is unable to find anything there, and when he looks up, Emil Winge is sitting on the edge of the bed with a look of hopelessness, papers strewn in a wide circle around him.

"Ceton has scraped him bare. Every penny squandered. The house and lands are in the process of being parceled out. Only debts remain. If Erik ever gets out of here, all that awaits is debtors' prison."

Winge returns to Three Roses's side to coax him with unheard questions and Cardell lets him be until the words become less pressing. He puts his hand on Winge's shoulder and urges him to his feet.

"The boy is lost. Can't you see? Beyond our reach. And in the abyss into which his senses have been relegated, he believes that he was the one who killed his bride, even though it is that grinning devil who bears all the blame. We can't even give him that bit of comfort, and as long as Horn Hill exists, Ceton will be protected by it as safe from the law now as when we first began our search. And so our last bit of hope is gone. Damn it all to hell. Let's go."

A faint trickle can be heard from the chamber pot under Three Roses, and Cardell tactfully turns away to avoid Winge's look of horror and disgust. Cardell rubs his face, stretches his tender back, and rolls his hips from side to side, unused to the weight of the wooden fist that now again hangs under the elbow of his left arm, cleaned and scrubbed free of the guttersnipes' scribbles, shiny and new and no longer reeking of rotgut and dried blood, but instead infused with a scent that is both unfamiliar and reassuring: of forest and dew, spring water, moss, and soil; and of her and of her children, secure in his room now, and if not exactly warm, then at least warmer than they have been under the bare sky in the Great Shade.

84

The stump aches and stings, unaccustomed now to the hollowed-out space in the wooden arm from which it has been parted. Cardell has loosened the straps and hung it around his neck to give himself some relief. Through his shirt, he rubs the scarred skin gently in the hopes that the ache will subside. The feeling is still strange after all these years, impossible to get used to. It is subdued but ever present, and its endless patience makes it worse than anything else he has felt, to be forgotten only in those moments when something else manages to command all of his attention. Sometimes sudden tingles and tickling sensations come on that make his entire body jump as surely as if someone had poured a bucket of cold water down his collar. From time to time the pain moves into the flesh that is no longer his, and although he can see that nothing is there, the empty space where his missing arm once was burns where no relief can be applied. At its worst, the pain extends still further, until the viselike grip of the anchor chain once more seizes it, and the agony flares and spits like a guttering candle.

Next to him he hears Emil Winge's voice, and he can only manage to give him the barest attention. Scattered thoughts are being given voice, theories too quickly dressed in words. The reasoning runs in circles, the arguments all known. Of him, no answers are expected. Winge goes over the details in the hope that one of them will give way like a trapdoor suddenly revealed, and open up some hitherto unknown path.

It is as if a sixth sense alerts Cardell before his eyes can confirm the suspicion that they are being followed. Some soldier's instinct, long dormant, makes him cast a look over his shoulder as they pass through the tollgate, and in the corner of his eye he senses a deeper shadow in the falling twilight, someone who stops by a tree at the side of the road and remains standing until he has turned his head forward again. Cardell controls himself and allows their companion to pass unchallenged until he gets a better chance to confirm his suspicion. When they have drawn near to the Lock, they round a corner, and Cardell stops a few feet into the alley to shake an imaginary stone from his boot. He hears the intake of breath when the stranger realizes how close he has come to giving himself away and quickly steps back to put the corner between them once more. Next to him, Emil Winge has stopped of his own accord, distracted as always. For the hundredth time since they have said their farewell to Dane's Bay, he brings up his sister's name.

"I must consult with Hedvig."

Cardell takes him by the arm and leads him in the right direction.

"Maybe better advice will also come with sleep. I'll walk you home."

Cardell can still not be completely sure of himself. Perhaps it is only someone whom fate has sent along the same route as themselves, someone who has more innocent reasons to jump back at the sight of Cardell and his uniform. He takes the long way back and circles a whole block for no reason, and only when he sees that their shadow has done the same is he sufficiently convinced. He takes his leave of Winge and waits on the step until he hears the door close, silencing the voice that can still be heard mumbling to itself, before he continues down the street back the way they came, towards the Lock. A careful glance assures him that he still has company.

....

Down by the Stairs of the Master of Revenue, the boat-women have set out for the last time before the falling darkness will make it impossible to use their oars through the web of anchor ropes that stretch and tighten with the motion of the waves. Few people pass over the drawbridges, neither the red nor the blue, for the hour is late and the darkness a deep enough deterrent. The evening's revelers have long since selected their destinations, and anyone caught on the wrong side of the Lock would do best to adjust to what fate has determined. Cardell hums a little ditty as he walks along the road by the mill house. The low stone facade against the sea is broken up by a row of windows to give the millers and their customers enough light to see without risking any open flame. He turns the corner into the last street that the City-between-the-Bridges has to offer, or the first one that belongs to the South-ern Isle, depending on whom you ask. The stone rumbles under his leather soles, where the mill current rushes under hidden arches. The area is empty, as he had hoped, and he puts his back to the wall. The streams of water sing all around him, and he adjusts his stump and buckles the straps as hard as he can. He pricks up his ears for approaching footsteps, and waits.

....

He is ready to strike when the figure rounds the corner, just within reach as he had thought, and he lets his left arm go with force. The back of the wooden fist hits the face straight on. He doesn't need to see very clearly to know how well the blow has landed. There is a spurt of warmth, salt sting-ing his eyes, and the bite he feels in his stump, as if a wolf had locked its jaws around it, must be nothing compared to how it feels to be on the re-ceiving end. It is a grown man, as he can hear from the sound of the body when it hits the cobblestones once the legs have given way. He grabs the limp weight by the collar and drags it along the alleyway, where he bangs on a door until a frightened miller's apprentice, who has been assigned to stand guard, looks out. Cardell holds out a shilling in his palm.

"Good evening, dancing master, we have come to test your floor for a while, me and my friend here, if this entrance fee will suffice."

The boy nods with a grin and opens the door. In the light from his lan-tern, Cardell sees the damage he has caused. The nose is but a memory, pink bone shards in a flattened ruin are all that remain. The upper lip hangs in tatters over a mouth where the front teeth are shattered. The blood still flows, as black as pitch in the light of the flame, and each bubbling breath has to fight to win passage. He drags the man over to where he wants him, gives the boy another shilling for the loan of the lantern, and asks him not to return until the hour is over. A scoop of water shows Cardell something of the facial features, and a few mumbled words come after. With an effort, Cardell can make them out as French. He gives the cheek a hard pat.

"You are Jarrick, I assume? Ceton's henchman. You tracked us from Dane's Bay. Were you assigned to wait there or was it chance that brought us together?"

The eyes open, the battered gaze brimming with hatred. The words come in the same gushing flow as the blood so recently did, and Cardell shakes his head.

"I don't speak French, but those kinds of words I'd know in any language. Are you casting aspersions on my mother's honor? Asking me to go to hell? I've heard it all, and worse besides. There's something else I'd like to know, and I didn't think you would be one to sing willingly, but let me show you something that has changed many a man's mind."

The mill houses four waterwheels, each double the height of a man. Two channels run through the mill, narrowing to a stone funnel where they meet the blades of the wheels, forcing them to turn on creaking axles. Cardell grabs a bunch of Jarrick's hair and lifts him until the pain forces limp feet to stagger forward, to the nearest wheel. Cardell holds him out over the current.

"Look down."

The water can't be seen but can be heard, loudly, a dark maelstrom boiling with rage at finding its way blocked.

"I want to see your master tonight, and you'll take me to him."

Jarrick makes an attempt to spit in Cardell's face but finds that his cracked lips can no longer purse enough for the task.

"I'll show you an old Stockholm custom, foreigner that you are. The guttersnipes do this for fun when they're bored, but make no mistake: each step could be your last. I have seen youngsters lose their footing and get lost under the wheel. If they're lucky, they are dragged around underneath and carried up to the surface on the other side, where their friends can fish them out with poles down by the quay, and turn them upside down to drain them of water. But they are small and limber, Jarrick, and you are fat and heavy. It wouldn't surprise me if you get stuck between the paddle and the bottom until the water grows strong enough to crack your spine and spit you out on the other side as food for crabs. Ready? A deep breath now, and so we dance. You can be Count Luxembourg, and I'll play the devil himself."

Cardell pulls until his muscles creak and sets Jarrick on the tumbling wheel. He learns the art quickly, for there is nothing to do but climb, to pass each slippery board faster than the wheel can turn. He finds his pace.

Each time his boot slips, he loses height and has to double down on his exertions as his own weight interferes with the progress of the wheel. Cardell leans up against a beam to watch, and sees Jarrick's defiance melt away as the cold water soaks his clothes and he struggles above the jaws of death that await, with greedy patience, the end of a battle that no one can win. It is time that works the trick, the long moments that tell him one of them will be his last and that beat down every other thought until only blind terror remains. And yet the screams for mercy come more quickly than Cardell would have thought, and he finds that such words are just as easily understood in any language.

85

Tycho Ceton takes his meal late, alone in a separate room at a table set for one, so far back into the Golden Peace that the noise from the main dining room can hardly be heard. For Cardell's sake, a second chair has been carried in; he has declined the food but not the wine. Ceton digs into the meal that is served, one course at a time, with gusto. Sauces and crumbs spill down onto his cravat from the extended corner of his mouth. From time to time, a red tongue tip wanders along his lips and onto the edges of the wound. By the glint in his eye, Cardell senses that his disgust amuses Ceton, but as always, he can't say for sure if it is a mocking smile on his face or only the play of the light. A candelabra holds twelve wax candles on arms of silver between them, and the small room is lit up as if by the sun itself. For a while, only the wet sounds of Ceton's sloppy bites can be heard, before he dries his mouth on a silk napkin, drops it on the floor, and with a single gesture lets the server in his neat jacket understand that he can fill their glasses before leaving them in peace. They both drink. It is Cardell who breaks the silence.

"So we've an agreement?"

Ceton empties his glass and fills it up again.

"Are you in such a hurry to leave my table?"

Cardell stares down at the tablecloth as Ceton continues.

"I have asked for coffee, and even here they are prepared to defy the prohibition as long as the customer pays for it. They burn strips of linen over the pot in order not to attract any zealous informer with the smell of the brew."

He lights a cheroot on one of the flames of the candelabra and puffs on the stem until the smoke almost obscures him from view.

"I shall tell you the price of our agreement; what you have to ignore in order to get your way. That is more than just, surely? That you be told all the details?"

He holds his mouth closed and lets the smoke seep out through his cheek, slender, ghostlike tendrils at the edge of the wound.

"My pills caused Erik Three Roses to nod off over his plate, and I saw to it that he was carried to the bridal chamber as discreetly as possible, before I sent for the bride. We escorted her up the stairs in strength, she still rosy-cheeked and laughing in the belief that the whole thing was a game. She was led into the chamber where her sleeping husband already lay undressed and tucked into bed. The gentlemen began to carouse, taking turns in increasingly intimate dances in which she was sent from embrace to embrace as they shed their clothes, and one could still see a vestige of hope in the young beauty that she had become the object of some drunken prank that had gone too far. They enjoy such ambiguity, the gentlemen do, like a cat playing with the mouse. No night can be made long enough for them. Clothes kept falling, and when the pallor she soon took on began to rob her of her charms, she started to get pinches and slaps, and I could see that she knew this night would cost her, but not as yet how much. Then they put their masks on, naked to a man, one with the face of a pig, another a monkey, a third a stag, each chosen at random. One may think such things shouldn't matter, but you'd be surprised: everyone knows everyone else from a long way back, but as the bacchanal rages it is not easy to remember after the fact who bore which mask, and who did what. The masquerade helps them to manage what self-consciousness may infringe on pleasure. Things went from bad to worse. Her bridal gown was reduced to crimson shreds; soon the girl was in her birthday suit. She bit and scratched whenever she could, refusing to do as she was told—as do all who are worth the effort, the connoisseurs agreed—and the gentleman in the monkey mask took her to task. At first he reached for a decorative porcelain case for a weapon, but this broke into a thousand pieces after only a couple of blows. Some brilliant fellow found that one of the carved posts of the canopy frame could be unscrewed, and that suited far better. And now, Cardell, there it finally lay upon her bloody and toothless form. She knew that the night would be her last, and that it would be all too long. It was like seeing some handsome vase fracture and crack: at first the appearance is the same, but it will never ring again when tapped. The party was frisky now, some who had been waiting their turn heaved little Erik from the bed and bent him over its edge to make what use of him as could be had. It was only then that she first cried in earnest. Well. You understand more or less what followed. Each one had satisfaction in accordance with his wish, and in the order of seniority. She had spirit, just as Erik himself had recorded in his recollections. They were able to make her last a long time, and even after the soul found its escape, what remained still provided them with enjoyment for some time. Afterwards only carrion remained."

Cardell forces his features into stillness. The only thing he has power over in this room is to rob Ceton of the pleasure of his open hatred for him.

"And you yourself, where were you?"

"On a chair by the door. I do not partake. My enjoyment lies in the observation, and when I had assured myself that matters had run their course, and that the groom would wake under the circumstances I had arranged, I bade all good night. On my way out, I saw a man I had often previously seen, then dressed in silk and velvet, gilt-embroidered and decorated with orders and finery, in conversation with the lords of the kingdom. Now? Naked on all fours with his rear in the air and his chest stained red, his mouth full of false teeth, mounted on one of Fauchard's feather-sprung metal frames and sharpened into points—the price of a fortune to the silversmith who fashioned it—howling like a dog under a full moon. His birth had provided him with all anyone could wish for, but only in such a moment could he be himself to the fullest extent. Remarkable, don't you think?"

....

Ceton blows rings across the table, where they break on the flames of the candelabra. The cloud stings Cardell's eyes. He tries to control himself, but leans across the table as if pulled by an invisible thread, into the smoke from Ceton, who is weighing back on his chair.

"I was there, you know, in the anatomical theater where you got your way with that student. I watched you. Right before the girl had finally bled herself free, I saw something in your face that I've seen too many times to mistake. I saw it in the war, as our men prepared for the enemy's fire. Fear. You were afraid, as frightened as anyone I've ever seen. As if you were going to piss yourself at any moment. As if it was your life that had reached its final moment, and not hers. You enjoy telling stories like this, but as far as you're concerned, there's another story to tell, isn't there?"

Ceton sits for a moment in speechless astonishment before he lets the front legs of his chair smash down on the ground and he grinds out the rest of his cheroot into the remains on his plate. His sputtering words make his wound spill over, its edges bright red and raw.

"I'll tell you why I'm willing to enter into this agreement, watchman. It's not on your account. I have seen men like you a hundred times over. You're ordinary. Nowhere on these islands could I throw a stone over my shoulder without hitting someone like you, someone whom only his mother could distinguish from his peers. I have nothing to fear from someone like you. Look at yourself. Your body all used up, a worn wreck that only obstinacy is keeping together. I am used to reading others, and you are no exception. A common man whose every action is easy to anticipate. No, it is for the sake of the other one that I am willing to meet you halfway. The thin little one. Winge. There is something wrong with him that I can't put my finger on. When I see him, I can't tell what's happening under the surface. If I were you, I'd stay away from him. Nothing good can come of mixing with his ilk."

Cardell stands up and stretches out his one hand, suddenly eager to seal their compact with something other than words, although his thoughts go to the sinking of the *Ingeborg* and the grip of the anchor chain that deprived him of his other one. He would rather have put his right hand next to the left in that same trap. But Ceton takes a step away and shakes his head.

"I don't shake hands. But I will keep my word just the same."

Cardell growls goodbye before he turns and leaves.

"If you don't, you'll learn that it is I and no one else who deserves your fear."

Maybe Ceton smiles in response, maybe not.

86

"It's over."

Emil Winge stands rooted to the spot in his rented room and fixes Cardell with uncomprehending eyes.

"What are you saying?"

Cardell turns his back in order to avoid having to look Winge in the face, and instead stares up at the light that falls on the wall behind him. Dust particles dance through the sunbeam, weightless.

"I'll go to Blom at the Indebetou tomorrow in order to void my arrangement with the Chamber of Police."

"No, Jean Michael, all hope is not lost. I have discussed it with my sister. I presented our situation to her and, after giving the matter a great deal of thought, she has promised to meet me at the Quayside."

"It's enough, Emil. You were the one who was right when you came to my room to say goodbye, and I should have had the sense to listen."

"And yet you disagreed. What's changed?"

"Everything, damn it! Everything! We've gone down every road, and each time found a wall that we can neither break down nor climb over. There's no hope left. Let's give up while we still have time."

"Jean Michael, please turn around."

"Why?"

"Please turn around and look me in the eyes when you say such things."

Against his will, Cardell does as he has been asked, only managing to retain eye contact for a brief second until he lets his gaze fall to the floor, cursing himself and his ineptitude.

"You are not speaking the truth, Jean Michael, or at least you are not telling me everything. What has happened?"

"Nothing's happened."

"You have blood on your sleeve, and the stains are fresh."

"The city is dangerous at night."

"Won't you tell me the truth? You are concealing something from me and without knowing all of the numbers in the equation, I have little hope of finding a solution."

Cardell takes a deep breath, makes a fist behind his back, hard enough for the nails to draw blood from his palm, and stares into Winge's eyes.

"I went to Maria graveyard late yesterday after my dinner, to Cecil's grave, and while I was standing there, remembering what he and I had accomplished together, it was as if everything you had said before finally fell into place, and a realization came to me. You're not who he was. You don't know what he knew. I was a fool to think you could fill your brother's shoes, even for a moment. I should have left you to drink yourself to death to your heart's content, because that's all you're good for. You're a disappointment to me, Emil, and I have only myself to blame, and now this charade is at an end."

He turns to walk to the door, his eyes tightly shut and his face screwed into a grimace. The voice that reaches him over his shoulder is suddenly weak and pleading.

"You gave me my life back, Jean Michael, and now that my usefulness has ebbed, you throw me aside like a spent piece of tinder. You can't leave me alone again. Don't you feel any responsibility?"

Emil Winge puts his hand on Cardell's shoulder to stop him, a touch as light as a child's, but Cardell sees red, turning on his heel and grabbing Winge by the collar with his right hand, forcing him to back over the floor until his head and his heels slam into the plastered wall, then lifts him until his legs dangle a foot above the floorboards. He holds him there, as if weightless, feeling the slender fingers claw at his wrists in helpless desperation. Face-to-face, Winge's with terror shining from his eyes, his own with murder in its gaze and teeth bared. His voice is low now, a menacing growl.

"You forget yourself. You forget who I am, and who you are. You're a failed student who has never accomplished anything beyond emptying bottles. I've been to war. Had I the inclination, I could break you into tiny pieces right now, and there's no one who'd grieve or pose any questions over your corpse. Go back from where you came. If we ever see each other again, pray to your gods that you see me first."

He lifts his wooden fist, as bloodstained as it's ever been, and holds it under Winge's nose, before striking the stone next to his ear. He allows the blow to land badly, not in the angle he favors, but straight on, so the wood grinds into the bone stump that the surgeon had little time to file smooth. The pain blackens his sight, a huge swell to drown out his mind for a few moments, enough to obscure what thoughts are there. The respite is all too brief. He lets go, and Winge falls to the floor. He slams the door behind him over the sobs that follow, hard enough to make splinters fly from the door frame.

87

Anna Stina carries Karl, and Cardell carries Maja, as warmed by her trust as he is terrified at the prospect.

"What if I trip and drop her?"

"Do you usually fall as you walk along the street?"

He has adjusted her on his right arm with the left in front as a shield against the world. At first she wriggles, disgruntled in her unfamiliar seat, but then it is as if she remembers their first encounter, his large body with its smells of sweat and blood and Stockholm nights, and accepts them. A sigh of relief escapes him and he is surprised at how much he dreads the judgment of a child. In the darkness of the burrow they accepted him, but back then they had no one else to comfort them in their mother's absence. Only when their way has brought them across the bridge, opposite the hospital and the Royal Mint, is he struck by something else, and his steps lag so that Anna Stina is far ahead. At the edge of the fields she turns around with an inquiring expression and he shakes his head in confusion.

"Sorry, it's nothing."

"Come on, tell me."

"It's my arm, I can't feel it anymore."

She gives him an amused look and shifts Karl in her arms to show him how.

"Change your grip if it's gone numb."

He lets her misunderstanding go uncorrected, but the girl Maja looks up, reaching her soft fingers towards flaking scabs and day-old stubble, and gives a burbling laugh as if she knew.

....

High clouds float lazily across the blue abyss, and the sun that is each day lower than the day before, as if growing weary of climbing the sky, shows itself in between. Although the air is chilly, its rays yet bestow some warmth. At each crossroads, Cardell nods in the right direction, and soon they see the house.

Anna Stina's eyes grow wider with each step. Soon they are down by apple trees, where the harvest is in full swing. Children in warm woolen coats laugh and help each other, some balancing among the branches on ladders, others standing ready to catch the fruit that is thrown down to collect in baskets. Everything that he saw during his first visit now becomes clear also to her. These children are unlike the others. Here is a place beyond the disease and corruption of the city. Here is hope and comfort.

"How can this be possible?"

"You shouldn't look a gift horse in the mouth. Your children will have a home here, the best one I can think of."

"Whatever must this cost you?"

Emil Winge's pale face, lined by fearful tears, floats up out of his memory, and Cardell feels his stump burn as if the wooden fist had just struck the wall of his room. Despite the pain, he knows that he has no other choice.

"I can never repay you."

"You'll never owe anything to me."

In the distance he recognizes the girl Klara Fina and the boy Joakim, and also sees the look of recognition in their faces as they wave and rush away. Soon they return with the bald Rudstedt in tow, who gives them a wide smile from the stairs of the house.

"Maja and Karl, I assume? You are expected. Dear children, be so kind as to greet your new sister and brother."

Joakim bows and Klara Fina curtsies, holding her skirt above the ground. Rudstedt bows to Anna Stina.

"Welcome to Horn Hill, ma'am. Cots for the little ones have already been prepared. Won't you follow me in to see for yourself?"

Upstairs, the smaller children have a separate room to that of the older ones. There is no trace here of the sour smell of the orphanage, of neglected little bodies collected in dirty and crowded conditions. It is as if Rudstedt can read her mind.

"The children themselves are in charge of cleaning, and scrub the floors every other day. If there's lice or vermin, we do what we can to find the ones who are affected, so we can wash them and comb them, while their friends smoke out the rooms."

Rudstedt gestures to a woman who is waiting in the room.

"Greta is one of our wet nurses."

She is young, but stocky, of robust build, with a commonplace face, dimples in her cheeks, and light brown hair under her shawl. She curtsies to Anna Stina.

"Ma'am, would you care to show me how your children prefer to be held?"

Rudstedt puts a hand on Cardell's shoulder and closes the door behind them. They go down the stairs. Rudstedt winds a scarf around his neck before he excuses himself and goes out into the orchard.

"It promises to be a good harvest."

Cardell sits down to wait on the bottom step. He closes his eyes and turns his face to the sun in order to make the most of the little warmth it gives.

....

When the girl Greta has pulled her blouse over her head and revealed her bosom, Anna Stina instinctively turns away.

"You don't have to be coy on my account, ma'am. Come and show me how they feed best."

Anna Stina puts Maja at the left breast and Karl at the right, just as they have always preferred, but Greta's arms are a stranger's, and they kick agitatedly in their attempts to settle in. Karl is the first to cry, a low wailing that slowly but surely grows louder as the color rises in his face and a heavy tear is pressed out of each eye, to hang on the ends of his long eyelashes. His sister soon follows, despite Greta's soothing. She tries for a while to get them to suckle before she changes their places and nods approvingly as their lips find their mark and they relax. She smiles at Anna Stina.

"That's funny. With me they prefer the other way around."

They still let go from time to time, bewildered at their new place and perhaps at milk of a different taste. They roll their eyes and look for their mother, whimpering sometimes and making small attempts to turn towards her. Anna Stina does as she usually does. Karl wants to feel a warm hand on his stomach, Maja wants to be stroked over the head, Karl wants to squeeze the ragdoll cat he has inherited from an unhallowed grave. Under his mother's familiar touch, they soon fall asleep. Karl has found her thumb and wrapped his fist around it, as he normally does. In his grip, she can feel the fast little beats of his heart. Gently, so she won't interrupt his rest, she coaxes her hand away and wraps his hand around Greta's finger instead. In his sleep, he doesn't notice the difference.

For a long time the only sound in the room is the rhythmic suckling of the children, halfway between sleep and wakefulness, peaceful and satisfied, until Anna Stina becomes aware of another sound, a strange whimper as if from the squeaking wheel of a wagon or some small, anguished animal. She wonders what it can be. Then she hears Greta's tentative whisper.

"Would you like to borrow my handkerchief, ma'am?"

Soon she feels Rudstedt's gentle hand on her shoulder, his eyes full of tenderness, and as if it were a turn in a slow quadrille, he spins her around and leads her out over the threshold.

"There, there, let us leave now, when they are so contented. They are still so young. They will soon forget."

When her strength leaves her legs and her knees buckle, he is ready to prop her up. Behind her, the door falls shut and hides the two little ones, rocked on Greta's knee as she sings them a little song.

"Little Karl, sleep now content, you'll wake in a while, soon you'll see how time is bent, and taste her bitter bile."

....

Her eyes are dry but red when Cardell hears her steps coming down the stairs behind him, meticulously wiped so he won't think her gratitude hasn't drowned in tears. He sees how things stand, and rises in silence. They start walking towards the road. A girl who has playfully tossed an apple core at another is scolded by the older children. The children's laughter dies away with the evening as they are called to the supper table and leave their brimming baskets in neat rows on the stairs. Only when they have climbed over the edge of the valley, out of sight of the house, does Cardell clear his throat.

"I wish I could say something, but I've never had a gift for words."

She takes him by the arm.

"If anyone should say something, it's me. I am so grateful for what you have done for me, Mickel, and I wish I could show you how happy I am. But my grief is larger."

"And now?"

"Tomorrow I go to pay a debt."

"Will we meet again?"

"Let's hope so."

Her first thought at the question she keeps to herself. If they were to ever see each other again, she is not sure that he would recognize her.

88

Anna Stina wakes in bed with the feeling that something is wrong. It is the cold that has awakened her. It has permeated her body until her shaking has brought her back to consciousness. The feeling is one she has known of old, familiar but made unfamiliar by the memories in between. Ever since the summer she has slept with a child on either side of her, and the collective warmth of their three bodies has been enough to fend off the cold for all of them. This is the first morning without them. Yesterday she left them at Horn Hill, she and the watchman.

Cardell's snores rise from the floor, slow and heavy and strong enough to be felt through the planks. Through the window, she sees from the sky that the sun has not yet risen, but that its approaching light is brightening the horizon. She turns the blanket aside and gets up slowly so she won't disturb his sleep. She is already wearing her skirt and blouse, so all she needs is to tie her kerchief around her head, sweep the shawl around her shoulders, and lift the sack from its corner. The clasp on the door allows itself to be lifted without any scraping, and then she is across the threshold. He has leaned his wide back against a corner with the stump under his arm, the hand in his armpit and his legs outstretched before him, one boot over the other. His scarred face is peaceful in its slumber as she carefully steps over his legs. The sweep of her shadow makes him knit his eyebrows in sleeping concern, searching for a louse bite with clumsy nails, muttering something inaudible, and wrapping his arms more tightly around his chest.

....

Out in the alley, there is a changing of the guards among the common people. The drunks stagger homeward as the industrious hurry along to try to make every moment of daylight count. She stands for a while by the gutter, the weight of her sack over her shoulder, and asks herself suddenly what it is even good for. She needs nothing now. Maybe it will be of use to someone else. She places the sack next to a wall. When she reaches the end of the block and casts a glance behind her, it is already gone.

No time has been set for her arrival. If there is one door that will always be opened for her, it is the one to which she is on her way. Morning, as well as night, they will always bid her welcome and show her into Petter Pettersson's open embrace, filled to the brim by the fond anticipation that has grown by absence. Anna Stina finds herself dragging her legs. A strange feeling of peace rests over these final hours. Time is circumscribed now, only the final debt to be paid. There is no responsibility or duty any longer; cause and effect have taken their farewell. She walks towards the Lock. The breeze from the water sweeps in under the greasy smell of the houses. She looks around for the last time and perhaps it is because her gaze has become that of another that she now lets it linger on things she has never before noticed in the City-between-the-Bridges. Its beauty is sudden and un-expected. The sunrise, red and stunning, lends its luster to the yellow buildings. A cock crows, gruff and hoarse. By her foot, a newly estab-lished plant has managed to find nourishment in the dirt between the cobblestones. Maja and Karl are safe, their future secure. If they wake, they each have the warmth of the other. What greater comfort could a mother ask? What right does she have to tears?

....

Anna Stina passes by the wharf, where a scruffy party is waiting for a skiff now approaching across the bay, one stroke of the oars at a time, and soon they are arguing with the boat-women over the fee. Those who are hungover are no match for the boat-women's impudence, and after coins have exchanged hands, the skiff sets off again. A girl not unlike herself, or as she must once have been, tries to offer her wares to a German. Not apples and lemons as she herself once did, but tinder sticks, six bunches for a silver coin. Anna Stina stares at her pale face from a distance. She recognizes the expression, the same mask she has so often worn. An ingratiating smile strained by hunger and desperation. The girl is skillful, knowing how to use her long eyelashes and dimples to coax a purchase, but the language proves a barrier to the transaction. The German becomes embarrassed and doesn't want anything, and the girl shuffles off without success. Anna Stina also walks on, powerless to help her.

89

Cardell stands on Castle Hill and stares at his own shadow, stretched long and thin by the morning sun shining low against his back. Out at the Quayside, the linden trees are leaning in the wind, and each time it grows stronger, dry leaves are torn from the branches and carried up in a great whirlwind, only to float down over the worn roofs that stand crowded together in poverty at the Meadowland. Bearing the coming winter in mind, Cardell is reminded of those fistfuls of earth that will be strewn over the lids of coffins. Soon the cold will tighten its grip around the city and start to squeeze, and before the season shifts, many come of dust shall to dust return, just as soon as the ground has thawed enough to receive their remains.

Down by the street corner, a group of journeymen are making a noise. They are all so drunk, they're swaying on their feet and have to brace themselves against the building from time to time. One of them is in a worse state than the others, soon made the object of their merriment. With an open mouth and vacantly staring eyes, he tries again and again to raise himself out of the gutter, only to lose his balance and fall back again. His companions laugh themselves silly at his efforts. Finally he resigns himself and sprawls on the ground, his body inert, burbling like a child. A disappointed silence spreads at the fact that the play appears to be over, before one of the journeymen steps closer on unsteady legs, unties his trousers, and lets his urine pour out over the fallen. Soon the others join him, and their laughter echoes down the alleyways.

Indebetou House appears different now to before. The building remains as it was, slanted and askew, drafty and neglected. The general level of chaos is also the same, the disorder as palpable, but under the new police chief, the mood has shifted. Magnus Ullholm crawls before power, and in his service, the chief duty of the police is to listen to informants and trace malicious rumors to their source. If the source can't be identified, they take the next best thing: better to punish an innocent than allow a crime to go unavenged. It'll serve as a warning to others, and now that it has grown too cold and risky to sleep under a bare sky, there is no lack of vagabonds who will confess to anything you like in exchange for a sheltered corner in a prison cell. Nor do they lack for witnesses willing to accuse others of any crime at all, merely to satisfy a grudge.

Cardell forces his way in through the shivering police constables and sergeants, with their shiny badges around their necks, laden as they are either with bundles of paperwork or freshly caught sinners. Here the smell of hangovers hovers as thick as fog. Yesterday's wine has soured into stains on shirts and trouser legs, the sharp odor of vomit stings the nostrils. He makes his way up the stairs. When Cardell enters his office, Isak Blom takes an alarmed jump back caught in the act of stuffing his stove with paper.

"Cardell, you just about gave me a stroke, damn it. Come in and close the door."

The plump secretary returns to his task, the papers that have been laid on the embers bursting into flame with a crackle, Blom rubbing his hands to the warmth.

"What logs we have to burn are not enough by far. In this way I can clean up the office and don't have to be cold, though it's a little like pissing yourself: a momentary comfort, soon regretted. My only hope is that I'll be far away from here the day someone comes to take an inventory of the archives."

Cardell shakes his shoulders to drive some blood into his limbs.

"What's happening in this city? I've seen my share of drunkards, but rarely so many this early in the day."

"Ah, you haven't heard? Malla Rudenschöld's punishment was not as well received by the people as our good Baron Reuterholm had convinced himself it would be. What you see is the baron's latest maneuver to curry favor with the commoners, whose displeasure he now fears as much as our late King Gustav did. The baron has ordered every pub to let the journey-men booze as much as they like, with the Crown footing the bill."

"Is the man out of his mind? If people are allowed to drink for free, the whole city will go under before the week is out."

Blom shrugs. He closes the stove door and crawls up in his chair, rais-ing the collar of his coat up to his ears.

"Let us hope that Reuterholm's frugality and the kingdom's poor fi-nances will turn off the tap before then. Well, speaking of money, have you come for yet another handout?"

"Quite the opposite."

Cardell stands with his back to the tiles of the stove and leans his weight into its warmth.

"I have come to relinquish my post, if that is the right term for our agreement."

Blom reaches into the desk drawer and takes out a half-filled bottle and two cups. He raises an eyebrow at Cardell, gets a nod in answer, fills both cups, and pushes one across the desk while emptying his own. Cardell throws his head back and tosses the drink down his throat to spare him-self from as much of the taste as possible. It can't be entirely avoided—the spirits are cheap and impure—but its strength can't be faulted, and its com-forting heat fills his chest. Blom carefully replaces the stopper in the bottle.

"I will show you the respect of not pretending to be surprised. The fact is that I have been expecting your visit."

Blom leans into the back of his chair and knits his fingers together over his belly.

"Your companion came up here yesterday in a very agitated state of mind. He made a scene on the stairs, and if I had not come to his aid, I think the patience of the constables would have worn thin and they would have clapped him in irons until he calmed down. He did what he could to convince me to reassign the mandate of the police authority to him alone."

"Emil was here?"

"It wasn't easy to grasp what he wanted. He was both upset and—if I am not mistaken—scared. Time and again he stopped speaking to lis-ten out for something, and I asked myself if I was growing deaf since I couldn't hear what it could be. But there was nothing there. I don't know what you were thinking when you decided to go into partnership with someone like that. Or rather, of course I do. They are very similar in appearance, him and his brother, isn't that right? Tell me, has he told you much of his background?"

"Not a lot. I don't know much more than what you yourself have told me. He was in bad shape when I first ran into him, drinking with abandon."

Blom nods.

"I have kept myself informed about young Mr. Winge ever since we last saw each other, from acquaintances who stayed on in Uppsala longer than I did, and who saw what happened later. Do you know that there is a third Winge, a sister older than the brothers? Hedvig, if my memory serves, a particularly willful and headstrong woman, if my sources are to be believed. Emil had a breakdown, as I said before, and in the end Hedvig Winge came to collect him, probably after receiving a message from one of her brother's professors. She took him to the Oxenstierna, in the shadow of the cathedral, and left him there to rot."

Cardell indicates his incomprehension with a shrug.

"A madhouse, Cardell. She put him in the madhouse."

Blom sees Cardell grow pale, and gives him the bottle while slapping his own shoulders to quell a shiver.

"If there is anything I would like to read in the story of Emil Winge, it is the chapter about his escape. You know, Cardell, that in those places the security is tighter than any prison. It's one thing if a robber contrives his escape, but no one wants a lunatic loose in the street: the deeds of a thief are the fruit of necessity, or greed, and can be somewhat predicted, but what the mad will do, no one can say. Not for nothing are madhouses called tombs of the living. Casanova's escape from a lead-lined cell can hardly have been more dramatic than Emil's, and I will tell you one thing, Cardell. The fact that Emil Winge managed to pull that off is the only evidence I need that he is his brother's equal in cunning."

"So you agreed to his request. Is that what you are trying to say?"

Blom makes a dismissive gesture.

"Dear God, no! When he did not want to accept my refusal, I told him to go to hell, and when that did not have the intended effect either, I had to ask a constable to show him the door. He's out of his mind, anyone can see that. I had heard as much beforehand. He made something of a spectacle of himself the other day. As you know, Cecil was known and respected here, and at first many thought that the Ghost of Indebetou was living up to his name when they first laid eyes on his little brother. Emil Winge wandered up and down the Quayside, right outside here, gesticulating wildly and raving as if to another. But there was no one else there."

90

Cardell pushes the door inward, until it bangs into a loaded chest that has been pushed up against it to keep it closed. He grunts in irritation as he puts his shoulder to the wood, shifts his weight, tensing his thigh muscles until the weight gives way and scrapes across the floor. Once inside, he finds that Emil Winge has hidden himself away in the furthest corner, sheltered behind the table. His face is pale and frightened. Panting from his exertion, Cardell rests his wooden arm against his knee and holds up his palm in a gesture that he hopes will exude reconciliation.

"Please be calm. I won't do anything to hurt you."

He waits until his breathing is steady enough to allow him to speak freely.

"I came here from Indebetou House. Blom let me know that you also paid him a visit."

Winge shoots him a defiant look.

"Jean Michael, the fact that you want to give up on our case as hopeless doesn't mean that I feel the same way. Justice doesn't change its appearance from one day to the next, and perhaps it is still within my power to help advance it."

"Blom's of another opinion, as far as I can tell."

Winge nods reluctantly, chagrined.

"He left me no room for doubt on that account."

"What about now? Are you ready to lay down arms?"

"Hedvig just left. She promised to think the matter through. If you didn't walk past each other on the stairs, you must have passed her in the alley. What about you? Have you come to threaten me into changing my mind?"

Cardell stretches himself and sits down on the bed.

"Come on, Emil. Come out from your corner. Since I've not had the pleasure of your sister's company, although we appear to succeed each other remarkably often, can't you tell me anything about her?"

"She is older, but you would never believe it. Her mind is as quick as no one else's. We have had our differences before, but are finally reconciled."

"Does she live in the city or is she only visiting?"

"She had heard through a family contact that I was here to see to Cecil's possessions. We met over Cecil's grave, where she had come several days in a row hoping to see me."

Cardell looks around the room.

"Tell me—your brother's papers, are they here? And have you gone through them?"

Winge shakes his head.

"Only to look for the pawnshop receipt he received for Father's watch."

"Will you let me have a look?"

"Why?"

Cardell gives him a shrug.

"It's just a feeling I have. Maybe there's something that can confirm or deny it. Surely it can't do any harm? Let me do this, and I promise to leave you and your sister to your plotting."

"Help yourself."

Winge points to a shelf where a thick pile of documents is sitting, wrapped up in brown paper and bound with string. Cardell gives it a look.

"Will you help me with the string? Knots are the constant nemesis of the one-armed man."

As Emil Winge watches, Cardell sits down at the table and begins to sort the documents into piles. He finds what he is looking for near the end: a letter inscribed at the top with the place and date. Cardell holds it up to the light in order to make out the elegant handwriting, and when he is done, he sets the letter aside, continues leafing through the rest of the papers and finds yet another letter to put aside. He hides his face in his hand and rubs his tired eyes.

"Oh, Emil."

Winge is awakened from his thoughts.

"What is it, Jean Michael? What's wrong?"

"Everyone tried to tell me, everyone who met you. That there was something wrong. The only one who has been blind is me."

"What are you saying?"

"You have no sister. She is dead, Emil. Four years dead."

"What are you talking about?"

Cardell pushes the letters across the table, one at a time.

"Here's her letter of farewell to Cecil, and here is a letter from the minister in the congregation who confirms the burial and offers condolences. She wrote her confession to Cecil. She took her own life, Emil. She hid her brother away in a madhouse before the rumors of insanity in the family could create a hurdle for the marriage that promised her a comfortable life, and when she started to notice the same signs of madness in herself, she decided to take poison while she still had the presence of mind to bring the bottle to her lips."

Winge blinks in mute shock, speechless, then pathetically stammering.

"Jean Michael, she was here; she left but ten minutes ago. She was just going to take a short walk to gather her thoughts, then she promised to return."

"The minister writes that she had mixed so much wolfsbane in her wine that her skin was gray and cracked when she was consigned to the earth. You have had the habit of walking together along the Quayside to confer, isn't that right? Isak Blom and others have seen you there. You were always alone, there was no one else. She is a figment of your imagination, Emil. It was only you the whole time."

"You are out of your mind."

"Not I."

Winge's gaze flits across the lines of text until his white hand crumples up the page in a paroxysm and his face twists in pain.

"She asked my forgiveness. She told me she loved me."

In Hedvig's last words to Cecil, there is no trace of doubt or regret, no desire for reconciliation, only rage at having seen in her mirror the same signs that she had noticed in her brother, and a bitter catalogue of the escalating pace of the condition. Sounds no one else can hear. Voices in the silence. The company of the departed. The disdain she has felt for creatures of this sort simmers between the lines and, rather than join their ranks, she chose a hasty farewell. Not once does she mention her youngest brother by name.

Emil Winge's thin shoulders shake, and his grief locks his jaw. Cardell is at a loss until Winge's legs threaten to give way, and he closes the distance between them to avert the fall. He puts his arms around Winge and they both sink to the floor. Cardell feels his head against his chest where the warm tears soak the fabric and find their way in towards his bare skin. They sit like that for a while, rocking from side to side, in a rhythm as old as mankind itself. When Cardell hears the sobs decrease in intensity, he whispers in a cracked voice.

"Come with me now, Emil."

"Where to?"

"Dane's Bay."

Terror gleams in his eyes.

"Not the madhouse, Jean Michael."

"No, Emil, not the madhouse. Never that. Only to the hospital, and to Doctor Näsström."

91

At the Scorched Plot, Cardell finds a barouche whose driver is willing to take them beyond the gates for a couple of shillings. Under its raised top, Stockholm flies past them, the Quayside and the Lock, the Southern Square, and the derelict slums beyond. The trip is uncomfortable, and each time the wheel hits a stone, they both veer to the side in unison. While Cardell falls back on muttered curses and does what he can to meet the sharp swerves with a firm grip on the side of the carriage, Winge can't be bothered to counter the irregularities of the road. His gaunt body sways back and forth like some stalk in a capricious wind. The crying that had contorted his face has abated, and he looks out at the landscape they pass without fixing on anything. Tears are still streaming, but down smooth cheeks now, with no attempt to wipe them away.

"Wine and wolfsbane. She knew her Socrates. Father always said that if she had only been born a man and had a little less reason, she could have been a great philosopher. I once saw a cat die of wolfsbane, Jean Michael, in the Oxenstierna, where they treated those who had been driven mad by the French disease. No one knew how the creature had come by it. Perhaps it had licked it out of a spilled bottle, perhaps it had been given by some spiteful boy. It howled terribly, dragging itself forward on its front legs and leaving behind a trail of slime that ran from its mouth in an endless flow. It bit into the stove handle with enough force to crack its teeth. A resolute manservant grabbed it by its hind legs, swung it around once, and dashed its head into the wall as hard as he could."

He rubs his red eyes with his knuckles.

"She was so real, Jean Michael."

Cardell puts his hand on his shoulder to comfort him, an act that comes naturally, and for lack of anything else to do, but which nonetheless appears absurdly inadequate.

"Come now. What help there is, we'll find soon."

Winge stares at Cardell with hollow eyes.

"I have been offered help of that kind before. What cures they have do more harm than good."

Cardell shakes his shoulder and leans closer to lock into his gaze.

"I haven't gone through life without encountering my share of charlatans. There are all kinds. There are some who practice their craft because there's nothing else they can do. There are others who enjoy the power they have over their wards, and the attention they receive. From time to time, you meet someone who seems to have made their way to their position out of consideration for their neighbor, however this miracle can be possible in a vale of tears such as this one. Näsström seems to me to be one of the few."

Winge shakes his head and remains silent for the remainder of the trip, until the driver pulls on the reins and swings the carriage around to let them off at the hospital fence. Behind the gate, the garden lies deserted. Not even the mill creek seems to have any life left, as if its flow has been stemmed, the sooner to be able to assume its icy dress and await spring. They end up waiting in the hallway of the hospital. Where it extends within, towards the nave of the chapel, mumbled prayers can be heard rising from the pews, and moans from the corridors leading out to the wings. It is cold here, made worse by the raw and the damp. It doesn't take long before a maid comes carrying a bucket and a copper kettle, and gives them an inquisitive look. Cardell stretches himself and does whatever he can to make as presentable an impression as possible.

"We are here to see Näsström, Doctor Näsström."

He receives a confused look in return.

"That's not a name I'm familiar with, but I haven't been here very long. If you gentlemen will wait here for a moment, I'll come back with someone who will know more."

They sit down in the last row of the pews while the maid hurries on. From the whitewashed and plain ceiling hangs an unlit chandelier. What light there is comes from arched windows on either side of the altar. The large room seems impossible to heat, and the cold rises through the floor from the wet stone foundation of the building and the stream that passes under it. Cardell wonders which came first, the stream or the house, and finds it as strange that a building would have been erected over the water as it would have been to construct a tunnel beneath it. Next to him, Winge remains silent, his coat wrapped tightly around his body, his arms crossed to hug his own thin chest. Cardell can feel his shaking through the pew, whether from the cold or his emotions, or both. In the rows in front of them they can see backs bent over clasped hands: a gray-haired woman at death's door who whispers nine words and shouts out the tenth; a man whose monotonous rocking of his upper body bears witness to some unknown ailment, either of soul or body. At the front, over the altar, is Jesus Christ, depicted at Golgotha, his outstretched arms a promise of a bloody embrace. Now and again some new hospital inmate comes shuffling along to show the altarpiece their respect, and then out again, having accomplished their goal. Someone clears their throat behind Cardell, making him aware of the fact that he has managed to nod off on a bench deliberately crafted to be uncomfortable in order to encourage the attention of the God-fearing.

"Are you the ones asking for Nässtrom?"

Cardell stands up on limbs that have quickly stiffened in the cold. The man before him is lanky and thin-haired, with cracked spectacles, stains on his waistcoat, and a smell of wine about him. Cardell can make out the telltale outline of a bottle in his coat pocket.

"Sondelius is my name, and excuse the trouble, but I simply want to assure myself that there is no misunderstanding. Are you sure of the name?"

"It was the name he himself gave us when we were here at the hospital as recently as a couple of days ago."

The man laughs, and shakes his head so hard that a loose glass shard in his frames makes a clinking sound.

"It's not possible. Doctor Nässtrom isn't . . ."

Sondelius's forehead smooths out as if by the light of inspiration.

"Ah. Will you be so kind as to follow me?"

He leads them out into the wind blowing in from the sea, on the path that leads them to the madhouse. In the entrance of the building he calls over an errand boy.

"Can you find Josefsson and ask him to bring Tomas here with him?"

They wait for a while before a noise is heard on the stairs, and then rushing steps at a wild pace. Down the stairs comes a man without breeches whose every exhalation is a howl. He is foaming at the sides of his mouth, and the tail of his shirt is flapping behind him. He windmills his arms to retain his balance as he bounces past them, jerking violently at the handle of the locked door that leads out to the courtyard, and then disappears down a hallway. Sondelius smiles and points with his thumb in the direction that the man has gone.

"Could that have been your Doctor Näsström, by any chance?"

Cardell has to concentrate in order to find Näsström's features in the agitated face that just passed.

"I'll be damned if that wasn't him. What's going on?"

Sondelius shrugs.

"That was Tomas, one of the inmates. He is tranquil most of the time, and since there is so much overcrowding he is allowed to roam. Many also find him amusing, not least because he often adopts new mannerisms and plays his roles with great conviction. This Näsström must be one of those, one whose acquaintance I have not had the pleasure of making."

Cardell throws up his arms in a simultaneous gesture of rage and defeat.

"Is both heaven and hell to be emptied of inhabitants simply to jest with the living? When it isn't a delusion, it's some damned charade."

More steps come down the stairs, though not with the same haste. Around the corner they can see a guard, the same one who earlier that summer had shown them to the room of Erik Three Roses. In his hand is a pole with a noose at the end, intended both to keep an inmate at a distance and force him to heel. The guard is red in the face and panting, and stops to lean over to catch his breath right in front of them as he stammers out the words.

"Tomas . . . Was he just—"

When the guard rises and for the first time sees who is in front of him, he opens his eyes wide with amazement.

"You! But how did you find out so quickly?"

Emil Winge speaks the first syllables he has uttered in over an hour.

"What do you mean? Speak clearly."

"The bouquet boy. Three Roses. He's gone rogue."

"How is that possible?"

The guard shrugs as if the question has answered itself.

"The only room we had to put him in had a broken lock; that's why it was empty."

"When we visited him last it was impossible to make any contact with him at all. Did someone come to fetch him?"

"The gates are easy to open from the inside, but not from the outside, so the best explanation is that his condition improved and he trotted off under his own power."

"When?"

"Sometime last night. I found the room empty this morning, so I can't give you the hour."

At the sight of Winge's alarmed face, the guard waves his arms and smiles wryly.

"I wouldn't worry unnecessarily if I were you. It's only the most harmless inmates who aren't kept under lock and key, and they tend to come back to us pretty quickly, either off their own bat or because someone else has found them, seen how things are, and given them a ride back. Well, duty calls."

His breath calm again, the guard disappears around the corner with his catchpole over his shoulder, whistling.

"Jean Michael, let us put behind us all that has happened these past few days, because we now need all the haste we can muster."

Cardell blinks uncomprehendingly, but Winge, pale and wild, gives him an impatient shove towards the exit before he himself pushes the half door open and starts to run down the path that leads past the hospital, towards the tollgate beyond. Anxiety seeps from his voice as he shouts over his shoulder.

"Can't you see what is happening?"

92

Erik Three Roses walks, every step an effort. His body feels awkward, mute in limb and joint, as if all he asks of it is to travel a long and arduous path before anything else happens. But it serves, if hesitantly. He walks dressed only in his shirt, shoeless, bare-legged. The ache in his head is terrifying. He has walked for a long time: in the past night, each new step was like a strike of lightning, and once the sun rose, it gave such blinding light that he was forced to shield it with his hands and could only look at the world through the grate of his fingers. When he touches his face, it is as if he is touching the skin of another, as if the metal that has pierced his skull has banished all feeling. His lips can hardly form words, but he only needs a single one, a last one, and he practices as he walks, over and over again. Only when he is struck by the realization that he has been deprived of the sense that once allowed him to feel her kiss does he give a howl of helplessness and anguish. He must stop to gather his thoughts, reminding himself of his destination.

Schildt wrote them all at the same time, one after the other.

....

In the night, he comes limping across the red drawbridge at the Lock, by the light of the moon. The City-between-the-Bridges never sleeps, and along the quay and past the Flies' Meet, people scurry back and forth, some arm in arm on their way to some pub or other, others hastening in urgent need towards the privies. Erik is not who he once was, and the world he sees is not the same as before. Rage and confusion. All is obscure, haunted by shadows. When they draw close, he sees them for what they are, grotesques with repellent features set around a greedy hole where meat goes down and lies come out. All alike.

Ceton has scraped him bare.

....

Those who take any notice of him have only a quick glance to spare, and what they see is nothing out of the ordinary: yet another miserable wretch who has drunk himself into a stupor and staggers forward draped in the rags of poverty, on a vain hunt for a corner where no one has vomited and only a few have pissed, to catch a few moments of sleep, ready to be dressed all in white for the grave by the night frost. Some have the misfortune to pass by at close quarters, where the cloud fragments to allow the moonlight, or else the wolfish eye of some street lantern, to scatter the night, and see in his stricken face something that causes them to recoil and walk around him. With the hand that works best he makes a claw, grabbing at whatever he can, and to those he catches, he whispers the sounds that he has been practicing ever since he left the madhouse. The name of a place. Sometimes fortune favors him. Some understand what he means and point him in the right direction, in exchange for their liberty.

He believes that he was the one who killed his bride.

....

Past midnight, he lurches over the bridge that crosses Klara Lake. The moon over the bay lights the crest of every wave on the black deep, an army of ghosts that march at his side, that sing to him a song of love and betrayal and retribution. At his back, the day will soon break. He passes the Seraphim Hospital, and soon there are no more stone houses to be seen, only simple cottages and wooden shacks among fields and pastures. He meets only a few, and those who see him at a distance in daylight sense trouble and put distance between them, so as not to get too close. The sun pierces him. It wanders low along his left side and keeps its business brief, as the time of year directs. Soon it is past him, in front of him. It falls lower in the sky, blinding his eyes, afternoon now.

It is that grinning devil who bears all the blame.

....

He reaches his goal. The house on its small knoll in the middle of the valley that slopes down to the water, surrounded by an orchard of apple trees. A few children who play hide and seek among the trunks catch sight of him, and laugh at the strange figure in the large shirt that flaps around his legs. They come closer and make him a part of the game, taking his hands and leading him around and around, dancing in a circle. He stammers out the same word as before, and they nod happily. Down from the valley, a bell calls them to supper, and they head off among the trees towards the house, but turn and wave when they see him linger by the road. He waits as evening falls, driving others inside, leaving him alone where he stands. Above him, the stars are out, and among them is her face, Linnea Charlotta, her voice in the bushes and the trees, urging him on with an assurance that it will soon be done, that thing that must be done. He can't feel the warm caress of the tears over his cheek, no more than his numb lips would now have felt hers, but her whisper carries a promise: soon we will be united, my love, and then our kiss will be your reward, the one you have awaited for so long, and when it comes, you will feel it as before.

As long as Horn Hill exists, Ceton will be safe from the law.

....

He makes his way down into the valley, along the path between the trees where fruit baskets lean, waiting for the harvest to continue. The house is dark, a single lantern burning next to the door to keep the steps lit for those who have to make their way to the outhouse with greater business than can be entrusted to the chamber pot. The flame beckons him closer, contorted behind the irregularities of the glass, and it borrows her voice to address him. Isn't it a kindness to all, that which he must do? What crossroads will life hold in store for these little ones, other than that where all of humanity must make their choice: to be the victim or the perpetrator? Better to sleep in innocence and never to wake. How much does he not himself wish that another might have shown him the same mercy? He stretches out a trembling hand to free what the glass holds captive.

93

Anna Stina lingers at the Russian Yard, where old memories return, and wanders over to the weighing scales to see the iron carried on bent backs that can only afford to feel the pain of the labor at day's end. Then onwards, as far as she can go, past Maria church and the territory that once belonged to the Dragon. She sees a funeral in the distance. The cantor stands in the garlanded doorway, the black-clad mourners bowing to the departed. Onward still. The Bridge of Sighs awaits, past the rank fish ponds where desolate captive shapes pass the time by swimming in circles.

When she sees to which side her shadow leans, she notices that the sun is on her other side now, and is surprised by how long she has taken on her way. The Scar lies at her feet; the spire of the workhouse church a thorn against the evening sky.

She allows the light to fade even more, and awaits nightfall, slowing her pace, but never fully. Each step carries her towards the end of the road, where the timber of the gate bars her way. She stands there long enough for her ears to grow accustomed to the silence and to sense what lies beyond: the sighing of the spinning wheels at the last hour of the evening shift, the clockwork cogs to measure the hopeless tedium of time. She stands waiting for the moment when the bell will mark the end of the working day. It soon begins to chime, and she raises her hand to knock once the echoes fade. But it is as if its final muted strikes never want to end. They go on and on until she rounds the corner of the workhouse in confusion, following the cliff to the crest, and there opens her eyes wide to make the best of the starlight. It is the bell of the King's Isle that is tolling, in three repeated strikes, each followed by a brief pause, over and over again. At its spire, lanterns glint, raised in threes. She knows only all too well what the signal means. She turns her eyes to the west, and it takes a while until she understands what she sees. The sun seems reversed on its course, to rise in the west. And now she runs.

94

Inside the Tessin Palace, the doors have been opened to dissipate the heat of the assembly. Tycho Ceton shifts in his chair and looks out at the knee-high boxwood maze in the garden, where some guests are strolling to further cool themselves. His eyes sweep past Minerva, hewn of marble in an eternal welcome, and he smiles. When he turns his head back, he catches a look from a well-dressed gentleman in the row in front, who blushes and directs his expression of disgust elsewhere. Ceton grins more widely: they don't want him here, his presence revolts them, and they know that he is not from the same class as them, but ambition and shrewdness have opened even these doors for him. All around him are crowded the highest in the land. Without any sense of urgency, he takes out a silk handkerchief and pats his cheek where his smile has opened his wound and dampened his chin. Later, when he is enjoying a smoke in the garden, he will take his place in their circle, the one they don't dare to deny him, and watch them squirm as he blows smoke straight out of his cheek, just to see them shudder.

The musicians are tuning their instruments, and the guests are settling into their chairs, exchanging the final words of their conversations and clearing their throats in advance of the performance. The evening's host introduces the piece: a century old, a Canon in D. The musicians play a note in unison, their eyes meeting over the coordinated stroke, and then the cello begins its two bars, an obbligato of eight notes, da capo. One by one, each joins in with their bows. The second violin echoes the first, the third the second, leaving the first free to lift its melody to even further heights to where the others must follow, each in turn, always in a new and astonishing harmony. The result is sublime, and as the hairs prick over Ceton's arms, he rocks back and forth to the steady pulse of the cello. He closes his eyes and leans his head back, not bothering to wipe himself when his wound weeps down his neck, and stains appear across his silk scarf. He is lost in the music, separate from himself and embraced by a marvelous and complete peace.

95

Cardell runs through the dusk, his upper body hunched so as to lessen the stitch in his side. The soles of his boots smack against the packed earth. Although the exertion has brought the taste of blood to his mouth, he is unable to gain on Winge's lead. He can still see his spindly figure outlined against the slopes ahead, and from time to time a shout is carried back through the darkness, an urging to hurry, hurry! He clenches his teeth, presses his fist against the pain in his midriff, and forces his legs to continue.

At the tollgate, Winge has presented himself in front of some horses to stop the carriage, and although Cardell's heart is beating so hard in his ears that no words can get through, a few quick glances are enough to apprise him of the situation. There are already some passengers in the carriage, a heavyset man and a younger woman. The driver does his best with the two tasks that an unkind fate has suddenly imposed upon him: to calm the horses frightened by Winge's appearance, and to defend the rights of his customers to the carriage that they have already reserved. Even in Cardell's ears, Winge's attempts at changing his mind sound like the ravings of a madman. He himself has to catch his breath before he can utter a single word. As the driver is preparing to brandish his whip at Winge, Cardell is finally able to speak, pointing first to the driver.

"If you so much as touch him with your whip, you will spend the rest of your days with that shaft so far up your arse that the point of it will tickle the roof of your mouth."

The entire group falls silent and awaits his next message. Cardell turns to the man in the carriage. He doesn't need to raise his voice. He has learned a long time ago that few seriously delivered threats need to be yelled.

"We're no highwaymen. The money you have paid will be refunded, but you need to get out of this carriage this instant. As yet you're free to choose how. Otherwise it will be nose first."

That is enough. The matter is settled, and then they are on their way. An expletive floats after them once its sender deems the distance to be safe. Winge sits up front with the driver, Cardell behind, his feet planted on the carriage floor. Winge gives directions and urges speed. When the pace is not fast enough, Cardell yanks the whip out of the driver's hand and lets the crack smatter around the ears of the horses until they break into a gallop, and the driver's protests give way to panicked profanities as he struggles to keep the wheels out of the ditch.

....

In the night before them, a long bell has begun to toll at regular intervals, three strikes at a time. It is the tower of Hedvig Eleonora that speaks of calamity. The message is spreading. When they are halfway across the bridge towards the King's Isle, the bellringer in Klara Church starts ringing the same strokes behind their backs. Both towers have raised lanterns in the night sky.

They reach the city outskirts, shrouded in darkness where the road can no longer be easily distinguished from bare ground. All they can do is narrow their eyes to keep the fencing in sight and hope that no sharp curve will come faster than they can parry. Soon the night gives way to a light before them, an illumination whose source still lies concealed behind the hills. It is strong enough to set the clouds aglow, and those beams that are sent back to earth again are enough to elicit a sigh of relief from the driver. The wind is shifting, and now they can smell the smoke. As can the horses. They possess senses that already allow them to perceive the danger ahead; they snort and show the whites of their eyes, breaking out of step as they chew on their bits and toss their manes as if to warn their master. Soon not even the whip will compel them to obey, and the driver can only shrug his shoulders at Cardell's scolding.

"The devil himself couldn't force them to go on. You see why."

Cardell draws a breath to continue berating the driver, but Winge has already left them behind. A panting cough makes him known through veils of smoke that waft across the ground in their shifting shapes, the ghosts of giants.

....

Cardell tosses his purse to the driver, along with a parting obscenity, and sets off along the road. He passes the last crest and almost immediately runs straight into Winge's back, come to a standstill to gaze at what is happening in the valley. Even at this distance, the heat can be felt on their gaping faces. Horn Hill is aflame, half of its roof on fire. Many windows have cracked in the heat, and through the blackening holes the inferno spews flames into the sky.

Cardell hears Winge call his name, now from behind him. He himself is far in front, running towards danger for all he is worth, down into the valley and in among the apple trees that have started catching fire like torches around a bonfire. The leaves crinkle, smolder, and then burst into flame, one by one as the heat drives the sap out of them.

Against his will, Cardell recoils at the yard in front of the door, filled with an ancient terror. The flames greedily lick the front of the building.

The two halves of the door have fallen from the frame, where glowing hinges loosen their grip. Behind them he can glimpse the hallway. The fire is established in the beams under the roof, and billows back and forth in impossible shapes. An outlandish breeze comes from all directions, straight into the house as the fire draws breath, strong enough to take hold of his jacket. Cardell keeps his hand in front of his face to ward off the heat. Then he regains control of himself and forces his legs to obey. He runs through arching flames, and jumps over the smoldering threshold.

....

Another world awaits on the other side. The glow is white and blinding, and although he squints, his eyes water in self-defense. Fire roars around him. The flames make sounds of their own, hissing and crackling as they crawl from meal to meal. Everything they consume adds to the mournful choir: wood that creaks and sags before giving way, glass and bottles that clatter before cracking with a high-pitched noise. The air sucks everything upwards, and makes every crack between the floorboards and walls whistle. Above him is a ceiling of roiling bubbles, an incandescent sea as if viewed from the deep. Cloth and paper take to the air on shining wings.

Cardell has encountered him before, the Red Rooster, when he devoured the ships that had been hit by the Russians' red-hot cannon balls, and his thoughts are the same now as they were then. This is a living thing, a primordial creature full of malice that has been biding its time, to all appearances docile when lurking in fireplaces and stoves, patiently waiting to be let loose to collect all its debts. When the old one's shackles are cast off, there is nothing to do but flee. But Cardell must run into the fire.

96

Erik Three Roses stands in the comfortable shade of a tree, where the air is warm and pleasant, at some distance from Horn Hill. He shares the place with a drinking trough for sheep, a discarded oak barrel that has been cut in half and is still full of water. From time to time he lets one hand sweep across its smooth surface. In expectant silence, he watches the timbers start to collapse, the ridge sink, and now the entire roof collapses with a crash, sending a cascade of sparks to light the pillar of smoke. He feels impatient, shifting his weight from foot to foot. He knows that he has completed his task, but not what comes next. Shouldn't she come now, now that what has been wronged has been made right, come to gather him in her arms and press her lips against his in the kiss he has been promised? Anxiously, he lifts his hands to his numb face yet again and wonders for the hundredth time if he will be able to feel it as once he did.

A hand is laid on his shoulder and he turns with effort and anticipation. Not her, not yet. It is a pale and slender figure. Familiar. Ah, the little fortune teller. The figure tries to speak with him, but the stammered words hold no interest. Soon he loses patience and turns back to the spectacle of the flames. And yet the figure does not leave him alone, but gets in the way and tugs at his ripped shirt to gain his attention. Simple gestures convey meaning. He recognizes a mimed strike of steel against flint, an accusing finger turned at himself. Erik Three Roses willingly nods his acknowledgment. The next time he looks around he is alone again, his temporary guest only a spot against the backdrop of flames, now calling out a different name to his.

97

Cardell shields his mouth and nose with the crook of his arm, sucking air through the cloth. He forces a mind made sluggish by fear to conjure up memories of the inside of the house and he rushes towards the staircase, as yet intact. He takes it three steps at a time, up into even hotter air. He is on the side of Horn Hill that hasn't yet caught fire. Here the inner walls still guard against the blaze, paint flaking, wallpaper peeling, woodwork blackening, and the smoke hovers like a thundercloud under the ceiling. He remembers where he is going. Doubled over, he presses on.

The fire seems to have robbed the air of sustenance. It is as if every breath is drawn in vain. His sight starts to go black and he is forced to his knees. The air is better there, and he continues crawling over floorboards so hot the flames must already have taken hold beneath, two inches of wood between him and hell itself. He senses that it is already gnawing at the joists. Soon the framework will lose all its strength and the upper floor will collapse. It will surely bring the rest of the house with it. But Cardell has arrived now, pushing open the door he thinks the right one, and sees what he is looking for: the two cots, left just as they were last time. Squinting, he feels his way over to their small waiting bodies, lifts them into his arms, and turns in the hope that the way out will still be clear.

Out in the corridor, there are flames spurting through the cracks in the floor, prized open by the heat. He draws a breath that sears his chest and hopes it will be enough, running back the same way that he just came, towards the stairs. Soon he is forced down again, to crawl his way along, and halfway to the stairs he notices that something is wrong, that his burden feels different and lighter than it was. The skin on Cardell's face has swelled and the smoke lies thick, but he gropes for the children with his hand. It is Karl, he can feel it by the hair that has always been shorter than his sister's. But something is missing, they have left something behind, something important, perhaps the cat made of knotted rags that Karl loves so much and that he always grips tightly in his sleep, and so Cardell fumbles behind him on the floor, searching for what has been lost. His fist soon finds it, but it feels different than he had been expecting. It is a tiny limb, an arm or a leg. One-handed, he struggles to fit it back in its place, but only succeeds in doing more damage, for the flesh is tender and collapses under his touch. The flames roar up around him and force him to hurry, and he gathers what he can and continues on to the stairs. He no longer has the strength to stand, so he closes his arms around the children and rolls down. Down on the floor of the hallway, he finds that more damage has been done, and he has to crawl back up, step by step, clutching to him all he can find, whimperingly trying to mold the children back into the shape they once had, into bodies where life can be coaxed to return, but his eyes can no longer be forced open and he cannot say for sure which part belongs to whom. Wherever he touches, he opens fresh wounds. They are like two pieces of meat that have been left to stew in a pot overnight, gray and soft. No firmness remains between the hopeless block of the wooden fist and the living hand, and everything he does makes things worse. He can no longer tell them apart. Soon all that remains is a pool of soft bones. While he sits bent over his hopeless task, the fire catches in his hair and burns his scalp clean. He has to hit himself about the head, hitting harder than he needs to, and feels bloody lacerations and blackening blisters spring up among the flames.

98

On bare feet that are bleeding but numb after the journey, Anna Stina crests the hill. At first she doesn't understand what she sees at the bottom of the valley. Where the house once stood, the one where she left her children, there is now only a dark red blot that shifts in color with the gusts of wind, a coiled serpent, sleepy after eating its fill.

The path in front of her runs like a silver ribbon between the trees. Where tears have blurred her vision, and fatigue her mind, she wonders if this isn't some ghostly apparition of the place she has seen so recently: the stream where two children had sent off their wooden boat, and the sound of whose laughter had just faded on their happy way down the forest slope.

"Maja?"

She calls their names as she runs, over and over.

"Karl?"

The night has no answer.

99

The air around Erik slowly cools as he waits. The inferno loses its intensity, and soon there are more embers than flames. Over the hill, a pump has arrived, pulled by an experienced horse who has learned not to fear the fire, and a group of men roll out their leather hoses under cries to keep the blaze at bay and the sparks from spreading. With axes and saws, they cut down trees and make brooms of the branches to drench in water and beat the ground.

Then a new figure comes towards him, down from the valley, aimlessly careening at first, but now it sees him and its steps become more determined. Its appearance fills him with amazement. It is hardly human, more like a monster birthed by the fire itself. The hair has been singed from the scalp and a wreath of smoke surrounds his head; the face is blackened, the clothes are scorched rags, the smoldering left hand glows red. A few steps away, it stops to stare at him. He meets its bloodshot gaze and waits. Some sense that he can't put a name to tells him that it is coming now, the reward for all of his effort, and he feels a tickle in his belly.

The figure closes the distance between them, and lifts him in its arms as if he were a child. The feeling is unfamiliar and dizzying, and for a while it is as if he is floating like one of the sparks towards the sky. And now water, wet and cold. He is pressed down under the surface. The feeling at first is of discomfort, but it is fleeting, for here peace reigns with silence and coolness, and he embraces the change. Only when he has to breathe does his body put up a struggle, but against the force that is pressing him down he can do nothing. The glow from the valley is enough to light the face above him, now distorted in a grimace. Finally he must draw breath, and the resistance he meets at first is strange, but once the lungs are filled there comes well-being, and he sees that the face above him is a different one now: hers! As enchanting as spring sunshine on slumbering meadows. It is she who leans over him now, and he smiles at her, for he knows what is coming. He doesn't need to worry any longer about his numb face. It is coming now, at any moment, the kiss that he so well deserves.

100

The music heightens, the musicians' fingers and bows fly over their instruments until Tycho can no longer follow the melodies. The lead part is played by a girl in the bloom of adolescence, easy on the eye, with clean features and a sharp little nose, her hair carefully pulled back behind her ears so as not to disturb the strings. She is lost in her playing, and the music sways her body to and fro as in a dance. Half-closed eyes under long lashes bound along the dots and lines of the notation. Ceton is filled with the feeling that he is witnessing a moment that is intensely private, something intimate and sensual. In the moment she is wholly and completely herself, as if she were alone, and the room empty. But the music takes over, and he must close his eyes. The voices of the quartet blend together in an irresistible whole, and which sound comes from which bow is no longer possible to say. He rocks on his seat in time to the music, his mouth open.

....

Someone is brusquely shaking his shoulder. The enchantment is broken, and in furious surprise he spins around in his chair. Jarrick, on his knees beside him, as misplaced as a stray dog, his face a mask of bruises and wounds. The liveried servants who have failed to prevent him from interrupting the performance stop at the back row when they see that he is Ceton's man, and while the shushing of the audience causes the cellist to lose his tempo, Jarrick grunts his message in Ceton's ear.

He feels all the blood rush from his face, his head spins, and he gets up abruptly enough to send his chair toppling backwards into the lap of the woman behind. He must lean against Jarrick's shoulder to keep his balance. He is lost. Enemies more numerous than he can count, recently locked into an enforced truce, will soon gather as the scent spreads. His defense ruined beyond repair, whether by accident or design. His sight goes dark. Only escape remains. Together they lurch towards the door. Many point and whisper, unable to contain their pleasure at seeing the state he's in. The fugitives hunch under the starry sky of Castle Hill, and hurry to take cover in the indifferent grid of the alleys, soon swallowed in the shadows that pass judgment on no man. Over the rooftops in the City-between-the-Bridges, the church bells ring from each tower. United, they thunder in the night as a call against approaching danger.

101

He smiles—he smiles, this arsonist—forming his mouth into a kiss down at the bottom of the vat in the midst of his drowning, and inside Mickel Cardell, there is a rage the like of which he has never before felt. He lifts his left hand and hears it sizzle with hate as the wood breaks the surface of the water, setting it against the smiling lips and putting all his weight behind it as he presses down. Underwater, a dark red rose blossoms, a submerged thundercloud of portent. White shards come whirling up before they sink again to rest on the bottom, and he presses harder, presses until the pain in his stump burns white, until there is nothing left to offer any resistance. Impossibly, Cardell can hear the killer scream, a wordless howl of pain and injustice, and it doesn't even end when he recognizes the voice as his own.

102

Down at the edge of the bed of embers, as close as the heat will allow, stands Emil Winge. The pale blue tongues of open flames are visible only in the center, and the hottest white only hugs the beams that once bore the weight of the house. He tries to count the lives that have been lost, to remember if Tycho Ceton ever gave them a number.

A hundred? More? Their remains make the falling flakes of ash fat and sticky.

....

Now he sees he has company. A young woman is sitting nearby on her knees, and although her sooty face is laced with tears, there is something in it he recognizes. Her expression reveals an anguish that makes him ashamed of his own. He scours his memory in vain until realization comes. It is she, the girl of whom Cardell spoke, the one he looked for in vain, the one whose face he described in the way that only one who loves it can. And with this recognition, he understands even more, he understands for what reason he has been cast aside and who it was who found her progeny refuge here. He shakes his head and turns to stare at the waning light before him.

The charred wood makes clinking noises, stirring in the deepest red. The hands he holds shaking in front of him bear the same color.

"Oh, Hedvig, without us none of this would have happened. How will we ever wash ourselves clean again?"

He turns around to better hear the answer, confused for a moment, but the one he has addressed is a woman he has never met before, and he remembers that the sister he once had chose a coffin rather than share in his trust and guilt.

....

Now he hears Mickel Cardell bellow, an alien noise, hardly recognizable as issuing from a human throat. He turns and hurries in the direction of the sound, under the maimed trees, trying to find the right way through the darkness that the dying blaze has returned to the night. False turns everywhere: to the left, to the right. The breeze whispers its warning in rustling leaves. Among the shadows, a danger lurks unseen, and he perceives it clearly with his entire being. A shiver slows his step. What he sees is almost before him now, hidden behind the gnarled trunk of an apple tree. It is close, there is only one turn he can make. The center of the labyrinth.

Winge opens his eyes as wide as he can, the better to see, and is at once struck lame by a dizzying fear as he recognizes Cardell's broad back bent over a vat of water. His enormous shoulders, his arms as wide as logs, his hand and wooden fist red—and there, on top of his shoulders, a bull's head crowned with sharp horns. But now, when Winge sees the beast with his own eyes, it doesn't scare him as much as he thought, and he closes the distance between them, and he takes its hand in his.

Acknowledgments

Fredrik Backman, brother in all but blood, two years ago you made me aware of the possibility of writing a continuation of the book that would not have been written without you, and it helped me to realize that it was also what I most of all wanted to do. You have been with me each step of the way, reading, commenting, and analyzing, and at each stage you said the words that I most of all needed to hear. I am deeply in your debt, as always. Thank you for everything.

Adam Dahlin, my publisher, and Andreas Lundberg, my editor, you have with diligence and conviction pointed out all of the problems that appear when ideas are to be harnessed by words, and without your assistance the shortcomings of this book would have been far greater than they are.

Stina Jackson and Sofia Lundberg, honored fellow writers, I am deeply grateful to you both for the fact that you have lent me your talents in offering your opinions of my manuscript. Your respective insights opened perspectives that I had earlier overlooked and gave me the opportunity to improve my text. Thank you, Stina. Thank you, Sofia.

Federico Ambrosini, my agent, thank you for all of your tireless efforts on my behalf, and for your friendship. Marie Gyllenhammar, thank you for all of your hard work and support.

Martin Ödman, I appreciate that you have once again taken the trouble to read and critique, and provide your clear-eyed commentary. Thank you also for lending parts of your je ne sais quoi to Jean Michael Cardell.

Anna Nordenfelt Hellberg and Tobias Hellberg, thank you for reading and providing commentary.

Thank you to my father for such critical acumen, and the same to my mother with particular thanks for careful copyediting.

Many thanks to my wife, Mia, and to my children for all of their love and patience.

Of all of the source material that has been used for writing this book, I want to particularly acknowledge Kirsi Vainio-Korhonen's *De frimodiga* (*The Courageous*), translated from the Finnish by Camilla Frostell, which describes in scrupulous detail the reality for midwives who were trained in Stockholm in the eighteenth century and the conditions for the mothers-to-be that they assisted.